IMMORTAL DUSK

WHITE HAVEN HUNTERS BOOK SIX

TJ GREEN

Immortal Dusk

Mountolive Publishing

Copyright © 2023 TJ Green

ISBN eBook: 978-1-99-004760-2

ISBN Paperback: 978-1-99-004761-9

Cover design by Fiona Jayde Media

Editing by Missed Period Editing

Contents

One

The clouds were heavy with the promise of snow over the narrow valley in the Yorkshire Dales, and Nahum was glad he was wearing a thick coat and boots. Especially seeing as Olivia Jameson, a collector employed by The Orphic Guild, had led him up a bleak hillside coated with frost to look over the small village nestled below.

"Couldn't we have done this in the car?" he asked her. "It would have been warmer."

"But less spectacular." She gave him an impish grin. Her cheeks were a rosy red from the biting cold, her face framed by the fur-lined hood of her jacket. "Besides, the exercise is good for you."

"I get plenty of exercise, thanks. Do I look unfit?"

"No. You look delicious."

Nahum laughed. He was used to Olivia's flirting and found that he liked it. However, that was all it was going to be. Olivia flirted outrageously with everyone—unless he'd become rusty with reading her signals. He shrugged it off. He had a job to do. "So, what am I looking for?"

"I just thought we could get a good impression of the place from up here. Make sure I wasn't missing anything."

"I thought we were planning on stealing from a vicarage, not a fortified castle?"

"I have learned from long experience that you should never presume." She frowned, her eyes narrowing as she studied the buildings below. "As you know, I have been searching for this reliquary for a long time. It has been very hard to track down. It's almost like it has a life of its own."

Nahum had flown to Leeds late the previous afternoon, collected his rental car, and met up with Olivia in the small town in the Yorkshire Dales. They had spent the evening in a boutique hotel they were both booked into, discussing Olivia's search for the reliquary, as well as answering her questions about his past. She was fascinated with the Nephilim and their history. In fact, they had spent more time discussing that than the job. Now he had a lot more questions. The reliquary was for one of Olivia's regular clients, but it had taken months to locate. She was convinced it was in the vicarage in the hamlet below, owned by the local vicar named Jacobsen.

He watched her profile, noting her tense jaw. "What aren't you telling me, Olivia? I sense that you are very capable, and I'm sure not averse to stealing from a vicarage. Why do you need me? Or should I say, a Nephilim?"

She cocked her head at him. "The more I've asked around up here—discreetly, of course—the more I've realised that this vicar is quite unusual. I'm wondering if he's a necromancer—or something of the sort. I thought backup might be important."

"A necromancer! You didn't think to mention this last night over dinner?"

She looked sheepish. "I wondered if I might be letting my imagination get away from me, but I've learned to trust my instincts."

Nahum hadn't wanted to pry too much into the background of the object they were stealing. It didn't seem necessary; it was just a job. As long as he understood the basic requirements, that was fine. Plus, he was only supposed to be there as a hired hand. The muscle. *But now...* "Why does it seem to have a life of its own?"

"The reliquary contains some of the remains of St Ignatius, an obscure saint who was originally from the Alps. He was a monk who preached the word of God in the surrounding villages, and lived in a monastery in the mountains, a small order that has long since gone. The monastery, too. It vanished, like many do. Anyway, he visited a village known for its paganism, and an angry mob turned on him and he was stoned to death. His body was collected and laid to rest in the monastery, and a while after that he was beatified." Olivia shrugged. "Well, his resting place became a place of pilgrimage. It was said he could cure madness. Draw out devils. His bones were split up and ended up who knows where, but his skull was placed in a highly decorated reliquary. Over the years it's been in different churches, and then a religious museum, but then it disappeared. Stolen, presumably. I managed to track it down by a lot of hard work."

"Revolting, of course, but that still doesn't explain why you say it has a life of its own."

"Well, now it seems that where the reliquary goes, madness follows. Odd outbreaks of violence or hysteria that the perpetrators can't explain. Not all the time, of course, just sometimes. I wonder if it's cursed or something, or can be manipulated by whoever owns it. Reliquaries are supposed to heal people, or offer solace..." She trailed off, perplexed.

Nahum stared down at the small hamlet with smoke pouring from its chimneys. It looked peaceful. "Has something happened here?"

"There's been a smattering of violence in the surrounding villages. Fights that came out of nowhere—pubs, schools, restaurants. A broad area—not small."

"Unfortunately, violence happens."

"But it all occurs around the area that this priest is in. It's not just the reliquary. He moves around, you see. Every few years he goes to a new church. Always small villages, remote, lonely. Attendance goes up, more convert to the church. I wonder if the priest is manipulating the reliquary somehow to swell his numbers."

"That sounds extreme! Besides, the monk, St whatever, didn't sound violent in life."

"Ignatius. No, he wasn't. Like I said, I suspect the priest is using it for his own ends. I've done a lot of research on this." A gust of wind whipped a strand of hair from beneath her hood, and she tucked it back inside again. "Let's walk a little higher."

Without waiting for his response, she led the way further up the steep sides of the valley, along a narrow track that weaved between heathers and ferns. Snow lay thick on the surrounding peaks, and suddenly the air seemed menacing. The wind tugged Nahum's hair and whipped his breath from his lungs. This was wild country. Remote, breathtakingly beautiful, and deadly if you misjudged the weather. If snow started to fall now, it would white out their surroundings in seconds.

Although he'd followed Olivia up the hill, he called out, "Olivia, wait! Let's turn back. There's nothing I can see up here that I can't from down there."

"Just a few more meters. Around the bend!"

Reluctantly he followed her around the rugged, boulder-strewn curve of the hill, and into the shadow of a ruined stone building. Immediately the wind dropped as they tucked themselves into its shelter. There was a small camping stool in there and the remnants of a camp.

Nahum laughed. "You've been spying on him!"

"Of course I have. It's sheltered, and I sit up here in the late afternoon and watch at night." She tapped her pack. "Night vision binoculars, as well as the usual."

"I'm impressed." He surveyed the area, the church a short distance from the village. "The vicarage is the old, grey-stone building by the church, I presume?"

Olivia nodded, binoculars already trained below. "He scurries to the church at night. Not every night, of course, but several. I see lights in the nave, long after everyone has gone to bed."

"That doesn't necessarily mean anything sinister."

She lowered the binoculars and clucked at him. "Really?"

"I'm playing devil's advocate."

Her eyes didn't leave his. "Something is very wrong here. I know it. I don't think it will be easy to steal this reliquary. I think he'll do anything to keep it."

"What does your buyer want it for?"

"To admire it, catalogue it, and fawn over it in private."

"Are you sure *he* doesn't want it for anything more sinister?"

"I've known Charles for a long time. He's a collector. That's all. I think it's better in his hands."

Glad to be out of the wind, Nahum leaned against the remnants of the stone wall, the roof long since gone. "Okay. Let's discuss the job. You think the reliquary is in the church or the vicarage?"

"I suggest we try the church first, but I think he moves it around. I should stress that it is not on show. No one actually knows it's here."

"So, we check out the church, and if it's not there, we go to the vicarage, make sure we keep Jacobsen secured, steal it, and go. The car will be close by, I presume?"

Olivia nodded. "Hire car, under a false ID. It's not my first clandestine hit. We drive out tonight. Job done. Couldn't be easier, right? If the worst happens, you use your fabulous wings and fly it out. I will escape in the car. Either way, we must get that reliquary tonight. I can't waste any more time on this. Besides, I've done my homework. I don't think there's much else to find out about this guy."

"Other than the possibility that he might be a necromancer, or using the reliquary to spread bad mojo, or something else..."

"Okay." She smirked. "I admit there's stuff I don't know, but I do know it's the right reliquary. I caught a glimpse of it. I've also tracked it historically—picked up where my client left off. As I said, strange events follow it. Unless you were looking for a connection—like me—no one would really know. And I've seen the priest. He's middle-aged, gaunt, not a physical threat. He'll be easy to deal with."

Nahum still wasn't convinced. He had an uneasy feeling about it, and it was obvious that Olivia did too, or else he wouldn't be there. But if the man was as odd as she suggested, and violence did seem to follow this reliquary around, then it was best they removed it. And he was a Nephilim. He could handle most things.

Finally, he nodded. "All right. Tonight, then. Now, can we get off this freezing hill and into a pub?"

Gabe watched Shadow put the final decorations on their huge Christmas tree in the corner of the living room in the old farmhouse in White Haven, distracted by her swaying hips.

"Can't we do something more interesting? Like, go to bed?"

She tossed her silvery hair over her shoulders as she turned to look at him. "This *is* interesting!"

"Not as much as your naked body draped over mine."

Niel groaned behind him as he entered the room. "Shut up! Other people are in the house."

Gabe grimaced. "I thought you were busy in the barn."

"I was, and now I'm here." Niel gave a malicious smile at seeing Gabe's disappointment. "Take it to your room!"

"Perhaps you should stop sneaking up on us!"

"I'm not sneaking! I can't help it if I'm naturally stealthy." He stared at the tree. "Please don't put an angel on the top of that thing."

Shadow had a mischievous glint in her eye. "Will it make you nervous?"

Niel's blue eyes turned to ice. "No. It will annoy me. As if my father would be watching over me benevolently!"

Gabe had already vetoed all angels from the house for Christmas decorations. Fortunately, Shadow had zero interest in deities of any kind, and was happy to dress the tree in a more naturalistic fey fashion. So far, branches of spruce and pine were festooned around the house. It was a huge fire hazard, but Gabe had to admit that it smelled good.

They were celebrating the winter solstice rather than Christmas, but like the previous year, they had agreed to exchange small presents...if they were even going to be at home. JD had called with a request—well, more like a command, because JD wasn't good with polite requests. However, Gabe had yet to break that news to everyone.

Reluctantly shelving the idea of spending a couple of hours in bed with Shadow, Gabe sat on the corner of the sofa. "Where's Ash?"

"Upstairs I think, researching the *Comte*—again."

Ash, always loving research and learning, had almost become as obsessed with the *Comte de Saint-Germain*, the man they believed to be behind Black Cronos, as JD and Jackson. He was helping in the search for possible bases, hoping to isolate a place that might be a centre of operations. It was Estelle Faversham and Barak who suggested that the *Comte* and Black Cronos might have an alchemical centre somewhere mystical, with history, energy, and power. A confluence of Ley Lines perhaps, or an old religious site. While that was a great idea, Europe and the UK were littered with such places. Some were easily dismissed; others, however, needed more careful screening. There were also hundreds of ancient castles around, many abandoned, but all offering discreet places to set up a secret headquarters.

Gabe's brothers were split doing various things at present. Barak was often with Estelle, in and out of London and The Retreat. Eli and Zee continued to work in town with the witches. The rest of them picked up occult-hunting jobs with The Orphic Guild. Currently, Nahum was helping Olivia Jameson, Harlan's colleague, steal a religious reliquary in Yorkshire. He was supposed to be there for only a day or two, but since yesterday, he hadn't heard a thing. Gabe, much to his annoyance, was being regularly contacted by JD, the demanding, immortal magician to Queen Elizabeth I.

Four months earlier, in the thick heat of August, they had found the Emerald Tablet belonging to Hermes Trismegistus in the Templar treasure hidden within Temple Moreton, and they had given it to JD. It was like all his Christmases had arrived at once.

However, after finding that vast treasure, they were still yet to receive any money for it. The collection was still being catalogued and valued, and no doubt there would be a lot of wrangling about money. Fortunately, Harlan and Theo were very good at dealing with the museum, something Gabe was glad to let them do. Shadow, of course, with her avaricious and shrewd, gold-loving heart, was also making sure they received their cut. He hoped they would, for their sake. Shadow was wont to exact retribution in any way she saw fit, usually at the point of her sword or the tip of her arrow.

"Why do you want Ash?" Shadow asked, her question drawing him back to the present.

"JD has a job for us."

Niel virtually growled. "I will not be experimented on!"

"Neither will I!" Gabe considered the weird conversation he'd had with JD about Alexander the Great and Hermes Trismegistus. "He wants us to go to Egypt. He thinks there's something there that will help him understand the Emerald Tablet."

He had Shadow's full attention now, her violet eyes wide with hope and excitement. "We're going on an adventure?" Her hands settled on her hips. "And you didn't tell me?"

"I just did! The details elude me right now, but once we go to see JD, I guess he'll explain everything. Just to be clear, I haven't agreed to it yet." And he wouldn't if he didn't like the job, no matter how much JD might sulk.

Niel still scowled. "Why can't he come here? Everyone runs after him!"

"He'll pay us. The least we can do is head to his estate."

"In a few months we won't need his pay."

"But we like the work," Gabe reminded him. "Unless you want to lounge around here all day, getting fat?"

Shadow marched over and poked Niel in his very flat abdomen. "Who knows? If he needs us to steal something, we may need a thief to help us. A small, petite thief..."

Any mention of Mouse, the thief who had captured Niel's interest only to seemingly betray him during their last big job, still made him scowl. "I think not. We can manage perfectly well without her. Besides, you're a thief."

Shadow grinned. "Just looking out for you."

"I'd rather you didn't." He turned to Gabe. "When are we going to see JD?"

"Tomorrow. Potentially, we'll fly out the next day."

Niel nodded, his gaze distant. "Fine. I'll tell Ash. I guess Egypt before Christmas will at least be warm."

Two

"A re you sure you're ready to go back to France?" Jackson Strange asked Lucien, seeing the uncertainty in his eyes. "If you want to stay here, that's fine. Barak and Estelle will manage without you."

"No! I am ready. I want to find the people who did this to me." The need for revenge was etched into the jut of his jaw and the tightening of his eyes. "I have mastered my changes now. I'll be fine!"

Jackson looked at Barak and Estelle, the only other two people in the room with them. "What do you think?"

Barak shrugged, the muscles across his shoulders rippling. "I think Lucien needs to get out of this place. Four months trapped in The Retreat is too long. Besides, I trust him."

"Me too," Estelle added. She sat in the chair in the corner of Lucien's room, eyes never leaving Lucien as he paced back and forth, nervous energy welling up in him. "He's already been here far longer than we ever anticipated." Regret crossed her face as she addressed Lucien. "I'm sorry, we had no idea how things would end up."

He finally sat down on the end of his bed. "I know. I don't blame you. I don't blame any of you. I blame only Black Cronos. The more I hear, the more I hate them. And the more I want to know."

Jackson knew that feeling well. The subject of Black Cronos was like a drug. It absorbed his every waking moment, and his dreams, his thoughts constantly circling them. He hated his own obsession, but couldn't shake it off, and understood Lucien's need to find them. He leaned against the wall, arms crossed, assessing the risks for what felt like the hundredth time. Since Lucien had been rescued by Barak and Estelle from beneath *Château du Buade*, he had been kept in The Retreat as a well-treated prisoner, with only the occasional trip to the surface at the beginning—accompanied, of course, by a security team. His semi-tattooed body had created unexpected and uncontrollable changes within him. Lucien had been as anxious to be kept safe as everyone else. His lack of control had terrified him.

Lucien had been studied, interviewed, poked, and prodded, and had endured all of it with good grace, as curious to understand the complex tattoos that had been etched into his skin as everyone else. Everyone was especially interested in the way they took over his mind, turning him into an automaton. Thanks to Layla, the team's doctor, the lab scientists, and the brilliantly irascible JD, they had made a lot of progress. The tattoos drew on astrology and constellations, all tied into Lucien's birth chart. It seemed that the tattoos connected him to the cosmos and the wheel of time. Jackson's head ached at the magnificence of it all. And thanks to an ingenious device designed by JD, Lucien now had control of his own body again.

As they grew to trust Lucien, the room they contained him in became a bedroom rather than a cell. Although, big metal brackets were still fixed to the wall, just in case they had to chain him up. It was also still in a section of The Retreat that was unused by anyone else. It had a small kitchen and bathroom attached to it, so his area was completely self-contained.

Jackson nodded at the thick metal bracelet on Lucien's wrist, a complex interweaving of metals that JD had constructed using alchemical means. The metals' magical properties had been enhanced and tuned to Lucien's energy frequencies. "Are you sure you're okay with that?"

Lucien's long fingers turned it as if for reassurance. "Yes. It has saved my life. I haven't changed at all without using my own will for almost two weeks. When I do change, I still have my reason."

"I still think it's too soon to be out there unaccompanied. It could be a blip."

Barak huffed. "He won't be unaccompanied. He'll be with us. And a big tranquilliser gun."

"But, say you find Black Cronos—or maybe that rat, Stefan," Jackson continued. "What if he can override that device?"

"There are a lot of what-ifs and maybes," Estelle reasoned. "There are in life, all the time. Eventually we must trust that the progress we've made will work. I think we should head outside now. It's a crisp, clear day out there, and London is full of Christmas spirit. I think it will cheer Lucien up. Let's have lunch after a walk in Hyde Park. What do you say, Lucien?"

"Yes, please! I'm desperate for fresh air."

Jackson smiled. Estelle had been a revelation. When they'd first met, her guarded, prickly manner and sharp tongue had been off-putting. An attitude, he now suspected, that had been long honed to deter friendships and to protect herself. However, every time he saw her, she now seemed a little softer. There were still flashes of obstinacy, and sharp responses still bubbled out, but mostly she appeared happier, and certainly every time she looked at Barak, she seemed to melt a little more. As for Barak, well, the big man continued to surprise him. He'd stayed for weeks, on and off in The Retreat at first, making sure Lucien was okay. Even now he visited weekly, and stayed overnight to check on him. On Jackson, too. On the occasions when Jackson had barely left The Retreat, Barak had persuaded him to go out, and Harlan had backed him up. Jackson tended to shoulder all of this on his own, and knew it was unnecessary.

"In fact," Estelle continued, "let's all head out." She stared at Jackson, her tone brooking no refusal. "My treat."

Jackson nodded, thinking a pint and pub lunch sounded perfect. "Fair enough. We can discuss our next plan of attack."

"France again, you say?" Barak asked.

"Yes. But I want the usual surveillance on it first."

"You said that about the last half a dozen places." Barak didn't look angry, just resigned.

"I know, but I've changed my search parameters, and I think this one could be it. Sorry…"

Barak cut him off. "It's okay. We'll get there." He grinned, the flash of white teeth bright against his dark skin, but his eyes were hard. "I look forward to making them pay."

Harlan Beckett, Collector for The Orphic Guild, was mesmerised by the Emerald Tablet.

It glowed on its stand in JD's library, unaffected by the cool winter light from the window or the firelight in the grate. JD, the immortal head of the guild, stood over it, also bathed in its green glow, and the scowl on his face made him look demonic.

Harlan was standing several feet away, but the tablet exerted a pull on him even from there; he shuddered to consider the monstrous power and knowledge it contained.

"JD," he repeated. "Did you hear me? They're going to Montferrier tomorrow. Any advice?"

JD finally dragged his gaze away. "What?"

Harlan had arrived ten minutes earlier, and it had taken that long for JD to acknowledge him. Once he did, Harlan stepped back, unnerved by his ghastly appearance. "Holy shit, JD. Have you slept lately? Or eaten? Or even had a shower in weeks?" He tentatively sniffed, but the room merely smelled of polish and old books.

"Of course I have, you fool!" JD strode to the cabinet of drinks and poured a glass of sherry. "I have a lot on my mind, and can do without disturbances."

"Well, if you answered your damn phone I wouldn't be here!" Harlan's temper, normally mild, was always raised to boiling point within minutes of being with JD.

"Stop being so prosaic!" He swung his arm around and pointed. "Look! The Emerald Tablet of Hermes Trismegistus is right there! The man named the Thrice Greatest—Thoth, Hermes the God, Hermes the Scribe! It's older than the ten commandments—and I have it!"

Chastened, Harlan nodded. "I know." He'd averted his gaze, but he forced himself to look at it and instantly felt dizzy. The heart of it seemed to swirl, as if galaxies were trapped within it. "It terrifies me." He blinked, forcing his gaze back to JD. The room seemed dim by comparison, almost bleached of colour.

JD took a ragged breath, and the anger drained from his eyes. "Yes, of course. Sorry." Abruptly, he caught up a cloth from the table and threw it over the tablet, banishing it beneath thick, black velvet. "I have to do that just to think clearly. There's something in there."

Shivering, Harlan walked to the fire, and accepted a glass of sherry from JD.

"Sorry, Harlan. It haunts me. My every waking moment, my dreams, my plans... It's a drug. I both love it and hate it."

"I couldn't bear it near me. Isn't there somewhere else you can keep it? Somewhere behind thick walls and a reinforced door? Somewhere that contains its influence." He laughed. "Sorry. That sounds mad."

"Not mad at all. I've considered it. I think you're right."

"You said there's something in there. What did you mean? Hidden knowledge?"

"Yes. No. Something else..." JD turned his back on the tablet, focussing only on Harlan and lowering his voice. "I feel it's been shrunk, somehow. I've seen illustrations and read old texts that suggest it's huge. I thought it was an affectation, but now..." His eyes were wide, appealing to Harlan for understanding.

Harlan also lowered his voice, as if the tablet could hear them. "You mean as if magic has made it smaller?"

"Something like that. I believe that if I could make it bigger, I could actually see what swirls within it. I think I need to unlock it, somehow..."

Harlan's mouth was very dry, and he sipped his sherry. "That doesn't make me feel any better about it. Besides, you've had it for months."

"I could probably have it for several lifetimes and still not understand its mysteries. Alchemists have been debating the meaning of its text for millennia."

"How would you even go about making it bigger?"

"I don't know. I've been observing it for changes during full moons, new moons, the past equinox and solstice, as well as several planetary events, but the time I've possessed it is too short to see anything significant."

"I'm surprised it's not in your lab."

"It was for a while. It affected my instruments—all of them..."

Harlan stared at it over JD's shoulder, feeling as if it was sentient. "If you're going to try to make it bigger—and I'm not sure you actually should—you need it to be outside. Under a marquee or something." In the face of such weirdness, Harlan liked to focus on practicalities. "That way, at least its influence would be outside of the house. As long as it doesn't affect your defences, of course."

"It doesn't so far, I've already checked." JD nodded to himself. "Yes. A marquee is a good idea. I'll get Anna to organise it. Something robust on the far lawn."

Harlan decided to shift the conversation back to Black Cronos. "What about the latest castle Barak and Estelle will look into? Any suggestions there?"

"Not really." JD topped their sherry up and turned to the long table covered in books and manuscripts. He shifted several aside and picked up an old, well-read, leather-bound volume. "I've been reading my old notes again. This is my own research into Germain that I've added to over the years. In the light of new knowledge and our current theories, I've gained a fresh perspective on his activities, especially about his friendship with another alchemist, Melchior Figulus. He was an ancestor of the current family who own *Château de Bénaix*. Descendants of Cathars. I presume you've heard of them?"

"Sure. A religious sect that was considered heretical, and consequently persecuted."

JD flicked over a few pages, searching avidly for a reference. "Exactly. Figulus lived many years after all that, and was an average alchemist, at best. Ambitious, certainly, but lacking the intelligence to be truly brilliant." He said it matter of factly, without malice. "That's probably why he and St Germain became good friends. I'd forgotten him until Jackson mentioned the name. Germain collected people, but was never truly friends with anyone who was his intellectual equal." JD gave Harlan a ferocious grin. "It would have been hard to exploit or dazzle them."

Wow. JD really disliked the count.

"So, yes," he continued, "I think following up on the Cathars is a good idea. If that castle isn't the right place, it may be at least a step in the right direction." His gaze drifted to the velvet-covered tablet. "And if I can unlock some of those secrets, I may be able to help even more. That's why I need Gabe and Shadow."

Harlan frowned. "Do you? What for?"

"I stumbled on something I'd forgotten when I went through these notes. A thought I'd had on Thoth and the tablet."

Harlan nodded. "The Egyptian God with the head of an ibis."

JD fumbled for another book, already open at the relevant page. "Here's an image of him. God of writing and knowledge, who also wrote about the afterlife. The Greeks equated him with Hermes. Anyway, I think the key to the tablet is in Egypt. That's what I want Gabe for. I think I know where it is."

"The key?" Harlan could barely believe his ears. "After all this time?"

JD looked at him in absolute seriousness. "Of course. If it's anything like the tablet, it will be indestructible. I need it. Perhaps you should go, too?"

"Me?" Harlan blinked with disbelief. "I have cases to cover!"

"I think you'll be useful. Gabe is coming tomorrow for a briefing. Why don't you wait and hear all about it?"

"Why don't you just tell me now?"

"Because I hate explaining things twice. And right now, you're going to help me take the tablet into the garden. It can go in the greenhouse for now." JD gave him a pleading smile. "It's a bit heavy for me and Anna. You can stay here tonight, have dinner with me." He cocked an eyebrow hopefully.

"Okay, as long as I can read some of your notes on this other alchemist."

JD swept his arm expansively across the table. "All at your disposal."

"Deal."

Three

The warm pub that Barak and his companions had settled in on the edge of Hyde Park was festive. There was a Christmas tree in the corner, and lights were festooned across the ceiling.

Although Lucien's mood had brightened when they left The Retreat, his fingers drifted to the bracelet on his wrist as his eyes darted around the room. Barak kept a careful watch on Lucien's eyes. They were usually the first to change when what they'd dubbed "the Black Cronos effect" took over. First, they glazed over and Lucien became distant, and then his entire eyeballs turned an unearthly copper-gold, showing no white at all. The change happened quickly. After that, his skin shimmered with a metallic sheen that formed a type of armour.

Once he was drugged and tied up, they found that his skin was still warm and fleshy—just super strong. Barak patted the small tranquilliser gun in the inner pocket of his jacket, a subconscious need to check that it was there—just in case. To need to use it would be a disaster. Fortunately, Lucien still looked like any other person sitting in the pub with a pint and a burger in front of him. He'd been well cared for in The Retreat, but the lack of sunshine meant his summer tan had long gone.

Barak's gaze drifted to Estelle who, although eating, also kept a watchful eye on Lucien, and finally shifted to Jackson. "So, where in France are we heading? I'm hoping it's that Cathar castle in the Pyrenees." He and Estelle had found it with Ash's help about a month ago, and all three thought it sounded promising.

Jackson nodded, swallowing his food before he spoke. "Yes. I discussed it with Waylen and JD, and the more we investigated, the more we liked it. Although, there are a few castles in that region that offer promise, and many are linked to the Cathars." He sipped his Guinness before having another mouthful of his steak pie. "It's not a great time of year to be going there, though. It will be cold, and there'll be lots of snow."

Estelle shrugged. "If it's the place, we have to act, regardless of the weather."

"Slow down," Lucien instructed, glancing between them. "Where are you talking about?"

Lucien had not been involved in their conversations about possible bases for Black Cronos. They had all worried about his loyalty, especially Jackson, who suspected he may be a spy that Barak and Estelle had conveniently rescued. Barak understood Jackson's concerns. He and Estelle had endlessly dissected how they had rescued him from the underground lab, but nothing suggested that it was a convenient set-up. Especially the fact that some of the lab staff had been killed. Barak was sure that would not have been part of the plan. No, everything suggested that Lucien was a prisoner.

In addition, Lucien was genuinely distressed about his capture and the changes he'd been subjected to against his will. There was also his background to consider. Lucien had split from his long-term partner, a man called Davide, and devastated, had been searching for change and meaning to his life. Barak felt sorry for him. He had been vulnerable, and Black Cronos had taken advantage of that.

"Sorry, Lucien," Barak said, shuffling his position to look at him squarely. "We're getting ahead of ourselves. As you know, we're trying to find where Black Cronos is based. We looked at many remote castles, strongholds that might provide a base for the Count, and there are hundreds of possibilities, as we mentioned. We factored in that the count is immortal, with many powerful connections, particularly to royalty and nobility. Someone, or many people, supported him in the past. He had no obvious money of his own. But Estelle had the brilliant idea of focussing on places of power, or that have religious or astronomical significance."

He nodded at Estelle who said, "We know that the *comte* is—*was*—fascinated by alchemy, astrology, gems, angels, religion, magic, spirituality, and many other esoteric subjects. He thinks differently. He's subversive. A risk taker. Our investigation went wide and far, and we drifted to the Cathars."

"The Cathars?" Lucien shrugged. "Who are they?"

Barak continued. "A religious group of people who originated in about the twelfth century. They were considered heretics because of their beliefs. They believed in two Gods, not one." Barak paused, finding the subject odd because of the way it intersected with his own background. "They considered that the true God was the New Testament God, and that the Old Testament God was Satan. It's complex, I won't go into it all now, but they were linked to the Templars, and like them, the Church wanted them wiped out. Their beliefs were considered heresy. They had a huge power centre in the South of France, particularly the Pyrenees."

A smile of recognition crossed Lucien's face. "Of course. I remember the name, but I know little about them. They were a type of Gnostic, yes?"

"Yes, favouring personal growth with God over organised religion." Jackson snorted. "They've been linked to all sorts of subjects and people. Some of it seems inflated, but there's no doubt that they were hunted and their castles destroyed. The remains are littered across the Pyrenees, and one in particular looks promising. *Château de Bénaix.* It's privately owned and was rebuilt a couple of hundred years ago. It's positioned high up on a ridge and has astronomical links. Its chapel is aligned with the summer solstice."

"It's also," Estelle said, pushing her empty plate away, "remote and defensible."

"Who owns it now?"

"A family called Voland. They can trace their lineage back hundreds of years. Admittedly," Jackson said with a sigh, "there's only a tenuous link to the count through one of their ancestors who was an alchemist at the same time the count was '*alive*', but even so..."

Barak started to feel the stir of the hunt. Eager not only to find out more about the *comte* and the Cathars in the Pyrenees stronghold, but to explore a wild and mountainous region unknown to him. Somewhere he could spread his wings without city lights glowing below. And of course, another opportunity to spend time with Estelle.

"Where are we staying?" he asked Jackson. "I presume you've made arrangements."

"Yes. And it was very tricky at this time of year. The place is full of ski enthusiasts."

"I love skiing!" Lucien said, smiling. "I'm good at it, too."

"I'm so-so," Estelle said, wiggling her hands. "But hopefully cars will suffice for what we need."

"Well, courtesy of government connections, I've got you a house in Montferrier. A chalet, actually, on the slopes below *Monts d'Olmes* ski resort. It's big, too. I suspect some of your brothers will need to join you. *If* it's the right place," Jackson said, looking at Barak.

"That's fine. They're more than happy to help. Although, I think JD needs them and Shadow for something, and Nahum is tied up in Yorkshire for a few days."

Jackson's eyes darkened with worry. "That's okay. There's still more we need to find out before we act. Time for them to get things wrapped up and join you."

Barak nodded, hoping that Jackson's assessment of their time scale was correct. If they were right about the *château*, they couldn't handle it alone.

⚶ ⚶ ⚶

Darkness fell and the temperature plummeted. Nahum shivered, despite his warm clothing, but he adjusted the binoculars and focussed on the church below.

It was almost nine in the evening, and after a hearty meal, he and Olivia hiked back up the hill to watch the church. Olivia was right about this being the best place to watch. They had cruised around the area in the car, but it was hard to get close for a long period of time without it being obvious that they were watching. The church stood along a slight rise, surrounded by trees. Within the village, but slightly separate.

Olivia nudged him. "See those lights!"

"I see lights in the church. It doesn't mean anything."

"But it's a strange glow."

"It could be candlelight!"

"There's no service tonight."

"He could be praying. That's what vicars do."

She nudged him again, harder this time, so that he bashed the binoculars against his face. "Olivia!"

"He's walking from the vicarage. I can see him. And he's carrying something heavy. It's the reliquary."

Nahum adjusted his angle, watching Jacobsen, the vicar, trudge up the path. "I presume he doesn't keep it in the church because it's either too eye-catching and he fears it will be stolen, or he doesn't want anyone to know he's got it." He frowned, watching the awkward way he walked. "It's bigger than I expected." As soon as he said it, Nahum realised how weird that sounded. "Not that I'm overly familiar with reliquaries or anything."

"Some are big, some are tiny. It depends on what they contain. It's the gold and other precious metals and gems that usually make them so heavy. The more important the saint, the more ornate the container."

They'd changed their original plan. Olivia's car was parked in the village. Nahum would fly them in, and he would fly back out with the reliquary after tying the vicar up. She would escape on foot, and then meet him on the backroad out of town. It was so dark without city lights that he knew he wouldn't be seen.

He had tried to persuade her to let him steal it on his own, but she insisted on going. She wanted to make sure that up close the reliquary was the right one. Plus, it was her job, and she wanted to see it through.

Nahum lowered his binoculars as the vicar entered the church and studied Olivia, who was still watching Jacobsen. She was an attractive woman. Soft curves, long hair that was currently tied up in a messy bun, and very feminine, despite the heavy boots and camouflage clothing that she wore. "Are you sure you're happy to fly down there?"

She snorted and lowered the binoculars to stare at him. "Are you kidding me? Flying with a Nephilim? I can't wait! Are you sure you want to? It means stripping off, and it's freezing." Her eyes drifted down to his chest and back up again.

"I'll be fine. When I extend my wings, it banishes the cold. It's a weird trick of genetics. We don't feel the cold winds when we fly."

"Really? Interesting." Her lips twitched in a smile. "You'll have to promise me a longer experience some time."

He laughed. "Maybe you should see if you like it first."

"Fair enough. I suppose we should get started." She patted the pack at her side and smirked. "I have the ropes and stuff. Anyone would think I did this all the time."

He laughed, sure she stole such objects far more often than he suspected. "Don't you worry about being reported to the police?"

"He won't report it. These people never do. How would he explain owning something that was last seen in a museum in the 1840s? You don't look that concerned, either."

"I'm not. Although, this man does intrigue me. If what you say is true, he could be dangerous."

"All the more reason to restrain him quickly."

Nahum stood and stripped off his jacket, t-shirt, and jumper, and quickly extended his wings. He was used to people's reactions to his wings, but he still smiled at Olivia's wide-eyed expression.

"I know I've seen them before, but holy cow, Nahum. They are really something else..."

He opened his arms wide, aware her eyes were roving over his wings and bare chest. "Ready?"

"Am I ever!"

She placed her backpack on and stepped into his embrace. Her grip was tight, and after clasping his arms around her, he soared into the sky. She gasped and tightened her grip further. "Holy shit!"

"Shush! I'm just going to sweep around once before I land."

He took in the village, noting the empty streets, and the warm glow of lights coming from the pub, and then ensuring that the churchyard was empty, angled downward in a rush of flight. He landed soundlessly within the churchyard, close to the entrance, and for a moment just stood there, Olivia still clasped to him. He needed to make sure there were no traps or watchers, just in case they needed to leave right away.

The churchyard was deserted, the only light coming from the stained glass windows.

His skin prickled as he sensed ancient power he hadn't felt in a long time. He froze, Olivia still tight within his arms, the urge to flee strong. He fought down his panic, taking deep breaths.

"Nahum?" Olivia's question was barely a breath, spoken so softly only he could hear it. She eased back, hands on his chest as she looked up at him. "What's happening?"

"I feel something...unusual."

"Magic?" Olivia's pounding heartbeat echoed his own. "Should we leave?"

He liked that she didn't hesitate to ask, rather than insist they continue. But he had no intention of leaving. "No. Wait here."

He released her and edged to the main door of the church, the way the vicar had entered. With every step he took, the feeling increased. It was magic, but not of a kind he was expecting. It felt more like his own. Innate. Exalted. *Angelic...*

The huge door was shut tight, but he eased it open. Relieved it didn't squeak, he slipped inside quickly. Olivia, disobeying his request and just as silent, followed him inside and eased the door shut. They were in a small, square vestibule, and the glow came from the nave.

He withdrew his sword and edged to the nave's entrance. Only the altar was illuminated. A man was kneeling on the hard stone floor, a row of candles in front of him. The reliquary was placed on the altar. The candlelight reflected on its burnished surface and glinted off the gems inlaid into it. *Emeralds, rubies, sapphires. No wonder Jacobsen hid it.* It was certainly priceless. But it was what lay inside that troubled Nahum.

As yet the priest hadn't moved, still kneeling in wordless prayer. Nahum edged forward, keeping to the shadows. He should attack now, while he was occupied, but something delayed him. Curiosity, perhaps. Or fear.

He was aware that Olivia was staring as much at him as the priest, her anxiety climbing. He took a mental grip of himself and walked on. But halfway down the aisle, Jacobsen rose to his feet and opened the golden box. Instantly, he heard whispers; urgent, entreating, coaxing. They tugged at his memories. Demanded fealty.

And then the voice whispered a warning.

Jacobsen spun around, clutching something in his hands, and a wild-eyed look on his face. At the sight of Nahum, he screamed and dropped to his knees, face planted on the floor. An object tumbled forward, ringing loudly on stone as it bounced to Nahum's feet.

It was a thick, gold ring, inset with jewels.

Olivia had been crouched behind a pew, but now she bounded towards Jacobsen, taking advantage of his prone position.

Forcing himself to focus, Nahum scooped the ring up, the metal hot in his palm, and shoved it into his pocket before helping Olivia. He secured the blindfold on the vicar and bound his arms. Jacobsen didn't resist, so they were gentle. He was whispering about angels and God. Nahum laid his hand on his brow, willing him to be calm. He was no healer, but his father's blood still ran through his veins. If he wished, he could impose his will on others.

Instantly the man stopped fidgeting, but he still muttered softly. Nahum could imagine how he must have looked, lit by candlelight, his wings spread behind him. It was a wonder the man hadn't had a heart attack.

Olivia was crouched on the other side of Jacobsen, eyes wide in her pale face. She mouthed, "*Are you okay?*"

He nodded and stood, and together they crossed to the reliquary.

The inside lid of the golden casket was inscribed with angelic words and symbols, and on a bed of red velvet, was a skull. Next to it was a bracelet—a golden torc, beaten, inlaid with mysterious symbols. He could still hear whispers, and he asked, "Can you hear that?"

Olivia shook her head. "Hear what?"

"A voice." He pulled the ring from his pocket and compared it to the torc. "They match. They belong to a Fallen Angel." He threw the ring inside the casket and shut it. Instantly the whispers vanished, but the power emanating from it remained. "Let's get out of here. I presume this is what you were searching for?"

Olivia nodded. "Yes, but...it's not quite what I was expecting."

Nahum just wanted to leave. There was time enough for discussion later. His eyes swept the altar, seeing nothing else of note. Nothing unusual. "Are you okay to drive?"

"Yes. Are you okay to fly?"

He nodded. "See you in my room."

Four

O livia had calmed down by the time she returned to the hotel, and her hands had finally stopped shaking.

She might not have been able to hear the whispers that crawled from the casket, but she experienced a gnawing sensation in her brain, and an itching beneath her skin. She was just glad that the damn thing was with Nahum now.

But how was Nahum? His blue eyes had blazed when he saw the reliquary. A mixture of anger and bewilderment. *And maybe a trace of fear...*

She looked for him overhead, the memory of the flight vivid. His hard, warm body pressed to hers. The muscles she longed to explore further. The tantalising V that ran down to his groin. And the flight itself, of course. The rush of cold air. The feeling of space and freedom, and Nahum's power that he kept carefully concealed when his wings were folded away.

Of course, the reliquary itself was also emblazoned on her mind. She wasn't lying when she said it wasn't what she was expecting. She had been searching for only the skull, not the jewellery of a Fallen Angel. She needed tact for what was to come. Compassion.

She found Nahum in his hotel room, his blue eyes stormy, the reliquary sitting on the small table under the thickly curtained window.

"Nahum, I'm so sorry. I swear I didn't know what was in that. I thought it was just—"

He cut her off, his voice brusque with emotion. "It's fine. It's a shock, that's all. I'm not angry with you." He was less imposing with his wings folded away and his bare chest regrettably covered in a t-shirt—but only just. His height and broad shoulders still dominated the room.

"Would you mind if I opened the casket again? Does it hurt you?"

He laughed, a short, sharp bark of incredulity. "No, not hurt. Herne's balls, I need a drink. You?"

"Yes. Whatever's in that mini bar."

While he fixed the drinks, she studied the reliquary, shining the table lamp directly on it. It was definitely the one she had been seeking for her client. But it seemed more...*everything*. The gold shimmered, the gems sparkled, and now that she was close to it again, she could truly feel its magnetism.

"Why can't I hear the whispers that you can?" she asked when Nahum handed her a drink.

"Well, with the lid shut, they have quieted, but I still feel the power. Ancient power. As to why you can't?" He shrugged. "I'm Nephilim. The son of a Fallen Angel. I'd know that power anywhere. I was born with it. It runs in my veins, and it commanded me many, many years ago."

She noted his blue eyes had lost that stormy look, and it calmed her, too. "Can it command you still?"

"No. We threw that yoke off millennia ago." His eyes, which had been on her, now drifted back to the golden casket. "But it's unnerving to find that a piece of their jewellery is here. In the present. In this damn room. It should be under a pile of stone, or at the bottom of the ocean. No wonder people are going mad. Humans aren't meant to be close to it—not for prolonged periods, anyway."

"Well, *I'm* not going mad, or being destructive," Olivia pointed out. "Although, the itching under my skin is really annoying."

"Itching?"

"Like a crawling sensation, I suppose. Or a cold ooze of something."

"Some humans are more susceptible than others. Your body recognises something powerful, but can't place it." Nahum ran his fingers across the designs on the surface.

"Do they mean something?"

"No. These are just ornate, but inside..." He cocked his head at her. "Ready?"

She gulped a mouthful of neat gin. "Now I am."

He opened the casket and immediately the sensation under her skin increased. She shuddered. "You can hear the whispers? Many voices, or just one?"

He nodded. "Just one." He picked up the ring and examined it, turning it over, his long fingers probing it.

"I didn't think the Fallen had real bodies."

"They inhabited the flesh of men. Not for long, though. They burnt them up if they stayed in too long. But they liked precious metals, and adorned themselves with them." He shrugged. "Much like we did, at one point."

"I find that hard to believe."

He smirked. "It was expected of us. Gabe was draped in the stuff when he wasn't in battle, and Niel. So was Ash, come to think of it. The others, I'm not so sure. I saw less of them in our other life."

She could imagine them oiled and perfumed, resplendent in rich fabrics in their palaces once they'd bathed the dust and blood of battle away, something like the torc on their upper arms. She noted the small indentations that marked the torc's surface, and the perfect gems. Mesmerised, she reached in and picked it up.

Images suddenly rocketed into her mind—flaming eyes, alabaster skin, wings of grey feathers, and what looked like a palace in the stars. Her legs collapsed under her, and she stumbled and would have fallen if not for Nahum. His arm wrapped around her, and he wrestled the torc from her tightly clasped fingers.

"Bloody hell, Olivia! What did you touch it for?"

"I didn't think!" She felt breathless. Sick. A thrum of power tingled through her fingers and up her arm, and the cold, oozing feeling intensified. It was as if a river of slime flowed under her skin. She lowered herself to the bed. "Sorry, that was stupid..."

"It's my fault. I should have warned you."

A film of sweat had gathered on her brow, and she wiped it away. "I need water."

In seconds Nahum handed her a glass and she drank it down in one go, her mind and body slowly steadying. The torc was now looking innocent on the table.

"What happened?" Nahum asked, watching her intently.

She described the image. "An angel?"

"Perhaps. Probably." He frowned, clearly annoyed at the jewellery and its effects rather than her. "No more holding jewellery for you." Nahum placed it back in the box, shut the lid, and sealed it with the catch.

"What's written on the inner lid? I don't recognise the language."

"A mixture of angelic and Aramaic script. Protection to control the power of the contents. The symbols are protective, too."

Feeling steadier, and a little foolish at how much the torc had affected her, Olivia reached for her gin, cupping it in her hands. "Do you think Jacobsen will remember your face? I dived for cover as soon as he turned."

"He will hopefully think he was hallucinating. That he saw an angel. I can't believe I went in there with my wings still visible. I was so shocked at what I felt that I didn't think." He sat at the head of the bed, puffed his pillows, and then leaned back, legs stretched in front of him.

Olivia shifted to face him, cross-legged. "It's good you did. If he'd have seen a normal man, he wouldn't have dropped to the floor. Do you think he knew he had Fallen Angel jewels?"

"I was about to ask you the same question! You said you didn't expect the jewellery?"

"No. I've read lots about this reliquary, including the various churches and museums it was displayed in until it vanished. My client has been following it, too. Strange stories have always been attached to it, but there has never been any recorded mention of the jewels. Just the skull."

Nahum frowned. "The inscription? The symbols?"

"Also never mentioned."

"Which suggests someone added them to the casket years later. During its lost years. When did you say it vanished? Or when was it stolen, should I say?"

Olivia had reams of notes, but without them at her fingertips, she couldn't remember details. "Mid-nineteenth century, from a religious museum in Italy. Overnight it just vanished, but rumours surfaced every now and again. A visitor to a minor nobility's palace in Italy recorded seeing it in his memoirs. Then someone else said they saw it in a private collection in Austria. Then it was rumoured that it was in a church in France. Breadcrumbs only. My client has undertaken extensive research himself. He never mentioned jewellery."

"And the madness and violence?"

"Seems to be something that started happening only in the last hundred years or so."

Nahum watched her, eyes steady before they drifted to the casket. "Your client doesn't know about the jewels."

"You don't want him to have them, do you?"

"No." He looked regretful but determined, his jaw clenched hard.

Silence fell, the only sound coming from the hum of the heating, and the tinkle of ice in their glasses. It was a comfortable silence. Olivia felt safe with Nahum. But she also felt the pull of attraction. He was so alive. Virile. Sexy.

She should go to bed.

"He'll never know," she eventually said. "If you think you should, keep them. Especially considering the effect the torc had on me. Unless, of course, my client is keeping things from me, but I doubt it. I just hope Jacobsen will be okay." She considered his prostrate body on the floor. "But what was he doing with the skull and the jewellery? Was he being compelled? And if so, why?"

"That's a great question. I need to identify which Fallen Angel it is. That might help us. I'll take photos of the casket and the writing before you leave, if that's okay."

"Of course." She drained her drink, wanting another. "Thank you. And now I should go to bed. I need a shower. I'm dusty. And I need to wash *that* off me." She nodded at the casket. "I'm not looking forward to driving with it for hours."

"You drove up here?"

She laughed. "I can't very well put that on a flight."

"I'll drive back with you."

She smiled. He was a gentleman. Thoughtful. "You don't have to."

"I want to. Even if I take the jewellery, I won't know if they've left any residual energies. Besides, without the casket to protect everyone from their worst effects, I might send the whole flight mad. I can book another car in London and drive home."

The offer relieved her more than she expected. "I'd love that. But only if you're sure."

"I'm sure." He stood and stretched. "I need a shower, too." In seconds he had peeled off his t-shirt, once again revealing abs to die for, and that V that disappeared into his low-slung jeans. She knew she was staring. She couldn't help it. Didn't want to help it.

Olivia scrambled to her feet. She wasn't a teenage ingenue, but right now, she felt like one. "I better go."

His voice was rough. Hopeful. "I was hoping you'd stay. It's a big shower, and a big bed." His eyes darkened with desire. Those gorgeous blue eyes that glowed like sapphires against his olive skin. "No strings. No hard feelings if you walk away. Fallen Angels leave me feeling wrung out. I don't want to spend the night alone. But neither should you feel obliged to stay just because of that. I'm a big boy. I'll cope."

"I bet you're a big boy." It was out before she could control herself. "Oops."

"Is that yes?" He smiled and stepped closer, and desire shot through her.

No strings, no regrets, no second thoughts.

It was definitely a yes.

Nahum awoke in the middle of night, suddenly alert, his body wrapped around Olivia's heat and her spicy scent wafting in the air.

He froze, his senses on alert for strange noises or movement in the dark, but the hotel room was quiet, and his keen eyesight revealed that nothing was untoward. For a second he couldn't place what had awoken him, until the image flashed into his mind again. The flaming eyes that compelled obedience and obligation.

Once.

Was it the power of the jewellery that forced these images into his mind, or was it the angel himself, somehow connecting to him? Nahum would rather not debate it now. He would prefer to lie within Olivia's warm embrace. She was a bold and confident woman and knew what she wanted, and he was only too happy to oblige—despite his earlier reservations. He still wondered why he had suggested they sleep together. The idea had popped into his head as she sat cross-legged on the bed, her hair tumbling around her shoulders, testing desires that he ultimately gave in to. Maybe it helped that she was such a flirt.

But he hadn't been lying, either. The power of the Fallen Angel contained within the jewellery really had affected him.

Easing out of her arms, he rolled onto his back, staring up at the ceiling. He was pretty sure that he knew which Fallen Angel the jewellery had belonged to, but he needed to know more. If the pieces hadn't been in the reliquary to begin with, how had they got there? As much as he didn't want to leave the bed, he knew he needed to return to the church, and Jacobsen. There were still hours of darkness left, and tomorrow he would be too far away. He'd been far too surprised earlier to ask any questions. And he'd feared keeping Olivia there too long. She was recognisable, and vulnerable. He was not.

Nahum rolled out of bed and pulled his jeans on, then slipped out onto the balcony. The area was deserted, and within seconds he was flying high above the huddle of buildings and toward the next town. He wondered if the church would be in darkness, but a dim light still glowed behind the stained glass windows. *Curious. Was Jacobsen still praying?* That would at least save him from having to break into the rectory to wake him up and question him. Regrettably, he'd have to leave his wings out for show. It would frighten him again, but as much as he hated doing that, Nahum needed answers. With luck, he'd think he was having a vision.

Once Nahum was standing inside the door of the church again, he heard a low voice. But it was strange. There were gaps, as if the vicar was conversing with someone rather than praying alone. His voice rose with a plea. Frowning, Nahum edged to the door, seeing the church lit as before, candles on the altar, the vicar on his knees. At least the man had been able to free himself from his restraints. The ropes lay on the floor, cast aside.

Something, though, was very wrong here. The presence of the Fallen Angel was still strong. *How, though?* The Igigi had said they had restricted their movement on Earth.

Hating his decision, but knowing he had to make an impression, Nahum stepped inside the nave, extended his wings, and flew to the darkness of the roof. He then lowered his voice, injecting power that he hadn't used in years. "Jacobsen, I have questions that you must answer."

Emitting a startled gasp, the man on the floor squirmed, looking up in alarm. Nahum hovered, arms outstretched, knowing the candlelight made his feathers glow, and exploiting it. He dropped and hovered over the altar, his blue eyes pinning the man to the spot.

Nahum spoke commandingly. "Did you hear me, Jacobsen?"

Jacobsen's eyes widened with horror before cunning settled into them. "You're not Him."

"Who? God?"

"No! The angel I speak with. He told me you would return."

"You speak with him still? Even though I took his belongings?"

And then Nahum saw what he'd missed earlier. The clasp at the neck of the man's surplus that had been hidden by his fall—unless he hadn't been wearing it then. *Another piece of the Fallen Angel's jewellery.* Aware of Nahum's piercing stare, the vicar's hand flew to cover it. "It's mine."

"How can you wear it? Or even bear to touch it?"

"Because I have been *chosen*." Fire flashed in Jacobsen's eyes, and he staggered to his feet. "He says you drowned. That you have no place in this world."

A chill raced across Nahum's skin that had nothing to do with the cold church, and he unleashed his anger. "*I* have no place? And what of the one you talk to? He fell and was never supposed to walk on Earth. How dare he presume to talk with you?"

"I am His messenger!"

"Delivering *what*? Death? Madness? Cruelty? I met your supposed master once. I remember him because I fought his offspring. I won. You can remind him of *that*." Nahum withdrew his sword, a slow, deliberate hiss of menace as the blade whispered from its sheath. "Do I need to use it again?"

"You cannot hurt me!" But Jacobsen scuttled backwards, dark eyes uncertain.

"I most certainly can. Tell me how you found the jewellery."

"What does it matter?"

"I'm curious." Nahum landed in front of the altar, eyes darting everywhere, fearing some trick. "Tell me the name of your master."

"He won't let me."

Nahum laughed. "I'll make a guess, then. I'm sure I'm right. But first, tell me about the jewellery." He placed his blade beneath the man's chin. Jacobsen shot back so quickly, he hit the pew behind him and sat down.

"I found it in the casket."

"Liar. It never used to be there."

"I found them there!"

"In the reliquary you stole? That's not very worthy of a man of God."

"Neither is holding a sword to my throat, Nephilim."

"This *is* my job. You know that. I was the eyes and ears of the Fallen. The deliverer of rules, laws, and death to those who did not obey. Until I too rebelled. Give me answers." Nahum pressed harder, breaking the delicate skin beneath the man's chin. "If you think he will save you, you're wrong. Only your answer can save you now."

And as the man began to spill his secrets, Nahum knew he couldn't allow him to live. He contained too much darkness. Too much of his master—because he was in thrall, no doubt of that. Nahum had not envisaged having to dispense justice this night. He hoped Olivia would forgive him. And that her soft curves would drown it out afterward.

Five

S hadow was looking forward to the group's new job, but was far less enthusiastic about seeing JD. She tried to hide her impatience with him. She failed.

"You mean you haven't worked it out yet?" She gestured to the Emerald Tablet placed in the centre of the greenhouse in his extensive grounds. Due to the season, it was mostly empty, except for the plants kept in there to overwinter, and a selection of seed trays.

He glared at her, lips curling with disdain. "No! How many times do I need to explain this? It has hidden its mysteries for millennia, and no one has seen it since *their* time!" He jabbed his fingers toward Gabe, Ash, and Niel. "I'm brilliant, but not a miracle worker. Don't you ever listen?"

Refusing to be chastened, she shrugged. "I block out whining."

Gabe intervened with a pleading glance. "Shadow, shut up. This isn't helping. JD, focus please. The job? Egypt, you say?"

JD turned away from Shadow to face Gabe, his irritation still bubbling. "Yes. That's where I hope the key to this will be. I've done extensive research, and I'm sure of it."

"The thing is, JD," Ash started cautiously, "Egypt has been investigated by teams of archaeologists for years. How can you be sure that the key hasn't already been found? Or that it's there at all. It's a long way to go on a hunch."

"Not a hunch!" JD repeated, looking smug. "*Research*. Besides, it's already been found. I just need you to steal it."

Shadow's irritation turned to delight. "Theft is one of my favourite jobs! This sounds better by the second!"

Niel snorted. "It depends where we're stealing it from!"

"Ah. That's where this gets tricky," JD admitted.

"Of course it does," Gabe said with a sigh. "Go on."

"A few years ago, a team of archaeologists discovered an ancient pharaonic city built along the banks of the Nile. Many treasures were recovered, and one of them was a curious emerald disc with an ibis sitting proud of it." JD fished in his capacious pocket and pulled out a dogeared image that highlighted several Egyptian treasures, one of which was the disc. Unfortunately, the image didn't reveal much detail. "Not much has been posted about it since, but it resides in The Museum of Egyptian Antiquities in Aswan. It was once a private mansion, but now houses many Egyptian artifacts. I didn't give it much thought before. Not until I received the tablet. Can one of you help me turn it over?"

Niel was closest, and he waved JD away. "Let me."

"Put it on this bench—carefully!"

A soft velvet cloth had been laid across the wooden bench, and effortlessly, Niel picked up the heavy tablet and flipped it on its side.

JD tapped the base. "See? There is an indentation in it."

They all leaned forward to see better. A circle, about a handspan in width, was carved into the bottom of the tablet. In the centre was another shape, and if Shadow squinted, she could see a bird with a long beak. When it was upright, it was impossible to see due to the cloudy interior of the stone. The interior, that under a certain light, appeared to contain swirling clouds or stars.

Confused, she asked, "An ibis is a bird?"

"Yes. It represents a few things, including the Egyptian God, Thoth. He made the tablet."

Even more confused, Shadow said, "I thought Hermes did."

Unexpectedly patient, JD explained, "Thoth is also known as Hermes to the Greeks."

"Could it be a flaw in the emerald?" Ash asked. "It doesn't look that clear cut to me. The circle could just be a mount. Are you sure it's an ibis?"

"I considered that," JD admitted, reaching into his pocket again. "Until I pressed some plasticine into it. I made a mould." He withdrew a small clay disc. "I've considered making a gemstone replica, but I know I need the real thing."

Harlan whistled. "That's an ibis, all right."

Gabe nodded. "Okay. At least we know what we're looking for."

JD grimaced. "There are no details on the museum's website, or in fact any recent images at all. I just know it's listed as being on display. The museum has certainly not linked it to the Emerald Tablet. But it's just too much of a coincidence…"

"I agree," Niel said. "An emerald disc with an ibis relief that matches this. It has to be it." He eyed his companions. "It's worth trying, at least."

Ash didn't look convinced. "The ibis is a popular motif. It might not have anything to do with this at all. And there's no mechanism." He ran his fingers along the base of the tablet. "There's nothing to twist. No locking system. I mean, what could it do? More importantly, is it dangerous to put them together?"

Harlan folded his arms across his chest, a speculative eye on JD. "JD thinks the Emerald Tablet is supposed to be bigger. He thinks this key will magically make it grow. Perhaps it will. That thing is weird."

"Make it grow?" Shadow said, incredulous. "I suppose it could happen. Magic can achieve many amazing things. And the tablet is very odd. It has a compelling magnetism to it." Her eyes drifted to it, despite her attempts to look elsewhere. She noticed her companions were drawn to it, too. They glanced at each other for seconds only before their eyes slid back to the tablet.

"I have also seen the ancient images," Ash said, nodding. "Some do show that it is easily twice the height of a man."

"I heard stories about it way back," Niel said immediately. "It had a certain mystique, even then. There were whispers about its powers."

"And its size," Gabe agreed. "But I never saw it myself. But JD, why do you want to make it bigger?"

"That's easy. Because I sense there is something hidden in there that can only be seen when it's at its correct size." A gleam of desire kindled in his eyes. "I need to see what that is if I'm to even begin unlocking its secrets."

Secrets that perhaps might be better remaining hidden, but Shadow wasn't about to voice that.

Gabe addressed the team. "Do we want the job?"

"Of course we do," Shadow answered immediately.

"Not so fast, madam." Gabe stared at JD. "How big is the museum? Security?"

JD had the grace to look sheepish. "I'm actually not sure. It's a museum, so I presume that of course they take their security very seriously. I was rather hoping that you would find all of that out yourself..." He bristled. "It's part of your job."

Gabe nodded. "I guess that's true."

Ash was already searching on his phone, and he showed them a photo of a large, attractive mansion with a courtyard on the banks of the Nile. "It doesn't look like a fortress—unlike The Nubian Museum."

"I don't care how much security it has." Shadow grinned. "I love a challenge! I have fey stealth, you three have wings. How hard could it be?"

"Hold on!" Harlan said. "First of all, I will be of no help on this job, but I do know practicalities! How are you going to get it through airport security? If you're searched, you'll be in big trouble. You can put your weapons in checked baggage, but you can't risk that."

"All in hand, my dear boy," JD said breezily. "Years ago, I had a box made for me for just such events. I may have done a bit of smuggling in my past. I had a very nice witch friend of mine spell a box with disguising and hiding spells. It's very effective. You will take that." They all looked doubtful, but he just smiled smugly. "Trust me. You are far more useful to me out of prison than in. I have also arranged your transport through Jackson. You already have a flight booked tomorrow on a government plane. Some diplomats have business in Egypt. Please be discreet, and try not to cause an international incident."

Estelle admired the view that surrounded the chalet in Montferrier and shivered, despite the warmth of the house.

It was cold, brutal weather outside. The snow-capped mountains were spectacular but deadly. A night outside, without shelter, would mean certain death. The suspected stronghold of the *comte* would be high up and hard to access. Tackling this in the summer would make life so much easier.

The group had arrived only hours earlier, driving from the closest airport. Lucien hadn't travelled so far in months, and he was worried and wary, as were she and Barak. But the trip had gone well, and now Lucien was resting. It was something they had observed about him. When he was tired, he was more vulnerable to shifting into a super-soldier.

She heard the soft-footed approach of Barak moments before his arm snaked around her waist and pulled her against him. She smiled, twisting to look up at him, her lips seeking his.

"You're always so quiet!"

He kissed her and then grinned. "Always?"

"Well, except for when you're singing or laughing. Then, you're very loud!" Barak had an excellent voice and loved to sing, serenading her sometimes with the worst music just to make her laugh. And he had the best laugh. Loud, energetic, and infectious. She was lucky to have him, and that made her frightened to consider what they faced now. She would die to protect him; she knew that now. The intensity of her feelings shocked her. She had never felt that way about anyone else in her life.

"You're worrying about the job," he said, releasing her and leaning against the window frame.

"I'd be mad not to. Look out there! It's beautiful and harsh, and if we're right, we'll be fighting Black Cronos in their own space. They know it well. We don't."

His eyes drifted to the breath-taking view and the high peaks. "I know. But we can't afford to delay. They're already strong, and for all we know, are getting stronger. More unfortunate men—or women—like Lucien could be getting kidnapped and experimented on right now. At least we know that we managed to shut down one place."

They had returned to the *Château du Buade* a week after they had rescued Lucien with the rest of the Nephilim. At night, they entered by the rear doors that led to the lab, but the place had been cleaned out. It had been frustrating, but also a relief to know that base was finished. As for the *château* and the family, other than the placement of the base, there was actually nothing to link the family to it, other than the historical connection to the count. It might have been on their property, but there was nothing that would stand up in court. The family was so powerful that the local police refused to interview them without concrete evidence. It was a dead end. Jackson had used experts to investigate their finances, but everything was neat and tidy, and any pressure that he'd been hoping to exert from that side was a dead end, too.

Estelle sighed. "True, but how many more places are there?"

"Let's just worry about this one for now. We need to decide on our next step."

"Reconnaissance. But that will be tricky."

"Not for me."

"But you'll be on your own!" Estelle argued against him—again. They had discussed this earlier on the flight. Barak was going to fly over the old citadel to assess the activity there, and had refused to take her with him.

"I'll be swift, manoeuvrable, and high. I can fly just as easily in the cold as in the heat."

"And if they have lookouts with crossbows as they had before, and you're shot with poison?"

"They won't see me. I'll stay high. It's just reconnaissance." He held her gaze, his brown eyes steady and reassuring. "I'll be fine. The best way you can help me is by studying the map of the area. I think I hear Lucien stirring. There's a huge table in the kitchen, let's set up there. I'll cook while we work."

They had stopped at a supermarket and bought a mountain of food and drinks, and the kitchen was well-stocked. Barak had made his mind up, and on this she knew he wouldn't change it. He was being protective.

"Okay. Done."

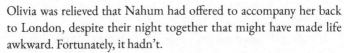

Olivia was relieved that Nahum had offered to accompany her back to London, despite their night together that might have made life awkward. Fortunately, it hadn't.

Although the casket was in the boot of the car, she was aware of its presence, and she blocked it out by talking about anything and everything rather than the night before.

She knew he'd left in the middle of the night after she woke to an empty bed, and it was obvious where he'd gone. When he returned, he looked hollowed out, but she didn't say a word. She'd just opened her arms and comforted him. She knew that what they'd found that night had changed everything.

A Fallen Angel had found a voice.

It was now mid-afternoon, and they had stopped at a service station on the A1. Rather than eat in the café though, she had taken food back to the car. Nahum sat with the casket open on his lap, and as she slid into her seat, he shut it.

The insidious feelings were already trying to dominate her thoughts. She passed him his coffee and a pre-packaged sandwich. "I'll be glad to see the back of those jewels. However, I think it's time we talked about last night. The hour that you were missing."

He sipped his drink, eyes wary. "You'll hate me for what I did."

"I don't think I could ever hate you. What happened?"

He looked at her, his blue eyes once again darkening, but not with desire this time. Memories, more likely. "I killed him."

Olivia chose her words carefully. She could see that Nahum hated his actions. "You're not a monster, Nahum. You obviously felt that you had to. Tell me why."

"He was in thrall to a Fallen Angel. People were dying. It wouldn't have stopped. In fact, I'm sure it would have become worse. I couldn't reason with him, even though I tried."

"That's hardly surprising. You told me the Fallen are strong. *Were* strong." She tore off a piece of her sandwich, finding it hard to meet Nahum's intense stare. She forced herself to anyway. He needed to be heard. "We shouldn't have left straightaway. I should have been there with you."

"No way. I wouldn't have wanted you there. I had to go alone. But I only went back to question him. Get some details. But he was talking to the Fallen. He was in his head."

Recalling the insidious feel of the whispers crawling over her skin made her shudder. "I guess that can never end well. But we took the jewellery, so how could that happen?"

"Because he had another piece that we missed. A clasp on his surplus. It confirmed that the angel was Belial." The name seemed to hang in the air, a dark cloud between them. "Even though I took the clasp, I could see Jacobsen was still affected by him."

Olivia swallowed. "I think I've heard of him. He's bad news, I presume?"

"Very."

"Why?"

"He was one of Sammael's closest. Sammael's other name is Lucifer."

"As in the devil. Great..." She sipped her drink, but her hand shook, and she placed it in the drink holder. "So, we're facing some kind of Armageddon?"

"No. I wouldn't go that far." Nahum smiled and squeezed her hand. "Sammael had a bad rep because he caused the Fall. He was the first to walk out. He wasn't all bad, though. He just wanted independence. Belial, who has been conflated with Sammael over time, was meaner spirited. Freedom went to his head, and he exploited his power. All of the Nephilim that he fathered were the worst of all. They were known as the Sons of Destruction. The House of Belial. That's what the families were called, you remember? Houses. Remiel, my father, hated Belial. We were sworn enemies."

Olivia nodded. Nahum had told her about this over dinner the other night. "And you were of the House of Remiel. You had more brothers than just Gabe?"

"Yes. There were hundreds of us."

"And therefore, there were hundreds in the House of Belial."

He nodded. "We were armies, bringing destruction, until some of us rebelled." He flashed her a grin. "Rebellion runs in our blood."

"Mine, too. And the jewellery?"

"It was common for all of the Fallen to fashion some, but as I said, no human could sustain a Fallen Angel for long. But Nephilim also had jewellery made, and weapons fashioned to our design, with the emblem of our house upon them. All long gone of course, until now."

Olivia took another bite of her sandwich, and the food made her feel better. A memory suddenly struck her. "Not *all* long gone. The Temple of the Trinity had weapons there."

"You're right. I'd forgotten that! I guess because they were buried when the temple was destroyed. But it's surprising what parts of the past survive." Nahum finally relaxed and started to eat. "That's why museums are so fascinating."

"Which suggests that if Belial's jewellery has survived, others' could have, too. Jacobsen is dead, but what about Belial now that he has no acolyte?"

"Great question. We thought the Igigi had dealt with them, but Belial was always wily. Taking his jewellery might be the end of it, but I need to talk to my brothers—if I can get us all in the same room together."

"You still haven't told me how Jacobsen found Belial's jewellery. Or why a seemingly respectable vicar stole this priceless reliquary."

"He didn't. It was donated to him by a mysterious benefactor. The jewellery was already in it."

"Really?" Olivia squirmed in her seat to look at him. "You know, I don't often ask questions when I 'retrieve' objects. I can't, most of the time. My end objective is to get whatever it is and get out. However, I'm pleased you went back. This casts a whole new light on the situation. So, what now?"

"You give the casket to your buyer, and I..." he shrugged, "think about Belial and these *trinkets*."

Olivia liked the hunt, and she liked Nahum—not that she was expecting any more bedroom antics between them. The previous night would stick with her forever. However, she certainly didn't want to be left out. "But then what? Will you need help?"

He levelled his gaze at her. "I'm not sure this is something you should be involved in."

"Oh, Nahum. How little you know me. I already am!"

Six

Barak's raven-black wings blended in perfectly with the thick clouds that gathered over Montferrier, and after taking a moment to orientate himself, he flew to the *Château de Bénaix*.

These mountains were riddled with old castles, many crumbled ruins. He flew further than he first intended to take in the vista spread below. Thick snow blanketed the heights, making it hard sometimes to discern the true landscape. But the ruined buildings stood out, like a chain across the peaks. Defensible, tough, and remote.

Barak had read about the Cathars and felt sorry for them. They had been hunted only because they had strayed from the word of the Church. It seemed impossible that they had vanished into history after seeing these mountains and impressive buildings. He had never needed to fight in such extreme cold, but he'd certainly had to attack such fortifications before. They never fared so well when Nephilim attacked. Their angelic abilities were no match for men, although other paranormal beings certainly put up a fight—such as the Igigi and the servants of other Gods.

However, the Nephilim didn't have to contend with modern warfare. Although trebuchets hadn't been invented back then, spears were deadly, as were arrows when they came into close enough range. Of course, there were always paranormal weapons, too. *But what defences did the count have—if this was even the place?*

He swept around, approaching the citadel from the south. It stood on a steep-sided peak, a winding road meandering to a huge gate set into a thick wall. Within the walls were extensive courtyards set around a huge, sprawling castle, its many towers reaching towards the cloud draped sky.

Barak dropped lower, turning in a wide circle. The walls had broad ramparts, and where the walls turned, he saw lights in square towers, containing guards, no doubt. Lined up along the walls were huge bows and weapons that looked like cannons. That suggested they were correct in their assumptions. Whilst most occupied castles would surely have some kind of security, this seemed excessive. Especially when considering the remote location. A few guards patrolled the walls, wrapped up against the cold.

An area to the east of the building caught his eye. A large expanse that stretched to the perimeter wall seemed to have markings on the ground—all swept clear of snow. Barak had come prepared. He pulled binoculars from a pack strapped to his chest and studied them. It was a huge series of concentric circles, all marked with sigils and signs. It looked like JD's device, only it was vast in comparison. They denoted the astrological signs, planets, metals, the elements, and many other things. He recognised angelic symbology and ancient languages, too. And then he realised something else as he studied it further. *It was aligned to the compass.*

He felt sure he was looking at the centre of the *comte's* organisation, and that potentially there were layers of buildings, caves, and tunnels beneath the castle. The largest tower caught his eye next. A gleam of light shone within the highest window, and what appeared to be a communications array jutted from the top. He flew to it, far from the lights below, and settled into deep shadow. He could afford to stay here and watch for a while. See what scuttled below.

Gabe lowered his binoculars and considered their options. There weren't many.

The Museum of Egyptian Antiquities was set in a beautiful building with gilded courtyards and long balconies, all surrounded by large, landscaped grounds. These were also filled with sculptures and ornate walkways. And all of it was actively patrolled by guards.

Shadow wasn't put off. "I told you it would be fun."

"That's because you're nuts."

"You know I'm right. You love this stuff. We can afford to set off alarms and just fly out of there. They won't catch us."

"That's reckless and stupid, and I know that you are neither of those things."

She grinned. "But it would be so much fun! However, stealth is always best."

"And no deaths! *No one* needs to die. They're just guards doing their job. Understood?"

He loved Shadow, but there was no denying her ruthless streak. It was unnerving, and it was even more unnerving that he, a Nephilim, should think that.

"I'm not a complete monster!"

"No. Just a little bit of one."

She leaned forward and kissed him. "You say the sweetest things."

Their flight had arrived a few hours earlier, just before the museum had closed, and their team had managed to enter and see some of the halls. The problem was that they hadn't found the green disc of Thoth, and there were still many halls to search. With a deep sigh, he twisted in his seat on the top of the high wall bordering a neighbouring private garden, and turned to face the Nile. The rush of the current over the cataracts was loud in the still night. They were away from central Aswan here, out in the suburbs. He had never been here in his first life, as they all called it, but he knew Barak and Ash had.

Ash had studied the city with his cool, speculative gaze, his golden eyes taking in all the changes. His conclusion was that it was better before. Gabe was glad he had nothing to compare it to. Memories sometimes got in the way.

"Come on, madam. Time to go." He stood and opened his arms, and Shadow stepped into his embrace. He lifted her and she wrapped her legs around his waist. Even on top of a wall she stirred deep desire within him. But he launched into the air, wings extended, and crossed the warren of dark lanes to their rental car. Niel had been monitoring the area from above, and he swept down to join them.

"Anyone watching us?" Gabe asked. No one should be. This had nothing to do with Black Cronos—hopefully—but they were taking lots of precautions, regardless.

"Nope. All quiet around here. What's security look like at night?"

"As you'd expect. Patrols, guns, alarms, gates, lights. The works."

They joined Ash in the car, and Niel said, "Right now, I'm starving, but I'll come back later and watch for a few hours. Get an idea of patrol times and security patterns. That will help."

"Not if we can't find the disc in the museum," Ash said. He checked the mirror and pulled away. "If it's in storage, we're in trouble. Those places have endless rooms of stuff they haven't looked at in years."

Shadow huffed. "We haven't seen all the halls yet. That place is bigger than it appears. There are plenty of other areas it could be. Calm down. We'll find it tomorrow."

Her blithe confidence always amused and reassured Gabe. "You're right, there is still plenty to see inside. One way or another, we'll find it. We just have to be careful not to show our faces there too often. We'll visit once more tomorrow, so we need to be thorough."

Gabe watched the lights of Aswan sliding past the window, the streets becoming busier as they entered the main town. Aswan was a large city, the centre of commerce for old Egypt, and a popular place for tourists. Small islands crowded the river, as well as huge, abandoned temples and palaces. Many of the temples had been moved, brick by brick, years before. When the Aswan Dam was built to control the river flow, it had flooded part of the valley, creating the largest man-made lake, Lake Nasser. All of the old temples had been moved and rebuilt. Ash had had trouble reconciling the old with the new.

Gabe felt the familiar catch at the back of his throat that he'd felt in Mardin, back in Turkey. Here their own past was too close. Too raw. As much as he liked to visit these places, and to connect with cultures similar to his own, it was also too painful. Living in Cornwall, close to the quaint fishing villages, made life more comfortable.

"But we do the job tomorrow, yes?" Shadow asked, interrupting his thoughts. "There's no point in delaying."

"Yes. We do it tomorrow. The big question is, Shadow, will that box really hide the disc as we go through customs? If not, and we're searched, we'll be arrested for antiquities theft."

She patted his knee placatingly. "Have a little faith."

Niel just snorted. "I'd do better flying it out."

"Across how many countries?" Gabe asked, wishing Niel would be realistic. "It would take weeks."

"Just saying." He spread his hands wide as he twisted in his seat to grin at Shadow. "I'll grab it and make a run for it while Shadow gets arrested. Then you'd wish you'd gone with that plan." He winked at her. "I'd miss you—maybe..."

She scowled at him. "As if airport security could hold me."

Amused, Gabe let their banter wash over him. Niel and Shadow always bickered, winding each other up constantly, but he knew they would also defend each other to the death. They all would. He hoped it wouldn't come to that over the next twenty-four hours.

Harlan eyed Jackson over his pint of ale, noting how tired he looked. His shaggy hair needed a wash, his clothes seemed even more dishevelled than usual, and he had dark circles under his eyes.

"You need to get some sleep while you can. Lucien is out there with Barak and Estelle. He has control of his abilities now. Your babysitting time is over."

Jackson huffed into his Guinness. "Easy for you to say."

"Easy for you to do." He turned to Olivia, who was sipping a glass of white wine and looking preoccupied that evening. "What do you think?"

"I think as mere mortals, we need to trust them. We certainly can't protect them. Not in any physical way, anyway. You're exhausting yourself for nothing, Jackson."

Jackson shook his head, leaning back in his seat as he eyed the room. "I can't just switch off."

They were in a crowded pub near Hyde Park, and it was close to closing time. Conversation was loud, Christmas lights were twinkling, and festive music played in the background. Harlan's own mood was good. He hadn't needed to go to Egypt, which was a relief. As much as he would have loved some winter sunshine, getting arrested was not his idea of fun, and he certainly had nothing to offer Gabe's team. He'd left JD musing over the Emerald Tablet and returned to The Orphic Guild and his London flat. Olivia had phoned him earlier that evening and suggested a drink, and now they were all caught up on each other's news.

Harlan looked at Olivia. "So, your client didn't say a word about the casket's missing items?"

"They weren't 'missing,' remember?" She grinned. "No. He was very happy with the casket and the skull. But now I can't help wondering who gave the damn thing to Jacobsen."

"Someone who wanted to unleash a bit of devilry, obviously," Jackson said. "How long did he have it?"

"Close to five years. I'm surprised he hasn't gone completely mad in that time." She corrected herself, clutching her wine glass as if her life depended on it. "*Hadn't*. You saw the news, I presume?"

Harlan nodded. The news report had said a vicar had been found murdered in front of the altar in his church. The murderer had been decried as a cruel madman.

If only they knew.

"Nahum did the right thing, all things considered."

"What if he'd recovered over time?"

Harlan gave a dry laugh. "Like you just said, we need to trust them. Nahum is a good man. He considers things. He wouldn't have killed him if he didn't think he needed to."

"I know."

"So, what now?" Jackson asked her. "Will you follow it up?"

"I'm not doing anything as far as the jewellery goes. That's all on Nahum and his brothers. What could I possibly do, anyway? However," she paused, sipping her drink again, "I'll continue to make discreet inquiries into the casket. Based on the pattern of behaviour around it, I think the jewellery has been in it for some time. I really want to know who gave it to Jacobsen. And why *him*? I won't delve into the Fallen Angel side of it, obviously."

Jackson looked incredulous. "You can't separate the two! Leave it to the Nephilim."

A challenge flared in her eyes. "And what about you and Black Cronos? Like you can let your grandfather's disappearance rest! Or you, Harlan, and the business of the Emerald Tablet and how that might help the fight against Black Cronos? We're enmeshed in all of this, no matter how much we might want to disentangle ourselves. We can't."

Harlan was relieved he could discuss all of this with Olivia and Jackson. And Maggie too, when he saw her. He had formed an even closer friendship with her after the events with the Storm Moon Pack. A little band of humans in a paranormal world. *Their own pack*. He laughed at the idea.

"What are you sniggering at?" Jackson asked him.

"I'm laughing because I've just realised that you two and Maggie are my pack. I thought it was The Orphic Guild, but it's not. May the Gods help me."

Olivia raised an eyebrow, her eyes twinkling. "Who's the alpha? Maggie, right?"

Harlan was about to protest, then groaned. "Yeah, she so is."

"We should have invited her out tonight."

"Next time. It could turn into some kind of AA meeting. Like we're confessing our sins."

Jackson drained his pint. "Well, I'm going to take your advice and get some sleep. I might actually clean my flat, too. That can wait until tomorrow, though."

Olivia also finished her drink. "That's great advice. I didn't sleep too well last night." A trace of pink graced her cheeks, and she tried to appear a little too casual.

Harlan looked at her suspiciously. "Really? The theft?"

"Of course!"

Harlan didn't push, but he had a feeling he knew what that meant. Reluctantly, he also finished his drink. He may as well go home, too.

They were all heading for the same tube station and they walked together, still chatting, taking a short cut down a side street, when a large black van cruised into view ahead. Harlan's conversation faltered. Neither of his companions seemed to notice, and he told himself he was being paranoid. Black vans were everywhere in the city. It didn't mean they were Black Cronos.

And then he heard a vehicle slow behind him. He turned, mouth dry, hoping he was wrong. But there, at the other end of the narrow side street was another black van, and four tall men with broad shoulders were already climbing out of the side door. The gleam of copper and silver eyes was already visible.

Black Cronos had come for them.

Seven

The only two of Nahum's brothers still in the country were Eli and Zee, and both glared at Belial's jewellery.

They were in their farmhouse in Cornwall, on the moors above White Haven, gathered around a roaring fire in the living room. The Christmas lights twinkled, and a few presents were already waiting under the Christmas tree. Outside, the wind howled, and rain battered the windows. Nahum felt shut off from the rest of the world, but knew it was an illusion. Belial might be watching them right now.

"I always hated that devious bastard," Zee said, scowling. "I should have put money on him being the one to find a way past the Igigi's spell—if that's even what we call it."

"Whatever we call it, he found an agent to help him. If he were walking the Earth now, we'd know about it," Eli said. "He swaggered...liked to put on a show with his destruction."

"True." Nahum nodded. "There was no *show* last night, or over the years that his jewellery has been circulating. Just insidious madness instead."

Zee snorted. "There's nothing new in this world. That happened in our time, and it's happening now. The Fallen had nothing to do with madness or evil. Evil lies within the heart of everyone. Most suppress it. As for madness...well. Mortal bodies were always fallible."

"True, brother," Eli agreed, voice dropping. "But the Fallen were adept at manipulating weakness. Just as some angels were able to offer strength to resist it. It's the age-old battle of good against evil. All Gods and their acolytes have a stake in that."

Nahum ran his hand across his stubble. "You're both right, obviously. But now we have proof that Belial is manipulating again. I saw him and felt him. How do we find his agent?"

Zee looked confused. "You killed his agent, surely, last night. Jacobsen."

Nahum shook his head. "No. Someone gave him that casket. Delivered it right to his door. Maybe they thought that as a man of God, he would be more susceptible. Why *him* still eludes me. Something must have marked him as useful."

Zee was sitting cross legged on the rug in front of the fire, but he stretched his legs out as he pondered this. "Why not use the other agent, then?" he huffed. "This all sounds ridiculous. Unless..." Zee's eyes widened as understanding dawned. "Jacobsen was expendable. The other person was not."

"That's an interesting suggestion." Nahum knew this would get ugly. This was just the start. "If Belial has found a way, others will, too. Perhaps his true agent is another supernatural creature."

"Someone who will want Belial's jewellery back," Eli pointed out.

Zee grimaced. "He'll have more than just those three trinkets."

"Not necessarily," Nahum said, hoping time would have erased most of them.

"We need to ask Newton or one of his team to investigate Jacobsen's background." Eli leaned forward to study the jewellery, hesitated, and then picked up the torc. A shudder ran through him, but he didn't let go. "Its power has dimmed over time. I didn't think that was possible."

Nahum had thought similarly, but hadn't wanted to presume. "I'm glad you said that. That's good news. Something to work with. Maybe something about Jacobsen's belief made him more vulnerable."

"But again, why him out of all the holy men Belial could choose from?" Zee said. "Unless there are several out there."

Nahum felt steadier with his brothers around him. More in control of his emotions. Last night had unnerved him because it was totally unexpected, and in a moment of weakness he had sought solace with Olivia. That was unfair of him. She wasn't a tool for his enjoyment or to drown his sorrows in. He had once thought of women that way, but not any longer. He should apologise. Then he thought of the way her eyes and hands travelled down his naked body. *No, they were all square there*. Shaking off his memories, he turned to practicalities. "Let's ask the witches for help. A finding spell, perhaps. Or ask Alex to locate him."

Zee looked incredulous. "Are you insane? Asking him to connect to Belial! No way. I won't let you!"

"Alex is strong, and well used to crossing to other realms and dealing with demons and spirits."

"This is no demon. This is *Belial*. Alex is my friend—and I thought he was yours! I won't allow it!"

"*Allow*?" Nahum felt himself firing up. "You're not my master! I'll ask. It's up to him whether he says yes or no."

Suddenly Zee was on his feet, eyes flashing. "You'd risk Alex? What kind of man are you? Oh! I forget. You're *Remiel's* son. His house was always known to risk much to gain the upper hand."

Nahum leapt to his feet too, almost upending the coffee table between them. His ears were buzzing, and a need to exact violence and vengeance that he hadn't felt in years raced through him.

They were suddenly shouting and pushing, and the air was thick with anger.

And then Eli intervened, strange words looping in the air. Words of protection. Words of healing. The buzzing vanished, and reason returned. He found himself on the floor, Zee beneath him, with Zee's hands at his throat.

Eli pried them apart. "Nahum. You've spent too long around the jewels. We haven't been exposed to them in years. They got to you. Both of you."

As understanding dawned, Nahum stood and extended his hand to Zee. "Sorry. That was..."

"Terrifying? Yes." Zee took his hand and pulled him into a hug. "Time has weakened us, brother. Let us not let that happen again."

The jewels were now inside a swiftly drawn circle on the floor, a sprig of pine next to them. They looked innocent now, the Christmas lights bathing them in a rosy glow.

Eli glowered at his brothers. "Lucky I didn't lose my head, too, or we'd have probably killed each other. Are you all right now?"

Nahum ran his hand through his thick hair, tired and exasperated. "I will be. Zee, you were right. I can't expose Alex to those. They made

Olivia feel weird too, and they were still in the casket most of the time. She touched the torc and saw him—well, elements of him."

"Actually," Eli said softly, sitting again now that the atmosphere had returned to normal, "I think we must ask Alex for help. Or maybe all of them. We need answers, and have no other choices. And if that fails, we have one other option that I'd rather not use, but there's no doubt they're powerful enough. The dryads."

Nahum laughed, and then stopped as he saw Eli's expression. "You're serious? The ones who have bound you to them for guardianship? What might they exact for *this* piece of advice?"

"I did say I'd rather not."

Zee grabbed his beer and took a long drink, then wiped his lips with the back of his hand. "That is the absolute last resort."

"I should call Gabe," Nahum said, reaching for his phone. "We have to speak to him before we do anything." He knew he wasn't planning on pulling off the heist that night, not after his earlier phone call. "Maybe he'll have a better idea."

Barak's limbs were stiff because he had been stationary so long, but at least he was warm. His wings were wrapped around him, blending with his black skin, and in deep shadow high up on the tower, he felt confident he hadn't been seen.

Barak just hoped the castle didn't have defences like JD's, or he'd either be zapped from existence or trapped if they were activated.

But his persistent watch had paid off. He had studied the number of square towers populated by guards, and had watched them patrol across the ramparts at regular intervals. Always two of them walked the castle walls before returning to their respective towers. Fortunately, most patrolled at the same time, and they didn't linger. No doubt the freezing temperatures were putting them off. They scanned the skies and the steep slopes and then retreated. They felt comfortable. Safe. The guards did not expect anything untoward. But he'd seen at least a dozen of them, and there were probably many more inside.

Just when Barak thought it was time to leave, voices echoed up to him, and he heard the slam of heavy doors. A couple of men walked across a courtyard below, vanished for a moment beneath arches, and then appeared on the periphery of the huge circle. They paced its perimeter, and one stopped to study the sky. The clouds were clearing, revealing the swathe of glittering stars above. Unfortunately, although he caught snatches of their conversation, he couldn't hear the words. Just mumbles. He wished he was lower, but that would be impossible.

After another animated discussion, one of them pulled a phone out and called someone, and within seconds a huge rumble broke the larger silence. Stone grated on stone as a couple of concentric circles started to move and realign. Light emitted from some of the sigils. Astrological symbols were aligning with the wheel of the year.

Of course. Yule was only a week or so away. It must have significance for them. Maybe a ritual that would give power.

And then a shaft of moonlight caught the face of one man, and Barak gritted his teeth. *Stefan Hope-Robbins*. The Oxford professor who had escaped from the Dark Star Temple and the Igigi's underground city. Barak studied his companion, noting the man's short hair and angular face. He was taller. Thinner. Barak didn't recognise him.

Stefan looked to the arches as another figure stepped into view and crossed the grounds to join them, and Barak's blood ran cold. She looked like the mirror image of The Silencer of Souls. Long limbed, lithe, and deadly, her hair a cascade of silk down her back. The first one had warned there were others, and here she was. *But why was she so similar? Was she a clone? Were they sisters?*

Barak was tempted to launch himself from the tower and try to kill all of them, but ultimately knew that would be a suicide mission. The tower guards would surely see him and attack. Not only would he risk death, but they would know their stronghold had been identified. He must wait. Now more than ever, Barak wanted to know what lay beneath the castle. If there were tunnels, rooms, and huge mechanisms, there would be other entrances, and they may not be as well guarded. Or at least as visible.

That was the next night's task, then. He would return with Estelle and Lucien to identify as many other entrances as possible, and hopefully his witch could veil them in an invisibility spell.

Olivia heard Harlan's warning shout on the narrow side street and looked around in alarm. She immediately saw the men exiting the black van ahead, blocking their escape.

Harlan tugged at her elbow. "There's a van behind, too. We need to move!"

"Where? I presume these are your bloody Black Cronos soldiers?" Unless they were Belial's agents, but she doubted that. Heart pounding, she spun around, looking for an escape route on the narrow lane. There were a few doors, but all were shut. "For fuck's sake. I was having such a good night!" She reached into her bag and found her pepper spray. It wasn't much to defend herself, but it was better than nothing. She didn't go anywhere without it.

Jackson, however, had pulled a gun from his pocket. "I really, really hate these guys."

"You have a *gun*?" Harlan spluttered.

"You know I do! I've just started carrying it more often."

"Thank the Gods for your paranoia," Harlan said, running towards the closest door and tugging at it. "It's locked."

Jackson fired at the lock without hesitation, the blast loud in the confined space. Rather than scare off the soldiers, they quickened their steps. As Harlan wrenched the door open, Jackson fired at the advancing men. Olivia was impressed. He was a good shot. A couple stumbled and fell, utter shock on their faces, but that's all she could take in as she ran inside the building. From the meagre streetlight, she could see a short passage and rooms ahead, and using the torch on her phone she ran onwards. More shots sounded, and then the door slammed behind them.

"Block the bloody door!" Jackson shouted.

"With what? My body?"

"No, you American moron! The bloody boxes!"

Olivia sought another way out. They were in the back of an up-market furniture shop. She could see the store front to one side. It was large, a big glass window. *Oh, shit*. A shop near Hyde Park. *That meant...*

An alarm peeled out into the quiet night, the high-pitched whine painfully shrill. *At least that would deter Black Cronos...* She hoped. Unfortunately, there was only one other way out, and that was through the front door. Right on cue, half a dozen black-clad soldiers, a mix of men and women, appeared in front of the windows. They extended long, slender weapons from their palms and smashed the window. *So much for the alarm.*

She raced back to the corridor and spotting stairs leading up, yelled to the others, "Move it! Now!"

Olivia ran up the stairs, trying to ignore the sounds of splintering glass and thundering footsteps, and behind that the squealing of police sirens. They just had to keep moving for a bit longer. On the upper level, she skidded into another room.

Harlan was right behind her, and he yelled, "Jackson!"

They were in a storeroom, and there was furniture inside that they could use to block the door. But Jackson wasn't with them. She shot Harlan a look of pure desperation and ducked back into the corridor. "Where the hell is he?"

The alarm was insistent, and so loud she could barely think straight, but they both returned to the top of the stairs. With horror, she saw Jackson still at the bottom, firing his final rounds. "Jackson. Get your arse up here!"

But it was too late. A Black Cronos soldier tackled Jackson to the ground, and his gun tumbled to the floor. Olivia threw down the closest thing at hand to help, a huge glass statue. It fell short. Harlan followed it up with another. That missed, too. The soldier punched Jackson, and dazed, he fell limply on the floor. The soldier scooped him up and ran for the exit.

Only seconds before Olivia had wanted to barricade herself in, but all that was forgotten as she screamed, "*No!*"

They both raced down the stairs, desperate to save Jackson.

Harlan cursed loudly. "Stupid bloody man! What the fuck was he thinking? We're all going to get caught and turned into damn lab rats."

Another soldier was waiting in the doorway of the shop. His dispassionate silver eyes showed no mercy as he blocked her, intending to capture her, too. She unloaded most of the pepper spray in his eyes. Roaring in pain, he stumbled, and she kicked him in the groin. Harlan vaulted over him, racing after Jackson.

The sound of sirens was louder now, and it was the only thing that saved them.

The wounded soldier regained his feet and shoulder-barged into Harlan, knocking him into some furniture and clearing the way to the door. He staggered to the waiting van, and in seconds they accelerated down the road.

Jackson was gone.

Hot, sweet tea burned Harlan's throat. He would have preferred a large shot of bourbon, but this was better than nothing. *Screw this stupid British obsession with tea.*

Maggie was growling like a feral cat as she stalked around the furniture shop's kitchen. "You're both bloody lucky! You could have died!"

"They didn't want to kill us," Olivia told her, also cradling a hot cup of tea. "They wanted to capture us, just like Jackson. I'm so angry, I feel sick. If they hurt him..."

"Let's hope he's a bargaining tool," Harlan said, quickly intervening. He'd had those same thoughts, and wanted to push them away. "I've always been paranoid that they'll strike. Convinced myself I was crazy."

"Well, one thing is for sure," Maggie said. "You can't go home, either of you. You need to go somewhere safe. Perhaps The Retreat?"

"No!" Harlan shook his head. "They've been attacked before, and we don't want to lead Black Cronos back to their door again. We either hole up in my favourite hotel—"

Olivia interrupted him before he could finish. "The bloody Mandarin Oriental? Don't be moronic!"

"There's logic to hiding in plain sight! It's big and busy. Or, if you'll let me finish, we stay at JD's. Or join Barak and Estelle abroad."

Maggie finally sat down, eyes bleak. "You said they think they've found the count's base?"

"Yes. They're investigating the place now."

Maggie rolled her eyes. "You're a fucking idiot. First, you're moving yourself closer to their potential power base, which is insane. Secondly, you risk blowing their cover too, *if* they're watching you."

Dread ripped through Harlan, and he ignored her jibe. "What if they already *are* watching them? We're all spread out. Separated, and therefore weaker. Maybe the last few months of quiet have been to lull us into a false sense of security."

Maggie leaned on the table, her chin in her hands. "It's possible. Maybe you should start making some calls. Let them all know what's happened here."

"But it doesn't make sense to come after me," Olivia protested. "I haven't been involved in any Black Cronos stuff."

"But you have been working with Nahum over the last day or so," Harlan reminded her.

"Yes, but not on this stuff. He was helping me look for my reliquary!"

"You might have just been caught up in this because you were with Harlan and Jackson tonight," Maggie told her. "It could just be bad timing. Plus, if they've been watching Harlan, they know who you are and what you do. Seeing the three of you together might have been a big attraction. Maybe they think you're useful now. And all of that makes me feel very worried about us staying here any longer. I've got your statements, so you're free to go. I'll start following up with traffic cameras, looking for black vans. Unfortunately, I'm pretty sure we won't get far. They're too good. Any thoughts on where they could have taken him?"

Harlan shook his head. "No. We think they have multiple bases, but I guess logic dictates that he must be in England."

"Unless they have a private jet," Maggie pointed out. "Money does not seem to be an issue for them."

"Poor Jackson. This is a nightmare." Olivia raked her hands through her tousled hair, attempting to smooth it out. "But where will we go? And how?"

"I'll drop you off wherever you need," Maggie said, flashing a smile of reassurance that Harlan didn't even know she possessed. "I'd like to know you're safe. Even you, Harlan!"

He choked out a laugh. "Thanks. So, I guess I was right in saying I thought of you as part of our pack, earlier."

"Really?" Maggie snorted. "I could go for that. Only if I'm the alpha, though."

"Yeah. We thought that's what you'd say. But we're a member down right now. We need to find Jackson."

"Leave that with me. But warn the Nephilim!" She emphasised her message with a jabbing finger. "Now, let's decide where you should go."

While Maggie and Olivia discussed options, Harlan felt more and more uncomfortable as the shock of the attack wore off. He didn't want to go anywhere. He wanted to find Jackson. To do that meant they had to act quickly, so he interrupted their conversation. "I have a better idea. I found Jackson's scarf on the floor, and that means we can use a finding spell to locate him."

Olivia looked at him, startled. "That needs a witch. Who could we use?"

"The Moonfell witches." He cocked his head at Maggie. "What do you think?"

She held his gaze for a moment, and he could tell she was weighing up their options. She exhaled slowly. "I suppose that is a good idea. *If* they'll help."

"Why wouldn't they? They helped Maverick."

"Hold on!" Olivia intervened, puzzled. "The Moonfell witches? The ones you met last month? You hardly know them!"

Harlan shrugged, impatient to act. "Yes. The ones who helped the shifters fight the therians. We need a finding spell, and they're powerful. Our White Haven witch friends are too far away."

He had met the Moonfell witches the previous month when he'd helped Maverick Hale's Storm Moon Wolf-shifter Pack after one of the members had been brutally killed. The three Moonfell witches had helped find his killer. Moonfell was the name of their Gothic mansion situated near Richmond Park. Birdie was the oldest, nearly blind with cataracts, and she had two granddaughters, Morgana and Odette. Cousins, not sisters.

He pulled his phone out and found Morgana's number. "I had a long chat with them on the return trip from Wales. I like them. I'm sure they'll help. I'll happily hide out at JD's later." His Mortlake Estate was the only place with defensive systems strong enough to hold back Black Cronos without any other paranormal support. "Right now, I need to try to find Jackson while the trail is hot!" Neither Olivia nor Maggie liked to back out of a fight. He appealed to them. "You both know I'm right. And you, Maggie, are always saying how limited your resources are. Are you with me? I'll do this alone, otherwise." He squared his shoulders defiantly.

Olivia rose to her feet. "Of course. That's actually a brilliant idea. I met Morgana once, years ago, but I doubt she'd remember me. Let's do it."

That left Maggie, and Harlan stared at her, a challenge in his eyes.

Maggie huffed. "Bollocks. I just wish I'd have thought of them first." With her characteristic belligerence she charged out the door, yelling over her shoulder, "Don't forget to phone the bloody Nephilim!"

Eight

After Niel completed his survey of the museum, he settled on the roof of their hotel and admired the glittering vista of Aswan and the dark waters of the Nile.

He knew he wouldn't sleep. Too many things swirled in his thoughts, and for once, one of them wasn't Lilith. Instead, it was the news of Nahum finding Belial's jewellery that worried him. He was sneaky, mean, and one of the most powerful of the Fallen.

When he couldn't stand thinking of Belial anymore, it was Mouse that preoccupied his thoughts. The thief with the beguiling eyes, slender body, and treacherous soul. He wondered what she might be stealing now. Maybe she was hanging upside down by a rope, or vaulting over a wall, or creeping through a silent museum. As long as it wasn't Aswan's Museum of Egyptian Antiquities, she could be anywhere she liked. But she wouldn't be there. No one except their own small group could possibly know their whereabouts. JD was more paranoid than they were.

However, he watched a black van crawl along the road in front of their hotel before shrugging it off. Lots of people drove black vans. Then again, it was almost two in the morning, and the roads were much quieter now. It was also the same make and model as those used by Black Cronos, and they weren't that common in Aswan. He cricked his neck and rolled his shoulders. *Could it be them?* He paced to the far end of the roof and studied the road below. The hotel was big and modern, sitting squarely at a junction. There was another van down there, too. However, no one emerged.

Unable to shake off his unease, he decided to keep watch. It was highly unlikely to be Black Cronos, and even it if was, it was madness to attack a big hotel. He pulled his phone out to call one of his brothers, just as it buzzed in his hand. It was Harlan. That cheered him up. He liked Harlan's dry wit, and the way he teased Shadow. "My American friend. You're up late."

His next words though were like ice. He listened carefully, and when he hung up, his thoughts no longer drifted. They were razor sharp. Jackson had been taken by Black Cronos, and they might be coming for all of them. No longer feeling so paranoid, he called his brothers, including Barak and those in Cornwall. In minutes, Ash, Shadow, and Gabe were with him. They had all been asleep, but were now dressed, alert, and armed.

Niel pointed to where the black vans had parked on the roads bordering the hotel. "Those two. No one has exited. It might be nothing, but..."

Ash pulled his hair into a ponytail as if preparing for battle. "And it might be everything."

Shadow shook her head. "It doesn't make sense. If it's them, it would have been better to attack us on the back lanes around the museum. Here it's just too busy."

"They're determined. Maybe they think a big hotel with people coming and going will be good cover," Gabe suggested. "Even at two in the morning, there are night staff and cleaners about."

Niel snorted. "They're soldiers. They don't look like cleaners!"

"Cleaners don't put up much of a fight though, do they?" Shadow pointed out. "And we're supposed to be tucked up in bed."

As Niel watched the road, he saw another black van pull up not far from the others. "There's another."

They all watched in silence, rewarded moments later when black-clad men and women exited the vans and assembled on the street. Seconds later they crossed to the hotel, some circling around the back to cover all exits.

"Damn it," Gabe muttered. "How the hell do they know that we're here? And does that mean they know *why* we're here?"

"If they steal that disc before us, we're screwed," Shadow said, watching the activity below. "Unless they're already there..."

"There's no way they know *why* we're here," Ash said, shaking his head. "We snuck that Emerald Tablet out from beneath the Templar Church, and no one knows about it except a very small group of people I'd trust with my life. This is an opportunistic attempt on us."

Gabe was still watching the last of the soldiers slide into position. "Which means we are being watched, and we didn't know. That's unacceptable. I feel like an idiot. And on top of that, there's Belial's crap to deal with. The farmhouse boundary alarms should work, but we still need to warn our brothers."

"I've already called, and so far, there's nothing going on there," Niel reassured him. He started to laugh, feeling like they might actually have the upper hand despite the nearly two dozen soldiers circling the hotel below. "They won't make a scene downstairs. They just want to find us, and we're up here. If they go in, guns blazing, the police will arrive. They won't want that. Let's leave them to it, and go steal the disc right now."

Shadow grimaced. "Damn it. Now I'm torn between wanting to kill lots of Black Cronos soldiers and stealing from a museum."

"My poor sister," he mocked. "Decisions, decisions..."

Ash cut in, moving things along. "There is no decision. Let them turn our rooms upside down. They won't find a thing there, and we have our weapons on us now. I think it's a great idea."

"But we haven't brought our packs with the other tools we might need," Gabe pointed out.

"I have my skeleton keys for the display cabinets, but I need a bag to put the disc in, and the packing," Shadow pointed out. "We can't risk it getting damaged."

"But we have pockets." Ash patted the fatigues that they were all wearing.

"Exactly. We'll improvise with the rest," Niel said, hoping he wouldn't regret the suggestion. "To go to our rooms now risks us being caught. Let's go get that disc."

Nahum, Eli, and Zee were still up, musing on Belial, when the calls from Niel and Olivia came through, literally within minutes of each other. They had immediately turned off the lights in the farmhouse, grabbed their weapons, and prepared for the worst.

"How much faith do you have in our new system?" Nahum asked his brothers as he stood at the window looking out on to the courtyard and the drive.

"A lot," Zee answered from the window to the rear of the house. "The witches did it, and they're brilliant."

"But Black Cronos are brilliant, too," Nahum pointed out. However, nothing moved outside, and only the usual night noises broke the silence of the countryside around their house.

A few weeks earlier they had decided to set up enhanced protection around the grounds. With their efforts to find Black Cronos intensifying, and after their encounter with the ancient Templar order in Temple Moreton, they had decided that they could be vulnerable to attack, especially as they were often spread out on different assignments.

They had debated putting in cameras and a standard security system, and had decided to place a couple of mounted cameras at the front and rear of the house, but for the larger area, they preferred something magical. The witches had been happy to help. They had warded the boundary of the fields immediately around them, and then added more wards within metres of the house. It had taken them several days to complete, and once a week one of them came over and reinforced them. Usually it was Alex or Briar. It was essentially a protection circle, enhanced with powerfully charged gemstones buried in the earth. The Nephilim, Shadow, and their friends could come and go with ease, but anyone else would encounter a type of forcefield they couldn't pass—they hoped.

Zee shouted from the kitchen, "The perimeter protection field has been activated!"

"I see it!" Eli replied.

Nahum left his own post—hopefully the last place that any intruder would get to was their front door—and headed to Eli's side. At the far end of the field, where Shadow had taken out several soldiers months earlier, a blue shimmer illuminated the oak tree.

Nahum nodded, already gripping his sword. "I see it. Damn it. I really hoped it wouldn't come to this."

"That they wouldn't attack us here again?" Eli huffed. "It was inevitable. But I think Niel is right. They know we're separated. This is a coordinated attack. And that means they've been watching us."

"Let's worry about that later."

Another spark of blue further along the field had Nahum marching to the kitchen, Eli on his heels. Zee was readying his crossbow, and he grinned at their arrival. "Time for some target practice. I'll head up to the roof."

Eli positioned himself at the back door. "If they find a way through, and they're spread out like last time, we're screwed. Unless we just take off. But that effectively means surrendering our house to them, and I won't do that."

"It won't come to that, I'm sure of it," Nahum reasoned. "Eli, what say we edge a little closer. Zee, watch the front of the house while you're on the roof."

He nodded and called over his shoulder as he left them. "Of course."

"I have one last suggestion," Eli said, just as Nahum was about to head out of the back door. "Let's take Belial's jewels."

"What?" Nahum spun around, Black Cronos pushed to the back of his mind for a moment. "Are you nuts?"

"There are only three of us. We could probably draw on his power to enhance our own—if needed."

Nahum hesitated, his normal revulsion at anything related to the Fallen pushed aside in favour of necessity. *Perhaps they could use Belial for some good, after all.* "Fine. But we need to be careful! He's strong."

"Brother. The time for care has passed. The time for battle is upon us." And with these most unexpected words coming from Eli, the lover and peacekeeper of their little family, he went to fetch the jewels.

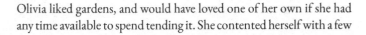

Olivia liked gardens, and would have loved one of her own if she had any time available to spend tending it. She contented herself with a few pots on her small balcony. The garden at Moonfell, however, was very unusual.

Gravel crunched beneath their feet as they approached the Gothic mansion. High up, a window in a turreted tower glowed with a soft yellow light like a beacon. Or a lighthouse, warning them away from rocks that could kill them.

Huge evergreen topiary statues marched down either side of the drive, lit up by the occasional spotlight. Others revealed themselves in glimpses between the shrubs. A few were elaborate mixtures of round balls, spirals, and pyramids, but amongst them were shrubs sculpted into leaping cats, dragons, snakes, and what appeared to be sigils. *Someone was a very skilled gardener.*

Other trees—not surprisingly, considering it was mid-December—had bare branches that rattled together, sounding like cackling old crones. They reached towards the house, tapping the walls and windows as if announcing their arrival. Olivia longed to explore, seeing fallow beds, and others with frost damaged plants wilting in the cold. She sensed secrets in this garden, and she shivered.

"It's watching us," she declared to Harlan and Maggie. "Assessing us."

"For fuck's sake," Maggie grumbled. "This place is weird enough without you making it worse."

"I can't help it!" Olivia kept her voice low, and wished the gravel would crunch quieter. "I'm a bit freaked out, but I'm excited, too. Have you ever been in the house before? Either of you?"

"Nope." Harlan shook his head. "Not entirely sure I'll be coming back, either. Now I wish I had called first."

"We did the right thing," Maggie reassured him. "It's harder to turn us away now that we're here."

The huge, wooden front door was made of thick timbers and set between two ornately carved pillars. The door knocker was a raven made of burnished brass, and what looked like a bone in its beak.

Saying nothing, but casting them a long look of apprehension, Harlan used it to rap on the door.

The boom was loud, and for a while, nothing could be heard inside. And then the door swung inward on silent hinges, revealing a huge staircase and a long hallway beyond it. All three froze on the covered porch, goosebumps erupting along Olivia's skin. No one was there.

Thick rugs covered the floor, the slim edge between rug and wall revealing ornate tiles in rich colours that glowed in the subdued light. Dim lights from open doorways lit the hallway in stripes. Incense hung in the air, and occult imagery lined the walls. Power resided here. And more secrets.

Maggie bristled with impatience, but Harlan smiled and said in an aside, "Arlo told me that Odette likes a dramatic entrance." With a firm voice he shouted, "Odette! It's Harlan. I'm here with friends."

A slender woman with shoulder-length hair falling in soft curls stepped from the room to the left and smiled, her teeth gnawing at her bottom lip with regret. "Harlan. Such a spoilsport!"

Maggie huffed and stepped in front of him. "DI Maggie Milne. Don't you have some dramatic music and the sound of bats, too? Maybe wolves?"

Odette's eyes sharpened, and she folded her arms across her chest. "Next time, perhaps, DI Milne. I remember you from Storm Moon club. You watched us treat Arlo. Is this a social call? It's quite late." And then she took a sharp intake of breath. "Darkness stalks you. Come in." She hustled them inside and shut the door. "Put your coats on the rack under the stairs and come to the kitchen. We don't stand on ceremony here." Then she gave a sneaky little grin. "Well, sabbats notwithstanding, and spells, of course. We have plenty of ceremonies for them."

"Odette," Harlan said, shrugging off his three-quarter length woollen coat. "This is Olivia, my colleague at The Orphic Guild, and a good friend."

Odette had cast only a cursory glance towards Olivia, but now she looked at her properly. Olivia noted her soft brown eyes ringed with amber set inside her heart-shaped face. She was beautiful, but her eyes reminded her of an owl. A predator. And Olivia was prey. For some reason Olivia couldn't explain, she felt wary around Odette, almost an instant dislike, and she couldn't fathom it. She had no problem with witches. She admired their magic.

But before she had time to consider her response further, Odette had frozen, transfixed, eyes looking deeply into Olivia's own. She grabbed her arms with her cool hands and pulled her under the light. Something within Olivia recoiled, and then flared in anger. A hard, jealous, resentful anger that craved destruction.

Odette's sharp voice was accusatory, like a slap. "By the Goddess. Something dark resides within you. What have you been doing?"

Olivia floundered, trying to push her weird thoughts aside. "I haven't been doing anything! Except being chased tonight, and almost killed! That's why we're here!"

"Chased by who? What I see doesn't seem possible!"

"Woah, slow down!" Harlan went to place a calming hand on Odette, but she flung it away. Chastened, he said, "That's why we're here. We encountered an old enemy. Well, a new one, actually. Is that what you see? Black Cronos? Alchemical monsters?"

Odette's face wrinkled with distaste. "No, that is not what I see. It's older. Far older." She focussed on Olivia, repeating her earlier question. "What have you been doing?"

Olivia suddenly felt very scared, and knew exactly what Odette could see. For some reason, however, she didn't want to answer. She had to force a response, her body seeming at war with itself. Her voice sounded gruff when she answered. "Nothing. I helped a friend, that's all."

"*No*. You lie. There is more than that. He's extending his influence, even now. It's a good job you came, Olivia. Before it's too late. To the kitchen, quickly." Her arm threaded through Olivia's as if she didn't want to let go, and she hustled her down the corridor.

The others scurried after them, Harlan calling, "Odette! What's going on? We came for help to find a friend! Will you help us?"

"Of course I will, but this is more important."

Olivia squirmed in her tight grasp. "Actually, it's not. Jackson is more important! He's been kidnapped."

"And you have a small splinter of a Fallen Angel inside you, and he's itching to get further in." Odette stopped again. Her amber-ringed eyes peered deep into Olivia's, and then beyond her, seeing something else. "Oh, my old enemy, I see you. But not for long." She blinked, smiling at Olivia, her thousand-yard stare vanishing. "He's hanging on by a thread, but he is tenacious. If we don't act now, it will be harder to get him out. But don't worry," she squeezed Olivia's arms again with her strong hands, her smile infectious. "I love a good battle, especially at midnight. The witching hour."

Nine

S hadow slid from Gabe's warm embrace and solidly muscled chest as he landed softly on the tiled roof of the museum.

She pulled her fey magic around her, embracing the dark night and the song of the museum's garden. The night sounds were different here, loud and voluble, despite the chill weather. Its exoticness reminded her of the Realm of Fire in her own world. But now was not the time to reminisce. They had work to do.

She adjusted her slim-fit leather jacket that moulded to her body, her fatigues tucked into sturdy leather boots, and extracted her daggers. Their cool familiarity calmed her nerves and sharpened her senses. She studied the uneven rooftop, its skylights and vents scattered across the large building.

Gabe folded his wings away and pulled on his jacket from his pack as Ash landed next to them. Niel still circled above. All three crouched in the shadow of the tower over the east wing on the roof. This was their way in. A couple of guards patrolled the high-walled perimeter, and the gates at the end of the drive were locked.

Ash's eyes were narrowed with worry. "This is a big building, and we barely saw half of it earlier. This is insanity. We have only a few hours before daylight. We should have waited."

"I think it adds an extra little fizz of fun to our endeavours," Shadow said, silently lifting the air vent's hatch and peering inside to assess the narrow space.

They had noted the vents high on the walls when they walked around earlier. They hoped they weren't alarmed like the doors and windows, but maybe that was naïve. If they were, they would just have to fight their way out. The east wing was one of the areas they hadn't reached during the daylight tour, and it seemed to have the easiest access, too. Although they had spotted cameras, they suspected that they weren't real-time monitored at night, and would instead record everything. They planned on disabling the system once they were inside.

"I'll go first to check the space." She eyed the two large Nephilim. "You might have trouble getting in. Perhaps you should wait here."

Gabe shot her an impatient look. "You can't search the entire place on your own. Carry on. We'll follow."

The next few minutes were hazardous and awkward, and she negotiated a long drop, which necessitated her walking crablike down the narrow vertical vent, and then having to slide into one that ran horizontally. It quickly became clear this was very difficult. From the grunts she could hear above, the men weren't faring any better. She shouted at them to back up, and in ten minutes they were all back on the roof, now very hot and grumpy.

Gabe looked furious. "I knew that was a stupid idea!"

"Well, at least it wasn't alarmed!" she hissed at him, aware their voices could carry to the guards.

Ash huffed. "That gives us very few options. We just have to break in, set the alarms off, and get out. We should have contacted Mouse for this."

Shadow scowled, not liking to be defeated, and even worse hating to think someone else could do the job better. "No! There has got to be a better way. We needed more time to prepare."

"Well, tough," Gabe said, still grumpy.

She knew he was worried about Belial. Once again, Gabe's fears regarding their fathers' interference in their new lives, after months of feeling like they had gone for good, had resurfaced. All of them were worried, actually. Ash and Niel had fallen into uncharacteristic reflection. At least this theft was a good distraction.

The soft glide of wings was barely perceptible in the brisk wind that was blowing off the river, and Niel landed next to them, dragging all of them down into a crouch. His blond hair was in a top knot, and his piercing blue eyes swept across them. "What the hell is going on?"

Gabe glared at him. "We got stuck. And you're supposed to be watching our backs."

"I'm watching you fail! But I have a solution. A pair of guards are heading to the museum's side door, I presume to patrol inside. I saw them enter that way last night, but hadn't realised they did it every couple of hours. I suggest you get down there now, let them disable the alarm, and then incapacitate them. North side, centre. Get on with it!" Without another word, he launched back up into the air.

"I guess that's option two, then," Gabe said, stripping to fly again. "Time to go."

"Drop me behind them," Shadow instructed. "I'll take one, one of you can take the other."

Ash nodded. "Deal. But wait until the alarm is disabled."

They circled high, spotting the two men that Niel had referred to. They were crossing the lawn along a path that snaked between sculptures, talking to each other and laughing. Gabe swept in low and dropped Shadow, and sticking to the deep shadows beneath the palms, she followed them silently. It would be far easier to just kill them, but Gabe was right. No one needed to die tonight—except maybe Black Cronos, who had forced their hand in all of this.

The side door wasn't as imposing as the front, but it had a security camera and a keypad, as well as a huge metal gate in front of a sturdy wooden one. Impatient, and as close as she could get, she watched them unlock everything and swing the door wide. A moment more, and she heard the beep of the alarm.

With lightning reflexes, she raced across the remaining short distance, knowing her fey glamour kept her concealed. One man was still on the threshold, the other just inside. She crept behind the nearest one, wrapped her arm around his neck, and pulled him backwards before he even realised what was happening. Using the butt of her dagger, she hit him at the precise point required to knock him out instantly.

While she silently dealt with him, Gabe landed and wrestled the other man backwards and out the door, leaving Ash to step inside and make sure the way remained clear. In seconds it was done, and they dragged the unconscious men inside.

"In here," Ash called from a side room. "We can lock them in."

After securing them as best as they could with what little they could find, they locked the door, hoping they would remain insensible for a while.

Once back in the corridor, Gabe said, "I'll find the camera feed and cut it. You two start searching. I'll join you soon. We have a couple of hours, at most," he reasoned. "Can you remember the different areas of the displays? We've searched the most obvious, but any ideas?"

"Let's just split up," Shadow said, impatient already. "We have no time to waste!"

"You're right, but thinking logically will be quicker," Ash reasoned. He was looking at her, clearly surprised. "You're a thief! Surely you're used to this."

"Usually I have more preparation time!" In the Otherworld, her team did extensive research before their heists, and Bloodmoon was the one who tackled all the security issues. She was relying on Ash and Gabe to do that now.

Ash sighed. "Fine. Let's just get on with it. The west wing is done, so I'll take east, Gabe go north, when you're done. Shadow, south."

"Suits me." She wiggled her phone. "I'll call."

"Do nothing until we're with you," Gabe warned her. She knew that he both admired and feared her headstrong approach to life.

She winked and blew him a kiss. "Later."

Zee liked his perch on the farmhouse roof. It gave him an unobstructed view of the countryside.

First, he focussed on the front of the house. The protective boundary was at its closest point to the house there, extending behind the barn and the outhouses to the end of their short drive. The last time they had been attacked, the soldiers had come at them from all directions. Their courtyard and barn had become a killing zone, and it had taken days to hose away the blood. Now, however, that way appeared clear.

So, what was Black Cronos's plan now? To kill them or capture them? They must have reasoned that approaching over the field was the less obvious route. He focussed on the edge of the field and the glowing points of light that showed where their attackers were trying to get in. Another fizz of blue illuminated an additional attempt.

Zee's unease settled. *This would be fine. Their defences were too good.* For several minutes, he watched their attempt to get in, debating whether to fly over them and take them out that way. However, that was pointless if he left the front of the house exposed.

Nahum and Eli were poised at the edge of the field close to the house, also watching their attempts, no doubt hoping they would retreat.

And then a loud explosion dispelled that hope. Rock and earth went flying, and a dozen soldiers dressed in black raced in through the breach. Zee raised his crossbow and fired, taking out at least three men before a strange *whump* drew his attention overhead.

A helicopter was approaching from the sea, and it was coming straight for them.

Black Cronos had obviously decided on another strategy to offset their lack of wings.

Zee couldn't be in two places at once, and he was loathe to leave his brothers. They were good fighters, but no match for another dozen men. Eli and Nahum were already running to meet them, weapons raised.

Black Cronos weaved across the field, their progress slow because of the mud, and Zee shot a few more. So far, no one approached the front of the house. But with the helicopter closing in, he had to deal with that imminently. He extended his wings and took to the air.

The helicopter swept closer, and he made out a couple of figures in the cockpit. He aimed his crossbow and shot, but the helicopter veered to the side, and his shot went wide. A soldier leaned out of the side door and shot at him in return, using one of their strange, silvery weapons that had almost killed Shadow.

Fortunately, Zee was more manoeuvrable than a helicopter. This was his natural element. He flew low and quick, raised his crossbow, and peppered the helicopter with bolts, once again dodging more fire from above as the helicopter swung wildly over him. He swept around the rear, soaring high above the enemy. Then, his wings behind him, he plummeted like a bird of prey, aiming for the side door.

Disorientated and confused, the soldier fired wildly, aiming below initially, before finally spotting Zee. But he couldn't aim in time. Zee sailed under the blades, hauled the soldier out, and promptly dropped him to the ground. He entered the cabin and found another three soldiers and the pilot.

This was going to get interesting.

Eli charged across the grass, sword raised. But he had only advanced a few metres when a flash of light arrowed straight for him.

He dived to the side, rolling in mud, barely having time to regain his feet before another shot had him diving for cover again.

Damn it. They had come armed with advanced weaponry. He knew they could target different energy signatures. It must be how they had finally shattered the witches' defences. It also meant they had a lot longer range than his sword. At this moment, he was pretty sure they wanted to kill them, not capture them. They were too deadly in their approach.

The soldiers spread out, advancing on him and Nahum.

Eli launched into the air, sword extended. His rise was so swift that their shots missed him, but the next singed his wings and burned his arm. Still, he advanced, aiming for the more vulnerable at the back, without the big fire power. But they still had crossbows, and a bolt grazed his side as he flew low, managing to kill one and injure another. For the next few minutes, he fought furiously, but was unable to make progress. He killed a few more, but couldn't get close to the ones at the front who had almost reached their house.

A boom resonated across the fields, and the loggia burst into flames.

The house will be next.

He flew high again, meeting Nahum up above the field, hoping they were out of range of their weapons. Nahum was bloodied and breathing heavily, but his eyes were sharp and focussed.

"Nahum, they'll destroy the house! We're outnumbered, and Zee is busy." He nodded toward the helicopter that was veering wildly over the moors. "We need to use the power trapped within Belial's jewels." He could feel it calling to him already from where he'd placed it in his pocket.

There was a flash of fear, but also resignation in Nahum's eyes. "I don't like this at all, but you're right. We have no other options."

"Then let's unleash Belial's power. Destruction and madness."

"And if *we* end up fighting?" He gestured between them. "Like earlier?"

"We stay focussed on them!"

"Since when did you become so willing to take such crazy risks, Eli? This isn't you!"

"Since I made White Haven my home. I fear our friends will be next. Ready?"

Nahum nodded.

Eli pulled the torc from his pocket and placed it around the bicep on his right arm as Nahum settled the ring on his finger. The power he had felt earlier magnified. It was a strange, compelling power rooted in the magic of the old God. Already it infiltrated his brain and altered his vision. A sharp, predatory hunger filled him, and a wild urge to destroy took root in his mind.

White flames raced across his body and filled his wings with incandescent light. His skin couldn't contain it. Neither could Nahum's. Both were like stars. *Fallen stars*. He could just about see Nahum's shape through the flaming white glow.

Vengeance filled his soul, and the certainty of inflicting death reigned. An old feeling he thought never to experience again. He arrowed himself downward, sword outstretched, with Nahum next to him.

Deliverers of justice, just as their Fallen fathers intended.

The next few minutes for Nahum were like a dream.

No, a nightmare.

In general, he took no pleasure in killing. It was a job, and he executed his opponents quickly, taking no joy in it. And yet, in those few minutes, there was a glorious feeling. The wash of blood, the mayhem, the screams, the satisfaction. The horror in the eyes of those they killed.

Black Cronos soldiers were not cowards. They were ruthless killers, but they visibly quaked as the brothers descended upon them. Their fire power was repelled by Belial's, or it burnt out before even reaching their bodies.

In minutes, their enemies all lay dead. Limbs strewn, blood draining into the mud. Nahum stood in the field of battle, having barely raised a sweat, covered in blood himself, and feeling nothing but vindication. Eli was a short distance away, face turned skyward, and together they watched the helicopter plummet, their brother leaping clear before it hit the ground and exploded, flames blistering the night.

Zee approached them warily, circling wide before landing a short distance away. He gripped his sword, the crossbow slung across his shoulder, his wings still outstretched. "Brothers. You're still glowing with Belial's power. I suggest you put it aside."

"I wish I could," Nahum said, breathing heavily as he sought to return to normal. It was like wrestling a snake into a match box. He looked at Eli. He was a vision from the Old Testament and all those illustrations. *Was that what he looked like? A weapon of God.* "Eli?"

Eli's warm brown eyes, normally so full of calm wisdom, were like burning coals, and when he spoke his voice was rough, the old language infecting his accent. "Brother. It feels odd again, does it not? Like slipping into our old skin."

"A skin you hated," Zee reminded him, stepping closer still, hand still gripping his sword. "Put it aside. You don't need it. The soldiers are dead."

Nahum wrestled for control, a madman laughing in his head at the power they had unleashed. It took all of his concentration and will, but finally the white-hot angel's power faded, and he felt like himself again. "Focus, Eli! Think of our friends. Newton will be here soon, no doubt about that. With his sergeants. Maybe the witches, too. You don't want to hurt them."

Eli nodded, his face contorting. His muscles corded and strained, veins visible across his skin as he sought control. Finally, the heavenly glow seeped away, and he sagged to his knees in the blood and the mud. He pulled the torc from his arm and flung it in front of him. "He's still in here." He tapped his heart. "I feel him. You need to get Briar."

Zee swallowed and nodded, eyes finally drifting to Nahum. "And you?"

"He's under my skin. Faint, but there. Just as Olivia said. Like an itch."

"Throw his ring away from you. On the ground, over here."

Nahum wrenched it off his finger and threw it at Zee's feet.

Zee took a breath. "I'll find something to put them in."

"You'll lose them."

"No, I won't. I'd feel them half a mile away." Zee cleared his throat, tension finally seeping from him. But only slightly. He pulled his phone out as police sirens sounded in the distance. "In the shower now, both of you. I'll call the witches and Newton."

Ten

E stelle paced the living room of their chalet, unable to settle as she
waited for Barak to return.

He'd been gone for almost two hours, and with every passing
minute, she worried even more.

"Estelle, please sit down. You're exhausting me!" Lucien remonstrated.

He was seated in an old-fashioned armchair by the fireplace, oc-
casionally prodding the logs. He looked better after his rest, but his
eyes were still haunted. Distant. Estelle could barely imagine how
tumultuous the past few months had been for him.

"Sorry, I can't." She paused at the window and twitched back the
curtains to look outside. The clouds were clearing, allowing the occasional shaft of moonlight to stripe the snow-covered peaks. It was
charming and picturesque, but she wasn't really focussing on the view.
She watched for Barak's return.

"You watching won't make him come back any quicker."

She finally turned away and sat on the sofa, reaching for the glass
of wine that she'd barely drank. "I know. I'm running through our
options if he doesn't return. Storming the castle with just us two isn't
really an option, but I will if I must."

He regarded her silently for a moment, a sad smile on his lips.
"You love him. That much is obvious. It's terrifying, isn't it? To love
someone so much. When they've gone, you flounder. It's like your
heart has been ripped from your body." His hand pressed to his chest.
"I'm not sure mine has come back. And now I'm something else. Even
if we were still together, he wouldn't love me now."

"That's not true! Love transcends everything." Even as she was saying it, Estelle wasn't sure she believed it. Her love for Barak was so huge, she couldn't imagine that he could love her as much. It seemed impossible. And yet, he constantly told her in so many ways. Her worry for him renewed, but she remained in her seat, wanting Lucien to reassure her.

He grunted out a mournful laugh. "You say that because your love is young and new. It feels invincible. I hope yours does last. Mine didn't." As if he sensed her fear, he said, "Don't worry. He adores you. He'd die for you. He watches you. Shelters you. Ignore me. I'm just jaded and heartbroken. Disillusioned. And then to be kidnapped and abused like this..." He gestured to his tattoos. "Well, it certainly tests your faith in mankind."

Estelle felt horribly selfish for her own preoccupations, but his observations allayed her fears about her relationship. "My family certainly jaded my faith, but it's not too late. My brother has decided to resurrect our faltering coven. I thought it was pointless. But, surprisingly, he's right. Things are improving." She smiled. "Life is never stationary. It ebbs and flows, and the tide will turn for you. Surely your time at The Retreat has restored your faith in people?"

"A little. Mastering my changes has helped too, of course. This is just a different version of me, right?"

"Exactly. The new you. And someone will love you for it."

He nodded, turning back to the fire. "Stupid that I should be worrying about that, right? We have more pressing concerns. Like ending these monsters."

"Unfortunately, I think that will be far harder than we imagine."

A noise outside the front door had them both on their feet, magic balling in Estelle's hands, but then Barak called out. "It's just me."

Her fears expelled in a rush as he crossed the room to the fire, carrying the scent of snow with him.

Estelle headed to his side, searching his face for news. "I didn't hear you arrive! You were gone a while."

"I settled on one of the towers to watch." He huffed, his jaw tight. "We were right, they are there. I saw Stefan Hope-Robbins and the new Silencer of Souls or whatever she's called—or at least one of them.

They have a huge wheel of correspondence in one of the courtyards. It's enormous!"

"But that's brilliant! We finally found them!"

"Well, yes, it's good, but there are guards all along the walls, and no doubt below the castle, too. It's strongly fortified, and the only place I could land with any safety was a very high tower. I think it houses their communications."

Lucien had gone to the kitchen to get more beer, and he returned, passing Barak an uncapped bottle. "Yet, you don't look happy at finding them."

"Because I realise just how hard this will be. The reality of it. And how few there are of us in comparison."

"But we have time to plan our attack," Estelle reasoned. "To watch and prepare."

"Maybe." Barak's eyes settled on hers. "But the winter solstice is close, and I think they're planning something. Some ritual, perhaps."

"Why?" Lucien asked.

"Because while I watched, the wheel turned—or some of the rings, at least. There must be a huge mechanism underneath to move it. Some of the sigils lit up."

Estelle was very familiar with the solstices and equinoxes; the Sabbats, as witches called them. They were powerful times in the calendar of the year. Times of celebration, also used for spell work and rituals. "I guess that as an alchemist it makes sense that the *comte* and Stefan would utilise them. But they would use them regularly, just like witches do. It doesn't mean anything particularly untoward."

"Maybe not."

"So, what now?" Lucien asked, sitting in the armchair again.

"Now we explore the ridge that the *château* is on. I suspect there are entrances lower down. I didn't loiter, though. I didn't want to test my luck. I thought perhaps, Estelle, that we could use a cloaking spell tomorrow night."

"Absolutely. I have a few ideas." She'd been mulling on spells for weeks, honing the ones she thought would be useful.

"Good. I'll call my brothers tomorrow to alert them. Let's hope Gabe and the others can wrap up the theft quickly." He sat back in the chair, staring into the flames. "We'll need them. All of them."

Ash quickened his pace as he progressed along the museum's displays, all too aware of the advancing time, and the fact that other guards might come looking for the ones they had imprisoned.

He hoped that Gabe had found the set-up for the camera system. The blinking red light still flashed from the cameras, but hopefully they weren't recording anything. With luck, no one was watching from afar, either.

The weight of the past pressed upon him. Row after row of arte-facts, sculptures, chunks of stone from long collapsed civilisations, and fragments of text. He scanned them all, fearful of going so quickly that he missed what they needed to find.

And then, after a few more paces, there it was. Or rather, there *they* were. Half a dozen discs of various sizes were displayed together, all made of precious gemstones, but only three were emerald. Several were the size of a small plate. Ash groaned. *Half a dozen of them?* JD hadn't mentioned these. *What if, for some weird reason, the missing piece wasn't made of emerald?* Some were completely flat with no raised area at all, and had different animals etched into them. However, three pieces had a raised circular area with the image of an ibis sitting proud. Two were made from emeralds. They were all described as decorative objects to honour the Gods, but no other function had been ascribed to them. There was certainly nothing to signal them as being important or related to the Emerald Tablet.

He searched the rest of the room quickly, but nothing else looked remotely similar. One of these had to be it. He called Gabe and Shad-ow, studying the glass case that protected the display while he waited for them. It was large, coffin-sized, clipped in place, and alarmed. The movement detector device was attached to one of the glass sides. Ash had read up on alarm systems, and there were many varied types that all essentially did the same thing. They detected movement inside the case. If the case moved, it would go off. It was battery operated and linked to a central system. Guards would be alerted immediately if disturbed. Unless, of course, Gabe had the key to the display cases among the bunch he had stolen.

The light tread of footsteps alerted him to the arrival of Shadow and Gabe, and before Ash could speak, Gabe groaned. "You have got to be kidding me! There are loads of them!"

"I know, right? What are the odds?"

"The Gods are screwing with us. Bloody typical!" Gabe glared at the display as if it was laughing at him.

"I have no idea which of those three could be the right one," Ash said, explaining his reasoning. "Although potentially it will have a quality to it that we'll recognise, much like the tablet has."

"And if it doesn't?" Gabe said, a frown creasing his forehead.

Shadow shrugged. "We have only one option. We steal all of them."

"And get them all in the box?" Gabe looked sceptical.

"Let's worry about that later." Ash pointed to the keyhole that would unlock the mechanism. "If we have the key, that will make life simple, but we can't isolate the alarm."

Gabe pulled the bunch of keys from his pocket, but it was obvious from their size that none would fit the cabinet. He huffed with disappointment. "I guess that makes sense. The guards just need the door keys."

Ash watched the entrances to the room, but no one appeared, and no alarms sounded. Nothing that they could hear, anyway.

Shadow rummaged in one of her pockets and pulled out her skeleton keys. "No problem, I'll just use these. I used them all the time in my world. Not this particular set, obviously."

"Wait." Ash put a restraining hand on her arm. "Let's talk escape plans. The alarm will go off anyway, I'm sure of it. We need to know the closest way out." He quickly consulted a guide of the museum they had picked up from the reception area the day before. The museum was an old mansion, designed around one large courtyard, with three small ones. Several double doors led into the courtyards, but he had noted they were locked and chained. "The mains doors are close, but there's another door to a courtyard two rooms along. That's the best way out. I'll check it first." He stared meaningfully at Shadow. "Just wait for me to give the go ahead. If it's impossible, we'll need another way."

"Fine! But hurry up!"

Gabe rolled his eyes, trying to quell his amusement. "Don't worry. We'll wait."

Ash crossed the gloomy rooms, lit only by bars of strip lighting under the displays. The statues and colourful masks looked lurid in the half light. He found the exit, but it was barred by another waist-high display. A chain looped around the inside bars of the courtyard doors, securing them together. If he tried to remove the display, he would set more alarms off. Then again, they were already setting them off, anyway.

At least he could break the padlock and unhook the chain first. He should be strong enough to do that. He gripped the padlock, twisting it within his strong fingers, only seeing the fine wires that connected it to an alarm system too late.

In seconds, the alarm sounded, booming overhead.

Niel groaned as the alarm erupted below him. *They had thought it inevitable, but even so...*

He circled over the museum, heading to the outpost at the top of the drive where the guards were stationed. It was a brick building, set into the tall stone walls that surrounded the grounds, and the solitary guard was already exiting, speaking into his phone. No doubt trying to contact his colleagues.

But there were no other guards, and no sign of the police yet. They would have to come from the main centre, and that would probably take at least ten minutes. After watching for a few moments more, Niel decided the man was waiting for the police. The huge gates were still closed, and he wouldn't want to leave them open. Perhaps he figured the thieves had nowhere to go.

He wheeled around and flew back over the museum. He groaned again. Huge steel doors had sealed off the front door. A quick scout around revealed every single entrance had been sealed with similar, shuttered steel doors.

Landing on the roof, he called Gabe, and when no one answered, he tried Ash. He figured that if Gabe was deep inside the museum, the signal might be poor. Hopefully they all weren't together. But his second call went unanswered, too. *Where were they?* Exasperated, he moved positions, flying lower, and was finally rewarded when he heard a dull banging from one of the courtyard doors.

He landed on the ground. "Hello? Gabe? Ash?"

A muffled voice shouted back. "It's Ash! I need help to lift the screen!"

Niel snorted. "You lost your strength, brother?"

"Clamps have sealed it in, you moron! Magnetic, I think."

"Sure! You keep telling yourself that. Stay back!"

Niel repeatedly smashed the frame at the base with his axe. It buckled and warped, and he put his axe aside and wriggled his hands under it. Ash's hands were immediately in the gap, too, and with a grating squeal of metal, they dragged the door partway up. He wedged the axe in place and propped the door open. Ash slid through, dust streaking his face.

"Where are Gabe and Shadow?" Niel asked, crouching to look inside.

"On their way, I hope. They're securing the discs in another room."

"Discs?"

"More than one, I'm afraid."

"Of course there are," Niel said, resigned. *Nothing was ever easy.* "Do they need help?"

"I hope not. I'll give them another few minutes."

"They set the alarm off, I suppose?"

"No, actually." Ash looked embarrassed. "That was me, trying to secure our exit."

"Nice, brother. You did well."

Ash gave him the finger in response. "I suggest we wait here—just in case something else takes us unawares."

"I'll leave that to you. The police are coming. I'll go keep watch." Niel took to the skies again leaving Ash to wait.

"Bollocks to the lock," Gabe said, growing more frustrated as the alarm pounded into his skull. "I'll smash the glass."

"No, you won't! Broken glass might damage the discs," Shadow protested.

She persevered with the pick, her nimble fingers turning the lock with practised ease. In seconds, the case was open, and she reached inside to grab the discs. As soon as she picked them up, another alarm sounded, and the whirr of a mechanism had Gabe spinning around. With horror, he saw a barred gate drop into place on both doors.

"You have got to be shitting me! Herne's fucking balls!"

"Go lift it! I'll get these!"

"Yes, of course! I'll lift it, just like that!" Gabe sprinted to the gate that led to Ash, relieved to see that only their room had been sealed off. He should have known it. Of course emerald discs the size of plates would have extra security. *Damn JD and his crazy requests...*

Gabe tried to lift the barred gate. It was solid, and brutally heavy. Knowing he was stronger with his wings open, as they enhanced his paranormal strength, he ripped his shirt off, and stuffed it in his pocket. With great effort he managed to lift the gate. He shouted at Shadow. "Hurry up!"

"I am being as quick as I can!"

"Shadow!" He glowered at her. "The guards are on their way, and I'm about to have a hernia!"

"It will all have been for nothing if these are damaged! Besides, the guards are Niel's job."

Gabe knew she was right. Heists weren't his forte, so he should just shut up and do as she said. Besides, he quite liked her being bossy. Not that he would tell her that, of course. If anything, it made her sexier.

In another few moments she raced towards him and slid under the gate. "Your turn."

With immense effort, he lifted the gate higher, braced himself, ducked under it, and finally released it with a thunderous clang. "That way!"

They crossed the floor and headed to the exit. The courtyard doors were partly open, and a mangled metal screen was warped beyond it. Gabe and Shadow slid through the gap and found Ash standing outside, gazing up at the stars, his phone pressed to his ear. "They're here. How's it looking, Niel?" He nodded, wings extending, and ended the call. "Half a dozen cars are on the way. Time to go. Got them?"

"Yep," Shadow said, a smug smile on her face. "Now we have to hope that Black Cronos has gone. Otherwise, where to next?"

"One problem at a time." Gabe opened his arms. "Let's go."

Eleven

"**I** still don't understand," Harlan complained to Morgana, "what a splinter of a Fallen Angel is! It sounds insane! Ridiculous." He tripped over his words, finally settling on, "Impossible!"

Morgana sighed heavily, eyeing him with impatience. She looked imperious in her flowing black dress with her hair loose down her back. "It's not impossible, because clearly it has happened. Although, perhaps splinter isn't the best word. It's hardly like Belial has a physical presence. Thank the Gods."

Maggie snorted with disdain. "Hasn't he? It sounds like he has to me. Him and his bloody agent. And the dead vicar!"

"But Belial has no physical body," Morgana explained. "He never had. He's all light and energy. All angels were. *Are*," she corrected herself. "But their spirit was so powerful it was almost a physical presence. Nothing like a ghost."

They were in the kitchen at Moonfell. It was a large room at the rear of the house, half kitchen, half dining area, with huge, gothic arched windows that overlooked the garden. He and Maggie were talking to Morgana, while Odette worked on Olivia in the dining half of the room. A confused, slightly panic-stricken Olivia, who was clearly trying to remain calm.

Everything about this house is dramatic, Harlan thought, taking it all in while Morgana talked. From the three witches who lived there, to the house itself. The kitchen was modern, with black tiled walls and dark wooden cupboards and work surfaces. It suited the gothic style perfectly. A fireplace blazed at the dining end, and books, newspapers, and plants covered the table and filled shelves. Even though it was late, something bubbled on the large, five-burner hob top. He was pretty sure it wasn't food.

Beyond the windows, some of which had stained glass images depicting leaves and plants and the menacing grin of the Green Man, were the dark shapes of plants. Like the front garden, the occasional spotlight picked out the unusual topiaries. The scudding clouds revealed glimpses of huge trees with bare branches and big garden beds. It was all very intriguing. Everything about the house made him want to explore it. To uncover its secrets. His attention was drifting, as if the house was calling him. He shook his head and focussed on the conversation.

Maggie showed no evidence of being distracted. "So, what's a better word for splinter?"

"You're being very prosaic, Maggie. Magic and witchcraft are not paint by numbers."

"I'm well aware of that. Are you saying that an angel is magic and witchcraft? I'm not sure they'd like that!"

Morgana grinned and it made her look younger, more mischievous. "No, I'm sure not. They were servants to their God, one amongst many. They just threw their weight around a lot more. And there were loads of them." She opened a cupboard and started to pull out jars of dried herbs and put them on the counter. "It was when a few of them fell that the real trouble started. However, I prefer not to dwell on them. The Goddess who they tried to suppress is someone I have far more affiliation with. But, to answer your question, Belial has such a strong presence that he has buried a part of himself in Olivia. We must exorcise him."

Harlan thought he was hearing things. "You're exorcising an *angel*? Is that even possible?"

She turned her sharp, intelligent eyes on him. "Of course, with the right words. Besides, it's only a very small part of him. A fragment of his influence."

"Morgana!" Odette summoned her attention. "Olivia said her friend was there, and that he was influenced, too."

"But he'll be fine," Olivia insisted, eyes wide. "He's, er, not quite human. He'll be able to resist far more than me. Although, I feel nothing! I'm fine."

Odette shook her head. "You're *not* fine! That's Belial's influence. Fortunately, I can tell. One of my skills. Neither should we take your friend's ability to resist for granted. You must warn him."

"I can call him." Olivia reached for her phone, glancing nervously at Harlan as she did so.

"Good. Tell him to act quickly." Odette stood, leaving Olivia to make the call, and crossed to Morgana's side. "We need Birdie."

Morgana was weighing and mixing herbs, but she nodded. "Certainly. He'll resist, of course. Even a small part of him is strong. It's lucky," she said, glancing at Harlan, "that you came so soon."

Harlan nodded, feeling like the night's events were spinning out of his control. Being attacked by Black Cronos almost seemed a breeze by comparison. "But we came for a different reason. We need to find our friend, Jackson. He's been kidnapped by Black Cronos."

Morgana paused her preparations and stared at him. "Who are they?"

"An organisation that is obsessed with alchemy." He explained their previous encounters as succinctly as possible.

"Alchemy?" Morgana said thoughtfully. "How intriguing. It's one of my interests. An organisation with an immortal head..."

"We think," Maggie qualified. "Nothing is certain."

"Nothing ever is in this world. You have something that belongs to Jackson?"

Harlan nodded. "His scarf."

"Good. We shall try." She swept the herbs she'd prepared into a glass vial. "I need some fresh ones, too." She thrust a large jar of salt at her cousin. "Take them to the tower, please."

Odette nodded. "I'll start preparing the space."

"Where are you going for fresh herbs?" Harlan asked, not caring that he was being nosy.

Fortunately, Morgana looked amused. "The glasshouse. Want to come?"

"Yes, please!"

She handed him a small basket. "For the cuttings. Don't touch anything!"

Odette called to Olivia. "Time to go. Did you reach your friend?"

"No, but I left an urgent message." Olivia's face was creased with worry, and Harlan wasn't sure whether it was for herself or Nahum. *Maybe it was both.*

While Odette escorted Olivia and Maggie through a door in the corner of the room, Morgana led Harlan to a panelled door not far from the fireplace. In moments they passed from the warm kitchen to an ambient glasshouse lit by clusters of fairy lights. Harlan gasped at the sight of what appeared to be a faery garden before him.

The glass house was a half dome constructed entirely of iron and glass. The glass panels were a variety of different shapes—arches, hexagons, circles, squares, triangles—all designed with great skill. Within it were potted plants, gravel paths, and beds dug straight into the earth, as well as raised ones. A peculiar scent hung in the air. Something sweet and sickly.

"Are those lilies I smell?"

"There are some. The scent comes from many things." Morgana progressed down the path, aiming for a raised bed in the centre of the space. Harlan hurried next to her, hand reaching out to stroke a feathery frond. "Don't touch!" she shouted.

Startled, Harlan dropped his hand. "Sorry! I forgot. What is it?"

"Hemlock. Several beds here are full of poisonous plants. Prepared incorrectly, they will kill. Prepared correctly, however, and they will heal."

"Unless of course you *want* to kill someone," Harlan said, thinking it was a poisoner's dream.

Morgana smiled. "Of course, but I try not to kill my clients. Or send them mad or put them in hospital. Not often, anyway…"

From the twisted smile on her face, Harlan wasn't entirely sure that she was joking. "Would your clients ask for such things?"

"They might. I would say no," she said, pulling gloves on and snipping leaves from a large, bushy plant. "Vengeance is a poor man's game. I would rather give my clients the upper hand. There are other ways to do that." She didn't elaborate, and Harlan didn't ask. She dropped the plant into the basket Harlan carried and nodded. "All done. Time for some midnight magic."

Zee had the feeling that his brothers had unleashed a monster. It looked like Newton, the Detective Inspector of the paranormal team, and Detective Sergeant Kendall thought they had, too.

All three stood on the edge of the field next to the farmhouse surveying the bodies of the dead. Again.

"Making a habit of this?" Newton asked, his tone sharp and sarcastic. "How did you three manage to kill so many?"

Zee sighed. "Like I said, Nahum and Eli had a moment of madness. They called on Belial's power. Through those." He kicked at the jewels that were in a box at his feet. "Don't touch them!"

Kendall, long-limbed and dark-haired, crouched and shuddered. "I won't. They have a presence, don't they?"

"Unfortunately, yes. Belial's."

"What will you do with them?" Newton asked. "If you let them get into the wrong hands, anything could happen."

"Anything has!" Zee said. "For a long time, they have been causing insidious behaviour, deaths, and madness, although it wasn't attributed to these until Olivia and Nahum found them yesterday. And tonight, well..." he sighed. "Tonight made things a whole lot worse. I think that by using them, the jewels have only become stronger. To be honest, though, if Nahum and Eli hadn't used them, we would all be dead. Or we'd have fled, and our home would have been destroyed." Like the loggia's blackened, fire-damaged timbers.

Newton dragged his gaze from the dead to stare at Zee. "They knew you were alone."

"Perhaps. Probably. But me and Eli have been alone many times, and we haven't been attacked before."

"But you said it was coordinated?" Kendall asked.

"Yes. Harlan, Olivia, and Jackson were targeted, too. Jackson has been kidnapped. And the team in Egypt have had their hotel surrounded. They're okay, though, as far as I know." Zee's thoughts were all over the place. He was worried about all of his brothers and Shadow.

However, it seemed that although Barak and Estelle were camped out on the *comte's* doorstep, they were fine.

"And them?" Newton pointed to the smouldering helicopter in the distance, police cars, fire engines, and ambulance close by, the blaze of their lights bright despite the distance. DS Moore was with them, overseeing the investigation.

"Another team, come to block our air escape. I was lucky. I killed the pilot and managed to get out before it crashed." *Lucky might be a stretch.* One of their spears had pierced his side, but his body armour had protected him from the worst of the thrust. Even so, it ached.

Behind them, the sound of engines indicated the SOCO team had arrived. Newton sighed. "I'll deal with them, and then take your statement, Zee. Best do it now. Kendall, head inside and see what's happening with the witches." Newton waited until Kendall had left them. "How bad is it? Your brothers and Belial? Don't lie."

"It's very bad. They had so much power, they could barely contain it. Belial was the angel best known for death and destruction. Sammael's right-hand man. They were both lit up with his energy. It wouldn't surprise me if people saw them. They looked like falling stars, Newton. Bright! And deadly." He closed his eyes, but the image was burned on his mind. He opened them again, and found Newton still staring at him. "They killed all of our attackers, barely exerting themselves."

Newton clenched his stubbled jaw, his grey eyes unfathomable in the darkness of the terrace. "Were they in control of themselves?"

"Only just; even I kept my distance at first. I could see it in their eyes. The old bloodlust that our fathers had given us."

"I thought angels were supposed to be forces for good."

"Many were, but we're talking about the Fallen. There were many things they disagreed about with the old God, and one of the biggest were humans. The Fallen considered them a scourge on the planet. Of course, you know our role. We were their weapons."

"Because they couldn't walk on Earth."

"Exactly. Not for long, anyway. And then the old God came to see their side of it. He endorsed the destruction we unleashed. Until He had enough of all of it and sent the Great Flood." Zee sighed, fearing he wasn't explaining things well. "We all absorbed the powers of our

Fallen fathers. We all could look like my brothers did tonight, if we chose. But it clouded our minds and judgment. We rebelled against that as much as anything. Their control. When we cast it aside, it diminished us, but left us whole of mind."

"I understand."

Newton looked through the kitchen window to watch Briar prepare her herbs at the counter. Her shoulders were hunched as she ground them, as if she were taking out her exasperation on them. The other witches were inside, all gathered in the living room. Zee should be there to protect them, just in case. He took a deep breath and tried to be rational. The witches could cope, and his brothers would not attack them.

Newton interrupted his thoughts. "Is this the start of something?"

Zee shrugged. "Honestly, I don't know."

Olivia couldn't help but be unnerved by Birdie, the small, wizened woman who was Morgana and Odette's grandmother. She was the epitome of an old crone, although she felt mean for even thinking that.

She had a tiny frame, shoulders rounded, her eyes milky from cataracts. But energy radiated from her as she directed Morgana and Odette's preparations. She was pretty sure neither of them needed her directions, but they acquiesced all the same. Every now and again, Morgana would suggest something, and Birdie would nod, and then Odette would offer a change, too. Between them, they completed their preparations quickly.

All the while, Olivia sat quietly, trying to subdue the rising panic she felt inside, and the insistent impatience and spite she noticed bubbling up along with it. Harlan sat next to her, a calm, reassuring presence, and she soaked him in. Despite her protestations, she knew that something was very wrong. Ever since Odette had called her out on it, the strange presence inside her—Belial, she couldn't deny it any longer—had become increasingly...alert. Maggie, however, was on the other side of the tower, watching every move avidly.

The round tower was a fascinating place, like something from a fairytale. Like the other rooms she had glimpsed, and the kitchen they had been in, these windows were gothic monstrosities of stone and stained glass, stretching up to the vaulted ceiling, the details lost in darkness. A fireplace danced with flames, and in the large space in front of it, the thick Persian rugs had been rolled back to reveal a pentagram scored into the stone floor. A large salt circle was around it. A couple of towering cases of books and armchairs were in shadows, witnesses to the events, but the rest of the space was empty.

Within the circle was a chair. Her place.

Birdie walked to Olivia's side, her gait slow and unsteady, her stick tapping the floor. "Time for you, my dear." She was so short that she was barely taller than Olivia, who was sitting. She peered into her eyes and muttered, "Enter the circle now. Don't hesitate, just do it. Give him an inch, and he'll take all of you."

Terrified, Olivia almost ran into the salt circle, feeling her legs drag with every step. But Birdie's words rang in her ears, and she didn't hesitate. She had visions of turning into a spitting monster of fire and light.

Morgana and Harlan entered with her, and Morgana said, "Sit down, Olivia."

But she couldn't. Olivia could feel herself rebelling, her limbs shaking as she disobeyed Morgana's order. And then a commanding voice screamed a language in her head that was so unearthly, she thought she'd go mad. The scream became her own, and she grabbed her hair as if she would tear it out, the voice along with it.

Harlan forced her into the chair, and Morgana uttered a word of command, her hand on her forehead. The room swiftly vanished, leaving only darkness.

Twelve

"**W**hat the hell have you done to her!" Maggie yelled, horrified, as Olivia slumped over in the chair.

"I've saved her from madness," Morgana replied calmly, as she helped Harlan tie her to the chair. "Good. Thank you, Harlan. Out of the circle. Now."

Morgana sealed the circle with more salt as they left Olivia alone in the middle, her head lolling onto her chest.

Maggie was horrified and fascinated. She had seen the flash of fire in Olivia's eyes before Morgana did...*something*. She rounded on the three witches. "You've made it worse! She was fine tonight!"

Odette, the most unnerving of the three in Maggie's opinion, with her strange, vacant expression that swept over her sometimes, turned to her. "She was *not* fine. He was lurking in there all the time. As soon as he knew I had seen him, he started to become stronger. Unfortunate, but inevitable. Left unchecked, he would have done so anyway. Better we tackle it now, before he's entrenched."

"But you said he was a splinter! How can he have grown bigger?"

"He's one of the Fallen, Maggie. One of the most powerful. An archangel. Even a splinter is enough in our weak bodies."

Maggie hated not being in control, and she was itching to boss everyone about and yell. But that was pointless. In this situation, she was powerless. She just had to shove her own annoyance and feelings of inadequacy aside, and help as best she could. And she couldn't deny the flash of fire in Olivia's eyes, or her shout in that strange language.

She took a deep breath and exhaled slowly, looking to Harlan for moral support. He shrugged his acceptance of the situation, eyes grim.

This was harder for him. Olivia was an old friend. His colleague. One of his pack, as he'd called it earlier. A pack of which she was supposedly a member. The alpha, of all things.

It was as if Harlan could read her mind. His normal air of devil-may-care insouciance had gone. "We've lost one friend tonight, Maggie. I can't lose another. I trust them. You must, too. You can't deny what you've just seen."

Maggie huffed. "We have not lost Jackson. That is temporary. We will find him."

"Yes, we will. As soon as this is done."

"We haven't time for debate," Odette instructed. "Stand over there, by the bookcase, and do not move, or try to help, no matter what you may see. It will be...difficult. Frightening. But exorcisms are my specialty."

"Even of Fallen Angels?" Maggie asked, ever sceptical.

"Hard, but not impossible. The Goddess will help."

Birdie cackled as she took her place around the salt circle. "The three aspects will come tonight. Crone, mother, maiden, embodied in us three. Then he will know what a fight is."

Of course, Maggie reflected as she stood next to Harlan, *the three witches were of the right age for the triple Goddess*. She may not know a huge amount about witchcraft, but she knew that much.

The witches, led by Odette, began their preparations, each taking a place around the pentagram, and each holding a staff that was as tall as the women. Every staff was different, with a strangely carved head inset with gemstones, and marks scored on the shaft.

Odette intoned a spell in her strange, sing-song voice that became even more hypnotic as she progressed. The language was unusual, of which Maggie only caught the occasional word she knew. As the words poured forth, the air thickened. A bowl of water in the circle that was filled with herbs, including the fresh leaves that Morgana had harvested, began to shimmer.

Odette's voice grew louder, the other witches joining in. She cracked her staff onto the floor and then lifted it, pointing it at the roof. The ceiling had been in utter darkness, but now sigils revealed themselves, fire racing along them. They reflected on the floor, revealing other sigils there. Maggie gasped and edged back, but the walls also filled with marks and signs, and she grabbed Harlan's arm. The whole room had become a spell.

Why was she even in here? They should be outside, surely. She felt as if she would be consumed.

The witches, however, didn't budge. Odette's voice grew stronger and more commanding with every word. The hairs on Maggie's arms stood up, and she felt Harlan's muscles clench. She didn't dare look at him. She was transfixed with the activity in the centre.

Suddenly, power cracked into—or maybe out of—Odette's staff as if it was a lightning bolt. It split, hitting the other two staffs that the witches carried, and suddenly they became more than just women. They were positively supernatural. A face was imposed over their own. Old, middle-aged, and youthful.

The Goddess is here.

Their voices weren't their own, either. They were all using one, powerful voice that resonated with magic, and seemed to be all around them and within them. The scent of blossoms filled the air, and a wild magic seemed to drag the breath from Maggie's body.

Only now did Odette address Olivia, pointing her staff at her. Again, the language was unintelligible, but the intention was clear. It was a command to leave. Olivia's neck muscles strained as she raised her head. Her eyes flew open, and they were filled with fire. Her face contorted, the muscles rippling, her mouth opening in a silent scream.

Maggie was horrified. Now she understood the true nature of possession. It was something she hadn't fully grasped before. *But why should she?* She hadn't witnessed it before.

Olivia's skin rippled with an inner fire, too. She writhed against the bonds that restrained her. Out of nowhere, huge fiery wings appeared behind Olivia, barely encompassed by the salt circle. Where the tips touched, the circle blazed into life. Inch by struggling inch, a creature of fire and light twisted out of Olivia. It curled around her in a wreath of smoke. But as the strange echoing voice continued its commands, the creature twisted upwards. A face blinked in and out of view, blindingly handsome and terrifyingly remote. The marks that the witches had drawn on Olivia's skin blazed with a white light, and the speed that the angel left her body increased. Maggie could hardly believe what she was seeing. A Fallen Angel, or a part of one at least, was twitching out of Olivia, pulled by the magic of the Goddess, summoned and embodied by the three witches.

A roar of anger seemed to come from everywhere, and Maggie shielded her eyes as the winged creature exploded with light. The room shook and glass exploded, and Harlan tackled her to the floor, covering her body with his own. It felt like an earthquake had struck.

And then in seconds, it was over. The longest seconds of Maggie's life.

Maggie finally lifted her head as Harlan eased off her. The sigils still glowed with a faint light, illuminating the room. The three witches were on the floor, their bodies twisted and twitching with spasming movements.

But Olivia was motionless on the floor, the chair she had been seated on splintered into fragments.

Eli felt strung out, as if he'd spent days drinking instead of minutes wielding Belial's power, but Briar's calming energy was restoring his equilibrium—slowly.

Briar was a petite earth witch, but her small frame contained a huge amount of power and knowledge. He had shakily made himself and Nahum a cleansing tea before she arrived, but as soon as she walked through the door, she had cast a palpable cleansing spell over them. Now she was working deeper magic.

They were seated at the kitchen table. The other witches were in the living room with Nahum. Briar had insisted on seeing him alone, even though he was worried that Belial's influence hadn't quite gone. He thought Briar was trying to demonstrate her trust in him. It was potentially dangerous.

"By the Goddess, Eli! What were you thinking?" She'd been in bed when she received the call, he could tell. Her long hair was loose, lightly curling as it spilled over her shoulders, and she wore minimal makeup. But her dark brown eyes were ringed with green fire, a sign of her agitation. Her hands ran over his body, bare millimetres from his skin. "Your aura is all over the place. And you feel..." she hesitated. "Violent."

"I was violent." He laughed. "I *am* violent. You know that. It's my nature."

"I know you cast it aside and spend your time healing now. You're an apothecary, remember?"

"I know. But it's still inside me. Normally, I control it better."

Briar sighed. "I know you use it to protect yourself and those you care about, and that's only right. What's the point of your abilities, otherwise? That's what happened today."

"That is *not* what happened today. I willingly absorbed some of Belial's power, using what he had bound into his jewellery. Jewellery I knew to be dangerous, because of what Belial is—was—and what Nahum had discovered. But I was so determined not to let Black Cronos win that I risked everything to stop them."

She lifted her face to his, so close that he could smell the sleep on her breath. "It wasn't about them winning. It was about them killing you and destroying your home. I'm so sorry this happened and that you were forced to make that choice."

He refused to be exonerated. "I had other avenues. I chose this one. Have you seen what I did?"

"You weren't alone. Nahum did it, too."

"It was at my suggestion."

"I saw the body parts and the blackened remains. There were many of them. It must make me horrible to say that I'm glad it was them and not you. Besides, what would your harem do without you?" Mischief sparkled in her eyes.

"Funny."

"Anyway, like you said, it's not the first time you've killed, and they deserved it. It's the manner of it, and what that means. I certainly don't think badly of you using something you thought would help. Admittedly, it was crazy, but sometimes desperation forces our hand."

Her warm presence reassured him. Invited confidences. He clasped her hands within his own. "It was almost like I *wanted* to experience it. Like a sudden craving for a drug I gave up. Maybe that's why I stopped doing this millennia ago."

"But you didn't use Belial's power years ago. You used your father's. You're getting maudlin, Eli. That's your out of whack aura talking."

"But he's still under my skin."

"Just his power, though, right? Not him."

"Yes. He can't possess us—although that feels like a very fine distinction at the moment. It's just residue."

"Then I'll keep flushing him out. I have spells and herbs for that." She smiled. "I'll give you the day off, too."

He then voiced the other issue that had preoccupied him for weeks. "I'm wondering if the dryads have some part to play in this. I think they have bewitched me."

A few weeks ago, Eli and Zee had made a pact with the dryads to help the witches defeat Wyrd and the mad wizard who had tried to change their fate. It meant he had promised the dryads guardianship. He had felt fine with that at the time, but now he wondered about his choices. Events had progressed quickly, and recently the dryads had escorted them to one of their sacred groves that only they could access, where the saplings grew. These were the trees they would plant in ancient forests across the country. But the dryads whispered in his dreams, where he wandered among dark forests that echoed with birdsong and streams and secrets.

Briar pulled her hands from his and reached for her herbal tea, studying him over the rim of the cup. "You're a Nephilim. I doubt that's possible."

"I'm not so sure. They are fey. Ripe with power that's rooted in the earth."

"So are you."

"We're different. Of air and flight."

"You've been listening to Shadow and her sylph theory."

"I know that angels, especially the Fallen, are not sylphs, but you know what I mean. Our magic and paranormal abilities are different. Lately I've been feeling as if they have seeped under my skin, too."

"They, or *she*?" She cocked an eyebrow, a knowing smile on her face.

There was one dryad they talked to all the time called Nelaira, and Eli would be lying if he said he hadn't had carnal thoughts about her, but equally, the idea terrified him. He loved women, so that was just weird.

"You're very discreet about your women, but it's obvious you like your relationships uncomplicated. I think Nelaira fascinates you. She is utterly unlike any woman you have met before. I think she has beguiled you, rather than bewitched you. Or maybe...it's love."

"Not funny, Briar."

"Is that so scary?"

"You tell me."

"*Touché.*" She smiled again, but it was brief. "Perhaps she fascinates you deliberately. It is their nature. Have you discussed this with Shadow?"

"No. It's the last thing I want to do."

"She knows dryads better than anyone. She must know about your pact."

"She was scathing." Shadow was horrified, actually, but maybe she hadn't told Briar that. She had berated him and Zee for weeks over their decision.

"Well, it's something to think about, but I honestly don't think you should worry about it too much. Belial worries me more."

"You look frightened of me." He hated that. Briar was gentle and kind, and he enjoyed working with her. She was a friend, and he had made a new life with her help.

"Not frightened, and not *ever* of you. But I am worried." She put her tea down. "More cleansing, I think, and then it's Nahum's turn."

Shadow took the three emerald discs from her pockets to show to her companions. They were now gathered on the roof of a hotel close to where they were staying.

She tapped one specifically. "I think it's this one. It feels different. Not as powerful as the Emerald Tablet, but it has...vibrations."

Niel snorted. "That's great, but getting it out of the country now, after that fanfare of alarms, will be nearly impossible. Security in airports will be tight. Maybe one of us should fly them all the way to the UK."

"Niel!" Gabe looked incredulous. "Stop suggesting that! It would take *days*! Weeks, even! Weeks we haven't got."

Niel had bullish tendencies, and that's why they got on so well. Like Shadow, he just wanted to get on with the job. But in this case, he was wrong.

Shadow calmly wrapped the discs again. "Don't be ridiculous. JD's box and my glamour will work fine."

Niel folded his arms across his huge chest. "There are x-ray machines and scanners and all sorts of things. How do you know for sure?"

"Because I put my knives and a small emerald trinket in it coming over here—all in my hand luggage. A test. It worked."

Gabe glared at her, but Ash laughed. "Priceless. And if you'd been arrested?"

"It would have made the trip more interesting."

Niel, however, looked impressed. "You got your blades through? They didn't know?"

"Nope. JD's box works."

"So, Miss Smarty Pants," Gabe said, leaning against the air conditioning unit they were sheltering next to. "Where's the box now?"

"In our room, obviously! Like I had a chance to pick it up after we'd been summoned to the roof!"

"And if Black Cronos has taken it or destroyed it?"

A flash of fear constricted her heart. She'd never considered that. However, she put on a brave face. "What would they want with a wooden box? They might not even be in our rooms."

Gabe, always the planner, exploded. "Herne's fucking hairy balls! Without that box we're screwed!"

Ash cleared his throat, and they both stared at him. "So sorry to interrupt your cosy discussion, but perhaps we should also be worried about passports? In our haste to get the discs, we really didn't think this through at all."

"We're travelling in a government aircraft. That should have influence," Gabe said.

"But we'll still need passports just for ID," Ash pointed out.

Shadow groaned. "This world is so full of rules! It's tedious."

"Tough. Get used to it." Niel rose to his feet. "I'll check to see if the vans are still there."

After the elation and adrenalin rush of the theft, reality set in, and Shadow, Gabe, and Ash considered their options.

"Regardless," Shadow said, "of where Black Cronos is, we need to return to our rooms. For passports, the box, our bags..."

"And if they're there, we'll end up fighting," Gabe reasoned. "And that means deaths."

Ash nodded. "But if we hide their bodies—like up here, on the roof of another hotel—then it's all good. We could check into a new hotel, maybe next to the airport. Or Jackson can change our flight." He hesitated. "Shit. No Jackson. Maybe Waylen could."

Gabe was watching the sky, Niel a distant dot. "I doubt we can just hop on another government plane."

They waited impatiently, running through possible scenarios until Niel returned, looking hopeful. "There are no black vans, so they've either given up, or a team is lying in wait, which sounds much more likely."

"Let's hope for the former." Gabe stood and extended his hand to Shadow. "Ready?"

"Always."

Thirteen

O livia woke to warm darkness, the only light a flicker of orange on the far side of the room. For a second, she couldn't work out where she was. However, she was lying on something soft, and she was deliciously cocooned.

She should be panicking, but Olivia felt so safe that the emotion never crossed her mind. She stretched, and then winced. Every part of her body ached. *What had happened?* However, the more she struggled to remember, the more her memory resisted. Despite the aches, she shot up in bed, her breath shallow.

"Woah! Take it slowly." Harlan's voice emerged from the shadows, as did he, rising from a chair to her right. He looked shattered. His normally neat hair had a rakish, ruffled charm, and his clothing looked like he'd slept in it for a week. He laid a calming hand on her arm. "I'm right here, and you're safe."

"Where am I?" She looked down and found she was wearing a cotton night slip over her underwear. "What the hell is going on?"

"Don't worry. I didn't undress you. The witches did. We're at Moonfell, remember?"

"Moonfell?" The name was familiar. "You said witches?"

"You're in a spare room in their impressively gothic house."

Olivia's eyes adjusted to the light. She was in a huge, four-poster bed on what felt like a feather mattress. The quilt and pillows were thick, and she smelled lavender around her. The room beyond the curtained bed had a fireplace containing a small fire, a huge window covered in thick curtains, and a few pieces of bedroom furniture. Oliva thought she'd gone back in time.

"But why am I in bed?"

He moved from the chair to the edge of the bed, watching her. "What's the last thing you remember?"

Something had happened. Something unpleasant. She remembered being in the pub with Jackson and Harlan. That was fine. *But then...* "Being chased by Black Cronos, and Jackson being kidnapped." She groaned. "Shit! We came here for help. But then..." There was something else; a buzzing in her brain that was evading her. She tried to think back before the drinks in the pub. She had worked with Nahum, and, *wow*, had slept with him. How could she have forgotten that? *And the reliquary.* "Belial!" she shouted.

Suddenly her breath seemed stuck in her chest.

"It's okay! Breathe!" Harlan grasped her arms and pulled her to face him. "He's gone. The witches did a *thing*."

She wrestled a hand free and patted her head and her chest. "I'm whole. But his eyes. I remember him. Like something lurking!"

"A splinter, apparently." Harlan eased away, giving her space, appraising her. "I have never seen anything like that in my life. For a splinter, he was insanely powerful."

"I have gaps," Olivia confessed. "I remember sitting in a circle of salt, in a strange tower, and then nothing."

"Oh, the tower. Yep. That *was* strange. And the three aspects of the Goddess. That was also something." He shrugged in his teasing, nonchalant way. "Yeah, you know, I saw a Goddess summoned today. She battled with an archangel and kicked his ass back to where he belonged. Somewhere beyond our realm! Yeah. Very cool. The windows have no glass now, the witches were half-dead when it ended, and me and Maggie had to shelter from a magical explosion. You were unconscious on the floor, after looking like you were about to explode. Normal, mid-week kind of stuff. What Odette called the witching hour. Yeah, that was something..."

He was making light of it for her, wondering what she remembered. "Sounds terrifying."

"Nothing more terrifying, though, than seeing you possessed. Those witches are really powerful. I will never underestimate them again."

"But all day I felt so normal!"

"Apparently, once Odette saw him, he grew more potent."

"I must thank them. Where is everyone?"

"In the kitchen. Maggie is making calls about Jackson." A shadow of worry crossed his face. "The witches are trying a finding spell for us later. They're recovering right now."

"I feel like I've been hit by a bus."

"I'm not surprised. You wrestled with a Fallen Angel." He pinched his thumb and forefinger together. "A little bit of one. Not a physical being, so I've been told. Just a touch of his spiritual presence."

Olivia plumped her pillows and flopped back onto them. "It was when I touched his jewellery. I felt him then. Like residue. That's probably an understatement, considering what just happened. Have you heard from Nahum?"

"Oh, yes. He and Eli had a moment of madness and used the power in Belial's jewellery to defeat Black Cronos who attacked them, too. They have the five White Haven witches treating them now."

Olivia sat up again, heart pounding. "Is Nahum okay? And Eli, obviously?"

"They're both alive. Chastened. Blood-spattered."

"I don't get it. Why voluntarily do that?"

"Desperation. There were three of them against a whole platoon and a helicopter." Harlan passed her a glass of murky water. "Drink up. Witches' orders. It has herbs in it and will help you. And then you should sleep some more."

Sleep was already beckoning, her lids growing heavy. "What about you?"

"I'll text Maggie, let them know you're okay, and then sleep in the chair. I don't want to leave you alone."

Olivia patted the bed. "Sleep here. I promise not to molest you. You can't sleep well in the chair."

"Damn it. No molesting? Where's the fun in that?" He winked. "Kidding. Are you sure? The chair is fine."

"I'm sure."

Olivia wanted to phone Nahum herself, just to hear from him what had happened, but it could wait. She'd call him in the morning. Right now, she just hoped that Belial's compelling eyes would not appear again, because if they did, she doubted she'd have the strength to resist.

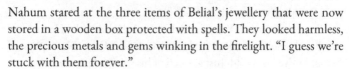

Nahum stared at the three items of Belial's jewellery that were now stored in a wooden box protected with spells. They looked harmless, the precious metals and gems winking in the firelight. "I guess we're stuck with them forever."

"No volcano you can throw them in?" Reuben asked, deadpan.

Alex groaned. "Tit. It's not *Lord of the Rings*."

"It might work. You can unmake them." Reuben cocked his head, a goofy grin on his face. "If you unmade angelic jewellery, would the entire world melt down? Would we all be stardust again?"

"Herne's horns!" El, his blonde girlfriend and a witch, remonstrated. "Has your bloody familiar, Silver, been waxing lyrical again?"

"Don't think you can break our bond. We're like that." He kneaded his hands together. "You're just jealous, but there's room in my life for two."

Everyone laughed, and Nahum was glad of Reuben's humour. He was always able to add levity to a situation. Even one as grim as this.

The five White Haven witches, plus Newton, Eli, and Nahum were gathered in the farmhouse's living room. He and Eli had been cleansed, spelled, and declared free of Belial's influence, although Nahum wasn't sure he could as easily cast the memory aside. He felt more guilty and worried about Olivia, though. For some reason he felt responsible, like he had endangered her, when the reality was that it was no one's fault except Belial's.

"We can't get rid of Belial's jewellery, unless we can bury them at the bottom of the sea," Eli said. "No human should ever touch them. They're too dangerous, especially considering what we know about Olivia. At least *we* can't be affected like that. What worries me even more," he confessed, staring at the witches, "is what would happen if someone like you touched them. Could he manipulate your magic?"

Avery, the pretty, red-haired witch who was Alex's partner answered immediately. "It's very possible. It seems to me that Belial is after a slice of power again, and he'll try any means to get that. We would be a decent way."

"I don't get any vibes from them now, though," Alex said. "Those protection spells have worked."

"The reliquary must have been spelled, too," Nahum said. "The lid was inscribed with protection sigils and angelic words to help mask their power. I want to know who put them there."

"So do I." Newton had been listening to the conversation in grim silence. His sergeants and the SOCO team had gone home, much to Kendall's annoyance, who was keen to stay. "Was it a human who put them there, or another paranormal creature?"

"Whoever it was," Zee said, "that will have to wait. Black Cronos is on the offensive. We've beaten them back, but we're about to attack their base. We're needed in France."

Briar shook her head. "That seems like suicide."

"We're reaching an impasse. Jackson has been kidnapped, the rest of us targeted. JD has the Emerald Tablet, and hopefully Gabe and Shadow have the key. That might help us. Barak is on the count's doorstep, with only Estelle and Lucien to help. Right now, we're scattered and vulnerable. Black Cronos is either still tracking some of us, or all of us. How?"

"Maybe," Newton suggested, "it's as simple as monitoring your phone. Or maybe it's a spell. A tracking spell. Or a covert team. Or a mole..."

Nahum's immediate thought was Lucien, but he had been thoroughly vetted, and he trusted everyone else. "No. There is no mole."

"You sound very sure."

"Because I am. The only possible person would be Lucien, and he's out for revenge." They all knew his background, because the witches and Newton had been kept abreast of their business.

Zee shrugged. "The Order of the Midnight Sun thought the same, yet they had one."

"Barak and Estelle have spent months with him, and Jackson," Nahum reminded them. "They considered that, but he's clean."

"Maybe Jackson, then," Newton suggested.

"He's been kidnapped!" Eli said, all three Nephilim staring at Newton. "He has a desperate urge to find his grandfather."

Newton was unfazed. "Maybe he contacted them, somehow. In his desperate need for answers, maybe he made a deal. Frustration can sometimes have weird consequences."

"Like getting kidnapped on purpose?" Briar asked, confused. "How does that benefit him?"

"Maybe he offered up Harlan, Olivia and himself, and it went wrong. They put up a bigger fight than he expected."

Nahum considered Jackson's shabby, gumshoe appearance. It didn't seem possible. And yet, he knew where all of them were at any time, roughly. He was at the heart of everything. He'd helped them, advised them, recruited them. Had even been appalled and stressed when he found out about his grandfather's colleague. "No. I don't believe it."

"But he hid his involvement with the PD very well," Zee reminded him. "Harlan never knew. That says a lot."

"But Harlan didn't know Jackson that well last year. He just knew him as another collector."

"Until we encountered Black Cronos."

Eli sighed. "I don't want to believe it, but the kidnapping could be a ruse."

"Harlan and Olivia could have been killed! He wouldn't have risked them, surely?" Nahum asked, hoping they'd agree.

Newton looked regretful, but his eyes were hard. "Who does Jackson report to? Maybe whoever that is betrayed you."

"Waylen Adams? The director?" Nahum expelled a sharp breath. "It can't be him!"

"Why not? If he's the boss, he'll probably know everything. Unfortunately, all my years as a policeman have told me that people hide things, all the time. At this moment, I wouldn't discount anything or anyone."

Gabe crept down the staircase that led from the hotel's roof to their rooms, Shadow next to him. The team had two connected rooms. Ash and Niel were approaching from the other end of the corridor.

It was four in the morning, and they still had at least two hours of darkness left.

The hotel was quiet. No guests stirred, and the corridor was empty. Gabe had debated flying and entering through the window, but if the doors were locked and Black Cronos was inside, smashing glass would be loud. This way, they hoped, would be quieter.

He eyed the other doors as they passed, wondering if the soldiers were waiting in empty rooms, but nothing piqued their senses. Ash and Niel approached them, Ash shaking his head. No one was waiting from that direction, either.

They reached the doors of their rooms, and Gabe pulled the key from his pocket. *Did they enter the conventional way, or burst in?* Being loud meant alerting the guests. He looked at Shadow and his brothers. Ash placed a finger on lips and pulled their key out, too. *A quiet entry, then.*

In tandem, they swiped the electronic keycard, pushed open the door, and ducked. Nothing happened. No shots. No charging soldiers.

Gabe edged inside, Shadow next to him, all her fey glamour wrapped around her. He could barely see her. They had a large room, but it contained only the usual furniture, an ensuite bathroom, a balcony, and nothing else. The interconnecting door was on the right, and it was closed. There weren't many places that Black Cronos could hide. It took only seconds to confirm that the room was empty.

Niel threw the connecting door open. "No one is here. The room looks undisturbed."

"Ours, too," Gabe confirmed. "Check your passports."

"Well, this is unexpected," Shadow said. Her blades were in her hand as she checked the wardrobe and under the bed. "Maybe they're coming back."

Gabe headed to the safe where their passports were stored, sighing with relief to find them still in there. He put them in one of his pockets. "Let's just grab everything and go. Is the box still there?"

Shadow searched her pack that she'd left behind after Niel had summoned them to the roof. "Yes. But I don't like this, Gabe. Did they get the wrong room?"

Gabe didn't answer. Like Shadow, he couldn't fathom it.

Ash appeared at the connecting doorway. "We have our passports. This is too weird. We didn't imagine seeing those soldiers."

"Unless," Niel said, looming behind him, "there was another target in the hotel. But that would be an insane coincidence!"

"Maybe there's a bomb?" Gabe suggested, eyes sweeping the room, but this time slowly, looking for details he had missed before. "If they didn't know we'd seen them, they could have planted one, thinking we'd be completely unsuspecting."

"I like it. It's sneaky. But where?" Shadow asked. She'd frozen in place, like everyone had, suddenly scared to touch anything. "If it were me, I'd want my target relaxed. Maybe I'd wire the wardrobe, so that when I opened the door it would detonate. Or the bed. Plenty of places to hide a bomb under the mattress. Pressure sensitive, perhaps."

"Or a trigger. If they've seen us come in."

"Too unreliable," Niel reasoned. "They'd have no idea how long it would take to get to our room. Maybe a timer."

"While I hate to add to our list of possible places," Ash said, "our luggage is also a good option."

"I hope not," Gabe said, eyeing it warily. "Let's get out of here. We touch as little as possible, and then find another hotel."

"I like that plan," Niel said, vanishing into their room.

Gabe checked his overnight bag, while Shadow lowered herself to the floor, and looked under the bed, edging closer than she had earlier. She used her phone's torch to scan the base. "I'm pretty sure I can see something that shouldn't be here. A small, metal box."

Ash had been waiting at the door, watching her, but now he turned to leave. "I'll check under ours."

Gabe slid next to Shadow. She angled her torch for him. "See? Right there."

"Fuck it." The small box had a winking red light on it. They edged back, careful not to touch anything.

Ash called over. "Yep. Niel's bed is clear, but there's one under mine. We need to warn the hotel. People will die."

"Or we could set it off and pretend we're dead," Shadow suggested, rising to her feet.

"And still, people might die," Ash pointed out. "We could have neighbours!"

"I haven't heard a sound from that side for hours earlier," Shadow said, pointing to the left. "One of you could fly out and check the windows. Then we'd know."

"To be honest," Gabe said, annoyed and wondering why they were still in the room, "I'd rather we have this discussion outside, just in case someone pushes the trigger. Grab our stuff carefully, and let's get out and discuss this down the corridor! Ash, tell Niel to get moving!"

Shadow, like him, had packed light, and had barely taken anything out of her luggage. She grabbed her bag and her backpack and headed to the door, Gabe right behind her.

But they were barely through the door when a boom threw him into the corridor, through a wall, and the floor collapsed below him.

Niel was on the balcony, grabbing his pack from the table where he'd left it earlier, when glass and brick exploded outward, throwing him over the railing. He hurtled through the air, plummeting a couple of floors, dazed, before extending his wings.

He swept around and flew higher, keeping away from the flames that poured from their room. Although, there wasn't really a room anymore. Most of the walls had blown out, exposing their level and part of the floors above and below it.

Screams erupted, and ignoring the fact that the light from the fire would illuminate him, he tried to see through the thick black smoke to the inside of the room. *Where had Ash been? And Gabe and Shadow?*

Unable to get close due to the searing heat, he flew to a balcony a few doors down, smashing the glass door with his axe. The room's occupants were already in the corridor, shocked and terrified, running towards the stairs. Doors were thrown open, and loud screams and shouts filled the air. Heading against the tide of fleeing people, his wings tucked from sight again, Niel marched towards the flames that were greedily consuming everything in their path.

The area where their rooms had been was completely destroyed, the surrounding rooms obliterated, leaving ragged holes of plaster and metalwork open to the elements. Unable to see his brothers and Shadow, he clambered down over the rubble, the hot metal searing his skin, to the floor below.

He yelled, "Gabe! Ash! Shadow!" But it was impossible to hear anything over the screams and the roar of the flames. The building creaked around him, and another chunk of rubble crashed down.

A persistent screaming to his right had him running to investigate. It was a young woman, pinned by metal and brick onto her bed. Flames licked the ceiling, and it was so hot that it was hard to breathe. Niel raced in regardless, hauled the rubble off her, and lifted her gently. He took her halfway down the corridor and found a man running towards him.

"Here!" He thrust the woman at him. "Take her out. She's injured."

He didn't even wait to see what happened next. He headed back to the flames. Piles of rubble could be hiding bodies, and he started to haul chunks aside, shouting all the time. And then he saw an arm protruding from the dust, and he redoubled his efforts.

It was Gabe.

He dug him out, fingernails ripping and hands bloodied. Gabe merely groaned.

"Brother! Wake up!"

Gabe shifted and moaned, blood pouring from a wound on his head. Twisted beneath him was Shadow. Niel had never been more grateful for his strength. Some of the fallen masonry was in huge blocks, but adrenalin fuelled him, and he tipped them aside, allowing Gabe to crawl free.

"Gabe, can you get Shadow out? I need to find Ash! More of this building is coming down, and if I don't find him now…"

Gabe nodded, still dazed. "Go. I'll get her. I'll meet you on the last roof we were on."

Niel headed deeper into the destruction and then took stock, noting where the rooms were above him, and where Ash could be. Ignoring the flames that were licking all around him, he looked up through the hole to the floors above and saw columns of writhing black smoke. Ash could have been thrown upwards, rather than crashing down. Just in case he was wrong, he hurled a few chunks of rubble aside, but there were no bodies beneath. Niel headed down the corridor to the edge of the fire, and then started to clamber up again. The place looked deserted, and the screams receded.

He shouted again, all the while cursing Black Cronos. They were a disease, and they had to eradicate them. *If they had killed Ash...* He could barely contemplate the idea as he searched.

And then he heard a weak, "*Help!*"

Eyes adjusting to the flickering flames and darkness, he caught an odd shape high up on the wall, pinned behind masonry and huge pieces of metal. Flames were encroaching, and the smell of burnt flesh was strong.

"Ash?" He rushed forward, stumbling over a blackened body on the floor. For one heart-stopping moment he thought it was his brother, and then another faint shout summoned his attention. His head snapped up, and he saw that Ash was pinned to the wall, a huge piece of metal skewering his shoulder.

Ash looked to be in agony. He was half embedded in the wall, the masonry beneath his feet helping to support him. *At least the flames hadn't reached here. Yet.* But they were close, and the air was so hot, it was searing his lungs. Niel scrambled up the fallen masonry to his side.

Ash was gasping for breath and covered in sweat and grime. His golden eyes seemed feverishly bright. "I tried to pull it out. I couldn't get a grip." Ash's fingers were slick with blood.

"I'll get it. Don't worry."

"It's pinned in the wall. I think it's melted in."

"I don't care! I'll get it."

Niel was still bare-chested, and tearing his t-shirt in two, he wrapped his hands and gripped the piece of rebar. But it was wedged in deeply, and still hot. Ash's shoulder was blistered and raw, and his golden eyes seemed to dim.

"Ash! I swear if you die, I will never forgive you!"

"Leave me and save yourself."

"Shut up!"

Niel extended his wings as fully as he dared, aware that his smaller feathers were already smouldering. He braced his legs on either side of Ash, grabbed the jagged metal, and pulled, using his wings as leverage. The metal groaned, ripping through the skin on his hands, and searing his palms.

Ash yelled in agony. Niel didn't dare stop now that he had momentum. Inch by inch, he dragged it from the wall and out of Ash's shoulder. Finally, he flung it aside, catching Ash as he fell.

Another explosion sounded overhead, blowing the closest window out. Oxygen poured in, and the flames swelled, rippling across the ceiling. Niel flew out of the window, Ash in his arms, as the flames leapt out to consume them.

Fourteen

B arak paced the living room of their chalet, unable to sleep.

He'd spoken to Zee a short while ago and was still processing news about Belial. It didn't seem possible that his jewellery, his *tokens* as the Fallen used to call them, could have survived all these years. Especially considering that many Nephilim had actively tried to destroy as many of those tokens as they could, once they rebelled.

But like many of their things, they were indestructible. Made of precious metals and gems that were crafted to the finest qualities and imbued with angelic magic, it was probably surprising that more of it hadn't survived.

Unless they had. Advances in the field of archaeology meant that more of the past was being discovered every day.

However, Barak hadn't the time to think about that yet. Not until Black Cronos had been defeated. They were caught between the enemies of their past, and the ones of the present. While Barak hated to be negative, he doubted they could destroy Black Cronos entirely. They were too big. The count was too powerful. But they could weaken him.

Of course, it depended on what Black Cronos were planning. The more he thought about it, the more he was convinced something was going to happen on the winter solstice. That moved their timeframe up.

Barak knew he should sleep, curl around Estelle and let his dreams take him, but fearing he would toss and turn, instead he headed to the TV and put the news on. He'd been watching for a few minutes when he saw a breaking news headline.

An explosion in a hotel in Aswan.

He phoned Gabe, Ash, Shadow, and Niel. None of them answered. Then he phoned Nahum. After a few minutes of hurried conversation, they had decided only one thing. Barak needed to wake Estelle and Lucien and leave their chalet. They had to move to a new place.

The others had been compromised, and they could be next.

"Well, this has been an eventful night," Maggie declared to the three witches gathered in the kitchen around the large, wooden table.

She tried not to stare at Birdie, but like Odette and Morgana, she found it hard to look away.

Birdie looked twenty years younger now. Her eyes were bright, the milkiness of the cataracts vanished, her skin was tighter, and she was no longer a small, wizened crone. The other two witches had also been affected by the Goddess, but not as much. Morgana and Odette seemed to have a glow of youthfulness to their skin, and although Morgana still had a grey streak in her hair, her jawline appeared tighter. Odette, perhaps because she was the youngest, was the least affected.

Birdie laughed. Less of a cackle now. "The appearance of the Goddess always makes for an eventful night."

Maggie had so many questions that she didn't even know where to start. She had spent the last hour on the phone. First, she called Waylen Adams, the Director of the Paranormal Division, then Stan and Irving, her own two Detective Sergeants. She had rattled Waylen out of bed. She had done all of this in what she called the poison palace, keeping her hands well away from any plants, and eyeing the witches through the partly open door. She spent five minutes more in there than she needed, settling her nerves before returning to the kitchen.

She drank one large whiskey and immediately needed another. She didn't want to confess that she'd been scared witless by the night's events. Maggie had tangled with many paranormal creatures over the years, but she had never experienced an event like she had earlier. The news that Olivia had briefly woken provided some measure of reassurance. Maggie's hip still ached from where she'd crashed to the floor with Harlan on top of her. *Big lump. Sweet of him, though.*

Maggie reached for the bottle of whiskey and topped up her glass, glad that her hands were steady. She blamed the adrenalin, not nerves. "I take it," she said, addressing all three witches, "that you don't normally summon the Goddess?"

"No, and I didn't summon her tonight," Odette admitted. "I called upon her influence. That's very common in witchcraft. She came of her own free will." She cleared her throat, eyeing her relatives. "That's what we've been discussing while you've been plotting. We're wondering what it portends."

"Portends? Fuck me! That word makes it seem so much more ominous," Maggie said, scowling. "How, and why, are you younger, Birdie?"

"The Goddess gives, and she takes away." Birdie picked up the small hand mirror at her elbow and held it to her face, turning to see all angles. "I confess, I did not expect this. But we never expected her to come at all." Birdie was still petite, as her name suggested. Short, small-framed, and slender. Placing her mirror down, she flexed her fingers. "My arthritis has gone, too. I wonder if there'll be a price to pay."

"A price? But you didn't ask for this."

Morgana answered, her hands around a cup of tea steaming on the table in front of her. "No. But a gift such as this usually requires payment, even though I have been a loyal admirer of the Goddess all my life. All of us have. We have altars to her throughout the house. Even in here." She pointed to a collection of candles and winter branches on a shelf close to the fire. "She is always welcome."

Maggie rubbed her temples, a right royal headache threatening. She needed to go home, and yet the thought of leaving this house and crossing the cold garden to her car was not attractive. But she needed a few answers first. "What is the tower room?"

"A spell room, that's all," Odette said, shrugging nonchalantly as if everyone had one. "It's amplified by sigils and signs of protection, devil traps, and other useful things. It is where we work our most powerful spells. It was the only place we could have cast that spell tonight."

"And that spell was what, exactly?"

"An exorcism, just as I said, but a complicated one. It was not an ordinary spirit or demon. But you know that."

"I didn't think it was any kind of spirit at all. You said it was a splinter. An impression left on Olivia's mind. So how did..." She floundered for words as she considered the flaming wings and eyes that had manifested from Olivia. "How could Belial appear so real?"

"Because he is an archangel. Powerful beyond measure," Birdie explained. She frowned, her fingers drumming the table. "It was an example of what even a tiny influence of him could do, just by touching his jewellery. If I'm honest, I'm not sure any of us fully understand it." She glanced at the other witches, and they nodded. "But he imprinted himself on her. I think a curse would be the most appropriate explanation. I would like to see those items. I gather there were three of them. It might help us understand."

"I think that would be a recipe for disaster, and it's a good job Nahum took them," Maggie retorted. "Can he come back? Can he target you, or any of us?"

"No." Odette didn't hesitate to answer. "We broke his hold, although he resisted very strongly. The Goddess saw we were struggling and helped. There is no love lost between the Goddess and the angels."

"Why is that?"

Morgana huffed. "Don't you know your history? Or religion? The Christian religion suppressed all mention of the Goddess. It is a one-sided religion. It lacks balance."

"I suppose you're right," Maggie admitted, thinking she really needed her bed. There was nothing she could do about the Goddess, or her battles with a misogynistic God and his angels. "Dragging us back to more earthly matters, we came here originally needing to find Jackson. Our friend who's been kidnapped by Black Cronos."

"While I appreciate that it's important," Birdie said, "we are tired now—although my appearance may not suggest that. I think we should all sleep, you included, before we perform that spell. If we slip up, we could send you in the wrong direction. Besides, will you really charge after him tonight?"

"Unlikely," Maggie admitted. "However, my sergeants are following what scant leads we have. But you're right. It's late, and I'm shattered. I just hope Jackson is okay. I presume if they wanted him dead, he would be already. It's what else they may do to him that worries me." *Like alchemical tattoos that could change him forever.*

"You must sleep here," Birdie insisted. "I think we owe you a debt. Or I do." Her eyes sparkled with delight as she stood. "Thanks to you and your friends, I've regained years of my life."

"It's not our doing," Maggie protested, standing too. "Although, I'm pleased for you, obviously. And I can't stay here. I will go home. I can't impose."

Morgana gathered their cups and glasses and headed to the sink. "Nonsense. We have a huge house, and you'll just have to come back in the morning. We'll put you in a room next to Olivia and Harlan. I promise that you'll be safe." She looked amused. "Besides, I know you're very curious about us, DI Maggie Milne. This is your chance to find out a little more."

Maggie couldn't deny that, and the thought of falling into bed within a few steps sounded brilliant. "Thank you. I appreciate it."

As Maggie followed Odette upstairs, she just hoped that when she woke up the next morning, she wouldn't be a frog. And that Jackson wouldn't be partially transformed into an alchemical soldier.

The concrete roof felt cool beneath Ash's bare skin as Niel laid him down, and yet it still felt as if fire raged in his shoulder.

His memories were hazy. One minute he was in the hotel room, the next he was hurtling through the air, battered by rubble, and pinned to the wall by a piece of rebar. He had passed out, with only Niel's roaring voice dragging him back to consciousness.

"Here, let me," he heard Shadow say. His head was lifted and then lowered onto something far more comfortable. Something that smelled of summer woods. Shadow's face loomed above him, and her cool hand rested on his injured shoulder. "Brother. Let me help."

"Shadow. I hate to say this, but you look half dead yourself." She was covered in dust and streaked in blood, chunks of plaster wedged in her hair, but her eyes were bright.

"I may have been flattened by stone and Gabe, who is a considerable weight, but I'll survive. And so will you."

Now that his head was slightly elevated, he could see he was on the roof of a building, and Gabe and Niel were standing at his feet, locked in furious discussion. He glanced at his shoulder. It was an ugly mess of torn and blistered flesh. No wonder it hurt so badly. But Shadow's hand was still pressed against it, and a cool feeling passed from her skin into his wound.

"What are you doing?"

"Sharing my fey magic with you. I'm not a healer, but magic is magic, and it should help."

"It does. Thank you." He wriggled to get a little more comfortable, and then wished he hadn't. Everything ached. He had broken ribs, he was sure of it, and there were cuts and gashes all over his body. "Where are we?"

"On the roof where we rested earlier, but we can't stay here much longer. It will be light soon, and we need to get to the airport."

"I hear sirens."

"The street is full of police and fire engines. Our hotel is ablaze."

Ash focussed on the sky, and as his senses sharpened, he saw the red glow and thick smoke from the fire over to his right. "They really wanted to kill us."

"With luck, they'll think they have. Let's hope no one caught our escape on camera. Winged creatures will make a great headline."

"Is that likely?" Ash asked, horrified.

She gave him an impish grin. Upside down, she looked demonic. "Not really. We circled wide before landing. Everyone's focussed on the burning building." Her grin quickly vanished. "Death will suit our purposes well. I will kill them all for this."

"Maybe that's the trouble. Maybe we need to compromise—somehow."

"You think that will stop them from making alchemical monsters?"

"They don't see themselves as that. They are superhumans. Everything evolves, Shadow."

"I know that, but they're doing it to people without their consent. That's my issue."

She had a point; one he couldn't overlook. He was exhausted, and it was obviously addling his judgement. But the thought of fighting Black Cronos again seemed to sap all of his remaining energy. They needed to find another way.

Gabe and Niel ended their discussion and crouched on either side of him. Gabe regarded him with compassion, but anger blazed behind his eyes. Gabe would not seek a compromise.

"We need to fly again," Gabe told him. "I know it will be uncomfortable, but we must get off this roof. We're going straight to the airport. Niel will carry you. We'll find a quiet spot to land."

"I'll cope. At least I'm alive." He looked at Niel. "Thanks to you."

Niel's face was like stone, his blue eyes chips of ice. Niel wouldn't compromise, either. They were on the verge of war with a large, private army. However, now was not the time to discuss alternatives. He needed to heal, and then they would make plans.

Gabe was already moving on. "You and Shadow will return to London, as planned, with the discs."

"They survived all of that?" Ash asked, surprised.

"I'd put them in the box already," Shadow said. "My body shielded it. I have a box-shaped bruise on my arse now."

Ash laughed. "That's something, then. And the passports?"

Both Gabe and Niel tapped their pockets. "On us, and safe—if battered."

"Where are you two going?"

Niel answered for them both. "France. Barak needs us. He's on the move with Estelle and Lucien, finding a new place to stay. They found the castle, though. We'll take the battle to them."

Ash struggled to sit up, fearing an ill-thought plan would get everyone killed. "But you'll wait for all of us?"

"If we can," Gabe answered.

"You'll wait for us," Shadow told him, "or lose your balls."

"And our brothers in Cornwall?" Ash asked, worry growing by the second.

"That tale can wait for the airport," Niel said, already flexing his wings. "Let's move."

Fifteen

"So, what do you think?" Zee asked Alex at The Wayward Son, early on Friday morning before the pub opened.

"I'm thinking lots of things, and none of them are very good right now," Alex said, leaning against the kitchen counter in the small staff room. "You're playing a dangerous game."

"Not by choice." Zee hoped Alex wasn't about to wash his hands of them. "Well, not entirely."

Alex smirked. "You mean notwithstanding Eli and Nahum's crazy decision to invoke Belial's power. Herne's hairy bollocks, you guys really know how to liven up Christmas."

"At least you're smiling."

"I'm trying to make the best of a bad thing."

With the events of the last twenty-four hours, Zee had almost forgotten that Yule was only a week or so away, and that Christmas loomed after that. Although, with White Haven bursting at the seams with Christmas trees, lights, decorations, the Green Man, and the weird, wizened gnomes that seemed insanely popular, it was hard to ignore. Blood and guts around the farmhouse were apt to do that, though.

"But finding Belial by using his jewels, somehow, is that possible?"

"Bearing in mind we shouldn't touch them? You tell me!"

Zee winced. "I know. I'm sorry. And after what happened to Olivia, we absolutely can't risk you."

"Nice to know I'm not expendable. Coffee?"

"Extra strong."

Alex busied himself filling the coffee machine, while Zee, unable to settle, cleaned the work surfaces. He liked Alex, and considered him a good friend. *Did he even know that?*

"You know," Zee started, aiming for humour, "we don't want you hurt, or any of the witches. We just need a lead. I like my job. I don't want to kill the boss."

"Thank you."

"I mean it. Without you guys, we wouldn't be here at all, or have the life we have now. It's a life we don't want to lose. Finding Belial's stuff was a shock. He's a slippery bastard."

While the coffee machine chugged and steamed, Alex turned to face him again. "Just to change the subject slightly for a moment, Simon is leaving after Christmas."

"Simon the bar manager?" Zee spluttered, surprised. "He's been here years."

"I know. To say this is bad timing is an understatement." Alex raked his hands through his long, dark hair. "It seems that the paranormal activity around here has finally got to him. Last night's event was the final straw."

"The crashing helicopter?"

"The bright lights over the moors that looked like two angels. Christmas come early."

"Oh, no."

"We knew it was possible that someone had seen that spectacle. Simon phoned me at eight this morning. I'm hoping his call is not the first of many."

"Shit. I'm sorry, Alex." Zee dropped into a chair under the window. "What have we done?"

"Don't worry. It's just one thing amongst many. I can't blame you. I've been caught up in enough supernatural weirdness to last a lifetime. Guaranteed, Ghost OPS will be on the phone soon."

"Yeah, but they'll be happy."

"Anyway," Alex said, hands shoved in his jeans' pockets, eyes fixed on him, "I have come to a very quick decision. Do you want the manager job?"

"Are you serious?"

"No, it's a nasty joke. Of course I'm serious!"

"You'd trust me to do it?"

"Again, of course I would! I don't know anyone who I'd trust more. The staff like you, and so do the customers. They respect you, too. But equally, I know that you have a lot going on. No hard feelings, if not."

"No! Yes!" Zee crossed the room in almost one bound to shake Alex's hand. "I really want the job! I'd love the job!" He couldn't quite get over how much he liked the idea. It would give him roots. Purpose. A way to pay back Alex for all his help and trust.

Alex pulled him into a hug. "Good. Great, in fact. I have to advertise it, obviously, but it's yours."

Zee stepped back, overwhelmed almost by his excitement. "You know I just need to tie some stuff up first..."

"I know. Just don't get yourself killed. That will really piss me off." Alex turned aside to the coffee, and then handed him a cup. He chinked it with his own. "Cheers, and thank you. You need to go to France, I presume?"

"I was hoping they wouldn't need me, but after last night..."

"We reinforced the protection spell on your house, and will head back there later to add a few extras. I'm a bit gutted Black Cronos got through it."

"Me, too. I was feeling smug on the roof with my crossbow."

"How is Eli this morning?"

"Preoccupied. Nahum is looking into flights."

"And Ash?" The witches had still been at their house when Gabe called with news of the attack in Egypt.

"Stabilised. Not happy that he's going to London with Shadow, but he just needs to heal."

"Do you need Briar?"

"Nahum will drive her there later today. There are other witches he could see, but he only wants her."

"The ones who helped Olivia, you mean?"

Zee nodded. "A group of three family members. They sound fascinating."

"When you know more about them, you'll have to tell us."

"I will. So, Belial's jewellery? Will it help you find him?"

Alex cocked his head. "He's not human, and not on an earthly plane. It will be impossible. All we can do is limit his sphere of influence by potentially binding his power in the jewellery. Sort of muffling it. That will be *really* hard."

"But brilliant!"

"We might be able to help in other ways. Last night Nahum talked about the fact that there might be an agent acting for Belial. We could potentially find this person. *Potentially*," he stressed. "But it will take time."

"Excellent." Zee sighed with relief, feeling like they were making some progress, and shifted his attention to other matters. "What can I do today?"

"Nothing, just your shift. I know you need to pack." Alex's lips tightened. "Look, we really want to help you fight Black Cronos, but we can't. We hoped we could travel to France to support you, but we're all so busy at this time of year—"

Zee cut him off. "Don't apologise. It's fine. Besides, it's probably for the best. We don't know if Black Cronos will return, and it's unwise to leave White Haven unprotected." He shrugged, wishing the witches could help, but knew it was impossible. "You never know—Estelle might have asked Caspian. They seem a bit closer recently."

"I hope so. Make sure you don't give them an inch, Zee."

"We won't. We can't afford to."

One slip could cost them their lives.

* * *

Estelle studied the map of the area around the *château*, and the photos that Barak had taken, feeling overwhelmed at the task ahead of them.

They were in their new place that was now surrounded by protection spells, all three gathered around the kitchen table of the chalet they were squatting in. It was on the outskirts of a place called *L'Aiguillon*, one of the towns around *Bénaix*. Barak had found it in the early hours of the morning. He had set out after the phone calls with his brothers, none of them willing to take chances after Jackson's abduction. This place was furnished, secluded, and empty. *But maybe not for long.* If the owner turned up for a skiing holiday over Christmas, they would have a lot of explaining to do.

"Is there any shelter at all on the slopes beneath the castle?" she asked Barak.

"The valley is wooded, and some of the slopes are, but some of the sides are so sheer that it's just rocks. The base of the ridge is more exposed. That's why we need your shadow spell."

Estelle sighed. "I can absolutely use my shadow spell, but it means all three of us will have to stick together. That's probably safer anyway, now."

Lucien was on the laptop, also scrolling through images of the area. The *château* was one of many Cathar *châteaus*, all famous landmarks, and there were plenty of photos online. He tapped the screen. "Look how steep it is, though! No one would see us right at the base."

"Unless they have lookouts down there, too," Barak pointed out. "It was difficult to tell last night. My night vision camera didn't pick up anything."

"Bloody hell." Estelle shook her head at the sight of the craggy ridge. "They picked the place well. I can't imagine how hard it would have been to build there."

"I guess rich owners wouldn't care about that. We could wait and move at night again," Lucien suggested. "I realise we'll lose time, though. Is there another ruin or place close by where we could watch from?"

Barak frowned. "Like setting up a blind, you mean? Like for watching animals? Perhaps. Like I said, that wasn't my priority last night. I could have missed something."

"What about traffic in the area?" Estelle asked. "There must be cars around. We could sightsee. That's what regular visitors do, right? It was something we discussed."

"Absolutely. There are roads that wind through the valleys, and lots of hiking trails. They won't be used much in this weather, though."

Lucien leaned back in his chair, eyes clouded with worry. "Do you think they'll take Jackson there? I can't believe they've taken him at all. Or," he shot them a belligerent look, "that he would betray us."

Estelle had been trying to ignore her nagging fear about his safety ever since Barak had told her the news, but now it all came flooding back. "I don't believe he'd betray us, either. No way. He was too angry with them. He hated them. Especially when he found out about James Arbuthnot."

Barak ran his fingers over his shaved scalp as he gazed out of the window and onto the pine-dotted slopes outside. "Unless it's a ruse."

"What do you mean?" Estelle asked, confused.

He faced her. "Maybe he saw an opportunity to get kidnapped. I mean, it wasn't a set-up, but perhaps he just let them have him. Maybe he wanted to get inside."

"That's a hell of a suggestion," Estelle acknowledged, "and ballsy, on his behalf."

"And insane," Lucien added. "Look what they did to me! And it doesn't answer how they found him in the first place. Or Gabe and Shadow."

"That's easy. Magic," Estelle said. "Alchemists are magicians. That's what they called John Dee. They might not have natural witchcraft abilities, but they have a way of manipulating matter. They must have used a type of finding or tracking spell. We've encountered them enough that they would have our blood or some kind of body matter. It's a horrible thought, but probable."

"I guess that makes me feel better," Barak said. "Better than thinking someone betrayed us or is tracking us some other way. Will your protection spell help conceal the house?"

"It should. I have brought supplies with me, and also have other spells I can use. I'll craft something more personal." Estelle hated to feel as if she couldn't cope, especially after all they had faced previously, but maybe more magical help would be a good thing. "I could see if Caspian will help us."

Barak smiled. He knew the issues she'd had with her brother, but Barak liked him. "I think that's a great idea."

"And your brothers?" Lucien asked Barak. "When will they arrive?"

"Gabe and Niel will be here as soon as they can get flights. I think it's proving harder than they thought. Shadow will come with Ash, hopefully today, but maybe tomorrow. She has taken the emerald discs to JD."

Estelle had heard all about the theft and the attack. The footage of the bombed hotel in Aswan had been on the news. Deaths had been reported, but no names had been released. She squeezed Barak's arm, hoping to reassure him. "I hope Ash will be okay."

"Me, too." Barak stood abruptly, anger and concern sweeping across his face. "I need to do something useful. Let's see what we can find below the *château*."

Harlan sipped his coffee while he sat at the scrubbed wooden table in Moonfell's kitchen on Friday morning. *At least the witches made great coffee.* Not that he'd seen much of them.

When he entered the kitchen at just after seven that morning, they had all left to do various jobs, including casting the spell to find Jackson, with instructions to make himself at home—with reservations. "Don't touch the plants in the glasshouse, and don't mix the herbs to make teas.*"

Did he look like a tea man?

While he waited for Maggie and Olivia to join him, he reflected on the night's events, simultaneously envying the great gothic kitchen filled with state-of-the-art kitchen appliances—nothing old-fashioned about them. He wondered how long the house had been in the witches' family. Generations, he suspected. The place felt soaked in magic. Through the open kitchen door, other rooms beckoned. Harlan wished he had more time to explore. Or the energy to.

He'd spent a restless night at Olivia's side, worried about sleeping too deeply in case something happened, but also haunted by what had transpired. He was broadminded, but the appearance of the Goddess had shaken him. And Belial, of course. Perhaps the spell wasn't quite on the scale of the Green Man making Ravens' Wood, but it was damn close. He'd *seen* the Goddess. Or was it *a* Goddess? *No matter.* She had fought Belial, banished his spirit, and saved Olivia. She had slept uneasily, too, tossing and turning, and moaning in her sleep. Nightmares, she'd confessed when she woke up.

It hadn't helped that they were in a great gothic mansion that was very unusual, far more so than Chadwick House. He and Olivia had found that place unnerving, with the dead collector's array of arcane objects, but it was nothing compared to this place. For a start, Moonfell was more castle than mansion, and although he was sure it was his overactive imagination, Harlan had heard creaks and groans all night. He blamed the heating system and old wood settling.

When his companions finally joined him, Maggie was as lively as a box of frogs. She had obviously slept well. Somehow, that did not surprise Harlan. He imagined she would sleep well anywhere; she was too stubborn not to. She was already texting furiously to her colleagues, her lips warped in a scowl and her hair slightly unkempt. Olivia was horribly quiet, in comparison. Her answers were monosyllabic, and her fingers played with the grain on the kitchen table. The witches may have banished Belial, but he'd left an impression.

Harlan's heart sank as Birdie entered the kitchen at Moonfell, her face grim. He'd been putting a lot of hope in the witches finding Jackson. *Too much.* Her long, grey hair was plaited and wound on her head like a crown, but wisps escaped, framing her face. He tried not to get distracted by her more youthful appearance, but it was disconcerting. Her shoulders were no longer hunched, and there was an air of determination in her step.

"Well?" he said by way of greeting as she sat at the table. "Did you find him?"

"No. Not a trace." She leaned on the table, her chin on one hand. "I've tried several spells, including using scrying, as well as more traditional methods. I'm getting nothing, and it's very frustrating."

"Is he dead?" Maggie asked, as usual striking at the heart of the matter.

"Not necessarily, although that is possible. I think they have just protected him well. You said they're alchemists?"

Harlan nodded. "Some of their group are. It's how they make the soldiers. They have labs, and alchemical wheels and things." He ended vaguely, feeling inadequately educated on the subject. He rubbed his face. "I choose to believe he's alive, or they would have killed him last night." He shot a smile at Olivia. "We have to hope, right?"

"Right." She nodded, but he could tell she wasn't really paying attention.

Maggie huffed, gearing up to her usual, belligerent state. "We'll rely on old-fashioned policing methods, then. I'll head back to the station and see how my sergeants are getting on."

"I'll keep trying," Birdie reassured them, "as will my granddaughters. I'm invested now. If you hear anything new, you must tell me."

"We will," Harlan said, finishing off his coffee. "Where are Morgana and Odette? I thought they were with you."

"Odette is appeasing the Goddess after last night. Morgana is preparing for the solstice, and probably creating spells for our clients."

"Not hexes, I hope?" Maggie asked.

"You came here for help," Birdie pointed out as she stood and walked to the sink with their empty cups. "Insulting me is not a good way to get it."

Harlan glared at Maggie, mouthing, "*Shut up!*"

She mouthed a silent, "*Fuck off.*"

Harlan had no desire to piss off a powerful witch. "Sorry, Birdie. Maggie has trouble with her big mouth sometimes. Ignore her."

"I'm trying." Birdie turned around and leaned against the counter, smiling. Fortunately. "She's hard to ignore, though."

"I'm right here," Maggie said, glaring at all of them.

Harlan had a feeling they were overstaying their welcome, and didn't want to see how much more insulting Maggie might get. "I think we should go."

"You two can," Birdie said, eyes narrowing, "but I think Olivia should stay. My dear, you look horrible."

Olivia blinked as if she'd been in a trance. "Do I?"

"Yes. I take it you had dreams?"

"Nightmares, really. Flaming eyes and wings." She swallowed, lips tightening. "Will he come back?"

"I doubt it. He'll be off licking his wounds somewhere. But, it has taken a lot out of you. Stay for another day. Let's get you right, first."

Olivia blinked. "Stay? But I have work to do."

Harlan intervened. "I can call Mason and update him on your current state. This is a result of work, anyway. He'd rather you be well." Mason liked Olivia much more than he liked Harlan. He turned back to Birdie, who was still watching Olivia. "What will you do for her?"

"Give her plenty of healing teas, and a little cleansing, too."

"But she'll get better?" Maggie asked, voice sharp.

"Yes. Think of it like the flu. Sometimes exorcisms take a while to shake off. Plus, she encountered the Goddess. Do you remember, Olivia?"

Olivia nodded. "I think so. A powerful female presence. It was like two people were at war inside of me."

"They were."

Harlan kissed Olivia's cheek and squeezed her hand. "I think it's a great idea. I'll see you later, okay? Once I've been to see JD with Shadow." She'd be arriving in a few hours, and he was acting as chauffeur.

"Okay. Don't forget." She offered him a wan smile.

After Harlan and Maggie had gathered their scant belongings, Birdie accompanied them down the hall. Once they were at the door, Harlan paused. "You're more worried about Olivia than you're letting on."

"It was a powerful spell. It has affected all of us. You two as well, I suspect, although in what way I'm not sure. Did you dream?"

"I tossed and turned," Harlan confessed, "but no dreams, not really."

"I slept like the dead," Maggie said.

"I think I'll prepare an amulet for you both, anyway. I can give them to you if you're dropping in later, Harlan."

"Great, thank you."

"Good. Later, then."

Birdie swung the huge door shut, leaving Harlan feeling diminished and exposed on the doorstep of Moonfell.

Sixteen

The previous twenty-four hours had been long and exhausting, and Shadow and the team had risked their lives to get JD's emerald disc. If JD didn't start looking more appreciative soon, she'd slit his throat.

"JD," she remonstrated, "we were almost captured by museum guards, blown up, and then Ash was skewered like he was a kebab! The least you can do is say thank you."

Actually, they would never have been captured, but JD really needed to understand the risks they had taken for him. Not only had the bombed hotel been on the news, but the museum theft was covered, too. The police suspected they were linked, but there was no hard evidence to prove it. They had announced the numbers of dead and injured, but no names had been released as of yet.

JD scowled. "I said thank you!"

"You mumbled it! Say it properly, or I swear that's the last job we ever do for you!"

He stepped back, hands raised as if in surrender, as she placed her knife at his throat. "Thank you! Very much! I am eternally grateful for your help, and as an immortal being, you'll know that counts for a lot."

"And say you are sorry that Ash has been horribly injured." She tickled his chin with the point of her blade.

JD's eyes widened and he stepped back again, hitting the long benchtop in the greenhouse in his grounds. "I am *very* sorry, but if I could just point out that I was not responsible for that..."

"Er, Shadow," Harlan interrupted nervously, "maybe it would be a good idea not to kill the boss?"

She didn't move, her dagger still lifting JD's chin, reflecting that Harlan should really hold his nerve for longer. "Just a grievous wound, then? A scar to remember this conversation."

"No!"

JD squirmed. "So sorry, Shadow. I forgot my manners. I was very preoccupied with the Emerald Tablet." His voice squeaked as he added, "Excellent thinking, too, that you brought several discs with you!"

"Well, I wasn't going back." Shadow finally lowered the blade. "And I avoided being arrested at the airport. Don't forget that."

Although she had every faith that the spelled box would hide the contents, it had still been a nerve-wracking exercise, even in a government aircraft. Their escorts didn't know what Shadow and the team had been doing there, and they didn't ask. If they had been caught, most likely they would be on their own. Friends with high connections were very useful, but only to a certain extent. Ash's injury also added to her worries. His natural healing skills meant he was already recovering, but it was proving to be a slow process. Potentially, Barak's healing capabilities might be able to help Ash, but as they hadn't tested that yet, they decided to play safe by using Briar instead.

"So," Harlan said, obviously wishing to move the conversation along, "what now with the discs?"

JD, after a final nervous look at Shadow, crossed to where the discs rested on the bench. They sparkled, even with the diffused light coming through the greenhouse windows. Shadow hadn't fully appreciated their beauty in the rush of having to steal them and then escape from the hotel, but all three were magnificent. And priceless.

JD rubbed his hands together as he studied them. "We now have to see which disc fits. This one looks and feels the most likely." He tapped the one that Shadow also had thought to be the right choice.

She nodded. "I agree. It has a certain quality to it."

"Are we going to try it now?" Harlan asked.

"I don't know." Perplexed, JD tapped his lip. "I'll run it across my alchemical wheel first. And perhaps move the tablet out onto the lawn. If it grows as I hope, it will smash the greenhouse."

"Then you'll have a huge tablet in the middle of your lawn. Has Anna arranged your marquee yet?" Harlan asked, cocking an eyebrow.

"I believe so." JD didn't elaborate. He picked up the disc. "Come on you two, bring the others."

Without a backward glance, he trudged across the garden, and they followed. The day was overcast, and a brisk wind carried an icy chill. They had already exchanged their news when Harlan had collected her and Ash from the airport and driven them to JD's. She'd offered to drive a hire car after successfully passing her driving test—and almost destroying Ash's will to live—but Gabe had broken out in a sweat and said, *"I wouldn't risk the roads in London. Leave it to Harlan."* She liked to think it was out of concern for her safety, but suspected it was more to do with a fear of her driving. She was erratic; she couldn't deny it.

Harlan, however, was preoccupied with the disc he was holding. "Do you think he'd let me keep this if it's not the one?"

"Are you kidding me? First, of course not! Secondly, *we* stole it and should therefore get to keep it!"

"I suppose you're right. It would look great on my shelf, though!"

"And link you to a heist. Probably not a good idea for either of us to have it. No one is likely to raid JD's house. He probably has a vault somewhere for such things. Which is actually a great idea. Maybe we should get one." Visions of precious icons, weapons, and jewels filled her thoughts. *It really was a brilliant idea.* However, the sound of a car engine drawing to a stop on the far side of the house brought her back to the present. "Sounds like Nahum is here."

Rather than following JD into his lab, they accompanied Anna, JD's housekeeper, to the front door, but Ash had beaten them to it. He'd been resting in JD's sitting room, propped on the sofa and supplied with tea. He hadn't even argued, which was a sign of how much his injury ached. Anna tutted and eased him out of the way, but Nahum swept inside, giving him a half-hug, with Briar right behind him. "Ash! Good to see you! I was worried."

Ash smiled. "I was worried about you, too, brother."

"And Shadow!" Nahum enveloped her in a hug, too. He smelled of spices. "Good to see you here in one piece."

"You, too," she replied, grateful for his hug that made her feel part of the family. Even after twelve months with them, and her relationship with Gabe, she sometimes felt like an outsider. "Don't think we haven't heard about Belial."

"Who?" JD had appeared silently behind them all after emerging from the stairs to his lab. His face was red with fury. "Did you say Belial? One of the Fallen?"

Everyone froze and looked at him.

"Sorry," Harlan stuttered. "I don't think I mentioned that with all the fuss about the discs."

"God's breath! You're all idiots! Nincompoops! Boils of a pestilence! Especially you, Harlan! *Belial*?"

Amused, Shadow watched Harlan's mood erupt. "JD, seriously, after the night I had, you can stick your outrage up your immortal ass!"

Nahum pushed forward, eyeing JD with grim dislike. "Is there a problem, JD?"

"One of the Fallen makes an appearance on Earth and you don't tell me?" JD placed his hands on his hips, managing to stand his ground as Nahum loomed over him.

"Oddly, whilst I was fighting for my life last night against a horde of deadly Black Cronos soldiers, I did not think to call you. Or this morning when I was driving here, worried about my brother! I suggest we discuss this later. My brother's health comes first. Agreed?"

JD looked as if he might argue, but then swiftly thought better of it. "Yes, later will be fine! Anna will provide everything you need. Harlan, Shadow?" He gestured at the discs.

Shadow decided that ensconcing JD in his lab with hours of experiments would keep him occupied and out of their hair. "Of course, JD. Nahum, Briar, I'll see you soon."

Resisting the urge to kick him down the stairs, she followed him.

Barak rested his back against the trunk of the pine tree, and adjusted his binoculars so that he could focus on the base of the ridge.

He, Estelle, and Lucien had spent the morning driving through the valleys of the Pyrenees, admiring the landscape and taking photos like dutiful tourists. In the daylight, it was easier to see the contours of the land and the road that wound up the ridge to the *château* at the top.

From the base, it didn't seem as if there was any kind of security, but partway up, nestled under an overhang of trees, they saw what looked like a stone building and a gate across the road. They all assumed it was some kind of guard house. Driving around the neighbouring ridge, they parked by the start of a trail and walked to where they had a reasonable view of the castle.

While Estelle waited at the bottom of the tree, Lucien and Barak clambered up the trunk. Estelle had kept the shadow spell around them all, even though they were disguised by greenery.

"*Merde. C'est impossible,*" Lucien complained. "The trees are planted so thickly it's hard to see anything on the slopes. But there are tracks. For wildlife, perhaps."

"There are darker areas, though, on the eastern slope," Barak said, studying one spot in particular. "Could be caves, or maybe just a cleft in the slope. The trouble is, Lucien, if we investigate, and we're right, and someone is guarding it, we give ourselves away before anyone is here to help." He lowered the binoculars to look at Lucien, wedged on the branch below and to the right. "We can't afford to do that yet."

"No, of course not. We should keep identifying them, though. They are all places to investigate. I presume we'll split the team when we attack?"

"Yep. I prefer not more than three teams, but it depends how we plan to attack, and how many possible entrances we find." Barak studied the ridge for what felt the hundredth time. "A team could attack the top, but that's the most exposed, even though we can fly in. There are probably too many guards at the top."

"Unless we attack from the bottom, and distract them first."

"I doubt it will work like that. And who knows what strange weaponry they have here? This is their stronghold, after all."

"And there could be traps all over that ridge," Lucien pointed out. He lifted his binoculars to the sky. "I hear something."

The whump, whump noise of rotor blades announced the approach of a helicopter, and Barak was glad they'd parked next to other cars at the start of one of the hiking trails. The sleek, black helicopter headed straight to the castle.

"I wonder who that is?" Barak said. "I hope it's not Jackson."

"It might be the *comte*," Lucien suggested. His voice grew thick with anger. "I really want to meet the man who changed my life forever."

"Be careful what you wish for," Barak said, starting to descend the thick branches. "I have a feeling he's the last one we want to meet. Let's get back to the house now, and then return tonight. With luck, Gabe and Niel will have arrived by then."

When the blindfold was removed from Jackson's eyes, he squinted against the harsh light. He hadn't seen daylight since the previous day. *If his abduction was even the day before.* He had lost track of real time.

He'd been knocked unconscious when he was captured, and when he'd awoke, he was blindfolded. His captors had barely spoken to him, except for issuing instructions. They had handled him roughly, but not cruelly, and he'd been offered water and basic food. He'd refused all of it, but that was hours earlier. Since they'd been airborne, they had said nothing at all.

When Jackson's focus returned, he saw a broad stone courtyard and an ancient castle ahead of him—a mass of towers, battlements, and thick stone. He knew exactly where he was. A mixture of fear and excitement flooded through him. *Château de Bénaix.*

They were right. This was the base for the organisation that had haunted his dreams for years. The fact that he was here surely proved that. Not that he would let on that he knew where he was, though.

His guards, two huge Black Cronos soldiers with impassive faces and muscles of steel, pushed him forward as the helicopter's engines cut out. He took the chance to orientate himself as he stumbled forward on numb legs that had been bound for hours. His hands were still bound in front of him, and a peculiar metal bracelet inscribed with sigils was on his wrist. Huge stone walls encircled the castle complex, guard towers placed at regular intervals. Vehicles were off to one side, as was a huge gate set into the wall. It was made of thick wood and bound in iron, looking Medieval in origin. *And perhaps protected by magic.* Sigils were everywhere. Giant ones were carved in stone and inscribed on metal.

Would Jackson find answers here? Or only death? *Or worse...* He eyed the soldiers that he knew were covered in tattoos beneath their winter clothing. *After all his raging and plotting against them, would he become one of them?*

He was pushed towards the huge entrance doors of the castle, also clad in iron and studded metal work. He was within feet of it when the door opened and Stefan Hope-Robbins appeared on the threshold. He hadn't changed. He looked mild-mannered in his tweeds and glasses, but still, Jackson faltered. The soldiers pushed him forward again.

Stefan smiled, but it didn't reach his eyes. "Mr Strange. Welcome to our *château*. We'd hoped to capture your companions, but you're all proving rather resourceful."

"We pride ourselves on it," Jackson said, lifting his chin defiantly.

The huge door clanged shut behind him, plunging him into the semi-darkness of an impressive entrance hall. A fire blazed in an enormous fireplace that was so huge a horse could stand in it. At least there was also central heating and electric lights; not everything was Medieval. Oil paintings and tapestries adorned the walls, and a huge double staircase led to the upper floors.

Stefan followed his gaze. "It's really something, isn't it? That's why I wanted to bring you through the front entrance. You need to appreciate all we have achieved."

Jackson stared at him. "Why would I need to appreciate that?"

"Because you need to see what you could achieve, too. Some of this wealth could be yours!" He raised his hands in a grand gesture. "You need only change your mind on your approach."

Jackson could barely believe his ears. "You want to convert me to your cause? You think I'm so pliable? I don't think you realise quite how much I loathe you and what you do!"

"Oh, I do," Stefan said. He removed the handcuffs from Jackson's wrists and led the way to a door on the right, his two guards dogging him. "Let's just say I have absolute faith in my abilities to change your mind."

They entered a much smaller but no less grand room. Another fire blazed in a stone fireplace, and the floor was lined with thick rugs. It was furnished in a mix of styles from modern to Medieval, a surprisingly pleasing juxtaposition. But it was the couple standing before the fire who Jackson focussed on. He drew a sharp intake of breath as he saw a woman who looked like The Silencer of Souls. The only difference was that her hair wasn't quite as dark, but her cold black eyes were exactly the same.

He faltered, confused. "I thought you were dead!"

It was Stefan who answered. "Your team killed her sister. There are several warriors who fulfil the role of The Silencer of Souls. Several have lost their lives in the course of their duties over the years. All consider it an honour. But you haven't met the most important member of our organisation."

Jackson's gaze shifted to the tall, slim man next to her dressed in an immaculately tailored dark grey suit. He looked to be in his mid-forties. He had light brown hair, tinged at the temple with grey, and his blue eyes fixated on Jackson like a hawk spotting prey.

"This," Stefan continued, his voice filled with pride and adoration, "is the *Comte de Saint Germain*. He has a proposition for you."

Seventeen

A sh winced as Briar deftly dressed his wound. Ash wasn't often aware of his height and build, but being next to Briar always made him feel like a giant.

She was petite and dark-haired, and for some ridiculous reason, probably the fairy stories he'd been reading to familiarise himself with different cultures, he had fixed her in his head as a kind of flower fairy. Seeing as he cohabited with a vicious fey warrior, he knew that was crazy. And yet, as she ministered to him, whispering healing spells while she worked, he had visions of her running through forests or meadows with flowers in her hair.

He must be delirious.

She looked up at him, the green ring around her brown eyes reminding him that she carried the Green Man within her. "You're very quiet, Ash. Are you okay?"

"I'm imagining you as a flower fairy. I think the pain is getting to me."

She sniggered. "Flower fairy? Herne's horns! And what do you mean, pain? You should be healing quicker than this. Although, I never saw your wound when it was fresh." He was sitting on a chair so she could reach his injury more easily, and she rocked back to look at him. "What aren't you telling me? Did something else happen?"

Ash hesitated, fearing to talk about what had preoccupied him for hours, ever since his injury. To discuss his fears aloud would make them more real. But they were alone in the ground floor bathroom. Nahum had gone to the greenhouse to study the Emerald Tablet again. Ash suspected he was putting off a discussion about Belial. Shadow and Harlan were with JD.

"Spit it out, Ash. What happened?"

He needed advice, and Briar was level-headed. "When the bomb went off, I was in the room that was ground zero. I should be dead, really. Anyway, I was blasted through the wall, with chunks of masonry and metal and furniture. Time can slow for us sometimes in moments of stress..."

"It can for us, too," she said. "It's weird, like everything's happening at a very slow speed. They say time is relative, right? Sorry, go on."

"Instinct kicked in, and I extended my wings. I smacked the wall in another room, and instantaneously was hit by lots of things, including the chunk of metal that pinned me to the wall. I retracted my wings, but they were damaged, and they wrenched, badly. Especially this one." He tapped his injured shoulder.

Briar frowned. "But your wings are magical, like you. Surely they've healed themselves?"

He summoned his courage. "I tried to open them earlier, in the sitting room when I was alone. The left one won't open." His fears came tumbling out, magnifying as he spoke. "If I can't use my wings, I'm not a true Nephilim. I'm some bloody half creature! I'm *useless*!"

"Shush. Calm down." Her hands cupped his face. "You are always a Nephilim, no matter what happens to your wings. They must have been injured before?"

"Minor only. Broken bones, burnt feathers. But this feels like something fundamental!" Panic filled him again. "It's not even like it hurt to use it. It won't manifest at all!"

"The body is clever. Injuries hurt because they alert us that something is wrong. To keep using a part of the body when it's injured is stupid! You will only aggravate it. Make it worse. Maybe your body knows better than you do. Perhaps your wing will stay safe where it belongs until it's healed. Wherever that is!"

He smiled, feeling ever so slightly reassured. The witches, and everyone else for that matter, always wondered where their wings went. It was hard to explain. They were always there, and yet, they weren't.

"Plus," she continued as she wrapped a large bandage around his shoulder and under his arm, "my magic works on many levels, as I'm sure your healing does, too. I suggest you don't try to summon your wing until you've healed a bit more."

"But that's the other issue. I should have healed more by now!"

"The bigger the injury, the bigger the shock to the body, and the longer it takes to heal."

"I've been stabbed by swords, spears, and daggers over the years!"

"But has your shoulder been pinned to the wall by a piece of red-hot metal?

"No, I guess not."

Briar tutted. "Stress slows healing, and all of you have been obsessed with Black Cronos, as well as being involved in other things."

"I'm a Nephilim. We're used to stress and fighting. We were bred for it."

"You are also half human! Honestly, Ash. How old are you? You know this! You're a scholar and a clever man."

"Not when it applies to me," he replied sullenly. He felt like a scolded child.

"Men! You're all alike." Satisfied that the dressing was finished, she leaned against the bathroom sink. "How does that feel?"

He flexed his shoulder. "Secure. Cool. The burning has subsided."

"Good. I used my special burn cream on it, and a few extras. The paste is packed with healing herbs, too." Briar hesitated, her teeth working on her upper lip. "I'm worried about all of you, actually. Especially after Eli and Nahum's behaviour last night. You all have your strengths and weaknesses. Niel is headstrong..."

"That's an understatement," Ash muttered.

Briar smirked. "So is Gabe, although he tempers it. That's his natural leadership quality, I guess. Nahum is more measured. Eli is a lover. Barak is a joker—and a bit of a romantic, I think. You are a scholar. Zee is a listener. What worries me is that those who I consider to be the more level-headed amongst you are being irrational! You're taking crazy risks! Stealing an emerald disc from a museum—several discs, in fact! Priceless artifacts that put you on the news! That's madness. Rash!"

"Finding Templar treasure put us on the news, too!"

"But that wasn't illegal. You were hired to do that! And," she continued, eyes blazing, "Eli and Zee made a mad pact with the dryads, which I appreciate was to help us, but even so!"

Ash saw her point. "Last night they were under attack with very few options, but I accept that it's been quite an interesting few months, hasn't it?"

"And then some. You're all scaring me a little, and the other witches."

"Scaring you? Why?"

"Because we care about you. You're our friends. Every single one of you. I know you arrived in this world under a storm cloud and things weren't easy, but look at what you've achieved! You must remember that you're not immortal—just long-lived, and yes, super strong and fast-healing. *But* you could still die, just like anyone else. You're surrounded by humans in a world where the paranormal takes a back seat. I understand that it probably clouds your judgment sometimes, but you're risking a lot!" He stared at her, unable to respond, because he knew that she was right—in part, at least. She sighed, humour once again returning. "That's it. Lecture over. I'm just worried, that's all."

He smiled. "Did you give Nahum an earful on the way up?"

"No. He was driving. I thought it might distract him."

"Lucky him."

"I say it because I care."

"Thank you. You're a good friend, Briar."

"I try."

"What will I do without you when I have to fly to France?"

Her impish grin returned. "Rely on Estelle. I'm sure she has a tender side."

He laughed. "Only for Barak! No, that's unfair. She's been good with all of us. She's even got a sense of humour!"

"A little love works wonders." A trace of sadness crossed her face, and Ash knew she was thinking of Hunter. "I'm just sorry we can't come with you."

"We'll be fine," he said, sounding as confident as possible.

As long as he healed. As long as his wings worked. The thought that he wouldn't fly again filled him with horror.

Nahum felt as if he'd betrayed his brothers as well as himself by using Belial's jewellery, and he suspected Ash thought so, too, which was why he was lurking alone in the greenhouse. He also sensed that Briar had been holding back her feelings in the car.

He tried to distract himself from worrying about their current troubles by studying the Emerald Tablet. Unfortunately, stray thoughts of Olivia kept popping into his mind. Her warm hands, smooth as silk skin, and soft, welcoming mouth. *Herne's horns. What had he done?* Belial had thrown him off his stride in more ways than one.

The trouble was, he had avoided sex ever since he arrived in this world. It had complicated his previous life; he hadn't wanted it to complicate this one. Unlike Gabe, his marriage was loveless, and he did not have children. His marriage was to unite the warring Houses of the Fallen. An alliance between him and the half-sister of another Nephilim. As he predicted, it had meant politics, manoeuvrings, arguments, and general annoyance. He had not been a faithful husband, but she had also not been a faithful wife. He continued to fight, drowning himself in blood, and then entered the courts of kings to negotiate peace. But the politics of that marriage had rumbled on.

That was one good thing about the flood—his marriage was over. He couldn't even say that he was scarred by it. He didn't harbour any feelings one way or the other towards his wife. Now, he sought to keep his life uncomplicated. And he was determined that it would remain so. Olivia was a woman of the world. He had stipulated the rules, and she had been happy to comply. It was fine. He probably wouldn't see her for months. *So, why was he so worried about her?* Because he was a friend, *obviously*.

"What are you talking to yourself about?" Shadow said, sounding amused.

He leapt around, sword drawn. "Herne's fucking balls, Shadow! Do you have to creep around?"

"I am fey!" She smirked as she leaned against the greenhouse door. He hadn't even felt a cold draught as she entered. "You were bobbing your head and muttering. You look quite cross!" She strolled down the gravel path towards him, hips swinging, dagger twirling between her fingers. "Are you chastising yourself for wearing Belial's jewellery?"

"Yes, absolutely." It wasn't a total lie.

In a split second her dagger vanished, and she wagged a finger at him. "I think it's more than that. Did something happen with Olivia?"

"*No!* What makes you say that?"

"Because you're all riled up, and you, Nahum, are never riled up." She prowled around the tablet, watching him, her figure sometimes blinking out of sight as her fey glamour soaked up the green earthiness of the greenhouse.

"I drew on Belial's power last night, in case you forgot. I was incandescent! Of course I'm annoyed."

"As insane as that was, I think it was a brilliant strategic move. You know he can't possess you. Unsettle you, yes. Worry he might have growing influence in this world, yes, but he cannot affect you unwillingly."

"No, but he's still powerful. He got under my skin, and he shouldn't have. And, it was horrifying to *feel* so powerful. I killed a lot of soldiers. I feel bad about it. They didn't stand a chance." As soon as he said it, he knew it was true. Killing vicious enemies was one thing, but they could barely respond to their onslaught.

"Bollocks! It was Black Cronos, and they were coming for *you*. They deserved what they got. They burned our loggia! But that's not what you're truly annoyed about, because you don't really regret killing them. Logically, you know it was right. So that means you are mulling over something else you did that bothers you a lot more. And you spent twenty-four hours with Olivia!" Her violet eyes sparkled with mischief.

"You are just obsessed with sex now that you're with Gabe!"

"Ha! I *knew* it! I didn't even mention sex, and that's the first thing you said!"

"You were implying it!"

"I implied *something*!" She leaned against the bench, arms folded across her chest as she grinned at him. "Well, well, well! Go you, Nahum!" She winked. "I bet she's like a wildcat in bed!"

"Shadow! Shut up! You can't speculate on someone's performance."

"People speculate all the time up here!" She tapped her head for emphasis. "Anyway, I don't need details. I'm just glad you're not denying it! In case you're wondering, Gabe and I have *great* sex. You probably don't need to hear that, but tough. Your brother—"

Nahum covered his ears with his hands. "No! Shut up! Shadow, you are exasperating."

Shadow was obviously beyond pleased with herself. She continued to grin at him. "Fine. I won't share details if you won't. She must have made an impression, though, or you wouldn't be so annoyed."

He lowered his hands, wanting to strangle her instead. "I would appreciate you not sharing this with my brothers."

"I have to tell Gabe, but fair enough. I won't tell the rest. You know they'll work it out, though."

"No, they won't. I am very discreet. It's only because you snuck up on me that you know anything at all."

"You're not denying that she made an impression, I notice."

"Don't push it, Shadow! We had fun, and that's all I'm saying. I'm worried because we're friends, and I don't want to ruin that. Sex can, you know."

"And obviously you're so irresistible she won't be able to keep her hands off you." She laughed, holding her own hands up to placate him. "I'm kidding! She's an adult, and very savvy. I like her. I can put up with her over Estelle anytime."

"You won't have to put up with her because we only have a working relationship. Nothing else."

"Fine. If you say so."

"I do! And, in case you hadn't heard, because of me, she ended up infected by Belial!"

"Harlan told me, but I'm not sure how it happened."

Nahum kicked the greenhouse bench in annoyance. "She touched his bloody jewellery. I didn't tell her not to quick enough, and to be honest, I'd forgotten how much it would affect her."

"I don't think I need to point out that it wasn't your fault," Shadow said, unexpectedly sympathetic, "but I understand why you feel guilty. What are we going to do about Belial?"

He smiled. "You want to help?"

"Of course! Gabe is furious about it all." Shadow's teasing manner vanished. "As soon as this business is over—Black Cronos, I mean—we will hunt for the agent who put his stuff in the reliquary. Although, you know that could have been done centuries ago."

"I suspect it's far more recent than that. But finding him, or her, won't be easy. And, by the way, I doubt very much if Black Cronos will ever be finished."

She shrugged. "You never know. The Gods might smile on us. Perhaps they already have."

"You never put your faith in the Gods. Or Goddesses."

"That's true." Shadow ran her finger along her blade. "I trust my companions and my weapons. And I include JD in that lot. Perhaps he will provide something for us that can make all the difference. But I was referring to Belial's very powerful jewellery. Maybe you found it for a reason. Maybe you're meant to use it on Black Cronos...again."

An uneasy feeling rippled through him. "I don't know if I, or Eli, would want to do that again, Shadow. It really shook him up."

"You don't have to. Perhaps Niel will, or Gabe. Maybe Barak?"

"I don't think they should, either."

"Nahum, we might not have a choice."

Harlan would rather not be hanging around in JD's lab. He would prefer to spend his time talking to the new arrivals, but JD seemed to want him there.

"You see," JD muttered as he adjusted his wheel of correspondences, "this is the alchemical signature of the Emerald Tablet. But this doesn't match it." He was referring to the emerald disc that they thought was the likely match.

"What does that mean?" Harlan asked.

"I don't know. Maybe it's not the one."

"Or maybe it doesn't have to match. Perhaps that's the point. It *adds* to the tablet. Enhances it, somehow."

JD gave him a sidelong glance. "That's an interesting suggestion."

"I know, right? I'm not just a pretty face."

JD tapped his lips while he stared at the wheel. "I noticed that the tablet has certain properties, but it's missing some that I would expect..." he trailed off, falling silent.

Harlan hated playing catch up. "Like what?" he prompted.

"Earth is missing. Elemental fire, air, and water are present, as well as a selection of metals. I won't bore you with the details." He went quiet again, but then yelled, "Ha! I am a fool!" JD moved the wheel slightly, making minute adjustments to all the concentric rings.

Harlan thought it a waste of time. "Why don't you just stick it in the base and see what happens?"

"Preparation is always the key!"

"But maybe you don't need to prepare anything."

Once again, JD didn't answer him directly. "'The power is complete when it is turned to Earth. Separate the Earth from Fire, the subtle from the gross, gently and with great ingenuity.'"

"What are you saying?"

"That is part of the script written on the Emerald Tablet. Alchemists have debated on its meaning for hundreds of years."

"You think it relates to the missing piece?"

"Perhaps. It could refer to many things. But no one has seen the tablet for, well, millennia. Only the script is known. So..."

Harlan nodded with understanding. "Everyone has debated its meaning, but it's intended for only one thing. The base!"

"Perhaps! One should not assume."

"And the other discs? Why are they so similar?"

"I don't know." He stepped back after adjusting the final circle. Nothing happened. He huffed. "God's pox."

"Not quite right?" Harlan ventured.

"No. Never mind, it was unlikely I would ascertain it's properties the first time around."

JD looked like he was settling in for hours of adjustments. All around him, jars bubbled and strange scents filled the room. One of these liquids could be JD's key to immortality. *Would he be so obvious about it? Would he share it if Harlan asked? Or did he assume, correctly of course, that Harlan wouldn't have a clue what it was, even if it was there?*

"I'll leave you to it then, JD."

"Wait." He focussed on Harlan properly for the first time. "What's this about Belial?"

Harlan groaned. He'd thought he'd avoided that discussion, but reluctantly outlined the issue as succinctly as he could.

"His power is in the jewellery? Interesting. True, angelic power, as close to pure as can be. I wonder if others could harness it?"

"The Nephilim did."

"I mean in another way."

"What about Olivia, JD? Does her health not matter to you? I witnessed something both amazing and terrifying last night. Olivia could have been killed! So could I!"

JD fixed his shrewd, hazel eyes on him. "I am very glad you both survived. But we shouldn't avoid these possibilities. I'll speak to Nahum about it later."

"I suggest you be quick about it. They're all heading to France soon. I'm hoping they find Jackson, because so far, it's as if he's vanished into thin air."

"Of course. They've done well to find that place. Interesting that it should be a base of the Cathars. They were considered heretics, you know." He scratched his nose with an ink-stained finger. "Which reminds me, I have something to share. Have everyone come up to my observation room in an hour."

Eighteen

Jackson didn't want to sit and drink tea with the *Comte de Saint Germain*. He wanted to punch him repeatedly in the face, but seeing as The Silencer of Souls was staring at him with fierce intensity, he settled for refusing to shake his hand.

The *comte* smiled, revealing white, even teeth. "Charmed to meet you, Mr Strange. It seems our organisation and yours have been at odds recently." His voice was smooth, his accent hard to place. It sounded vaguely European.

"Hardly at odds," Jackson shot back. "More like at war."

"Your term, not mine. I think you misunderstand our purpose." He sat, gesturing Jackson to sit opposite him. He crossed his legs, hitching his trousers as he did so to prevent creases. He was fastidious, and it instantly irritated Jackson even more. Unwillingly, he sat down. The *comte* continued, "I am an alchemist, pure and simple. I, like my colleagues, seek to understand the universe and the world we live in. How we are made. Not romantically so, as if we are stardust. No! Our essence. Our spirit! How we can all be a part of a greater consciousness!"

"Like the Borg?"

The count frowned. "The what?"

"Forget it! It's a pop culture reference."

"And that is the problem! Television. It's a distraction. I presume that is to what you refer?"

"Can you get to the point?" Jackson asked. "This is all rather tedious."

Stefan had disappeared after introducing them, but now he returned with tea in a fine, bone china teapot. He fussed and poured two cups, and then offered one to Jackson.

"No, thank you."

The count sighed. "I hear you have refused all liquids and food. That won't do at all. It's stupid, and you are not a stupid man. Have a drink."

"I have no wish to be poisoned."

"I am drinking it, too."

"You've probably acclimatised yourself to it."

"If I wanted you dead, you already would be," the *comte* snapped.

Jackson had to admit that his throat felt like sandpaper. He accepted the drink with a nod. *Fine. Let them play politely*. He was English, after all. It was in his blood. "Perhaps you'd like to explain why you've kidnapped me and brought me here, wherever this is!"

"This place is my home, where I first found my love of alchemy." He expanded his elegant hands. "My spiritual home, and the base of my work."

Jackson stared around the room, drinking it in, and preparing to lie. "But where is it? The Alps? It's mountainous. We thought your base would be on Ley Lines or something. We've spent months combing places like that. Centres of power! We didn't expect this." He studied the count, eyes narrowed, attempting to goad him. "If I'm honest I expected something a little more magical."

"I don't need magical! I create my own magic by bending the universe to my will." He leaned forward, eyes hard. "You're trying to provoke me. You won't."

"But this is the Alps, right? Which part?"

"Let's talk about why you're here." The count placed the cup on the occasional table that looked like an antique. "Your team, the Nephilim, have killed many of my soldiers. They are, admittedly, formidable opponents, especially for so few. And the two women. Interesting."

It sounded like the *comte* was digging, but Jackson just sipped his tea.

"Our fields of interest are, for the most part, different," he continued. "I'm suggesting a truce. We can go about our business, and you can go about yours."

"Your business being kidnapping and torturing to make enhanced humans—against their will?"

"Some sacrifices are necessary, but not all are opposed to it."

"Lucien didn't think so." Jackson didn't dare mention his grandfather. It might cause him to lose control, and perhaps give away too much of his own interests. "Lucien has been fighting to regain control of his own body for months."

"Your little team of two interrupted a process of transformation when you stole him. It was highly dangerous."

"I think you'll find the word is *rescue*. He's not an object. He's a person! And he is not very pleased with you." Jackson decided to test the count's knowledge. "He's been near death several times. I'm not sure we'll ever help him recover."

The count laughed. "Come now, Jackson. That's clumsy. We both know that you have stabilised him." His eyes flashed with annoyance. "Quite ingeniously, I gather."

Jackson's stomach twisted with dread. "So, we have a spy." He wondered who the spy was. Surely not Waylen.

Please not Waylen.

The count continued, taking pleasure in Jackson's angst. "I prefer to call it a convert to our cause. I won't tell you who, but suffice it to say he's far happier with our recompense than yours." His eyes glittered. "Your friends caused a lot of expensive damage to one of our facilities. In fact, they have caused an incredible amount of damage to our organisation as a whole."

"You started it when you attacked The Order of the Midnight Sun."

"They wanted what was ours."

"You *both* had a claim to it. Perhaps you should have negotiated for that, too. And we shouldn't forget the Igigi. You tried to destroy an ancient race. Kidnap them, too. And Ash."

"Like I said, sacrifices must be made for progress. But," the count smoothed his suit lapels, preening, "as I said, we must come to an agreement."

Jackson smiled. "Because we're winning. You fear what we'll do next."

"You're not winning. You're like flies that we continually must bat away." He darted forward, like a cobra, and Jackson shot back in his seat. "Do you know how long I've been an alchemist? How old I am?"

"From my investigations, I estimate possibly seven hundred years old."

"A better guess than some have made. Closer to nine hundred, actually."

Jackson blinked in shock. *He'd suggested seven hundred as an exaggeration, but nine hundred...* "How do I know you're not lying? You could be someone pretending to be the *comte*. He courted controversy. People often thought him a liar."

"I courted controversy? Ridiculous! Many feared me, because of what I knew. Of the secrets I kept. Others, powerful men and women, sought to use me." He shrugged. "It worked both ways. I used them, too. Used their influence. Their money. And over all that time, I never met your Mr John Dee. I kept away from the Elizabethan court during his *actual* lifetime."

Jackson decided there was no point in lying. "He met you, in what he thought was *your* real lifetime."

That seemed to delight the count. "He met me, and I didn't know? Interesting. We're talking about the 1700s, I presume?"

Jackson nodded. "I believe so. He kept his distance after that. Thought you were a charlatan, actually. Until recently, of course."

"Oh, good. How nice to confound one's enemies. I've known about him a little longer, maybe a hundred years or so. We immortals have developed very good skills of deception. Of course, our longevity allows us to make money, and acquire the objects of our heart's desire. Eventually."

Jackson had always thought that he would hate immortality. "It must be a long and lonely life. Have you offered to make other humans immortal?"

"I have never liked anyone enough to do so. Some people become extremely tedious, very quickly. Others, I miss. However," he gestured to The Silencer of Souls, "Deandra and a few other soldiers live much longer lives than a normal human. She is over eighty years old, and some are older. The two soldiers at the door, your escorts, are over a hundred. Part of the process of their transformation." He shrugged, a callous gesture, as if they were inconsequential. "With each enhancement, they live a little longer. My earlier experiments lived only twenty or so years longer than usual. Stefan has added a great deal to our endeavours."

"They live longer because they have a purpose to you. You use them."

"Like you use the Nephilim? Your own little army." The count smiled maliciously. "We are not so different."

Jackson clenched his fists, willing himself to be calm. "We are *very* different."

"Delusional, but have it your own way."

Jackson wasn't sure what he expected of the count. He wasn't even sure that he existed at all, despite their speculations. But looking at him now, hearing his smooth words and reasoned explanations, he wasn't surprised at his tone. He'd spent hundreds of years doing what he wanted to do, reasoning his way through his behaviour and justifying it. He was a sociopath, no doubt about that. JD certainly had traits of one, as well. The need to achieve and succeed, regardless of the consequences. Despite his revulsion, Jackson was also fascinated by him.

Jackson put his empty cup aside, deciding he should find out as much as he could while he had the chance. "Why didn't you approach JD? Another immortal alchemist could have helped you."

"John would never have helped me. I could tell." He looked amused. "His ideals and mine were quite different. He worked with that angel summoner, Edward Kelly. Now, there was a charlatan! But there was no doubt that John was brilliant, even though he was susceptible in his desperation to speak to angels." His eyes darkened. "As a mortal, he had the ear of a powerful queen—for a while, at least. But John also made a few bad decisions. Ended up penniless. *Fool*. And then he died, or so I thought. When I realised he had achieved immortality, he had already set up The Orphic Guild. We competed several times over the years. I, obviously, made sure to keep my distance."

Jackson had a sudden flash of insight. *The count was jealous of JD.* He was a brilliant rival. A threat. He must have considered other alchemists the same. In addition, to offer anyone else immortality would also be a threat to his superiority. *How did Stefan feel about that?* To be used for his own brilliance in alchemy, but never trusted with that final step of never-ending life. Unless he was hoping to steal the knowledge, somehow—or make the breakthrough on his own, like JD and the count had. Stefan was watching their conversation in silence, Jackson noted. He hadn't been invited to participate in the conversation and drink tea. Like The Silencer, Deandra, he was standing. While Deandra was impassive, Stefan's eyes darted between them. *Perhaps Stefan could be a useful ally...if Jackson ever had the chance to talk to him alone.*

Jackson forced himself to relax, and leaned back in his chair. "Why did you make your super-soldiers in the first place?"

The count shrugged. "Because I could. The more I researched, and the more I discovered how the universe worked, of its design, I knew that given time I could manipulate it. It was a challenge, and still is. There are things I still wish to achieve, but can't." His eyes hardened. "Like giving my soldiers wings. That continues to defy me."

"Maybe you need angelic intervention," Jackson suggested.

"I do not need help. I will get there. Eventually. But that brings me back to my point. These fights with your men hinder me. They are a distraction. We either end this, or I end them."

"But you've tried and failed. They're harder to kill than you thought."

"Oh, I don't know. It seems we successfully killed four of them last night."

All of Jackson's hard-fought composure left him. "What? *How?* You're lying!"

He smiled maliciously. "Of course! You have been trussed up and unable to see the news! Your friends were in Egypt on business. Gabreel, Shadow, Asher, and Othniel. Yes, I know all their names—thanks to our spy. We planted a bomb in their hotel rooms, one of my own design. And now..." He threw his hands wide. "*Gone!*"

Jackson floundered, horrified. "I don't believe it."

"The rest will be dead soon." The count's hands tightened on the arm of the chair, his knuckles whitening. "There was an unfortunate delay last night, but we will strike again. Unless *you* negotiate peace."

Jackson noted that throughout the entire conversation, the count had not referred to Barak and Estelle's close proximity once. *Did he know? Was he holding it back to taunt him about later?* He hoped that Harlan and Olivia were safe somewhere. *And what about the other Nephilim? He said there'd been a setback, but what?* Jackson's head was whirling with questions, and he didn't know what to do. He certainly didn't believe that Gabe and the others were dead. But he couldn't discount the spy. *What if they were gone?*

Jackson was, however, very certain of one thing. "I will certainly not negotiate for peace with you! A man who tortures humans and changes them without their consent. Who makes bombs and weapons! You're not an alchemist. You're a monster. You won't change. You'll continue to do it, unchecked!"

"I told you, Stefan!" The count stood and turned to the professor, who straightened in anticipation. "I knew he would be stubborn. The misguided and self-righteous always are. Take him below." He gave Jackson a glittering smile. "You have no idea of the scale of what I have achieved. What you see may change your mind. Then we'll talk again."

Nineteen

M aggie showed her police identification to the security guards stationed at The Retreat's entrance beneath Hyde Park, huffing with impatience as they scrutinised her badge.

She bit back her impatience. They were only doing their job. They were both humourless, although that wasn't surprising, seeing as they were stuck underground all day. She would rather shoot herself.

One guard lifted his gaze from the computer screen. "You have no appointment."

"I know. I'm the head of paranormal policing in London, and I need to see the director urgently."

"He sees no one without an appointment."

"He'll see me. It's about Jackson Strange."

She had decided to visit Waylen Adams, the head of the Paranormal Division, when her own enquiries proved fruitless. Irving and Stan had run into dead ends in their efforts to track down Black Cronos, and so had she. Their black vans had vanished, leaving no trace of Jackson's whereabouts, and she hadn't got the manpower to search through all the security footage in London. Nor would her boss sanction it. Not yet, anyway. And now, Waylen wasn't answering her phone calls. It infuriated her. His colleague and her friend had been kidnapped! The least he could do was answer his fucking phone.

Hence her grand plan to visit Waylen. She had met him once a few years earlier at an official police function. She couldn't remember exactly what it was for. He certainly hadn't been introduced as head of the PD then, but she knew his name from Layla Gould, the PD's birdlike doctor. She'd met her several times over intriguing investigations, and liked her a lot. Like Maggie, she was direct and forceful. Qualities she admired in anyone. That was her one and only meeting with Waylen, and she'd barely spoken to him since. Until the one call this morning to report Jackson's abduction. Fortunately, Harlan had visited The Retreat to see Jackson, and had told her where the entrance was located.

The second guard finally handed over Maggie's ID and then searched her bag slowly and methodically. Sarcastically, Maggie asked, "Do I need to bend over, too?"

Without missing a beat, he said, "No thank you, Madam. Your bag is quite sufficient."

While he searched, his colleague phoned Waylen. As far as she could gather, he didn't have a secretary. That seemed odd. Clearly, the PD did things differently. After a hushed conversation, in which the guard eyed her with suspicion, he finally nodded and ended the call.

"He'll see you."

"Thank you!"

He ignored her sarcasm. "Step into the scanner, please."

In another minute, after feeling like her privacy had been utterly violated, she was made to wait on a hard bench. With every passing second, she wondered if he would see her in the entrance and then dismiss her. She grew more and more angry, until a small, Indian woman walked up the long corridor, her heels clicking on the floor.

"DI Milne?"

"Yes!" Maggie leapt to her feet and shook her hand.

"I'm Petra. I've come to take you to Waylen. He's very busy, so sorry."

"So am I. If he answered his fucking phone, I wouldn't need to come!"

The woman stuttered. "O-oh! I guess he's been tied up." She walked down the corridor, looking at Maggie nervously. "I run the stats for England. I keep track of the paranormal activity in your area. We're all very upset about Jackson. Have you heard anything from him?"

Maggie softened slightly. "Not a thing. Those alchemically enhanced monsters have disappeared into the night. I need answers! Is Waylen always such a dick?"

"Er, no!"

"So, what the fuck is going on?" Maggie knew she was swearing a lot, especially at this young woman who seemed very pleasant, but she was exasperated. And the more annoyed she was, the worse her language became. She considered swearing a healthy exercise in reducing her stress levels.

"I honestly don't know!" Petra explained, darting nervous glances at her as they walked further into the labyrinthine interior of The Retreat. "I'm just an analyst. Me and Austin! It's all we do."

"You must see a lot, though."

"Only through reports," she persisted. "Jackson asked us to keep a particular vigilance for Black Cronos and their activities, but other than last night's attacks, they've been very quiet."

Maggie had been taking in the Art Nouveau features of the PD while they walked, noting side corridors, ornate mouldings, and inner, stained glass windows of what seemed like a lot of empty offices. There was a peculiar, hushed quality to the place, like it had just woken from a long sleep. It was nothing like a police station, with its ceaseless noise and bustle. Now, however, she stopped and stared at Petra. "Attacks? There were more? Where?"

"There was one in Cornwall. DI Newton's team dealt with it. Although, there was nothing much to deal with. Black Cronos's team was all killed in White Haven. There have been lots of reports of angels over White Haven recently. Christmas come early, according to some. A helicopter crashed there, too."

Maggie needed to call Newton. She'd been so busy that she'd barely paid attention to the news on the TV. "No civilian casualties?"

"None."

She ran through the events of last night, trying to work out what had happened. Olivia had phoned Nahum after they had been attacked, but couldn't get through. As far as she knew, he hadn't returned the call. Not that she'd heard, anyway. He lived in Cornwall and had returned there after dropping Olivia off. *Two attacks at roughly the same time...*

"Are you okay?" Petra asked.

"Just thinking what a strange coincidence two attacks are."

"I agree. It suggests prior knowledge of their whereabouts."

"Well, Black Cronos knows where the Nephilim live. They've attacked them there before. The Nephilim won that fight. However, I gather the Nephilim are split up at the moment." She huffed, feeling uneasy. "Let's see what Waylen thinks."

"He's in the lab at the moment, with Russell Blake."

"Who's that?"

"The Assistant Director, and head of the lab." She rolled her eyes. "He's becoming obsessed with alchemy. The alchemists in the lab are spending more and more time there. Russell asks me to update him on Black Cronos, too."

"You employ alchemists here? Why?"

"Because they're looking into Black Cronos and trying to understand their achievements." She laughed nervously. "It makes it sound like we have huge numbers of them. There are only two of them. They were just regular scientists who worked here, but when Black Cronos became more active again, they changed their studies. We have two labs, you see, side by side," she explained when she saw Maggie's confused expression. "One is more traditional, one is modern."

Maggie wasn't sure what she thought about that. It made sense, obviously, but she was starting to develop a dislike of alchemists altogether.

Petra continued to chatter nervously for the next few minutes, questioning Maggie on her job as they progressed deeper into the complex. Maggie knew the place was big, Harlan had said so, but this was vast. He hadn't fully relayed how big it was, although maybe he had and she hadn't been paying full attention. Hyde Park and Kensington Gardens were enormous. She really should have worked it out. They had passed the offices that were in use and had branched off down another passage when Petra announced, "Here we are. Layla works down here, too."

The noise of chatter and the hum of machinery replaced the hushed quiet of the corridors. They passed a series of offices, and then reached two well equipped labs with giant glass windows that were opposite each other on a broad corridor. It was obvious which was the alchemy lab. There was no fancy machinery present; instead, there was a dizzying arrangement of bubbling jars, tubes, and Bunsen burners. Yet, there seemed an air of sophistication to it. Huge white boards with scribbled symbols were on every wall, and a furious argument seemed to be taking place in front of the far one.

Petra hesitated. "Oh! This might not be a good time. Perhaps—"

Maggie cut her off. *This seemed like the perfect time.* "Who's Waylen arguing with, the guy with the rolled-up shirt sleeves?"

"That's Russell. He's been stressed lately."

"About what?"

"Getting results on Black Cronos's weapons. They seemed to be making progress, and then, all of a sudden, they weren't. Of course, that's made Waylen angry, too." Petra squirmed, seeming guilty about the admission. "It's been tense here lately, but I'm sure it will get better."

There were four others in there wearing white lab coats, three men and one woman. "Which ones are the alchemists?"

"The woman, her name is Lynn, and the man with the grey hair, Frazer. The other two are the regular scientists." Petra tried to pull her away. "Perhaps we should wait in an office."

"Let's not," Maggie said, and pushed the door open. The voices became louder.

Waylen Adams stood with his hands on his hips, glowering at Russell. "But I don't understand! You said you were making progress, and now it's failed? How?"

"This is alchemy! Like any science, there are upsets and failure."

"But we can't afford that to happen! We're playing catch up now, but we're actually getting further behind!"

Lynn interrupted him. "I must admit, I'm baffled. The latest run of experiments..."

"That's enough, Lynn!" Russell cut her off. "We'll just try again."

The woman looked outraged. "Russell! This bears debate! We've almost done a full U-turn!" She gestured to her colleague. "We were saying only a few days ago..."

Russell again tried to shut her down, but Waylen intervened. "Russell! Stop being so rude! I would like to hear Lynn's opinion!"

Russell looked furious and marched away, hands clenched. While Waylen questioned the woman, Maggie watched Russell. They were still only just inside the room, and no one had noticed them enter. She leaned close and whispered in Petra's ear, "Is Russell a scientist?"

She nodded. "Yes. That's how he got the job. He's been so weird lately, though. Grumpy. Short-tempered. The failures have been a huge issue. Especially after what they achieved with Lucien. Obviously, that funny little man called JD worked with them on that."

Maggie started to feel very uneasy. Black Cronos knew all about their enemy's whereabouts, and experiments were failing. She suspected that someone here was helping them.

"Any new staff here lately?" Maggie asked Petra, eyeing the scientists.

"No. They've all been here for years. Moved with us from the old place, after that was blown up."

"No breaches here, though?"

"No. But security is tighter. And besides," Petra shrugged. "No one much cares about us down here. The government mostly pretends we don't exist. Black Cronos causes issues, but they're not considered a national security threat, neither is any paranormal activity. It's just not big enough."

Maggie knew that. It echoed her own policing experience. "And Russell?"

"Been here years, too. He's Waylen's right-hand man. Knows everything about this place."

As the voices continued to rise and all the scientists joined in, Maggie said, "Time to intervene, I think."

She marched across the room, the strange smells and bubbling noises dogging her every step, as well as Petra. "Mr Adams! It's DI Milne. You agreed to see me."

Waylen turned, surprised to see her. "Ah, yes. You know, this may not be a good time..."

Maggie was potentially risking her job in challenging the head of the PD, but fuck it. "I think it's the perfect time. Jackson Strange has been kidnapped, I can't find him, and you're arguing about experiments. We need to talk." Maybe he didn't care because he knew exactly where Jackson was. *Christ. Had she walked into the lions' den?*

"DI Milne, I share your concerns, but this is important."

She met his stare with her own, refusing to backdown. "More important than your kidnapped colleague? We need to talk. Now. The sooner we talk, the sooner I'll be out of here."

An uncomfortable silence fell as everyone stared at Maggie. Waylen huffed. "Fine." He turned to the others. "I will be back. We have a major issue here that we need to get to the bottom of. We need a comprehensive investigation. Maybe an audit. I want a breakdown of every experiment on my desk by nine o'clock tomorrow morning."

As they gasped at the timeframe, he continued to rant, and Maggie was temporarily forgotten. She studied their faces, wondering if one of them had betrayed the PD. All she saw was anger and confusion.

Was she just completely paranoid? Had Black Cronos got to her, too?

Twenty

When Gabe and Niel finally landed in France, Gabe was tired and worried about his friends, as well as being furious at being blown up.

"It shouldn't have taken so long to get here," he complained to Niel.

"At least we *are* here!" he pointed out, as they walked through the airport to find the rental car companies. "I consider it a Christmas miracle."

"If it was a miracle, then we should have been here hours ago!"

The past few hours in Aswan had been a nightmare. After the bomb had exploded and they stabilised Ash, they had landed just inside the grounds of the international airport under the cover of darkness. Fortunately, the airport wasn't busy enough to be open twenty-four hours a day, and they hadn't needed to worry about incoming flights and control towers spotting them. It also helped that they were heading to the private area where the government jet had landed. Shadow had picked the lock so they could get inside. There they were able to patch Ash up, clean themselves up in the toilets, and wait until the place officially opened.

When they failed to reach Jackson on the phone they called Waylen, and he had been able to expedite an early flight for Shadow and Ash. He and Niel hadn't been so lucky. They ended up getting stranded for hours while Waylen tried to book them on a flight to France. They had kicked their heels, hoping not to get arrested for the museum heist, or somehow connected to the bomb that had gone off at the hotel. Security at the airport was tighter than ever. In the end, they flew from

Aswan to Cairo, and then boarded another flight to Toulouse. They had a few hours of driving ahead now, but the Gods had finally smiled on them.

"We need clothes," Niel reminded him. "I am not wearing this all day. I look ridiculous."

Gabe laughed, relief finally winning over his temper. As soon as the airport shops opened that morning, they swapped their dusty, damaged clothes for tourist t-shirts and hoodies. Niel's read, *I Love Aswan.* But they really needed jeans or fatigues. They couldn't find anything big enough in the airport.

"You stink, too," Gabe told him. "Sweat and burnt hair. Sexy."

"You don't look much better!" He gestured to Gabe's sweatshirt that said, *I love Mummy,* with an image of an Egyptian mummy on it. "Shadow will find you irresistible."

"Of course she will!" Gabe grinned at Niel. "Because I am."

Niel rolled his eyes. "Brother. That still revolts me."

"I'll remind you of that when you're mooning over Mouse."

"I don't *moon*, and I won't be mooning over her!"

Gabe just smirked as they reached the line of counters that served the rental car companies. He decided not to push it. Niel was still sore about the fact that she'd betrayed him, but hadn't really, and that Gabe had let her go. He'd made the right choice, and Niel knew it. He just didn't want to admit it.

He changed the subject as they joined the shortest queue and pulled out his driver's license. "I suggest we look as responsible as possible to get a car. And then, our first stop is a hypermarket." He checked his watch. "With luck, we'll be with Barak by late evening—and Black Cronos will be none the wiser."

Olivia had spent a strange few hours with the witches. Ever since she woke up, she had felt out of sorts and tired. She was finding it hard to concentrate, and her surreal surroundings exacerbated the experience.

Moonfell was odd, and undeniably beautiful in its Gothic, almost stage-set manner. She felt like she had stepped back in time. The witches had been happy for her to roam about the house, as long as she drank the restorative teas packed with herbs every two hours. She hadn't wanted to abuse their hospitality, but she certainly took advantage of it. She investigated every room, her keen eye noting valuable paintings, tapestries, sculptures, statues, and books. Even some of the furniture could have been auctioned off for a high price. Most of it was antique, a mix of styles through the ages, as well as more modern pieces. Some of the items were well worn, the tapestries bare in places, their jewel-bright colours faded. Somehow, it suited them.

The peculiar, timeless quality of the place was enhanced by the gloomy grey day outside, and the array of lamps that littered corners and work surfaces. And despite the vast number of rooms—sitting rooms, parlours, several studies, numerous bedrooms and bathrooms, and spell rooms—every room seemed to be in use. It was as if the witches were determined to utilise everything. Olivia approved. She finally realised that the house had been divided into areas for each witch, so they could live separately under one roof. There were even other kitchens on the first and second floor, although they were nowhere near as grand as the large kitchen on the ground floor.

The guest bedrooms and bathrooms where she, Harlan, and Maggie had stayed overnight were on the second floor, all beautifully furnished. Odd little side passages and short runs of stairs led to numerous towers and turrets, including the one where the spell had been cast the night before. There were also a few locked doors that she desperately wanted to open, but she moved on reluctantly.

Her favourite room, however, was the huge attic on the third floor that stretched the whole length of the house. Half was lined with cupboards filled with old clothes, beautifully wrapped and preserved. Gowns made of silk, velvet, and taffeta, both embroidered and plain. There were also lots of old portraits of men and women painted in oils, acrylics, pastels, pencil, and collages. All were witches. They wore witches' hats and sweeping cloaks, and were surrounded by witchcraft objects and occult symbols. Olivia, comfortable as she was with the occult, felt a shudder of wonder pass through her.

The whole of Moonfell contained a history of witches.

Olivia was lost in her thoughts when a voice behind her made her jump. "There you are. I was worried you'd got lost. And you're late for your drink!"

Olivia whirled around. "Morgana! I'm sorry. I was side-tracked by your beautiful house." Morgana had brought up a tray loaded with a plate of sticky cakes and two cups. However, it was Morgana's appearance that held her attention. She hadn't seen her for a few hours, and she had changed her clothes. She was dressed in a long, Medieval-style dress in dark green made of plain, heavy cotton, and her long hair with the grey streak fell loosely over her shoulders. Her eyes widened with surprise. "I love your dress!"

Morgana smiled. "Sometimes I need to embrace my ancestors. Especially after nights like last night. Let's sit and talk." She walked to a small table surrounded by a cluster of chairs, arranged under an arched window. She placed the tray on the table and ran her hand over the two drinks. They immediately started to steam. "That's better. They had gone cold. Nobody needs cold tea."

Olivia sat and dutifully sipped it as warmth ran through her. "It's lovely. Different to the others. I taste honey and cinnamon."

"Yes, plenty of warming herbs to try and revive you. You're still not right. I need some, too, after last night." Morgana studied her, leaning in to stare into her eyes. "You're getting there. He took a lot out of you."

"But he has gone?"

"Oh, yes. Not many can resist the Goddess."

"Or you either, I would imagine."

Morgana smiled and swept her hand out to encompass the pictures. "Oh, I don't know. I sometimes doubt that we are as strong as some of these."

"Your ancestors?"

"Yes. Some of these people were extremely powerful." She pointed to a middle-aged woman with thick black hair and a widow's peak. "She was said to be the most powerful of all. She advised King Charles II, but no one knew. Her name was Eliza."

"She lived here?"

"Yes. Most of them did; a few preferred to live elsewhere. At present, there are other family members who choose not to live here for various reasons. The house was gifted to us hundreds of years ago by a very grateful nobleman." She cocked her eyebrow. "He was in need of an heir, and he got one."

"Your family did that?"

"Fertility is one of our skills. Mine, in particular."

"Do you see women here? Or couples? Are you like a private fertility clinic?"

Morgana laughed. "No! Nothing so organised. But yes, word gets round. I help where I can. I have been said to perform miracles!" She winked. "Really just herbs and a little magic."

As Olivia sipped her tea, embraced by the ancestors who looked on, she started to feel a little better. "What do the other witches specialise in?"

"Birdie is good at finding things and scrying. New spells, too. She has a gift for contacting our ancestors. Her familiar helps."

"Her familiar?"

"You haven't met him yet. Hades, her cat. He can be quite gruff, so I advise you to steer clear. He's suspicious of strangers. Once he gets to know you though, he softens. *A bit*. He's large though, so you'll have a shock if you see him. He's in the garden at the moment, stalking pigeons."

"Okay. I'll bear that in mind." Olivia hoped he wasn't tiger-sized, although honestly, nothing would completely surprise her in this house. "What about Odette?"

"Ah. She has the Sight, but slightly differently to some. She sees to the truth of things. She's uncanny. You can't hide much from Odette. It taxes her, though. She doesn't always want to, but things seek her out. She's resting now after last night. She saw things that she would rather have not. She saw Belial, for example, far more acutely than we did. And the Goddess, of course. I would imagine, though, that you saw more too, as you were in the thick of it."

"It's fading now."

Morgana picked up a sticky slice of cake. "Take one, Olivia, it will help your strength. They're made from honey and oats, and they're excellent when warmed, which these are."

Olivia had been so caught up in the conversation that she had forgotten the cakes, but she took a bite and nodded. "Delicious."

"Good. So, did Belial speak to you yesterday, while we were closing the window he had opened?"

"No. I just remember him not wanting to go. I felt like he was grasping on to every bit of my mind. It felt like I was on fire. Then I felt the Goddess arrive. She was like a cool breeze, in comparison. Does that sound weird? I smelled blossoms."

"No, that's not odd at all. There are times, like last night, that her generosity knows no bounds, but we do have to work hard for that. There are also times when she's terrifying."

Olivia focussed on the gifts. "Like your skin, Birdie's age..."

"Yes. She also confirmed something that I saw, too. I see it even more now, as does Odette." She stared at her, weighing her up. "This might come as a shock."

"What? Has something bad happened? Am I ill?"

"No. You're pregnant."

Shadow watched JD line up several metallic objects of varying sizes and shapes and knew exactly what they were. "You've made alchemical weapons!"

"You're giving away my surprise!" he complained.

"I'm still surprised, if that helps," Harlan pointed out, attempting to pick one up.

JD slapped his hand away. "Not yet!" He smiled at Shadow. "My deadly friend gets first go."

"Deadly? I suppose you're right," she admitted, a sly glance at Nahum and Ash. "I am fey."

Nahum rolled his eyes. "Shut up, Shadow."

Briar and Ash just laughed, and Shadow was relieved to see that he seemed to be improving already.

They were all gathered in JD's observatory on the top floor of the house. The room had huge, sliding glass doors that opened out onto a flat roof. The garden beyond was melting into early twilight, and mist was already rising as the ground temperature dropped. Despite the plunging temperatures, JD urged them all into coats and led them outside, carrying the weapons on a tray.

"We are going to do some testing," he said, an air of eager anticipation in his voice. "I have of course tested them myself, and then aligned them to some general frequencies, but this will be a better test. I hope that if you feel they are useful, you can take them to France."

"Will they get past airport security?" Nahum asked, eyes lighting up.

"They should do, but best to put them in your checked baggage."

"Can I have one?" Harlan asked. "I was attacked last night."

"Of course. I feel we should level the playing field, don't you? Although," JD cast a speculative look at Nahum, "it seems you may have beaten me to it there."

He said nothing more on that subject, although Shadow guessed he was referring to the angelic jewellery. No doubt he had much more to ask, but he placed the tray on a table and selected a weapon.

"I have set up targets for you to fire at." He pointed to the middle of the far lawn where a row of bottles and bricks were lined up. "As you can see, they're at quite a distance, and rudimentary. I thought it worth testing their maximum range."

"But what are they?" Briar asked. "Are they made with magic?"

"Trust the witch to ask that." JD smiled at her benevolently, and it was very unnerving. Shadow preferred his sharp, impatient manner better. "Of a sort. Alchemy. A manipulation of matter and correspondences."

Briar nodded. "Like the elements? The building blocks of life."

"Exactly. Something we could discuss later, perhaps?"

"Of course."

"Excellent." He pointed at the weapons. Some were oval, some round, others more cylindrical, all made from a variety of metals—silver, gold, copper, lead, and others no doubt. "The different metals carry different vibrations and qualities. But that's not all. They have been aligned with planets, moon phases and many other complex things."

"But they can be used at any time of the day or week?" Ash asked.

"Absolutely. It merely means they have certain characteristics. All are deadly."

He marched to the wall that edged the roof with his selected weapon, adjusted his stance, and fired. A pulse of light with a narrow circumference blasted out and shattered a bottle.

"Good shot, JD," Shadow said approvingly.

"It looks like a laser beam!" Harlan said. "I can't even get my head around that."

"It's not a laser beam. It's not even light. It's a different kind of energy."

Harlan scratched his chin, perplexed. "How does it work?"

JD opened his palm so that the oval silver weapon lay in his palm. "The power is in the tip."

Shadow leaned in. On closer inspection, she saw the oval did have a slight, almost imperceptible point, and its surface was engraved with unusual symbols. "May I?" He nodded and she picked it up. "It has a tiny gemstone in the point."

"Exactly. That's what releases the power." He beamed at them. "But who would know? It looks like jewellery, or just an object of beauty. They also align with certain qualities. That one is designed to be used by humans." JD whirled around and picked up a cylindric copper weapon, also palm-sized, and passed it to Shadow. "This one is for you."

Shadow examined it, noting different engravings and a cluster of tiny gemstones on the tip. Careful not to point it at anyone, she gripped it, feeling it almost melt into her palm. It was so light, she felt it would just float away. "How do I make it work?"

"Grip it with your fingers, line it up, and squeeze your palm *with intention*. Gently!"

Shadow wasn't sure what to expect, but did as he said. Immediately, a jet of coppery light shot out and struck wide, missing the bottles, but hitting the lawn. A patch of grass sizzled and blackened. "Herne's flaming bollocks! I missed." Annoyed, she steadied herself and shot again. This time her shot was closer, but still missed. "Damn it!"

"Think of it like your bow and arrow," JD instructed, moving closer. "You're tense."

Aware that the others were watching, and priding herself on her deadly accuracy, Shadow did as he suggested. Her bow, like her sword and daggers, was an extension of herself. *This should be no different.*

She rolled her shoulders, took aim, and fired again. This time, the bottle shattered. She immediately fired at the next and shattered that one, too. She grinned at JD. "This is brilliant! *You* are brilliant!"

"Madam, I thank you." JD gave a small bow. "However, it has taken months to perfect, and I still feel I can make improvements." He turned to the others. "Come on. You must try yours, too. Even you, Ash. I know your shoulder is injured, but this should be easy for you to handle."

Ash looked uncertain but nodded anyway, and JD handed the weapons out, running through the instructions again. Even Briar was prepared to try. For the next few minutes, everyone practised. Initially, Briar was the most accurate, which surprised all of them.

"I don't know why you all look so shocked," she protested. "I do aim my own power quite accurately, you know." She arched an eyebrow at Shadow. "Events have been challenging!"

Shadow grinned. "Yes, they have, sister!" She pulled Briar aside as the others continued to practice. As of yet, she hadn't really had a chance to talk to her. "How is Ash?"

"He's worried that he's slow to heal, but he's doing fine." Briar's cheeks were flushed red with cold, her eyes bright. "I told him not to overdo it. A tough request, considering what you all will face over the next few days. I'm just sorry we can't go with you."

"It's fine. It's nearly Christmas, and you have your businesses."

"And we need to protect White Haven, in case Black Cronos returns. They have put White Haven at risk! I won't have that. My family is there. And my friends! But we feel terrible about not helping you. We'll never forgive ourselves if something happens to you."

"Please don't worry. We have resources, and new weapons. And as annoying as she is, we have Estelle. I gather she might be contacting Caspian for help."

"Good. We'll watch your home while you're away," Briar reassured her.

They were interrupted by JD, who summoned their attention by clapping his hands. "Any questions? Are you happy?"

There was a general murmuring of agreement and nods.

Harlan said, "I need more practice, but I'm impressed. Did the PD's lab help with this?"

"A little," JD conceded. "I worked with Russell Blake. He has a couple of test weapons there, too."

"Thanks, JD," Nahum said, turning his weapon over in his hands. "It's certainly effective. I still prefer my sword, but like you said, it offers us long range choices beyond Shadow's bow and the crossbows."

"Ah! That brings me to the ones I haven't shown you yet. Do you recall the weapons they could extend, as if from thin air?"

Shadow groaned. "I do! They seemed to make spears and swords out of nothing!"

"In that case, you'll be glad to hear I have made some of those, too." He turned to the small silver globes the size of tennis balls that they hadn't used yet. He placed one in his palm and swiped his other hand across the top of it. The metal stretched into a long spear, and JD twirled it like a baton. They all exchanged wide-eyed looks of appreciation, as well as perhaps some uncertainty. "Liquid metal, water, and air. I only have two, for now. These are works in progress. They're still too big. But these," he opened a large box that he'd set aside, "are game changers!" Inside the box were rows of silver balls that looked like golf balls. "These are grenades."

Shadow almost squealed with excitement. "Grenades!"

He picked one up, and they all leaned in. "See? They are in two halves. To activate it, you twist and lock it, and then throw." He turned and lobbed it into the grounds, and it exploded on his lawn. "Ten seconds to detonate, and the blast, as you can see, is big. Until activated, it's perfectly safe." He puffed up like a cockerel. "My own design. Another genius alchemical blend."

"Holy shit," Harlan murmured. "You could make a fortune in weapons manufacturing."

"*Could*, but don't want to," JD said briskly. "Besides, the set-up for mass manufacture would be exorbitant. However, what this means is that now I feel equal to meeting Black Cronos. And so should you, Harlan. You understand what this means?"

Shadow exchanged a nervous glance with Nahum and Ash, suspecting what he meant, but needing him to spell it out. "Not really, JD."

"If you've found the Count of St Germain's base, then I must come, too. I'm the only one who can truly understand his alchemical set-up. You need me."

Nahum stepped in. "You're not a warrior, JD. You're a brilliant scientist. That's a bad idea. You'll slow us down, just keeping an eye on you. It's about more than weapons. Taking them down is about strength, speed, and reflexes."

"And brains!" JD tapped his head, not the slightest bit offended. "I have plenty."

"But what about the emerald discs that we stole? Aren't you working on those?" Shadow asked, annoyed.

"That is still a work in progress!" JD pointed out.

Ash seemed as outraged as Shadow. "So then why did we have to get the discs now? We were literally blown up! We could have been with Barak sooner!"

"What if they were to be taken elsewhere, somewhere unknown? I couldn't risk that!" JD shook his head, utterly perplexed, and reluctantly, Shadow saw his point. JD continued, "You won't deter me. I'm coming, too."

"In that case, so am I!" Harlan said, although he didn't look half so eager as JD. "I need to find Jackson."

"*We'll* find Jackson," Nahum said forcefully.

Harlan huffed. "And defeat all of Black Cronos's soldiers in his fortress *château*? Come on!"

"We can't guarantee your safety," Nahum said quietly. "I can't even guarantee my own."

Harlan exchanged a look of solidarity with JD, unusual because they were normally at loggerheads. This time, it seemed they had common ground. "We know the risks, Nahum. We're coming anyway."

Twenty-One

J ackson presumed he would be led to a deep, dark dungeon and tortured, but instead he was escorted to a small, square room without windows that contained a single bed, a sink, and a toilet in the corner. Essentially, a prison cell.

However, he had no idea exactly where that was. He'd been blind-folded again, and all he knew was that there were twisting passages and lots of stairs leading down. He had been left there for a couple of hours, and had been provided with a basic meal and water. This time, he'd been sensible and consumed everything. If he was going to get out of there, he needed his strength.

Once he'd eaten, he examined every inch of his room. It had plas-tered walls painted white, a single, recessed light fitting set in a very high ceiling, and a concrete floor. Fortunately, it was warm. Placing his hands on the floor, he realised there was underfloor heating. *Interest-ing*. They clearly didn't intend for him to freeze or starve to death. He suspected he was in a cell that they usually kept their test subjects in. That didn't inspire confidence, either. And the place was very quiet. He couldn't hear anything. No footsteps or voices. The door was made of thick steel with a hatch in it. There was nothing he could use as a weapon, and no way of getting out. He threw himself on the bed, mulling over who their mole was, but despite his best intentions, drifted off to sleep. He was woken by the clang of the door opening.

Stefan stood at the entrance. "Time for a short tour, Jackson. Get up."

Jackson drank the last of his water, brushed his jumbled hair out of his eyes, and pulled his long mac on. "Is this the tour before I'm led to my death?"

"You're quite the dramatist," Stefan said, stepping back. "Deandra. The cuffs, please."

The woman stepped from the corridor behind Stefan, and with cold fingers, fixed cuffs on Jackson's wrists. They weren't normal cuffs, however; like many things here, they were covered in sigils, like the bracelet he still wore. Stefan had gloated earlier that it masked his energies, and that no one would be able to find him.

"No blindfold?" he asked.

"No. I think you're deep enough in the bowels of this place that you won't find your way out, anyway." He gave him a sly smile as he headed down a long corridor.

Jackson didn't bother to respond. He felt better after his nap, and he studied his surroundings, aware of Deandra behind him, monitoring his every move. He might be beneath a Medieval castle, but the corridors were plastered, and modern light fixtures were overhead. He passed multiple doors he assumed were other cells. It reminded him of how Barak and Estelle had described the lab beneath the *château* in France. All the doors were electronic, and cameras were mounted high on the walls. He looked up at one and waved.

"It's a sophisticated set-up," Jackson observed. "No expense spared at keeping your prisoners locked in."

"They're not prisoners!" Stefan said angrily. "The doors are to protect our *and* their safety. The process of transformation is not easy. You've probably seen that for yourself after stealing Lucien."

"Rescuing! You haven't convinced *me* of the merit of your cause yet, unlike your spy. Susceptible idiot."

"I confess, it always surprises me how little incentive some people need. It often comes down to money or recognition."

"It didn't do Barnaby Armstrong much good, did it?" He was referring to the secretary of the Order of the Midnight Sun. Another man who'd been swayed by the promises of Black Cronos. Now he was dead.

"Sometimes people outlast their usefulness." Stefan stopped in front of a row of three lifts and pressed the button to descend.

"Perhaps like you will, one day." Jackson watched his profile as he goaded him, but Stefan merely stared at the lift doors, waiting patiently. "You must work very hard for the count, and yet you seem to get none of the glory."

Stefan's mouth twitched into a smile. "I get to work in a properly funded alchemical laboratory, with access to precious metals, gems, an observatory, and a wheel of correspondences that, by the way, I enhanced considerably. My needs are well met. And," he stared at Jackson, "my skills are appreciated."

The doors of one of the lifts slid open, and they stepped inside, Deandra staying close to Jackson. He ignored her. "But you're not immortal."

"I have no wish to be."

"I guess you could discover the ability yourself, and then at least you'd have a choice. Sounds like the count guards some secrets very jealously indeed."

Stefan didn't answer, and the rest of the journey remained in silence. Jackson watched the number of floors they descended. They had entered on the floor labelled minus two, and were descending to minus five. According to the lift controls, there were another three levels. They must be in the heart of the mountain.

The lift shuddered and stopped, and the door opened onto a broad ledge that overlooked a huge cave. Despite his intentions to be unimpressed and coolly rational, Jackson's jaw gaped open. The cave was high-roofed and broad, making a huge, circular space. Within it were several large, intersecting, spherical metal bands that spun slowly.

Mesmerised, he walked to the wall that edged the broad ledge and looked down onto a vast series of concentric rings also made from a variety of materials, including metals. The largest was as thick as a road, and easily a hundred feet in diameter, set into a rim of steel. It was connected to the cavern wall at two points only. Within it, Jackson estimated there were about two dozen smaller rings, reducing in size to a circle in the centre. The metal bands passed around the giant wheel, continuing for some distance beneath it. Lights pierced from above, the whole range of the spectrum, and gemstones twinkled along the metals.

"I feel like I'm in an armillary sphere," Jackson said, barely able to breathe.

"Well done! That's exactly what it is. You're not a complete fool, then."

Jackson glanced at Stefan who was transfixed by the sphere's movements. "What does it do?"

"What any armillary sphere does—it models the objects in the universe, representing celestial longitude and latitude. This version is Ptolemaic."

"Which is what?"

"The Earth is the centre, encompassed in our wheel. If the sun was the centre, it would be called Copernican."

Jackson was stepping well beyond the bounds of his basic knowledge. "What do you do with it?"

Stefan dragged his eyes from it and looked at Jackson. He looked like he was drugged. "The rotating rings represent the Tropic of Cancer and Capricorn, the Arctic circle, the equator, the zodiac signs, the planets, and much more. It represents our universe. Many things that influence the alchemist."

"And the rings in the wheel?" He'd seen JD's, so he was pretty sure he knew what it was.

"Similar. A correspondence wheel. We can make many different alignments, and with the use of light, change energy. Create new life. And interesting weapons, too." He laughed. "I make it sound simplistic. It's not."

Jackson stared at it again, admiring the soaring metal rings, the shifting light, and its smooth movements. "It must have taken years to perfect."

"Hundreds. As man's advancements grow, so we incorporate the new with the old." Stefan warmed to his subject. "The metals are all slightly different. Some pure, some blended, all unique. All tested over years to make sure the proportions are correct. The crystals on them have been specifically chosen to enhance energies. When the wheel aligns beneath, we can manipulate energy. Matter!"

No wonder JD struggled to replicate the count's achievements. His wheel was impressive, but was tiny in comparison.

"We have a smaller wheel in the main courtyard," Stefan explained. "It's useful for simpler things, when we would rather work beneath the sun, moon, or the stars, but the true power lies here. This is the heart of the *comte's* genius."

"And beneath the wheel of correspondences?" Jackson strained to see below.

"Just the base of the sphere. The lift goes down to it for maintenance purposes."

Jackson knew this was what they had to destroy. *But how? Importantly, were Barak and Estelle and Lucien still alive? Were the others? Or did he somehow need to destroy it on his own?* "I presume the mechanism that drives it is down there?"

"Nothing *drives* it. It is self-driven, by the power of the universe that we have harnessed."

"And this is where you finalise your soldiers? Finish their transformation? Like with Deandra?"

She stared impassively. Her silence was unnerving. *Did she choose not to speak, or was she mute?*

"Yes, Deandra was a product of this. A combination of Mars and Venus, fire and earth, and other things. It is this which prolongs her life, too. At a certain time on the calendar, her powers are replenished."

Jackson's mind raced. *How could they destroy it? Un-align the spheres? Break the wheel?* But more unnerving was why he was seeing it. It could mean only one thing.

"I'm not here to negotiate, am I? The fact that you've shown this to me means you'll never let me go."

"Yes and no. We'd still like you to negotiate a truce. Call off your team. Explain the futility of their continued attacks. Under our guidance, of course. And then, this place," he extended his arms wide, "will be your home. If you behave, then you live. If not, then you die!"

"Transform, you mean?"

Stefan cocked an eyebrow. "Or that! Three options then, if that is your preference."

"Of course it's not my bloody preference!" Jackson exploded. "I want to go back to my life!"

"You think so small. Your existence is narrow, don't you see? You scurry away in your offices, chasing us around, and get outraged at our potential, when you could actually be part of it! This is what swayed Russell, in the end."

"Russell! Russell Blake?" *Fuck!* He had to tell Waylen. He was the PD's Assistant Director. "How did you get to him?"

"He was on holiday in September. It was a small matter of bringing him here."

"September!" Jackson felt an utter fool. For months Russell had been feeding Black Cronos information. *But what did he know of Barak and Estelle?* Jackson was pretty sure that he had only told Waylen where they were going, but what had Waylen told Russell?

Stefan laughed, a tight malicious grin on his face. "Yes. You think so small. That will be your downfall. Unless you join us, of course. Think about it for a few hours. I'm sure you'll come to your senses. If not, we have one more strategy to try."

"Why the hell do you care about my cooperation?" Jackson asked, clenching his fists. He desperately wanted to hit Deandra and Stefan, but knew that she would retaliate swiftly. Could he run somewhere? Hide? *No. He must bide his time. He'd find a way.* "What fucking strategy?"

Stefan smiled maliciously again. "You'll see."

Olivia felt as if a bomb had gone off under her. She stared at Morgana, utterly gobsmacked. "I'm *what*?"

"You're pregnant."

"I can't possibly be."

"I realise this is a shock, but I assure you that you are." Morgana narrowed her eyes. "I presume you have had sex recently? Or else this is way weirder than I expected."

Olivia immediately discounted Nahum. She had slept with him only two nights ago. It was far too recent. Three months earlier she had experienced a very enjoyable evening—actually, several enjoyable evenings—with a very handsome Italian man when she was on holiday with her friend in Italy. It was strictly a holiday romance, and they had used protection.

"It's impossible. I was careful, and besides I'm still having my periods. I can't be pregnant. I haven't put on weight, and I don't feel any different. I appreciate your skills and everything, but you're wrong."

"You're thinking this was how long ago?"

"Three months, when I was on holiday."

"Ah. No. It's more recent than that. This is a very early pregnancy, which is why you won't have noticed a thing."

Olivia froze, her drink forgotten. "How early?"

"A few days."

"How can you possibly know already? It's barely a collection of cells!"

Morgana smiled sympathetically. "I know, and so does Odette. She sees the truth of things, I told you. Yesterday, Belial was clouding everything else. Now that he's gone..." She hesitated. "It's rude to pry, but I presume there was someone recent?"

"Yes. A one-off night of very unbridled passion." She met Morgana's gaze and laughed. "It was the shock of Belial that did it. My conspirator."

Olivia stood, needing to walk and figure out what to do. She paced the room barely able to focus anymore on her surroundings. She had never planned on a pregnancy. Had never wanted children. Her career and travel were everything. *And what the hell would Nahum think?* He had promised nothing. It was a one-night deal. Would he think she had deliberately tried to trap him? No! What was she thinking? This didn't mean marriage! Or commitment. It was her decision. Or was it? She had to tell him. She owed him that.

"Fuck!" She turned to Morgana, who was still sitting and drinking her tea. "Are you sure?"

"Very. The Goddess saw it, too. It's a special baby, Olivia."

"Is it?"

"Yes. The father is...*different*, yes?"

Olivia didn't know what to say. She didn't know Morgana or the other witches. She'd met them barely twenty-four hours earlier. Although they'd shown her great kindness, and possibly saved her life, she couldn't tell them about Nahum. About who he was. That was too much. *Unless the witch already knew, somehow...*

Feeling foolish for standing in the middle of the attic and acting as if the witch ancestors were judging her, she sat down again, trying to compose herself. "Yes, he's a little different."

Morgana just sipped her drink and nodded. "I suspect that's why Belial clung on a little longer. Maybe he saw something, too. He craved that little window on your business. Best we got rid of him, for many reasons."

For some utterly irrational moment, Olivia felt afraid, and her hand flew to her stomach. "He knows? Can he harm me? Or the baby?"

"No! Rid yourself of that notion. He is spirit and air, powerless now to hurt you. Besides, you have gained our protection, and the Goddess's. If you choose to keep the child, of course. I don't judge, and can help you get rid of it safely if you choose to."

"I don't know what I choose. No, actually that's not true. But I'm confused."

"Go on. You can trust me. Olivia. I know you don't know me, but I am on your side."

Something about Morgana invited confidences. Or maybe it was the gloomy weather and the low lights that drew them closer together. Olivia felt like she was in a bubble. "I have never wanted children, but somehow, now, I can't bear to think of..." She struggled even to say the words. "Getting rid of it."

Morgana smiled broadly. "How lovely. Then it seems congratulations are in order."

Olivia felt a flutter that she thought was excitement, but it could have been dread. *Was she insane? Her life was going to change forever. There were so many things to consider...*

"Slow down," Morgana instructed. "I can see you're racing away already. One step at a time. All will fall into place."

But would it? Morgana sounded so sure, while Olivia was a whirling mass of emotions already. "I need time to think."

"And rest. Stay another night or two, please. For me."

The thought of being home on her own was terrifying. She couldn't even bring herself to tell Harlan or her best friend. Certainly not Nahum.

She found herself nodding. "Yes, please. That would be lovely."

Maggie huffed at the continuing argument in the PD's lab. Her attempted intervention had failed, and it seemed Waylen was avoiding her.

She turned to Russell Blake, wondering what his take was on all this, and saw that he was rummaging in a drawer. When he straightened, a strange silvery object was in his hands. He saw her staring, pointed the object, and fired.

Maggie dived under the closest workbench, wincing as a blast whipped past her ear and exploded some glass jars above her head.

Screams and shouts erupted, but she didn't have time to consider the others. She scrambled under the bench and out the other side, grabbing a stool on the way up. As soon as she regained her feet, she threw it at Russell.

Russell wasn't focussing on just her anymore. He was firing wildly at everyone. The scientists were running, Petra was screaming, and glass jars were exploding all around them. Hot liquid splashed everywhere, but Maggie stayed on her feet, grabbed a large metal pot, and hurled that, too. Both missed.

Unfortunately, one of the scientists hadn't been as quick to find shelter. The man was lying flat on his back, a huge, bloody wound in his chest.

Russell Blake was a murderer.

Russell sprinted for the exit, shooting wildly over his shoulder, and everyone ducked for cover. Petra froze in the doorway, and Maggie screamed, "Run!

But it was too late. Russell fired straight at her, and she flew backwards through the door, into the corridor. Russell kicked the door shut, sealing them all inside. There would be no chase through The Retreat. Russell was planning to kill them all.

"Has anyone got a fucking weapon?" Maggie yelled. They had seconds only before Russell would methodically march around the room, killing everyone. This was not how she intended to die. Not trapped like a caged rat.

By now, benches had been upended to provide cover, and the scientists were cowering. That wasn't surprising. They weren't used to being shot at or attacked. But she was. She dodged around the corner of a sturdy metal bench lined with cupboards in the centre of the room and saw Waylen sheltering at the far end with the female alchemist called Lynn. He crouched awkwardly, clutching his hip, and Maggie remembered that he walked with a limp. He must have aggravated an old injury.

She summoned his attention. "Waylen? Have you got a weapon?"

"No!"

"I know where one is!" Lynn said. She looked terrified. "In the drawers under the window. There's an alchemical one."

More shots exploded above her, and more shouts erupted around the room. Russell Blake laughed maniacally. "You can't win! You're stuck in here."

Maggie hissed at Waylen. "Keep him talking!" Their only hope now was to distract him long enough to get the weapon. He sounded cocky, like he had it all figured out. And they were a long way from security down here. No one would hear them. "And throw things at him!"

Waylen nodded and shouted, "Russell! We are old friends. What are you doing?"

"Doing what I should I have done years ago. Getting ahead!"

"Getting ahead doing what? I don't understand!"

"Getting more money. Getting recognised for my worth."

"By betraying your friends?"

Maggie crept along the benches while they talked, seeing glimpses of Russell's legs as he stalked around the room. Every now and again she grabbed an object she found on the floor—forceps, scissors, jars—and threw them in a flurry all over the room as distractions. Lynn saw her and joined in, making Russell skip and dance back. Unfortunately, he also kept firing, even though he was talking to Waylen. *But what was he shooting at?*

Maggie risked lifting her head above the bench and saw that he was methodically destroying his own research. Glass jars exploded, one after another, flames shot high, and colourful steam drifted over the benches. Maggie hoped they weren't poisonous. Russell didn't seem bothered.

She managed to make it to the drawer Lynn had pointed out. She risked lifting her head again. Russell was glaring down at someone. He pointed his weapon as a man shouted, "Russell! No!"

A pot flew across the room and smacked Russell on the head. He stumbled back, raising his weapon as he fell, and fired wildly again. He hit a huge plate glass window and it shattered. Russell dived for cover too, and Maggie took advantage of the destruction to search the drawers. There was nothing resembling a weapon. She wrenched the next drawer open, and then another. There was just a solitary silver sphere nestled in a velvet-lined box. *What the fuck was that?*

A sound of grating metal made her spin around, and she saw one of the scientists pushing a metal counter across the floor like a battering ram, aiming at Russell. Being nearly shot was clearly a very good motivator to take action.

Unable to work out what was a weapon, she chanced her luck. She raced across the room, intending to tackle Russell from behind while his colleague was attacking him. Waylen was still talking, trying to distract him.

Russell yelled, "Shut up, Waylen!" He fired at his colleague, and metal hummed and smouldered.

Maggie was halfway across the room now. A few more feet and she'd be on him. She had threaded through the chaos of the destroyed lab and into clear space when Russell spotted her. He swung around and aimed at her. But there was nothing now between them. Nowhere to hide.

Then there was another shout, and another shot, and the back of Russell's skull suddenly exploded.

Maggie stumbled back, willing herself not to collapse. Her eyes darted around the room, wondering who had fired. *A counterattack? Another enemy?*

Then she saw Layla Gould standing at the shattered window, a gun in her hand. For a moment their eyes met, and she saw Layla's terror, but also her steel. Maggie raised her hands, hoping she was judging correctly. "It's over, Layla. It was just Russell. No one else."

Layla nodded and lowered her gun.

It was over.

Twenty-Two

N iel approached Barak's new address cautiously. He and Gabe still weren't sure if magic had been used to find their where-abouts and was being used to track them now. So far, Barak's team had been safe. They certainly didn't want to give them away.

"I've kept a careful watch on the road," Niel said, glancing in the rear-view mirror again. "No one has followed us."

"With Russell Blake dead, that risk should be eliminated," Gabe pointed out. "Bastard."

Niel grunted in agreement. Nahum had phoned them earlier with the news of his betrayal and subsequent death. *At least that was one less thing to worry about*, Niel reflected as he stopped the car on a rise, just off the road that wound through small towns dotted along the valleys, beneath towering peaks. The sky was clear, it was freezing, and snow sparkled on the mountaintops. "There's not much cover for us to fly tonight."

"But not many streetlights, either. You want to see the *château*?"

"Don't you?"

Gabe nodded, scanning their surroundings. "If Barak thinks it's safe enough. Let's get there and assess it." Gabe laughed, unexpectedly. "I don't know what I need first...a shower or food."

"A shower—you stink!"

"So do you!"

"The heat of the car doesn't help," Niel complained, cranking the window down just a little so he didn't have to smell unwashed Nephilim. "At least we managed to find better clothes!"

They had stopped at a large supermarket that stocked clothing, and bought plain black t-shirts, sweatshirts, jeans, underwear, and overnight bags to store them in. They also picked up toiletries. The thought of a hot shower and fresh clothing spurred Niel on. In another half an hour, after winding along frosty roads, they found the secluded chalet just outside the small town of L'Aiguillon. Here, the Christmas preparations were in full swing. Lights were strewn in front of houses and festooned the streets, putting into stark relief their own grim objective. Gabe had phoned ahead to warn Barak of their arrival, and he greeted them at the door with a hug.

"Glad to see you in one piece." He grinned at Gabe. "You have a bad habit of getting blown up."

"Not by choice, I can assure you!"

Barak laughed as they stepped inside the wooden framed and lap boarded house into a high-ceilinged hall. "This house was a lucky find, as most places are inhabited. Some of you will have to share a bedroom because it's small. I'm hoping no one turns up here tomorrow, or we'll be in trouble."

"Have you visited the original place?" Gabe asked.

"No. I thought best to keep away, just in case."

Niel sniffed at the rich scent of garlic. "That smells fantastic! Who's cooking? Doesn't smell like steak, so I doubt it's you."

Niel was always wary of other people's food, as his own standards were so high. Although, he had to admit that right now, anything would do. A burger at the airport hours ago didn't cut it.

"Am I that predictable?" Barak didn't look the slightest bit offended as he led them into an open plan lounge and dining area. "Lucien is cooking, and he's seriously good!"

"I expect nothing less from a Frenchman."

Niel and Gabe had met Lucien a couple of times, but didn't know him as well as Barak or Estelle. He was hoping they could trust him. Ever since their attack, he'd been wary of everyone outside of their tight circle.

Niel must have looked worried, because Barak said in a low voice, "I'm sure he's trustworthy."

"I hope you're right."

Lucien and Estelle emerged from the adjoining room that Niel presumed was the kitchen, and Estelle walked over and hugged them—an unexpectedly pleasant gesture. "I'm glad you're here. We're planning on going to the *château* tonight once we've eaten. Interested?"

"Of course!" Gabe dropped his bag on the floor and shook Lucien's hand, and Niel followed suit. Lucien hung back, looking uncomfortable, as if he shouldn't intrude.

"Nice to be out of The Retreat?" Niel asked. Lucien had changed since their last meeting a few weeks ago. His hair had been shaved then, and now it was longer. He had also put on weight and some muscle. He might hate his tattoos, but they actually suited him, and he had fire in his eyes now, rather than despair.

He gave a typical French shrug. "Of course. I'm not so sure it's nice to be so close to the count, though."

"It will be worth it to end this."

"And that," Estelle said firmly, "will be hard. Why don't I show you the available bedrooms, and we can discuss everything over dinner? We have photos to share, and maps. Tonight is just for reconnaissance, though. You've heard that the others will arrive tomorrow?"

Niel nodded. "Nahum called us. I presume he told you about Russell?"

"Bastard," Lucien said forcibly.

Estelle sighed. "We trusted him. He always asked about Lucien, but he was never allowed near him, for safety reasons, more than anything. Of course, we didn't elaborate."

"I can't believe he killed Petra," Barak said. "She was a nice young woman. It's giving me even more motive to destroy Black Cronos—not that I needed much more."

Estelle reached over and squeezed Barak's arm. "I've asked Caspian to help us, and fortunately, he agreed. He might even be able to bring one of my cousins. I've left him organising it."

Niel gaped at that revelation. "You've asked Caspian to come?"

"We may clash sometimes, but I'm not an idiot. We're attacking a fortress."

"That bad?"

"Guards, lookout towers, a gated entrance. The works," Barak confirmed. "You up for a challenge?"

"Always."

"Good. But could I suggest one thing first? You both stink, and need a shower. And frankly, those sweatshirts are awful. I think being bombed has affected your style choices."

"Having my clothes blown up has affected my style choices!" Niel lifted his arm and wiggled his bag. "You'll be glad to know we have fresh clothes now. Just point me to the bathroom!"

Estelle laughed. "You'd better follow me. Then we can start planning."

Harlan pulled up outside Moonfell, hoping that Olivia would be looking better. At least that would improve his mood.

After more target practice at JD's house, everyone had left except for their host, who was travelling to London the next day to catch his flight. Harlan had just dropped Shadow and Ash off at Chadwick House. Ash was still recovering, and Shadow had offered to stay with him. Briar had driven Nahum's car back to Cornwall. It seemed he had vetoed driving to London in Briar's tiny mini. Nahum was flying out of London with them tomorrow, and Eli and Zee would fly from Cornwall. The flights were numerous and messy, but at least they had all managed to get seats. After Nahum heard that Harlan was going to see Olivia, he had asked to go, too.

Harlan was also still reeling from Maggie's news. She had phoned him a couple of hours earlier to tell him about Russell Blake's betrayal, and they had passed the news on to everyone. It was all they could talk about in the car after they'd left JD's house. Harlan was now plagued with worry about exactly how much he knew, and what he'd told Black Cronos.

"You need to stop brooding," Nahum said. "There's not much we can do about his betrayal now."

"I can't help myself. The good thing is that I'm pretty sure Russell didn't know about the Emerald Tablet. Jackson kept that to himself.

He didn't even tell Waylen why the team went to Egypt." Harlan shuffled to look at Nahum "You don't look that happy, either."

"I feel guilty for infecting Olivia with Belial. That's why she's here, in this gothic edifice, instead of her own flat." He peered out of the window. "You were right. It's a bit *Hammer House of Horror*."

"I promise that it's slightly less chilling inside."

"Only slightly?"

Harlan laughed. "I'm kidding. It's warm, and they're welcoming, if a little odd. And that house is as imposing on the inside as the out. But I like it. It has character, just like them. They are definitely weirder than your witches."

"The White Haven Coven? They're not *my* witches."

"You know what I mean. You have a badass coven on your side. That's great!"

"I know. I just wish they could help us now," Nahum admitted. "But it's also important that White Haven is protected. I don't put it past Black Cronos to strike again."

"Come on," Harlan said, and exited the car. "I need to get home and pack after this."

"Are you sure you want to come to France?" Nahum asked, as they strolled to the front door. "You didn't look quite as enthusiastic as JD."

"I'm not, but I must. It honestly seems wrong not to go. You have no idea what you're facing, and I need to find Jackson. Maggie said that he vanished into thin air."

"Of course, it's hard to question a dead man," Nahum said dryly.

"That's something else I need to do," Harlan said, making a mental note to do it before collapsing into bed. "Ask Maggie if the staff know anything. It was a bit chaotic when she called earlier."

That was an understatement. The call was hurried, and she was swearing a lot as she yelled instructions to others while also trying to talk to Harlan. He appreciated her updating them so soon. No doubt The Retreat was in a state of shock. He shook it off and focussed on Olivia.

Odette answered the door, her lips parting in surprise as she was introduced to Nahum. "Ah! I see it now," she said enigmatically.

"See what?" Harlan asked.

"Nothing to worry about." She smiled and beckoned them to follow her inside.

Instead of taking them to the kitchen, she led them down a passageway to the right. "We're in Morgana's sitting room. It overlooks the east moon gate," she explained, as if that would make any kind of sense. Harlan filed it away for another time.

The lounge was painted dark green, and one wall appeared to be a jungle. A squashy sofa took up a huge space in front of the roaring fire, but a couple of armchairs in differing styles flanked the other side, a coffee table in between. Curtains covered most windows, all except for double glass doors that looked out onto a spot-lit garden. Harlan barely took any notice though as Olivia rose to her feet from one of the armchairs, a book spilling off her lap and onto the floor. "Harlan, thanks for coming." She beamed, pleased to see him, until she also saw Nahum, and the blood drained from her face. "Nahum! I didn't know you were coming, too!"

Nahum crossed the room and pulled her to the lamp to examine her face in the light. "I was worried after I heard about last night. I'm so sorry, Olivia! Are you sure you're okay? I heard about an exorcism!"

"It's not your fault. And besides, I'm fine now. The witches did a great job of getting rid of him, and Harlan stayed with me all night."

"He did?" Nahum looked at Harlan, and for a moment, Harlan could swear he looked annoyed, before the expression vanished again.

"Sure, I did! I couldn't leave her alone after that. There was nothing funky going on! We're friends." Harlan couldn't believe he actually said that, but he felt like he should. *Just in case...*

Nahum floundered. "No, of course not. It's good. Yes. Very good." Nahum stepped back, and Harlan inwardly groaned.

How could he have missed it? Olivia looked awkward; Nahum looked awkward, and weirdly concerned. *They had slept together!* And Olivia hadn't told him. *Sneaky madam.* He cocked his head at Olivia, a knowing glint in his eye. "So, you're okay, Liv?"

She just stared at him. "I'm fine."

A cough came from behind them, and Harlan almost shrieked when he saw Morgana curled up in the corner of the sofa. "Holy shit, Morgana! You made me jump."

"I've been sitting here all along, Harlan. We're all just relaxing."

And then, as if out of nowhere, Birdie appeared in the other corner of the sofa. "Honestly Harlan, your eyes must be playing tricks on you."

He put his hands on his hips. "Oh yeah? I don't think so, ladies. Neat trick." Nahum was running his hands through his hair and shuffling like he was a child who'd been caught with his hands in the cookie jar. "Nahum, let me introduce you to the ladies of Moonfell. They have a rich sense of humour."

"Seriously, Harlan, I was just sitting there," Morgana said, rising to her feet. "The firelight casts long shadows. But you," she stared up at Nahum, "are hard to miss, even in a darkened room."

Nahum laughed. "I can disappear when I need to."

"Of course you can." Birdie also stood, appraising Nahum with her sharp gaze as she shook his hand. "Interesting."

Nahum's composure seemed to be returning. "I'm really not. We shouldn't have interrupted your evening." He looked at Harlan for support. "We won't stay long."

Odette, however, intervened, as she joined her cousin and grand-mother by the fire. "Your wings are magnificent."

"My *what*?" Nahum shouted before calming himself. "Sorry, what?"

A smile played on Odette's lips, and her hands lifted. Harlan had no idea what she did, but in the next second, Nahum's wings were glimmering in the half light, fully expanded. There, but not there.

"What the fuck?" he twisted and turned. "How?"

"Odette!" Birdie reprimanded. "Stop being naughty. Poor Nahum is not used to us yet, and you have outed him." She addressed Nahum as his wings vanished again. "Sorry. But she's right, they are wonderful. Our house has never been graced by a Nephilim before." She then turned to Harlan. "You must stay for a drink. Come and help us prepare something. Tea, coffee, something stronger? No matter. We'll discuss it in the kitchen. And maybe some chocolate cake. That's always good for shock."

Before he knew quite what was happening, the three witches had whisked him out of the room, leaving Nahum and Olivia alone.

Nahum turned to Olivia, feeling like he'd been stripped naked. "What the hell is going on? How did that happen? And why are you laughing?"

She giggled as she sat down again. "Your face is a picture, that's why. They're funny, aren't they?"

"They made my wings appear! They knew!"

"No. Odette knew. The others just found you interesting."

Nahum sank into the armchair next to Olivia, relieved they were alone. His awkwardness vanished. "Sorry. I should have said I was coming, but I knew Harlan was, so…"

"It's fine. It's nice that you care." Her guarded face returned. "Honestly, I am fine."

"Harlan explained to me what happened. The whole Goddess thing, and Belial's expulsion. You should have called."

"I just felt so tired today, I could barely think straight. And after nearly being kidnapped, too." She curled her legs under her, reaching for a glass of water. "It was quite a night for everyone."

He nodded at her glass. "No wine?"

"No. Just herbal teas and water for now."

"Witches love their herbal teas," Nahum said, nodding. "I hope I don't get offered one."

"Don't worry. They like other drinks, too."

He mulled over how much he should say about his decision to use Belial's jewellery and assume his power. The fire crackled and popped in the silence, logs shifting as they burned. He needed to be honest about it. He didn't know why, but he felt like he should, especially after being so cut up about the discovery. It made his initial shock seem lame. Like an excuse to sleep with her. He didn't want her to think that, so before he could change his mind, he told her what had happened.

"You don't need to explain your reasoning to me, Nahum. Under the circumstances, you made the right choice. Sometimes our best intentions are undermined, and life just screws with us. You need to see his jewellery as a gift. It saved your life, and it might have even pissed him off."

"Maybe. Well, I just wanted you to know, so you didn't assume anything." He looked around the cosy room, the leafy wallpaper seeming to move in the firelight. "This place is amazing. How long are you staying?"

"Maybe another couple of nights."

His head whipped around to look at her. "You must feel worse than you're letting on. You look okay. Still not yourself, though." For a start, she hadn't flirted with him once, but maybe that particular part of their friendship was over now.

"Actually," she swallowed, "there's another reason I'm here. It's why they've left us alone. Poor Harlan must be wondering what's going on."

"Is something wrong?"

"Well, I guess it depends on your perspective." She shuffled again, uncomfortable. "So, what I'm going to say will be a shock, but I just want you to know that I don't expect anything from you. I don't even think this is a good time to tell you. I mean, you're heading off to fight Black Cronos tomorrow. You certainly don't need distractions, but I've been told I must. The witches are very insistent, and they're probably right. Because, you know, I don't know when I might see you next."

Nahum was starting to get worried. And confused. "Olivia—"

She cut him off. "I'm pregnant, and the baby is yours. I'm sorry. It's an accident, and I don't want you to feel..."

Time seemed to stop. "You're *what*?"

"Pregnant."

His mouth was suddenly very dry, and he stumbled to get his words out. "How do you know so soon? It was two days ago!"

"The witches. Odette, again. It seems it's impossible to keep secrets from her!" Olivia raised her hands as if to calm him down. "But I just wanted you to know. You don't have to feel obliged to do anything. I have money and resources. I certainly don't want to trap you. But you're the father, so you should know."

"Oh fuck." Nahum collapsed into the back of the chair. Being a father had never crossed his mind. Well, not for years. *And how the hell was he to tell Olivia that the baby might not survive?* Nephilim children never did. It was their curse. He looked at her face and saw a glow of happiness. "You want to keep it?'

"Yes. It's weird. I never thought I would. But as I said..." He could see her withdrawing, trying to be strong.

"No." He leaned forward, his hand shooting out to grab hers. "You misunderstand. I will support you. Of course, I will. I would never let you deal with this alone! Ever!"

"Thank you, Nahum, that means a lot. But I promise, I'm self-sufficient."

"Stop apologising. We did this, not you. In fact, as I recall, I started it."

"I didn't need much persuasion."

He gave a shaky laugh. "No. But there's something you should know, too. I don't want to tell you now, because just saying it out loud feels like a jinx, but in the spirit of honesty and all that..." He took a breath, feeling like he was gabbling. "Nephilim were not meant to have children. It was part of our making. For those who did, well...the children died young. All of them."

The blood drained from her face. "All of them?"

"As far as I know. Gabe had a child, and she died when she was three years old."

"How?"

"They become sickly, and just sort of fade away." Olivia released his hand and stared into the fire, her features showing a war of emotions. Nahum hated himself. He should have just kept silent. *He might be wrong, but if he wasn't...* "It might make you change your mind about going ahead. You could save yourself a storm of heartache later."

"Yes, there is that. But I'd also deny myself an experience I might never get again." She looked at him again, her eyes dark wells of pain. "What if this is fate, Nahum? And medicine is so different to how it used to be back then! The advancements are huge!"

"That's true, of course. But it's what we were told. How we were made. Can science and medicine change that?"

"Perhaps. Or magic might." She leaned forward. "It's what Morgana does."

Nahum desperately wanted her to be right, because despite his initial shock and misgivings, this actually did feel right. As for whether anything came of his and Olivia's relationship, that was something else. "My brothers will be in shock about this. It will rock every single one of them."

"Will they hate it?"

"Of course not! But it will start a flurry of debate, and bad memories for some of them." He groaned, unable to see the room anymore, only his brothers as he imagined the conversation he was to have. "I won't tell them now, obviously. I'll wait. You're right. It could be a distraction."

Olivia squared her shoulders, suddenly practical again. "You must put it aside, too."

"Tomorrow. Tonight, we'll discuss it with the witches. What about Harlan?"

Olivia's hands flew to her face, cupping her cheeks. "Herne's horns! What the hell will he say?"

"He'll support you no matter what."

"I know. Once he's got past taking the piss about us sleeping to-gether. He knows already. He gave me a look!" She laughed, slightly maniacally. "Okay. We'll tell him now. Thanks for being so good about this."

"I'm not a monster, Olivia!" Nahum also hoped that Harlan wasn't about to turn into some heroic protector of Olivia, and question him about intentions.

And what about Belial? Despite his best effort, it was impossible to forget him. Belial could have more agents on Earth, spreading his destruction. *What if they found out about Olivia?*

What if they hunted her down?

Twenty-Three

M aggie had been in The Retreat for hours, and was now feeling seriously claustrophobic, despite its vast size.

How anyone could work down there all day, every day, was a mystery to her. But perhaps her experience was coloured by the catastrophic events of the afternoon. Three people were dead. The young woman, Petra, who had been shot at point blank range in the chest, the scientist named Ronald Larrington, who had been shot in the abdomen, and Russell Blake, the man who'd killed them, and had been shot by Layla.

The alchemy lab had been mostly destroyed, and the Scene of Crimes Unit had been picking through it, cataloguing everything. Russell's computer had been seized, and Waylen, despite his own injuries, had already facilitated a systemwide check on their computer systems and their staff.

The Retreat was currently sealed. None of the staff were allowed to leave. They were all gathered in the staff area, consoling each other, after Stan and Irving, her two Detective Sergeants, had interviewed them. All except for Layla Gould, who sat in front of Maggie in her own office, just down the corridor from the lab, and next to the mortuary. She was a small, elegant woman. Her hair, despite the events, still looked groomed, her makeup immaculate, and Maggie knew she must look unkempt in comparison. Layla had given a concise and professional statement, but had now fallen silent, staring at the wall. Maggie was sure she knew what she was seeing. It was a sight that haunted her, too. Seeing Russell Blake's brain splash over the lab.

"Layla," Maggie ventured, "I think you should join your colleagues in the staff room."

Layla shook her head. "I don't feel up to it. I shot Russell. I'm a doctor! These hands," she held them in front of her, "are meant to heal!"

"They also saved many lives, including my own. You're an excellent shot, by the way."

"Part of the PD training. I never thought I'd actually have to use it."

"Well, I am very glad that you took it seriously." Maggie had wondered if Layla's skills might be attributed to being a double agent, but had decided against it—mostly. Like Waylen, Maggie would do a huge amount of background checks. She suspected there would be big changes at The Retreat in the near future. Increased checks, maybe even increased staffing. Certainly new staffing.

With the formal part of the interview over, Maggie tried a different approach. "I'm really very sorry about your colleagues. Petra seemed like a nice young woman."

Layla nodded. "She was. An excellent analyst, too. I'm devastated, everyone will be. Especially Austin, her young colleague. They worked in the same office every day."

Maggie had seen him earlier. He'd been tearful, and then angry. She'd left him to Irving to deal with.

Layla continued, her voice faltering. "Jackson liked her, too. He'll be so upset—if he's still alive."

"I think he is, or they'd have killed him in the shop. I must admit, I wondered if Jackson might have been...*compromised*, security-wise. Now, I think not."

"I should bloody well think so!" Layla said, firing up. "He would never do that! Mind you, I also thought that about Russell. I saw him daily. I never suspected a thing."

"He was clever. You knew the dead scientist better than Petra, though?"

"Ron? Of course. Such a lovely man. Dogged, relentless. You say he was shot first?"

"Yes."

"Russell probably did that deliberately. Ron was the strongest. The most likely to tackle him." Layla's shoulders dropped and she started to cry. "He had a wife and children! Bastard."

Maggie gave her a moment to grieve. "What about Lynn? She seems smart."

"Very. The most capable alchemist out of the two of them. Creative. If Russell was destroying work, the chances are she can set it up again. She'll most likely have kept her own extensive records, too. She was meticulous."

"Good. I think Stan was interviewing her, so I'll check on that." Maggie stood. "Come on. You need to be with your colleagues, and I suspect they need you. With luck, we can release you all in the next hour. I'll arrange escorts to get you home."

Layla wiped her eyes and composed herself, and together they headed to the staffroom. Once she was settled with the others, Maggie walked to Waylen's office. The hushed silence of The Retreat had vanished as SOCO carried out their investigations. At least Waylen's office was in a main corridor and easy to find.

She knocked on the door and pushed it open. "Waylen? May I?"

"Of course!" He waved her to a seat. Waylen had cleaned himself up after being interviewed. He'd put a fresh shirt on and combed his hair, but he still seemed to be in pain. He sat awkwardly at an angle, favouring one hip over the other.

"I hope you'll be going to the doctor," Maggie said, again. She'd already nagged him about it earlier.

His response was the same. "I'll be okay. I just fell awkwardly. Old injury. It will be fine with rest and painkillers."

He was stubborn, and there was nothing Maggie could do about that. "Have you given any thought to my earlier question?"

"It's all I've been thinking about." Waylen huffed and leaned back in his chair, smoothing his hair automatically. "We've been friends and colleagues for years. It's fair to say that I'm devastated by his betrayal." He met Maggie's stare, his expression bleak. "But I can't for the life of me fathom why he did it, or pinpoint when it might have started. I keep examining every conversation, trying to see what I missed, but honestly, I don't know."

"Do you routinely check your security footage? I noticed cameras in the lab."

"No, but the feed will be stored electronically. Something else I shall have to start checking. If I had, I might have realised why we seemed to be going backwards, rather than progressing."

Maggie reached for her notebook, just to make sure she'd asked all relevant questions. "You suspect he has sabotaged the experiments."

"Unfortunately, yes."

"It makes sense. But wouldn't the other two alchemists have noticed?"

"Not if he was subtle. From what I gather, alchemy, like any science, requires extensive testing and minute changes to get results. It's utterly baffling to me."

"Which, of course, Russell would have known." She sighed. "Could he have brought anyone here with him? From Black Cronos?"

"No." Waylen was emphatic. "Security has been tight because of Lucien. It's meant that we've had an extra team in with him twenty-fours a day—until he left with Barak. Admittedly they were tucked away down a side corridor, but it still would have been too risky for Russell. One good thing, I guess."

"Did Russell have much to do with Lucien? Or Barak and Estelle?"

"Very little. Obviously, he knew that he was here. I've particularly agonised over that. The investigation into the latest *château* was firmly between me and Jackson."

"Why? As the Assistant Director, wouldn't he have known everything?"

"No. Absolutely not. He was very busy with the lab, and he had oversight of other paranormal activities. I supported Jackson with Black Cronos." He groaned, elbows resting on the desk. "Actually, he had been pushing to be more involved, but I refused. I didn't want him dragged into it because it's so distracting. I wanted him to remain focussed on the lab work. He was cranky about it, but I assumed that was the lack of progress."

"Good. Because hopefully that means that team is safe, and your entire operation isn't compromised." Maggie didn't know if Waylen knew about the team's job in Egypt. She knew they were up to something, but Harlan hadn't said what, and as it was nothing to do with

London, she didn't pry. The less she knew, the less she had to lie about, too. She decided not to mention it. "Have you had any updates from Barak or Estelle?"

"Not today. I trust everything is going smoothly, or Barak would have contacted me."

"That's good, then." She packed her notebook away after jotting down a few points, and then stood up. "You need to wrap up here. My team will probably be here tomorrow, too. This is a big breach. You won't be allowed in."

"I'm in charge!"

"There have been three deaths. You can come back when we're done."

"But how can I help the team in France?"

"You still have a phone and remote access to your computer?" He nodded. "Good. For now, Waylen, that will have to do."

Estelle cast her shadow spell again, making sure it was strong enough to protect herself and her four companions.

The spell was normally simple, but the Nephilim and Lucien had strong auras of their own that threatened the efficacy of the spell. It had taken several renditions and a tweak to cover all of them. Gabe and Niel's presence had vastly complicated things.

"Okay. You're all done. Happy?"

"This is downright freaky," Niel complained. "I can't see myself!"

"That's the point!"

"I'm going to fall over my feet!"

Barak sniggered to her left. "Are you a toddler? You don't need to see your feet!"

"Piss off, Barak. You've had practice!"

Gabe groaned. "Will you both shut up! Will it protect us from infrared cameras or night vision goggles?"

"Hard to say," Estelle admitted, "but I've added a cooling spell into it. That's why you might feel colder than usual. I'm hoping to mask everything."

"Colder! *Mon Dieu*. My junk has shrunk!" Lucien complained. "I'm hardly a man at all right now!"

That elicited a belly laugh from Barak. "My friend, you need Nephilim blood. It's less of an issue."

"You might regret that," Estelle pointed out, "if he's invisible and you're not. Now," she looked around the forest that bristled with night sounds, "should we move on?"

"For the love of the Gods, yes please," Gabe said.

Estelle led the way through the tightly packed tree trunks, following the path they had discovered that afternoon. She had marked the way with a few spells just in case the darkness confused them, and she led them steadily towards the base of the ridge the castle stood on. Like that afternoon, they had parked by a walking track, and hidden the car beneath the trees and another shadow spell. It was well out of range of the castle, but all of them were wary.

They emerged out of the tree line onto a rock-strewn field, the base of the ridge only a short distance ahead. Estelle tipped her head back and craned to see the top. She could just about see the battlements, but that was all from this angle.

"That is one big ridge!" Gabe complained. "That's a lot of ground to cover."

"Which is why we can't waste time," Barak said. "At least the winter gives us long nights. If you look up and to the right, about a third of the way up the ridge, there's a darker area I thought might be an entrance."

"But there's no path to it," Niel said.

"Maybe that's the point. Maybe it's only accessible from inside. But for us, that's not a problem. I suggest that I fly myself and Estelle there and we check it out. You guys should check the rest of the base. The road is around to the west. There's guard activity there."

"I'll check that," Gabe said immediately. "They'll be the first people we should eliminate when we attack tomorrow. Niel, why don't you search further to the east and north with Lucien?"

"Fine with me. But if we're spotted?"

"Don't be!" Barak growled, "or we might find the place impregnable tomorrow."

Estelle tutted. "You know the risks, Niel."

"I meant, do I kill them? But I know the answer to that. Of course I do. Come on, Lucien. Let's hike closer, and then we'll think about flight."

"Let's say three hours, maximum," Gabe suggested. "We meet back by the car. And if you think you've been spotted, just leave."

The others moved out, and Estelle used her binoculars to check the area she and Barak would investigate. "It's hard to see anything in this light."

"Time for an aerial view, then."

She stepped into Barak's arms, and in moments they were flying up the face of the ridge. Even now, she relished his embrace and how safe she felt in it, but she focussed on the job. Up close, the vegetation was thicker along the steep faces than she'd realised. Shrubs clung to the sides, leggy and windblown in places, while straggling pines soared high, their roots buried deep in pockets of earth.

"Those shrubs could be hiding many entrances, Barak," she whispered close to his ear.

"I doubt it. It would make them too vulnerable, even though it would take a mountain climber to reach them. Anyway, we only need one, although two would be perfect."

They both fell quiet as they reached the narrow cleft. Nothing stirred, and satisfied, Barak moved closer. He hovered for a while, and she knew his eyesight would detect more than hers.

"All good," he murmured, as he swept in and landed on the lip of the cleft. He released his grip, and they stepped inside.

It was pitch black, and Estelle waited for her eyes to adjust to the light, desperate to use a witch-light, but knowing she shouldn't. Barak, however, moved ahead confidently. Not wanting him to be alone, she advanced, stumbling slightly. It was freezing in the cave, the walls slick with moisture and ice in places. The cleft was narrow with a high roof, the other end in darkness. But there was no sign of it being a lookout for the castle's inhabitants. Within only a few feet, the ceiling and walls tapered in and down, until she crouched to advance. She bumped into Barak.

He grumbled. "Damn it. It's a dead end. Can you detect anything behind the walls? Any tunnels?"

Estelle placed her hands on the freezing stone, working her way back towards the entrance, but all she detected was solid bedrock. "Absolutely nothing."

Finally, they both stood on the edge again, looking onto the valley. It sparkled under the stars, the peaks white with snow. It was beautiful in its starkness. It was hard to think they were beneath the *comte's* castle, in a place that had been part of a religious war. A place that was very fitting for Black Cronos.

"At least we've eliminated it," Barak said. "And we have plenty more hours left. Ready?"

"Ready." She stepped into his arms again.

Gabe flew around to the west and found shelter in a huge pine tree. He settled into its thick greenery, the branches creaking beneath his weight. Fortunately, the wind was picking up, and the entire canopy creaked back and forth as if he was on the deck of a ship.

He had a good view of the road that turned up the ridge to the castle gates. The road was as steep as he anticipated, following the natural dips of the rock face as it switched back and forth. Precipitous, certainly. He lost sight of it at points, as it wound behind the trees. There was no security on the lower part, but he quickly spotted what Barak had seen. A third of the way up, a light came from a lodge at the edge of the trees, and a huge, wooden gate blocked the road. He adjusted his night vision goggles and saw a camera on one corner.

That was something they had to take care of—or avoid.

He focussed on the lodge. It had two levels, with a door on the ground floor and barred windows on each level. Although it backed onto the trees, three sides were clear, with a good view of the road leading to and away from the gate, and the gate itself. That would be a problem for Gabe and his brothers. They could fly over it, but they needed to take care of the guards before anyone radioed from the castle for help. *But how many guards were there?*

Gabe needed to get closer. Knowing he was risking a lot, and with his own words of warning in his ears, he flew behind the lodge and perched in a branch a few trees back. That's when he spotted another large, single-story building beneath the trees. A pocket was carved out of the hillside, the trees blocking it from view. Voices came from below as a couple of soldiers crossed from the guard tower to the building. He heard a door bang shut, and the voices vanished.

Gabe eased downwards, hand over hand, branch to branch, until he had a clear view of the building below. It looked like a barracks. It was impossible to say how many soldiers it housed without getting closer, but if there were bunks, or it went underground, there could be between fifty to a hundred soldiers down there. If this was just a small contingent, and there were more in the castle, they were in big trouble.

They were going to need a lot more weapons.

"There!" Niel pointed to an area to the north of the escarpment, a quarter of the way up. "Where the waterfall starts."

"I can't see your arm, you idiot!" Lucien complained.

Niel groaned. "This shadow spell is annoying!"

"Actually, I think it's fading. I can see a little bit of you. You're like a ghost."

Niel blinked as if his eyes were playing tricks, but Lucien was right. He could see his faint outline. They had spent nearly an hour tramping around the north side, investigating various crevices, and he'd hoped the spell would last longer. "We'd better get on with it, then. Look at the waterfall! There."

"It's a trickle of water! Hardly a waterfall."

"By definition, it's still a waterfall! Besides, it's the exit that interests me. It looks broad, like the entrance to a cave. Could be a way in."

"Or it could be a quick way to get lost and die in the dark."

Niel glowered at him. "We won't know unless we check. Ready for a lift?"

"While I hate to doubt your strength, I'm a man. I'm heavier than Estelle. I don't wish to be dropped and die."

"I'm a Nephilim. I can handle it. Or do you want to climb? Or even stay here?"

"I'm not a goat or a coward. So be it."

Niel flew them up the steep rockface, battling the strong wind coming from the north that kept trying to drive him into the rock. The spray of the water was icy, but Niel ignored it, angled his wings closer to his body, and swept into the cave it emerged from. Up close, the stream was broader and deeper than he had initially thought, running down the centre of the narrow cave.

He landed on rocky ground to the right. Beyond the entrance the roof sloped up, and the cave stretched back. "Watch your step," he warned Lucien. "It's icy."

Treading carefully, they advanced further in, following the stream as it twisted into the hillside. It seemed that Lucien's Black Cronos changes had improved his eyesight, because he seemed to see as well as Niel. They proceeded in silence until they reached a metal-barred gate set into the rock. A large cave opened beyond it, a pool of inky black water in the centre rimmed with ice. And something else.

Satisfied there was no sign of soldiers, Niel whispered, "Can you see the mechanism over there?"

"*Oui.* I can't make it out, though. Is it a lift shaft?"

"A lift? Down here? Sounds nuts." Niel strained to see further in, but the cave stretched to the right, well beyond his view. "Perhaps it's a maintenance area? It would make sense that they have dug into the rock."

"But this is a long way down!"

Niel studied the thick gate. *That would take a lot of strength to move. And destroying it would make noise and risk a rock fall.* "This could be our only way in, down here. They must have more security than just this!"

"Listen!"

They both fell silent, pressing their backs to the rockface instinctively. Niel heard a low, whirring noise coming from above, and became aware of minute vibrations around them. The longer they stood, the more the weight of rock seemed to press in on them, but there was no doubt something was moving. Something huge.

One thing was certain. They couldn't go any further that night, but they would definitely be back tomorrow.

Twenty-Four

On Saturday morning, Eli finished packing his bag to take to France, and carried it down to the farmhouse's living room. Immediately, he saw the box containing Belial's jewellery.

He could still feel the effects of Belial's strength, faint though it was. His sleep had been uneasy, filled with the images of one of the most powerful Fallen Angels in human form. Piercing blue eyes, long, white-blond hair, and high cheekbones that sculpted his face into ethereal beauty. An icy beauty, though. Unforgiving. His true, angelic form was spirit, not flesh, but the Fallen could always impose their will on the flesh of the hosts that they possessed. Belial was regal, tall, clad in armour that was richly engraved and moulded to fit his muscular body. Designed to impress and instil fear. And it worked. Men quaked at the sight of him. Usually before their death, from either his sword or madness.

Eli opened the wooden box the witches had spelled with protection. While he loathed Belial and all he stood for, his jewellery had saved their lives.

A footfall behind him announced Zee's arrival, and he said, "You should leave that shut."

"Should I? Or should we take it with us?" He turned to face Zee, seeing his brother's wary expression as he placed his own bag on the floor.

Zee's black hair was tied back, and he was dressed in black fatigues and a t-shirt, ready for battle already. "You know my feelings on it. I think you've been possessed by his madness."

"No. I have been blessed with self-preservation."

Zee crossed the room to his side. "Have you forgotten how much you needed Briar last night? You said you felt toxic."

"Of course I haven't forgotten. He's haunted my dreams. I still feel a tingle in my fingers, where his power flooded into my sword. But we are facing Black Cronos in their stronghold! Have *you* forgotten how you were nearly blown up in a crashing helicopter?"

"Hardly! Especially seeing as I can still smell burnt oil and hot metal."

"Then why are we having this conversation?"

"Because I saw you." Zee grasped Eli's arms as if to shake sense into him. "You were incandescent! You and Nahum. I'm your brother, and you scared *me*! I'm not ashamed to admit it."

"I would never have hurt you. I still knew what I was doing."

"Did you?" Zee searched his face as if he doubted him. "Because you looked lost to me. Drowned in Belial's power. And I almost got into a fight with Nahum last night because of the damn jewellery. You stopped us!"

Zee was right in some respects; he couldn't deny that. "It was overwhelming, but I was there all along. You know the feeling. We all experienced it millennia ago."

"That's what worries me. It narrowed our vision. Reduced our ability to judge."

"But we were still there. We were still us!"

Zee released his arms and stepped back. "We shouldn't allow them back. It might become a crutch."

"Like a drug."

"Exactly."

"But there is no *them*, only Belial." He smiled at Zee. "I'm a lover, not a fighter. When this is done, we find a way to dispose of these. Then we find the person who's behind their appearance."

Zee studied him, a wary acceptance in his eyes. "You are powerful in your own right. We all are. We do not need these trinkets."

"They're hardly trinkets."

"They are to me. We don't need them. We seven will fight together, and we won't need Belial to help us."

Eli knew Zee meant for the best, but he also thought he was short-sighted. "Would we have won last night without him?"

"Yes." But there was a flicker of doubt in Zee's eyes.

That was enough for Eli. He would pack the box, regardless.

Jackson stared at the soldier in front of him, wondering what new level of hell he was about to witness.

He was olive-skinned, broad shouldered, and brawny. His light brown hair was cut close to his scalp, and he had the usual impassive stare that all Black Cronos solders had. At least his eyes hadn't changed colour yet, which he hoped signified that he wasn't about to attack Jackson. However, he stood to attention, eyes fixed on the *Comte de St Germain*.

They were in a room in one of the guard towers on the walls surrounding the castle. The view was outstanding. Snowy mountaintops encircled them, their jagged peaks staggeringly beautiful in their own, deadly way. Their immediate surroundings were the lower ranges, a chain of castles stretching away. The last strongholds of the Cathars. He knew from his own research that many were now ruins, their inhabitants persecuted and slaughtered. Roads wound through the valleys below, and even though he couldn't see them, Jackson knew small towns dotted the landscape. Everything below looked tiny and insignificant, cars like ants crawling along the terrain. At least they had stopped blindfolding him now that he knew his fate.

After his breakfast, Jackson had been collected from his cell and marched along the battlements. Jackson had counted at least a dozen guards stationed at various points, all armed, and all wrapped up against the bitter cold. He wondered who else inhabited the castle. There must be more staff he hadn't seen yet.

It was a grey day, the mass of clouds promising rain, or maybe even snow. At any point he expected to be threatened with being thrown from the battlements if he failed to join the count's organisation or agree to call Waylen. But they had asked him nothing so far. He had been escorted in silence. As usual, Deandra was guarding him, and Stefan was there too, looking far too pleased with himself.

"Good morning, *commandant*. No need to stand to attention," the *comte* said. "Take a seat." He gestured to the hard wooden chairs gathered around a table. When they were all settled, he said to the guard, "Tell me, how long have you worked for me?"

"Sixty years, sir," he answered in English, but with a French accent.

Jackson gasped. "Sixty! You look barely older than thirty!"

The *comte* beamed at Jackson. "As I told you yesterday, age means nothing as a Black Cronos soldier." He turned to the soldier again. "Tell our guest when you were enhanced?"

"As a child. I was three."

"Do you remember anything of the process?"

"No. It was painless."

"How would you describe your abilities now?"

The *commandant* gave a hard smile. "I am exceptionally strong. Bound to my guiding planet and all its associations. I call upon my strengths to fight." As he spoke, his skin and eyes glowed like dull metal.

Rather than withdraw, Jackson edged forward to study him. He changed so seamlessly. It was uncanny. Under the edge of his clothes, he could see the beginning of tattoos that glowed like fire. He had only seen Lucien change so close up before. Despite his fear, and natural abhorrence, it was fascinating.

"Can you still think for yourself?" Jackson asked, interrupting the interview.

The soldier looked to the count for permission to speak, and he nodded. "Go ahead. Answer him."

"Of course I can."

"So why do you stay here, bound to this monster who made you?"

"Because it's who I am." The man laughed, looking at Jackson as if he was a worm. "I am superior in every way to you. Here I use my skills fully, and I'm well paid as a senior officer."

"To kill people? How very noble," Jackson spat.

"If necessary, I do. Otherwise, I guard the castle and our new recruits. Our job is to help them acclimatise to their new world."

"And if they don't?" Jackson didn't expect the question to be answered, and he turned to the *comte* and Stefan. "It's one thing to groom a child for this lifestyle, quite another an adult. You must do something to them to make them stay. They will have left lives behind. Family!"

Stefan tutted with impatience. "Jackson. Many have nothing to go back to! We give them purpose. Some were already mercenaries. Now they have new lives."

Mercenaries? That explained a lot. "You prey on the weak, as we suspected all along. And I know that during the Second World War, and other wars, no doubt, you used captured soldiers to experiment on." Jackson had tried to remain calm, but he felt his fury build again. "Why am I here? Do you think I'll change my mind? You haven't warped my mind like you have everyone else's here. It's like a cult! A cult to monstrosities."

The *comte* banged the table with his fist. "It's alchemy and my genius! Not a cult."

"That's what all cult leaders say. All of this makes you feel powerful!"

"I *am* powerful." The *comte* took a deep breath and leaned back, his gaze drifting around the room. "I was here when the Cathars were attacked by the Albigensian Crusade. That was followed by the Medieval Inquisition. Men have always sought to destroy what they do not understand. Particularly the Church. The Cathars believed that humans were the sexless spirits of angels, trapped in the human body. Trapped in the realm of the evil God. You're aware of the two Gods of their belief?"

Jackson nodded, wondering where the *comte* was going.

"It was quite a time. I've always been open to different beliefs. You should have seen all the castles when they were new. Strongholds of might. That's what started my quest, you know."

"What?" Jackson felt like he was on a merry-go-round.

"The sexless spirits of angels. I thought that if angels were trapped in human flesh, it was a brilliant thing to transform them. Try to free them from their mortal shackles. I wanted to be their liberator. I thought they would help me find immortality." He smiled at Jackson benevolently. "As it was, I discovered that myself, and as the Cathars fell, I also discovered that angels are not trapped in human flesh. They exist in their own sphere, along with the other Gods and deities, demons, and spirits. So instead, I sought to elevate humanity. Why should we be trapped in flesh that decays in so short a lifespan?"

Jackson was now convinced the count was completely insane. "And yet you haven't gifted mankind with immortality, have you?"

"Of course not. The planet would be overrun. Most people do not deserve it. Only a few of us are worthy." He stared at his hands, his long fingers flexing and stretching. "My soldiers are worthy of longevity. Not immortality. I still strive for perfection, but you know that."

Stefan cleared his throat. "Perhaps..."

"Oh, yes. To business. I presume you still do not wish to bargain for a truce, regardless of what I have shown you. The scale of my operation. What you are up against?"

"No. Despite the fact you have wheeled this puppet in front of me."

"Puppet. Interesting." The *comte* smirked at Stefan. "I see the resemblance now, don't you?"

"Indeed. I'm surprised Jackson cannot."

Unease rippled through Jackson. "What are you talking about?"

The *comte* flicked a finger at the soldier. "Tell him your name."

"My name is Laurent Strange."

Blood thundered in Jackson's ears. It couldn't be his grandfather. This soldier said he was three years old sixty years ago. "Just because he has my surname doesn't mean anything..."

The count smiled. "I assure you, it does. This is your uncle. Now, do you see why I have introduced you? You wage war on us, and you risk killing your own family. Now perhaps you will make the call?"

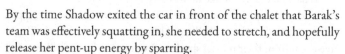

By the time Shadow exited the car in front of the chalet that Barak's team was effectively squatting in, she needed to stretch, and hopefully release her pent-up energy by sparring.

The journey had only taken a few hours, but by the time she factored in waits at the airport, clearing passport control, and then retrieving their weapons from checked baggage, it had seemed to take forever. Then they had picked up the rental car to drive there. That hadn't been fun, either.

Harlan had volunteered to drive. Once again, everyone looked horrified at the prospect of her driving. She found it all rather insulting. And to make matters worse, the atmosphere was weird. Nahum and Harlan were quiet and preoccupied, and Ash was mulling on his injury. It had been tedious. She presumed Nahum was brooding about Olivia, even though he'd said she was fine. Nahum was clearly more invested than he was letting on. *Interesting*. She had no idea what Harlan's issue was. She charitably decided it was concern for Jackson.

Seeing Gabe was a breath of fresh air. He was dressed entirely in black, and his thick, dark brown hair was swept back, revealing his perfect face. Perfect to her, anyway. He bounded down the chalet's steps to the drive to help with their luggage, and swept her into his arms.

"You made it! I'm very relieved I won't have to break you out of prison."

"You will never have to worry about that, Gabe Malouf. You missed me?"

"Always." He kissed her, and despite her best intentions not to be overly affectionate in public, kissed him back, her hands threading through his hair.

That is until Niel yelled, "Get a bloody room!"

She drew back, still staring into Gabe's deep brown eyes. "Let me stab him. Just once."

"Best not. He'd only be worse."

"I can hear you, sister," Niel said, startlingly close. She whirled around to see he was at the back of the car holding a bag of weapons in one hand, and an overnight bag in the other. His blond hair was loose, and he had a rakish grin on his face. "Need to let off some steam with some sparring? Or would you rather be soppy with my brother?"

Gabe groaned. "Herne's horns. Do you two have to start already?"

Shadow cupped her hands around Gabe's face. "I love you, but I need to beat your brother's oversized ego into submission."

Niel laughed as he carried the bags into the house. "I give you ten minutes!"

Ash forced a laugh, and after a brief nod of greeting to Gabe, followed Niel up the stairs without a word.

Harlan just said, "I need a shower. Catch you later, guys."

Only Nahum was left on the driveway, and Gabe turned to him, frowning. "Are you all right? You look like you bear the weight of the world."

"It's been a full couple of days, Gabe, that's all. Finding Belial's jewellery, and then using it has taken its toll. I'll put some coffee on. Then I'll be fine." He picked up his own bag and Shadow's. "See you inside."

Gabe watched him walk up the stairs. "What's up with everyone?"

"I don't know." She lowered her voice, even though they were alone. "It was a solemn journey. Everyone was preoccupied. I can normally get a rise out of Harlan, but today? Nothing!"

"I guess we've all got things on our mind. I'll talk to Nahum later. This Belial business troubles me."

"But we'll deal with it, right?"

"Of course." He smiled and kissed her again. "I've missed you. I thought we'd be stuck in Egypt forever. Anyway, come and see the others before you and Niel try to kill each other. Eli, Zee, and Caspian are here."

She followed him up the stairs, shivering in the bitter cold. "How are they?"

"Caspian is fine. Eli and Zee, however, are as distracted as the others. I didn't help. Eli and I had words."

"Oh! Then it's a good job we have a mission tonight. There's nothing like a battle to clear the head."

"Weirdly, Caspian seems to have lifted everyone's spirits. Even Estelle's. And Niel is cooking, so that helps."

"Good." Niel was an excellent cook. "And Lucien?"

"Fine so far."

Fortunately, the house was warm, and although the chalet was rustic, it was comfortable. After Gabe had shown her their room, they joined the rest of the group in the large living area.

Once Shadow had greeted everyone, Gabe addressed them all. "We're only waiting for JD now, so I suggest that once he arrives, we discuss our plans. If you need to shower, eat, or spar, do it soon.

And allow time for rest later! I don't see the point in delaying things. Tonight is going to be long and hard. We can't afford to get this wrong. We all know the consequences if we do."

He didn't need to elaborate.

Shadow thought she might pop if she didn't expend some energy soon. She caught Niel's eye. "Come on, then. Time to play. The rest of you should, too—even you, Ash. The sooner you know your limitations with that shoulder, the safer you'll be. I do not intend to lose this fight."

"None of us do," Estelle pointed out, voice dripping sarcasm. She never disappointed.

Shadow grinned at her. "I've missed you. Care to join us?"

"It will be my pleasure."

Twenty-Five

A s Barak watched his assembled brothers, Shadow, Estelle, Caspian, JD, and Harlan, he started to feel that perhaps they might have a chance at succeeding in destroying *Château de Bénaix*.

They were gathered in the chalet's living room, but Barak was worried about his brothers. Their moods were unusually grim. Zee was brooding about the jewellery that Eli had brought with them. Eli had weathered the storm of Gabe's fury on that subject, and now sat with Ash. Ash was clearly worried about his injured shoulder. He put Nahum's brooding down to finding and then using Belial's jewellery. Barak didn't blame him. He would most likely have done the same. Harlan seemed preoccupied too, and he figured that was nerves. Lucien, understandably, was worried about his own abilities, and about meeting Black Cronos again.

Caspian seemed his usual self. On his arrival, he greeted Estelle warmly and she reciprocated. For months, Caspian and Estelle had been at odds, but now they had reached a truce. For Estelle to have asked for his help said volumes. It was important to Barak that Estelle mended her relationship with him. He was not only her brother, but a good friend to all the Nephilim, and Barak was glad he'd agreed to help. Caspian would give her valuable magical support, and it eased Barak's concern for her. Because, despite all of Estelle's powers, Barak worried about her safety, and the thought that she might be injured or captured—*or worse*—filled him with horror. She returned his gaze, as if aware of his stare, and smiled. He winked in return.

Shadow had lifted everyone's mood. They had all had a vigorous and challenging sparring session in the chalet's garden that eventually left them hot, sweaty, and a good deal happier than they had been earlier. Shadow—bossy, exuberant, and as belligerent as ever—could always be relied upon to ignite the mood in one way or another.

And then there was JD. He had arrived on a later flight, which landed at a different airport, and he made his own way to them. At least he had brought new weapons that he had just finished demonstrating. Niel, who always loved weapons, was happy.

"JD! You have outdone yourself." Niel grasped the small, rose gold weapon in his large hands. "I prefer my axe, but this is next best."

JD preened. "It has a longer range. And these," he opened up a box containing silver balls, "are my own type of grenade."

Shadow grinned. "They are so good! I want one."

"Slow down!" Gabe said. "We need to work out who's with who, and who attacks where tonight. Then we decide who gets what weapon. Who has swords?"

There was a chorus of "I do" from every Nephilim, and Shadow. They had been able to travel with them in checked luggage after Jackson had prepared official government paperwork for them weeks ago. Niel had even been able to travel with his double-headed axe, and Shadow had transported her bow. It had made their life much simpler. And safer.

"How did you get those weapons through security?" Barak asked JD as he examined an oval, silver object like a squashed egg with a gemstone at the tapered end. It felt far too insubstantial to cause any damage, but after JD's demonstration, he couldn't doubt their worth.

"They're not weapons until they're activated. They just look like metal objects of art. Easy."

"And so unnerving," Harlan pointed out. "Bombs on board an aircraft. Just fucking perfect."

"You'll be glad of them later, I'm sure," Shadow told him.

"What about you, Caspian?" JD asked, fixing his intense stare on him. "You're a witch, you say?" JD had been sidetracked with his weapons and hadn't paid much attention to Caspian when they were introduced.

He nodded. "Yes. I'm Estelle's older brother, and I do not need weapons. I have my magic." He effortlessly conjured a ball of fire in his palms. "And I'm an air witch, so I can use witch-flight. Handy in tight corners."

"Witch-flight?" JD leaned forward eagerly. "What's that?"

"I can summon air and dissolve my body into it to transport myself somewhere else." Caspian frowned. "Not a great explanation. I'd best give a demonstration."

Caspian had been seated at the long dining table under the picture window, but he stood up and vanished in a swirling vortex of air, appearing again at the far side of the room.

"God's pox!" JD leapt to his feet and strode across the room to pace around Caspian as if he was a specimen in a lab. "That was magnificent! You use elemental air as a method of transport. Ingenious. I have never seen that happen before! In all my years..."

"Then you've clearly never met an air witch before. Or," Caspian grinned, "they've never trusted you enough to show you their skills. I assure you that I'm not unique. I can even transport others."

"Show me! How far can we go?"

"No more than a few miles, for safety's sake. It drains my power and might make you sick. Perhaps we should just cross the room for now?"

"Yes!"

By now the whole room was watching, amused, as JD pranced around like an excited teenager. Lucien was similarly awestruck. Caspian smiled at JD like an indulgent father, and he extended his arms. "Step close, then."

In another whirl of air that sent papers flapping, they transported to the other side of the room. Within seconds, JD was on his knees retching, and yet his eyes gleamed with a fervour that Barak was far too familiar with as Caspian helped him to his feet.

After enormous deep breaths, JD declared, "We must discuss this further. Your energies are clearly attuned to elemental air. Such symmetry. Such power."

Shadow rolled her eyes. "Beware, Caspian, he'll be running experiments on you if you're not careful. My affinity with earth magic had much the same effect on him."

JD threw his arms wide. "But this is what alchemy is about! The essence of life itself. And you embody it! Or an aspect of it, at least!"

Gabe coughed loudly. "Can we get back to the subject? We are planning an assault on Black Cronos! Or trying to..."

JD wagged a finger at Caspian. "We will talk later, young man!"

Caspian laughed. "Young man? I haven't been called that in a while, but of course." He turned to Gabe. "Sorry, should we sit down and plan our strategies? Time is marching on."

With a look of gratitude, Gabe sat, and everyone joined him around the table, stools taken from the kitchen when they ran out of chairs.

"Perhaps," Gabe suggested, "Barak, Estelle, and Lucien should lead this. Tell us what we know."

Between them, they outlined their months of investigations, and the recent confirmation that the *Château de Bénaix* was Count Germaine's base. What they hoped was the control centre of his operation. Then Gabe and Niel explained what they had found the previous evening.

JD stared at Niel and Lucien. "You heard a mechanism? Like an engine?"

Lucien shrugged. "Perhaps. It wasn't loud, unless the rock muffled it."

"I wonder," Barak suggested, "whether it works the alchemical wheel I saw on the roof. They moved some of the circles the night before last. I thought it might be to do with the solstice."

Niel frowned. "Perhaps, but we were two thirds of the way down the ridge. If the wheel is in the courtyard, surely that's too far beneath it?"

JD stared at Barak. "Set into the courtyard you say? How big was it?"

"Big! Fifty metres across, perhaps. I heard the grind of the stone moving while I watched. Some of the sigils lit up, too." He frowned as he recalled which ones. Like his brothers, he could speak any language and interpret signs and sigils. "The rune of Rowan, and the sign of Sagittarius, if I recall correctly."

JD worried his lip with his fingers. "A wheel like mine? The power that could generate would be huge. But if it's on the top of the ridge, then the mechanism would be beneath it..."

"Exactly," Niel reasoned. "I think that what we heard must power something else. There looked to be a shaft there, too, but most of the cave was hidden from sight. I'm more than happy to be part of the group who investigates that. But getting in will not be easy. The gate is made from huge steel bars set into the rock. I won't be able to get it out on my own."

Gabe nodded. "Okay. Barak, you found no other entrances?"

"Not one." Barak huffed with disappointment. "Just narrow clefts that went nowhere."

"Do you think we could have missed one?"

Estelle shook her head. "No. We were very thorough."

"Us, too," Lucien added. "Nothing northeast beyond what we found."

"It makes sense," Harlan said as he flicked through the photos they had of the castle. "No point in having an impregnable castle that features several entrances."

"Surely in the past they'd want an escape route?" Ash said. "Somewhere the women and children could use when they were under siege."

"I agree, Ash, and I have a theory," Gabe said. "As you know, I saw what I think were barracks behind the gate. What if there's a way into the *château* from there? The road loops around several times before it reaches the main gate. It would take a while to get to the top. Whereas a route underground would be so much quicker, and less dependent on weather, too."

"Sounds plausible," Zee agreed. "A separate barracks to supplement the one that must be in the main castle."

"There's plenty of soldiers there," Barak confirmed. "At least a dozen on the battlements, probably two, and plenty of buildings that could house them. The walls were thick. Six guard towers. Mounted weapons."

Eli looked puzzled. "I don't understand how you managed to get so close to see that, and not be shot out of the sky?"

"There was low, heavy cloud cover, and I kept very high initially. As the mist drifted in, I glided onto a high tower that looked to be some kind of communications nest. I think, for all of their available security, they are a little complacent here, or perhaps the cold has made them lazy. And of course, their elevated position offers them protection."

"No shadow spell?" Caspian asked Estelle.

"I wasn't with him. He has greater manoeuvrability without me. And I wasn't sure how long my shadow spell would last without me there. I did a lot of work yesterday to enhance it, and it still didn't last as long as I hoped."

Niel grunted. "Two hours tops, without you there to keep strengthening it."

"And I'd rather not be overconfident with it," Barak admitted.

"Okay, that's useful to know," Eli said, nodding.

"So," Gabe continued, "we have one sure way in. The *château* itself, which we can fly to, that has lots of guards. We have one way we *think* we can get in, the way Niel and Lucien found, but of course, that might be a dead end, too. And the barracks. Either way, all need to be targets. There are thirteen of us—let's hope that's lucky!"

"But what's our actual objective?" Nahum asked, stirring out of a deep, watchful silence. "To kill them, destroy the castle, or what? We all need to be clear on it."

Lucien answered quickly. "We need to stop them turning more humans into alchemical soldiers! If they have a master mechanism here, its destruction must be the goal. It doesn't matter how many satellite buildings they have, if this place is destroyed, they are no use!"

"Agreed," Estelle said, casting a dark look at Barak. "What we dis-covered was horrible. In all likelihood, we'll find more prisoners here, or at least a prison of sorts."

"And with that," Ash pointed out, "will come staff, kitchens, cells... There could be anything in that castle, or under it!"

"Are we insane?" Zee asked, looking around the room. "Thirteen of us to take on all *that*?"

"Maybe fourteen," Harlan reminded them. "Jackson could be in there. He could have been in that helicopter you saw."

"That's something else to consider," Zee said. "What if Jackson isn't there, and our attack jeopardises his safety? Hell, it could anyway!"

Barak knew Zee was trying to cover all angles, but Barak was cross anyway. "We can't back out now. We're too close. We may never have another chance again."

"I'm not suggesting we do!"

"We also have Belial's jewellery," Eli cut in. "That gives us the ad-vantage."

"I thought," Ash said, "we were trying to avoid them in this life, not *use* them!"

An uneasy silence fell, in which everyone, including JD, eventually turned to Gabe.

He sighed, hands cradling the back of his head as he leaned back in his chair. "You know my feelings on the Fallen, but we can't ignore the power they give us. Who amongst us, the Nephilim that is," he shot Shadow a quelling stare as she bounced in her seat, "is willing to use it? There are three pieces."

"I will," Niel said immediately. "That sly, angelic, slippery little shit won't get the better of me."

"He didn't get the better of *me*," Eli pointed out forcefully. "But I won't deny that I didn't like the feel of him again."

"I understand, brother," Barak said, meeting Eli's eyes. "I think you made a good decision under the circumstances, but I also know the cost. I have done it before and came out unscathed. I can do it again." He turned to Gabe. "*If* I have to."

Estelle took a sharp intake of breath. "Barak!"

"I'll be okay, Estelle. Trust me." Her lips were tight, her eyes wary, but she nodded, and Barak knew they would have a much fuller discussion on the topic later that day.

"Then I will take the third," Gabe volunteered. "Nahum and Eli have done their share, and Zee has made his feelings clear – and I don't disagree. But Eli also has a point. So, now that it's settled, you're right, Nahum. We need to be clear about our objective. It is not to search every inch of that castle and kill every single Black Cronos member, it is to destroy their ability to make more of them. And of course, weaken their organisation as much as possible."

JD laughed scornfully. "If the *comte* still lives, he will simply replicate it. He has money, that much is clear, and knowledge. We should kill him."

Gabe shrugged. "For once we agree, JD. Cut off the head and hope the rest withers. I presume, JD, you will be of most use if we can find where he transforms his victims?"

"Yes, absolutely. I should at least understand the set-up."

"Then you will go with Niel to the cave. Hopefully you can find a way into the heart of the complex. If you can't, come join us at the barracks. Perhaps two more members for that team? What about you, Ash? Your brains could help there. I want two Nephilim on every team."

"No problem. I'm sure my shoulder won't hinder us." He rubbed it with his palm. "Briar's magic has made a huge difference."

"I can offer you some more healing," Estelle said. "We have plenty of time before tonight."

He smiled at her gratefully. "Thank you. But I was also wondering, Barak, about your healing power? From your father."

Barak was surprised. It was something he'd barely considered trying before. It had only seemed to activate when he was near death, and he hadn't even realised it. "I know it healed me, when I was least expecting it, but I have no idea how to use it to help others. Although," he hurriedly added after seeing Ash's disappointed expression, "I'm obviously happy to try. Maybe Estelle can help me to use it."

"Thank you. I really appreciate it."

Niel changed the subject. "We need something to get us through that barred gate. My considerable strength," Niel flexed his biceps, "will not do it. And don't even suggest using Belial's trick so early."

"Then you need a witch," Caspian said. "Plus, if there are alarms or cameras down there, I can disable them."

"Glad to have you on the team," Niel said.

"Good, then that's settled," Gabe continued. "So that's Niel, Ash, JD, and Caspian assigned."

Harlan interrupted. "What about me? I will be no good fighting Black Cronos. They are far too skilled for me, and I'll just get in the way."

"Then you go with Niel. You can search for Jackson once you're inside. Someone has to assume responsibility for that, so that works for me. Although, obviously, we must all keep watch for him. But," Gabe warned him, "don't go off alone!"

"Nope! Scout's honour!"

"Okay. Then I will lead the attack on the gate and barracks. I *am* aiming to kill as many as possible there, because when we attack at the top, they'll call for reinforcements."

"Hold on," Zee said, holding his hands up. "Do we even need to attack at the top? Maybe stealth is the key."

Shadow gave her usual, feral grin. "We need them to panic! The more places we attack, the bigger the team they'll think we have, the more likely they will make bad decisions. I think a three-pronged attack is the best. And the barracks and rooftop attack must be simultaneous."

"Or," Gabe countered, "we attack at the gate, hopefully draw some of the soldiers away from the castle, which means it will be easier for the team to fly in."

Nahum shrugged. "I don't think it will be easy either way. The minute they know they're under attack, they'll be on alert. I think a simultaneous attack is best."

Gabe huffed, hands on his head again. "Fair enough. There is no best way. But I also agree with Zee. Let's be as quiet as possible for the first few deaths. Take out as many as we can before they know we're there. If Barak is happy to lead the aerial assault," he looked to Barak for confirmation, and he nodded. "Perhaps, Zee, you should join him. You brought the crossbow?"

"Yes, both. I am very happy to kill as many as I can. Who wants the other one?"

"I'll take it," Nahum said. He gave a rueful smile. "I don't think my aim is as good as yours, but I'll try."

Barak turned to Estelle. "If I carry you, think you can take out a few with magic?"

She grinned. "Sure. Just get me close enough."

Barak eyed his three team members. "I'll go over the set-up of the castle with you later, and we can decide our best strategy."

"Great." Gabe sighed with satisfaction. "That leaves Eli, Shadow, and Lucien with me."

"I am very happy with that," Lucien said, nodding enthusiastically. "I'm more comfortable on the ground."

"Great. Shadow, there's thick tree cover by the barracks. You should get some good shots with your bow. Perhaps you or I can attack from the air, too," he said to Eli. "Are we all happy?" At their nods, murmured conversation broke out, and Gabe eased back from the table. "That arrangement also works well, because it means every team has a piece of Belial's jewellery. As to whether it's a curse or a blessing, well, I guess we'll soon find out."

Harlan pointed out the window at the darkening landscape. "I don't know whether anyone's noticed, but the clouds are building out there. I think we'll have snow. That's good, right? It will hide our approach."

Barak grinned. "It certainly will. With luck, they won't know what's hit them."

Twenty-Six

O livia had spent a quiet, reflective day again at Moonfell, mulling over the events from the night before.

She had slept late, luxuriating in her four-poster bed, before descending the sweeping staircase to the main kitchen. None of the witches were around, but they had told her to help herself to breakfast and drinks, and treat the house as her own, so she had breakfasted alone. Huge copper pans, however, simmered on the hob, the rich scent of herbs drifting around the kitchen. Morgana must be somewhere close by, but Olivia was happy to be alone.

She spent time in Morgana's beautiful green lounge that seemed to rustle with her presence, even though she wasn't there. The fire crackled in the grate, and she found a leather-bound notebook and ink pen on the table by the armchair with a note. They were a gift from the witches, encouraging her to write a diary, and although she hadn't kept one for years, it suddenly seemed to be the thing that she wanted to do most.

Her day passed in a flurry of writing and reflecting on her current predicament.

Predicament! What a ridiculous word. She was pregnant! It wasn't something that would go away. *This was going to change her life forever.*

Her pen slipped from her fingers as she recalled Nahum's words about the Nephilims' curse. *Would she lose the baby before it even came to term? Or would it die shortly after?* It seemed cruel, and somehow impossible. *That might have been the case then, but now? Was he right? Should she save herself heartbreak and terminate it now?* She closed her eyes, unable to comprehend that. Already she felt so attached to it, and yet the idea hadn't entered her mind to even have a baby twenty-four hours earlier.

However, she had never been surer of anything in her life. It felt right. Thankfully, Nahum had been kind, thoughtful, and supportive. She wasn't alone. She laughed at the memory of Harlan's face. His mouth had dropped open, and he kept staring at her until he enveloped her in a hug that took her breath away. His words brought tears to her eyes. "*I'm with you every step of the way, Liv. Every step. And you,*" he'd whipped around to glare at Nahum, "*better not fuck up!*"

Nahum's answer was even funnier. "*Don't worry, Uncle Harlan. I won't.*"

When she opened her eyes again, the flames were flickering on a darkened room. She turned to the windows, and saw that the clouds had thickened, bringing twilight early. The huge, arched windows looked out onto a wintry garden, the east moon gate framing a large topiary crescent moon beyond. She had never seen a moon gate before, but they were magical, seeming to offer a portal to somewhere else. The gate looked as it sounded. It was a circular opening separating one part of the garden from another, with no gate at all. The east moon gate was carved out of a thick yew hedge, and therefore entirely green. The arch stretched above the hedge by several feet, and a stone path, thick with moss, led through it. Olivia rose to her feet, thinking to explore it.

Morgana spoke behind her, making her jump. "I wouldn't, if I were you. The paths sometimes change direction at night. You might find yourself lost, and it's bitter out."

Hand on her thumping heart, Olivia turned. "You're very good at being silent, Morgana. In fact, it's a trait you all have."

"It's just the house. It absorbs our sound, like a hug. It can't help itself." She smiled, her face all sharp shadows in the gloom. "Sorry. I didn't mean to make you jump."

Olivia sat down again, hands rubbing her face. "No, it's just me. I'm all at sixes and sevens. And what do you mean, the house can't help itself? It's not alive! And surely paths can't actually change directions on their own?"

Morgana laughed as she sat opposite her. "I think you've been here long enough to know the answer to that. This house is unusual. Look after it, and it looks after you. We make sure to look after it very well. But enough about us. How are you?" Her gaze fell to the open book, and she beamed. "You're using it! Do you like it?"

"I love it! It's so beautifully crafted, and I found myself pouring out my feelings. It has actually helped. I feel better. Lighter."

"Good. It usually helps to share, even if only to the page. I often think it preferable. It's you and words, pouring out and filling space with hopes and fears and dreams. This is a new phase of your life. I think it's appropriate to record everything."

"But what about what Nahum said about the child's survival?"

"Something to consider, certainly. However, I have skills, and the Goddess has blessed you. We have powerful support."

Olivia felt like she was an actor in a play. "Why does the Goddess care about me, and especially about a Nephilim's baby if she hates Fallen Angels?"

"Because she hates injustice, and the Nephilim suffered it in spades. Plus, it displeases Belial, and that makes her happy, too. And no, for the millionth time, he cannot harm you or the child."

"Okay. Then I shall see this through." Olivia flopped back in the chair. "I need wine, and I can't have it! For nine whole months! I love my wine."

"It will pass soon enough. I'm sure we have something alcohol-free that tastes just as good, somewhere." Morgana settled into the corner of the squashy sofa, gathering her skirts beneath her tucked legs. "Tell me about Nahum. He's very good looking!"

"Isn't he? I'm a terrible flirt, Morgana, especially with him. But I never once imagined…"

"Oh, I'm sure you imagined plenty!"

Olivia sniggered. "Well, maybe."

"He's a good man, I can tell. Honest, reasonable. Brave. He'll make a good father. He has brothers, you say?"

"Six. All good men, all very different. Well, so I gather. I haven't met all of them yet."

"Interesting. Lots of uncles, who I presume would protect you to the death."

"Don't say that. Not even in jest."

"The Nephilim had a certain reputation, that's all I mean. And it seems Harlan is on your side, too. An interesting man."

"He's amazing." Olivia sniffed as tears threatened. "What a whirlwind few days. I feel better, though. I think I'll go home tomorrow. I need to start planning."

"You have room?"

"Enough. But I have money and can get a bigger place."

"What if Nahum wants you close?"

"We'll work something out. I certainly won't leave him out of this. But I also need to work. I enjoy my work!" She shook her head. "Actually, I don't want to think about that now." Her serenity vanished as she contemplated that night's activities. "They are all at risk tonight. They are fighting a powerful group. They have witches with them, and they're strong, but Harlan is human, and he's headstrong, and he wants to find Jackson..."

"It's natural to worry. All you can do now is trust in their abilities." Morgana lifted her chin, listening, and then smiled. "Maggie is here. That's good. You can share your news."

Olivia groaned. "What will she think?"

"She'll swear a lot and then defend you to the death." Morgana winked. "You're not alone. Never forget that."

Jackson glared at the count, trying to contain his icy fury as they sat in the middle of a well-appointed sitting room on the second floor of the main castle.

The count, however, looked at ease. He adjusted his cuffs as he said, "You have had several hours in which to think on my request. It's time to make the call."

Jackson looked at his mobile phone on the elegant side table and decided it was time to act on his plan. He had raged in his cell after seeing his so-called uncle, kicking his bed and desperately wanting to punch walls. He decided that punching the count would be far preferable. He did not believe for one second that his grandfather had willingly become a Black Cronos soldier. He had desperately tried to work out why he had an uncle at all.

Initially, he had steadfastly refused to believe the claim, but the count had offered photographic proof. Images of his grandfather in a Black Cronos black uniform. Despite his best efforts, Jackson broke down in tears. All his hopes had been crushed, his worst nightmares realised, and the count had observed dispassionately. He was a sociopath. There was no doubt about that. Jackson had flown at him in a rage, but The Silencer of Souls and his uncle had leapt in, and The Silencer's cold fingers had ensured he was unconscious in seconds.

But once Jackson was back in his own cell, he ran through potential scenarios again. He had to conclude that his grandfather might have been tortured and had eventually agreed. Or he had been brainwashed. He would never know the truth, which was the horrible thing. *Never.* And meanwhile the count, the monster, was preying on his own fears and anger. Jackson used his anger and started to plot. The count had also said they had killed Gabe, Shadow, Ash and Niel. He needed to ask for proof of that, too.

Now Jackson swallowed, acting nervous, eyes darting to The Silencer, who regarded him with her dark, soulless eyes before studying the count again. He sat comfortably, his snowy white cuffs on show beneath his elegant jacket, tailored to perfection. His too smooth skin was like a mask.

Jackson tried not to overplay his hand. "If I call, you must promise to enact a truce. You won't harm my friends?"

"No, if they leave us to our own devices."

"But what if they don't listen to me?" Jackson argued. "I'm not their leader. I don't control the Nephilim. They have their own agenda. You said you've killed four of their team. They won't take that lightly."

"They will if they want the rest to survive." The count's eyes glittered with malice.

"I think you're lying about that. You've never shown me proof."

The count picked up a remote control and turned on a TV mounted on the wall. "I thought you might ask. This happened two nights ago. When we kidnapped you."

Jackson watched the footage of the destroyed hotel in Aswan that he knew Gabe and his team were booked into. The report detailed the rooms and the floor that had been affected, and said they were still searching for survivors—or bodies. Jackson's chest tightened again. *That was the place.* Russell must have known, but hopefully he wouldn't have known why they were there.

Jackson's fury exploded. "You bastard. They were my friends!"

"And my enemies. There was an interesting theft from the museum just beforehand. Know anything about that?"

Jackson looked him dead in the eye. "My business is with you. That must have been another job."

"Well, their looted objects have been destroyed with them." He tapped the arm of his chair, his eyes never leaving Jackson. "Emerald discs. Very interesting, indeed. I wonder what their significance is."

Jackson held his nerve. "I'm sure I have no idea, or if they are even connected to Gabe. You're just guessing now. Their bodies?"

"I have no doubt they'll find them." He picked up Jackson's phone. "Unlock it for me. I have decided that I will speak to Waylen myself. I think letting you speak would be quite hazardous."

"Phone him yourself. You must have his number."

"I wish to use your phone, so he knows I have you, obviously."

"But what will happen to me? You won't keep me here forever."

"Forever is a long time."

"You'll kill me!"

"Not as a Black Cronos soldier. You may as well agree now. You will eventually. Your grandfather came to like it."

Jackson felt his rage building again. "Then why are you giving me a choice?"

"Because you will be far more useful to me that way!"

"Waylen will want proof that I'm alive, and a guarantee of my safety."

"I think the threat of more deaths will be a bargaining tool enough. But yes, I'll allow you to confirm you're alive. I'm sure we can come to an arrangement."

"Then it's not Waylen you need to speak to. It's Barak."

"Why?" the count asked suspiciously.

"Barak, one of the Nephilim, is leading the search for you. He's the one you need to convince."

"Excellent."

Jackson held his hand out and unlocked his phone, quickly bringing up Barak's number. "I doubt you'll convince him."

"Let hope for your sake that I do."

Twenty-Seven

B arak was still seething hours later at the memory of the count's smooth, silky voice that oozed menace.

He had made his intent very clear. None of them would be left in peace if they didn't back off. He had crowed about killing Gabe and the others in Aswan, and Barak, although shocked to speak to the count, had played along. He had argued and sworn and raged, of course. He had to make himself sound believable.

And then they bargained hard. Barak had argued for time to talk to his remaining brothers. They were to return the count's call at midnight. Barak aimed to deliver the message in person.

The good thing was that they knew he was with Jackson, and that he was alive. *But was he in the castle?* Jackson's message had been short. He'd yelled, "Forget me. Move on. I'll be locked up in his damn dungeons forever." Then there'd been the sound of a scuffle and the count returned with a promise to call again at midnight.

Barak was sure that message meant he was in the castle. It had to. He could have yelled anything. He could have pleaded for his life, or urged them to violence. Or even revealed the location that they supposedly didn't know. But perhaps that would have been too obvious. They wanted to do nothing to alert the count.

So, they had proceeded with the plan.

It was dark, and snow was falling as Barak led his team to the top of the ridge. They circled high above the castle, the wind whipping around them, Estelle tucked close to his body. Snow settled on the battlements and in the courtyard, helping it melt into the landscape.

Only the glow of lights in the towers and the castle provided landmarks.

Nahum and Zee flew lower, crossbows ready. Unfortunately, the snow and bitter wind meant many soldiers were inside the towers, but half a dozen still walked the icy walls on their own.

Within seconds, they all lay dead.

No one had seen it happen. No other soldiers emerged.

"Damn it," Barak said in Estelle's ear, the wind whipping the words from his mouth. "I hoped they'd all come running and we could pick some more off. This means Plan B."

Estelle grinned. "Oh, goodie. I'll aim for the closest tower."

Before she could take aim, a muffled explosion sounded from further down the ridge.

Gabe's team.

Estelle released a volley of fireballs, bombarding the largest corner tower by the main gate. Stone blasted into the air, showering over the walls and courtyard. Seconds later, soldiers streamed out of all the towers, including the one that had been hit.

Immediately, Nahum and Zee took aim again, soldiers falling dead before they even realised what was happening. But that didn't last long, and they quickly manned the huge crossbows on the battlements, along with other more sophisticated weapons.

Barak swooped around and Estelle took aim, igniting fires along the walls and destroying the battlements and as many weapons as she could before a few fired in their direction. Fortunately, Barak was too quick, and as he swept away, Estelle kept firing, drawing their attention from Zee and Nahum.

A blast of energy sizzled past them, and a flurry of huge arrows almost skewered them. Barak flew into low cloud. When he circled back, Nahum and Eli had also been spotted, and were busy dodging the blasts from the weapons below. Despite the numbers they'd killed, reinforcements were coming.

All three Nephilim withdrew, disappearing into the ever-thickening snow. It was getting harder to see the castle, but that also meant it was harder to see them.

That is, until huge searchlights lit up the sky, a siren whined, and the volley of weapon fire began again.

Shadow had been thwarted in her efforts to shoot the guards at the gate. No one was stirring from the building, and the gate was securely locked, blocking the road.

It didn't help that thick snow was hampering her vision. *Time to use one of JD's grenades and hope it worked.* However, once she activated it, she would have seconds only to take the shot. She aimed her modified arrow that had JD's bomb strapped to it and adjusted her aim for the weight and the steadily increasing wind. Fortunately, her target was big. When she was sure of her shot, she activated the bomb, aimed at the window on the first floor, and released. The window smashed and a boom blew out the corner of the building. A fireball lit up the surrounding area, igniting the closest trees. *Herne's balls. What the hell had JD made that bomb from?*

As a second explosion ripped out of the sky far above, she knew the team up there had begun their attack, too.

Shadow focussed back on the guard tower. When soldiers ran from the building, and others jumped from windows, she took aim again, this time with her normal arrows, picking them off in the light from the fire. Shouts sounded from the building beyond the guard house where Gabe and the others were situated. She waited to see if any others would emerge before she joined them.

Movement to the right made her adjust her aim. *More soldiers beneath the trees. They must have evacuated the rear of the building.* She again picked them off. But then a flash of bright white light ripped out of the darkness by the gate and struck the tree she was perched in. With an ominous crack, it crashed to the ground.

Niel gripped the steel bars of the gate that was set into the thick rock beneath the castle.

"Any suggestions on how to get past this thing?"

JD frowned at the rock, hands on his hips. "We could try one of my bombs, but I fear it would bring the cave down on our heads."

"Yeah. Let's not do that."

"Or," JD persisted, "use my weapons to shoot it out. Aiming right at where the bars meet the rock. Effective, but not quite as destructive."

Harlan groaned. "I'm not sure I like that idea, either. We don't know what's around that corner! Anything loud could bring soldiers."

Niel nodded. "Agreed. Caspian?"

"I can try magic. Much quieter, too."

"What kind of spell?" Ash asked.

Caspian, like the Nephilim, was dressed in black, a change from his usual suits that Niel was so used to him wearing. "I've been thinking about that all afternoon. If only I'd have known, I would have asked El for her special blade that cuts through anything, but I'm going to try this."

Caspian laid his hands on the rock immediately to the right of the bars and murmured a spell. Cracks started to appear, and then the rock began to crumble. As Caspian pushed his hands further in, it was as if the rock melted at his touch, finally exposing the metal bars. But they extended deep into the rock, and the metal remained impervious to his magic.

Eventually, sweating and strained, Caspian pulled back. "The metal has been enhanced in some way. It's not responding as I hoped."

"And the rock is far too dense to make a hole through," Ash said. "It's at least four feet thick. It would take hours."

"Enhanced how?" JD asked Caspian. "By magic?"

"I can't detect magic. It's an unusual colour, though. Not just steel."

JD nodded. "A mix of metals, all alchemically done. In that case, we'll have to trust my weapons. I'll focus only on the bars themselves."

Niel was about to protest, but what was the point? They had to get in somehow, and he certainly wasn't giving up yet. "Do you need mine?" Niel asked him, reaching into his pocket for the strange metal object.

"No, thank you. I have a specific one in mind." JD had handed out most of his weapons, but he rummaged in his pack for the remaining ones.

Niel pressed his face to the bars, trying to see more of the space beyond. It was freezing cold and dark, but they'd risked using torches, or the humans wouldn't see a thing. Fortunately, the light had not attracted attention, and Caspian had thrown a couple of witch-lights in there, too. Small ripples disturbed the glossy black lake, and ice rimmed at its edge. A stream of water flowed out of the lake, across the floor and under the gate. Fortunately, their boots protected them from the icy cold water.

"What can you see?" Harlan asked him.

"Just the shaft as before, and bugger all else."

"Step back, everyone," JD instructed. "This will get hot."

A red beam of light shot out of the handheld device, and JD trained the beam on the edge of the bars, slicing down where they met the walls. The metal heated up and started to blister, the heat intensifying until everyone had to retreat several feet.

"Is that a laser beam?" Harlan asked, shielding his eyes from the bright red glare.

"No! Something much better, although, remind me to make a weapon that I can adjust in future."

Niel grinned at Ash. "I like this more every second. But I'd like it to be quicker!"

"At least it's quiet. Not that I think we need to worry this far under the castle. But," Ash shrugged and then winced and put his hand on his injured shoulder, "we can't be too sure."

Niel pulled Ash aside while JD worked. "Is your shoulder still painful?"

"It's not as bad as it was."

"But it should have healed by now."

"Brother, I think you forget how long some injuries take to heal."

It had been years since Niel had sustained a serious injury, and he'd never had a shoulder injury like Ash's. "I guess you're right. I take it Barak couldn't help?"

"No. He found it very frustrating."

"What about flight?" Ash hadn't flown earlier, insisting he needed to preserve his shoulder. They had travelled to their destination on foot, like the night before, and then Caspian had used witch-flight to take him and JD to the entrance, while Niel flew with Harlan. Flying with Harlan was nowhere near as pleasant as flying with Mouse.

"I'm sure it will be fine."

Ash's golden eyes met his own, but Niel saw doubt there. "What's going on?"

"Nothing."

Niel was about to question him further when JD's hoot of success drew their attention. He had finally succeeded in severing the barred gate from its moorings and it wobbled, threatening to crash to the ground. Caspian stepped in, and air whirled from his hands to cushion the gate. It landed as gently as a feather.

Niel pushed ahead, vowing to keep an eye on Ash. "Nice one, gentlemen. Stay close."

The cave opened to the right. It was long and low-roofed, the lake stretching for most of the cave. On the opposite side was the shaft he'd glimpsed earlier. Now that he had a better view, he could see the mechanism of hydraulics. The rest of the cave was empty, except for another hole in the rock wall at the far end, and a waterfall that streamed from the roof into the lake.

Harlan trained his torch on the shaft. "You were right. It's an elevator shaft." He stared at his companions, wide-eyed. "Is this for real? Can we just get straight in?"

"Maybe. But what's that?" Niel pointed at the round hole in the rock. "Another cave? A passage?"

"Perhaps, however there must be a natural spring somewhere in this rock," Ash suggested, focussing on the waterfall. "Very handy. A source of water during a siege. It might drive a mechanism further up. Or did, perhaps, years ago."

"Speaking of which," Niel said, "can you hear that hum?"

Now that they were in the cave properly, it was much easier to hear. Everyone looked up.

"It sounds big," JD mused. "Maybe it powers the castle. Their own turbine. That would be truly self-sufficient."

Niel quickly came to a decision. "Ash, JD, and Harlan, you check the lift shaft! Me and Caspian will check out the other exit."

He extended his wings and flew across the lake, landing mere seconds after Caspian, who threw a couple of witch-lights ahead of them. It was the start of a sloping passage leading upwards, hewn out of solid rock. Caspian walked up it, torch angled upwards. "It's pitch black. No lights at all. I imagine it's the way down, if the lift fails."

"But why dig this far into the ridge, anyway?"

"Perhaps there were natural caves throughout the rock, and they just added to them. Cathar strongholds would have needed places to hide. Places to store food and ammunition. Maybe the count has similar ideas. The question is, do we walk up, or take the lift?"

"The lift announces our arrival."

"But it's quicker, and we have no idea how the battle is going up top. If the fight has started, they won't be watching the lift," Caspian pointed out.

"Excellent point. Lift it is."

Zee swept around to the north of the castle, flying into the driving wind and snow.

The cold was exhilarating, as was the battle. The searchlights were powerful, but there was only so far they could penetrate, especially in a snowstorm. He let the wind take him, and as it drove him back to the castle, he angled his wings close to his body. He dived at the castle battlements, aiming for one of the search lights before it could swing around to see him.

He swept over it, wrenching it from its mount, and dropped it into the courtyard below. He swooped under the wall, so close that the soldiers had trouble seeing him, and then swept up again, picking a man up with ease, and dropping him from the battlements, too. He then decided to try JD's weapon. It felt clumsy despite his earlier practice, but he aimed at a soldier, squeezing, and firing with intent as JD had instructed. A blast cut through the air. He missed with the first shot, taking out only a chunk of battlements, but quickly adjusted and shot again. He hit the man square in the chest, catapulting him over the wall and onto the courtyard below. He then immediately sought cover as the rattle of gunfire split the sky.

The soldiers were shooting wildly. Estelle and Barak were still flying, and Estelle was hurling fireballs and glowing balls of energy with uncanny precision. He had no idea where Nahum was, but spotlights were being trained on the far side of the castle wall, and he guessed he was there. More and more soldiers were pouring out of the guard towers and onto the battlements. They had certainly drawn their attention. The newcomers immediately manned the remaining huge guns, swinging them up, and firing blindly.

Zee aimed at the entrance of the closest guard tower. As soldiers ran out, he shot the first few before they ducked for cover. He wheeled high again, the snow cloaking his movements. He flew around the north of the tower with nothing but the vertical face of the ridge beneath him, kicked in the window of the first floor, and threw a grenade inside.

Part of the tower exploded in a mass of rubble. Dodging the falling stone and debris, Zee decided to take the fight to the main castle and aimed for the yellow glow of lights leaking from the curtains covering a huge window. It overlooked the valley, not the courtyard, and there was no one firing at him. *Easy pickings.*

He hurled a grenade through the window, and in seconds the windows blew out and flames curled. It was only as he wheeled back to the fight above that he thought of Jackson.

Shit. Where was he?

Gabe's back was pressed to the wall next to the entrance of the barracks, waiting for soldiers to emerge. Lucien was on one side, Eli on the other, when he saw the tree that Shadow was positioned in topple to the ground. There was nothing he could do to help her.

The door to the barracks burst open, and half a dozen armed men rushed out, weapons raised. Gabe, Lucien, and Eli attacked them, Eli and Gabe slicing them down with their swords as Lucien used JD's weapon.

But the next batch of soldiers were more prepared. As the three turned to fight them, the soldiers' eyes turned dark black, and their skin became metallic. Lucien responded, his own skin and eyes changing as he drew on his enhancements. Gabe hoped he wouldn't turn on them. The next few minutes were chaotic as swords and weapons whirled, and the clash of metal and grunts of battle echoed through the trees.

Gabe knew they'd made a tactical mistake. They should have waited for more Black Cronos soldiers to emerge before attacking. That way they could have better assessed the numbers. But they had relied on Shadow being able to shoot from a distance, and that wasn't happening right now. He hoped that she wasn't crushed.

Flames crackled, and the fire spread. The main guard building was ablaze, flames and thick black smoke reaching into the sky. Potentially, it might set the barracks alight, and that wasn't the plan at all. They needed to get in to see if there was another route to the castle, and they couldn't even get close to the door. The heat was becoming unbearable. The smoke mingled with the snow, and visibility was poor. It was hampering them as much as the soldiers.

Gabe's fury and frustration grew as he saw his companions struggling, and heard the noise from the castle. He needed height and space.

Gabe extended his wings, seeing Eli do the same, and used them to beat a clear path around them. They crunched their attackers aside. Soldiers hit tree trunks, and flaming branches and ashes fell around them.

A spear seemed to come out of nowhere. He dodged it, but the sharp point grazed his ribs. A soldier emerged from the whirling snow, eyes flaming like the fire behind him, and flames rippled down the sword gripped in his hand.

That was new! Excellent. Flaming bloody swords...

Harlan studied the elevator shaft. Cables and rails ran down the walls, and buffers and a piston were on the ground.

"Damn it. There's no call button, and only the mechanism is down here. It's just the pit. We need to use *that*." He aimed his torch on the ladder that was bolted to a side wall. He stepped into the shaft and examined the space above him. The ladder extended a short way before ending at doors.

Ash stood next to him. "We can climb the ladders, open the door, and access the level above us."

"And if it opens on a nest of dragons?" Harlan asked.

"Then I'll be Saint George," Ash said, laughing. "Dragons? Seriously, Harlan, you need to get a grip!"

"I wouldn't put anything past Black Cronos."

JD had been examining the cables, but now he joined them. "Once we get through those doors, we can see how many levels there are. You're right about it feeling like a dragon's den, though, Harlan."

"*Dragons*?" Niel exclaimed as he arrived with Caspian. "You better be joking."

Ash laughed. "We hope we are. What did you find?"

"Another route up—we think, but we haven't explored it. Thought this might be quicker."

"We need to use the ladder and crank open the doors," Harlan explained.

Niel shouldered through and gripped the ladder. "Good. I'll go first and crank it open."

He quickly reached the door and used his axe to wedge the door open. When it was wide enough, he slipped his fingers in, pushed the doors wide, and clambered through the gap. "Come on. No dragons."

Harlan followed, hauling himself over the doorway and into a dark room. His flashlight revealed that they were in a storeroom that housed pieces of machinery. There were several shelves, and large boxes on the floor. He found a light switch and flicked it on so they could see properly. "There's a lot of stuff in here. Must be to maintain the elevator, and maybe other things for the castle, too."

"At least there's a call button here," JD said, pointing at the wall by the lift. "And no other exit here. That other way up that you spotted must bypass this one."

He pressed the button, and while they waited, Harlan gave the area a more detailed examination, but there was nothing that warranted their attention, and no cameras or alarms. None that were obvious, anyway.

They all waited, shuffling with impatience as the mechanism whined. The display above the door only showed a green light. It didn't indicate how many floors were above. Harlan gripped JD's weapon, heart pounding, but when the lift finally arrived, it was empty.

"Eight floors," Niel said, looking at the row of buttons in the lift. "Considering how far down we are, that's less than I expected. Where do we start?"

"Bang in the middle?" Ash suggested.

"Level six," JD countered.

"I suggest one by one," Harlan said. "There are only eight levels! Seven to go. Otherwise, we might miss something."

"That's slow!" Niel complained. Niel was all about mayhem and destruction; he wasn't known for his patience.

"We're here to destroy the damn place! We need to be methodical, or we risk screwing this up. And we need to find Jackson! Prison cells are likely to be low down. I am not leaving this place without him!" Harlan reasoned.

Caspian pressed level nine. "You're right, Harlan. Patience is a virtue. Let's see what lies beneath the *château* and bring the whole lot down."

Twenty-Eight

J ackson was lying on his bed, staring at the ceiling of his cell and
debating his fate after his attempted escape earlier.

The minute he had shouted at Barak over the phone, Stefan had
punched him, and taken his phone. By the time he had collected
himself, The Silencer of Souls was looming over him, her lips leaning
towards his. She'd miscalculated how conscious he was, so he punched
her, and she had reeled backwards.

He had scrambled towards the door, but Stefan pulled a gun from
his pocket and fired at his feet. "*Not one more move, Jackson, or you're
dead.*"

The Silencer was snarling like a wild animal, ready to pounce again,
but the count called her back. "*Wait, my dear.*" The count cocked his
head, looking at Jackson like he was an insect. "*Was that an attempt
at a clue? Foolish.*"

Jackson had staggered to his feet, wiping blood from his split lip.
"*There are a thousand castles with a thousand dungeons. Was it really
a clue, you moron, or was it just like I said? I'm not getting out of here…I
know that now.*"

The count had stepped closer, his chilling eyes cold and dispassionate. "*No, you're not. I was prepared to let you choose your fate, but now I
aim to break you. The winter solstice is in three days, and the team here
is already prepping a new batch of soldiers. You'll join them.*" He then
nodded at Deandra. "*Take him to his cell, and do not harm him!*"

And that was it. His fate was sealed. That was probably an hour or
so ago. It was hard to calculate, with no watch and no natural light to
go by. Then he heard voices down the corridor, and he rose to his feet.

The door opened and Stefan waited outside, flanked by two soldiers. "Time to begin the process, Jackson. Follow me."

He marched quickly down the corridor and Jackson followed, the huge, muscular soldiers barely a pace behind him. He'd rather be out of his cell than in it. This way, he could at least try to find a way to escape. When they reached the lift, Stefan took them down to another floor.

"You really are a fool," Stefan told him. "Thinking you can destroy us. This place is impregnable, and our organisation too big."

"Almost as big as your collective ego. Where are we going?"

"The lab preparation area, of course, for your tattoos, and...other things."

"The count said there were others. How many?"

"You'll see."

The lift shuddered to a stop, and they stepped into another corridor, but before they could progress, the ground rocked and a muffled explosion sounded overhead. All four froze and looked up, and then a siren peeled loudly as the corridor shook again.

Jackson laughed as hope leapt within him. "That sounds interesting. Or is it the count's armillary sphere?"

Stefan rounded on him. "What have you done?"

"I've been locked in a cell! What could I have done?"

Doors flew open along the corridor, and staff in lab coats evacuated. As the sirens continued to peel and panic spread, a couple headed to Stefan's side.

He had no time for them and yelled, "Get back to your work!"

A young man with slicked back, dark hair protested. "But the alarm! It's for an attack! We need to get in the shelter."

Stefan pushed him against the wall. "You'll do no such thing. Finish prepping everyone now!"

The crowd of outraged and panicking staff grew, and the two soldiers drew their weapons and pushed them back, their eyes already changing.

Then another dull boom sounded overhead, and the corridor shook again. The lab staff was spooked, and like a herd of elephants, ran for the lifts. Stefan was overwhelmed, and the soldiers started firing. But instead of being scared, the scientists were furious, and fights broke out as they yelled at the guards.

Jackson didn't wait to see any more. He took advantage of the confusion, pushed through the crowd, and ran into the closest room. He slammed the door shut and took stock. He was in some kind of central station with desks, computers, and observation windows that looked onto a series of open rooms. *Great. Lots of things to destroy.* He needed a weapon. But as Jackson advanced, he saw something far worse.

Lots of people strapped to beds.

Okay, change of plan. Rescue people, and then destroy everything.

Nahum took advantage of the havoc that Zee, Barak, and Estelle were causing on the battlements, and flew down to the courtyard.

The snow whirled in thick pockets, but as he descended, the wind dropped. He pressed himself to the wall of the castle. A few soldiers scurried out of the buildings and ran up outside staircases, but it was otherwise deserted. Nahum took flight again. He moved so quickly, and the sound of the battle was so loud, no one heard him. In seconds, they were dead.

Through the snow he saw a huge, dark shape on the ground. As he swept nearer, he realised it was a helicopter. It was unlikely that anyone would try to escape in it in this weather, but he decided to destroy it anyway. He hurled a grenade inside, and it exploded, showering hot, jagged metal over the courtyard. The blaze illuminated the huge, alchemical wheel a short distance away.

Shocked, Nahum realised it was already in motion. All the circles were realigning, from the large outer ones to the small ones in the centre.

This could not be good.

One by one the circles ground to a halt, and a section of sigils lit up with coppery red light. Beams shot into the air, forming a cone overhead. *No. A shield.*

Nahum blinked in surprise. Was he imagining it? If it was a shield, his brothers and Estelle could be caught in it. *Was it meant to kill them, or lock them inside?*

Or out, of course.

And then a bloodcurdling cry rose from above, and even though the thick snow and distance was hampering his view, he saw some of the soldiers change. Their skin was taking on the coppery red light. *Herne's hairy bollocks. Was this another enhancement?*

Nahum threw a grenade, but it evaporated as it hit the red light. *Shit.* He headed for the closest door. He needed to find the mechanism and shut it off.

Eli was cut, bruised, battered, and his wings were singed.

The battle was raging above them, and the snowstorm was getting worse, but they couldn't even get in the barracks to find a way to help. As he fought furiously, using his wings and every ounce of power and energy he had, he hoped that at least they were helping his brothers on the roof.

But then the soldiers' radios started to buzz with instructions, and a siren obliterated all other sound. Within seconds, most soldiers withdrew, leaving only a handful behind.

Eli squared up to face a huge-shouldered soldier with dead eyes, but an arrow whizzed past Eli's ear and struck his opponent in the forehead. He collapsed to the floor. *Shadow.* Lucien was fighting another soldier, but he was struggling. Lucien's skin may be metallic, but his fighting skills weren't as advanced. Eli was about to help him when another arrow killed that soldier, too.

Within seconds, all of their remaining opponents lay dead, and as Gabe, Eli and Lucien gathered together, Shadow dropped from a branch with lithesome grace and joined them.

She pulled twigs from her hair and grimaced. "Sorry. A fallen tree slowed me down."

"But you returned with a vengeance," Gabe pointed out. "And nearly burned the barracks down, too!"

"Don't blame me! JD's grenade had more of an impact than I expected!" She stared at the burning guard tower, a mixture of pride and regret on her face. "Remind me to get some more of those."

While Eli was relieved to see Shadow, his attention was on Lucien. He was taking deep breaths and seemed to be having trouble calming himself down. His skin and eyes still had a metallic glint. "Lucien!" Eli tried to keep his voice calm. "You're doing great. How are you feeling?"

"Uptight. I always struggle to bring myself back." He held his hands in front of him. "I can't switch it off."

"You don't need to right now, as long as you're in control. Are you?"

Lucien took another shaky breath. "Yes." He met Eli's eyes, and his normal eye colour returned. "Yes, I'm fine," he repeated. "I'm not as good as you guys. I can't keep up. But that was weird when I just...let go."

"You're doing great," Eli reassured him. "When all this is done, you should stay with us for a couple of weeks. A bit of sparring and training will help you in the future. But don't forget to use JD's weapon!" It was a reminder to himself, too. Using his sword was comfortable, but JD's weapons would give them another edge.

Gabe studied Lucien for a moment in silence, and then, seemingly satisfied, marched to the barracks' door and flung it open. "You'll do for now, Lucien. Don't beat yourself up. Stay close to us, and we'll help. Let's see where the others went."

They progressed through offices, a huge lounge area with sofas, chairs, a TV, and pool tables, all shockingly pedestrian. But then again, when they weren't enhanced soldiers, they still needed to be kept occupied. After that were some dormitories.

"So far, so boring," Eli concluded, throwing open doors to bathrooms and storerooms. However, a huge steel door at the end of a short corridor beckoned, and he hurried toward it. It was sealed shut, and a type of electronic keypad was next to it, but there were no numbers or letters. "Down here!" he yelled over his shoulder.

Gabe and the others hurried towards him.

Eli pointed to the sensor. "That looked hand-sized to me. It must be activated by a handprint."

"Or maybe," Shadow suggested, "a signal from an enhanced soldier. You know, something alchemically weird. We could grab a dead soldier and find out."

"Or," Lucien said, pointedly, "why don't I try?"

He placed his hand on the black screen and it immediately lit up with a red light. He kept it there, focussing his intention, and his skin began to shimmer as he accessed his enhancements. The screen blinked between red and green and then settled on green. The door clicked open.

Gabe placed his shoulder to it and gripped his sword. "Well done. Let's be careful."

Shadow squared up with her bow, and Gabe threw the door wide, leaping inside.

The room beyond was lined with racks that probably once contained weapons. Now they were virtually empty. At the far end was another door. This one was wide open, and a corridor stretched beyond it.

While Shadow and Lucien examined the remaining weapons, Gabe and Eli checked the entrance to the corridor. The blinking lights of a lift beckoned them, and next to it was a doorway leading to stairs.

Eli was eager to move on and help his brothers. "Looks good. I suggest we take the stairs. The way this place is exploding, I do not wish to get stuck. However, maybe we should check how many levels there are." He pressed the button to call the lift.

Gabe nodded, yelling over his shoulder. "You two, let's move!"

Gabe's expression looked strained, which worried Eli. "How are you coping with Belial's baggage?"

"I'm okay. He's getting rather insistent. Especially when I'm fighting, but I can handle it. Can you feel him?"

"A little. The other two seem unaffected so far. Despite everyone's objections, I'm still glad we brought them with us."

Gabe lowered his voice, locking eyes with Eli. "I'm relying on you to keep me in check if it goes wrong later, okay?"

"Of course." The lift dinged and the door opened, and Eli checked the buttons. "There are only three floors marked. *Lab*, *Cells*, and *Ground Floor*. I guess we start with the Lab."

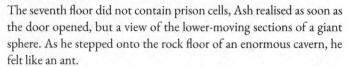

The seventh floor did not contain prison cells, Ash realised as soon as the door opened, but a view of the lower-moving sections of a giant sphere. As he stepped onto the rock floor of an enormous cavern, he felt like an ant.

As usual, when thrown into a situation he didn't anticipate, he swore in Greek. "Is this what I think it is?"

"If you think it's a giant armillary sphere, then you'd be right," JD said, advancing into the cave. "It's magnificent."

"It's freaky as hell!" Harlan complained. "What is it for?"

"Capturing the power of the universe on a massive scale." JD was transfixed, but to be fair, they all were. The biggest band of the sphere rotated above their heads, the others turning within it. It was mesmerising.

Niel gripped his axe as if he was about to start smashing things. "At least we know what's causing the noise."

Harlan looked up, head craning back. "But I can't see an engine."

Caspian gave a dry laugh. "That's because there isn't one. It's self-propelled. Can't you feel the magic? This is really something else."

Ash felt giddy and overwhelmed, but as he overcame his shock, he focussed on the details. Sigils and signs were not only etched on the bands, but on the wall and the floor, and high above him appeared to be a huge, metal disc accessed by walkways. "Up there. What's that?"

"Screw the lift," Niel announced. "Let's fly."

"Take me!" JD commanded.

"Sure, but don't struggle, or I'll drop you. Ash?" Niel cocked an eyebrow. "You up for it?"

Ash wanted nothing more than to fly, but he shook his head, terrified he might find that he couldn't. "I'll take the lift, but go ahead, I'll explore down here first. You can all go," he said to Harlan and Caspian. "I'll follow."

"I'd rather not," Caspian said, eyes narrowing with concern. "We shouldn't split up. But JD, is this the source of the count's power? Do we need to destroy this? Because that's a big ask that I don't even know how to answer."

"Destroy *this*?" JD looked outraged. "The thought is abhorrent."

"JD," Ash said, recognising the feral light of the fanatic in his eyes, "if this is what drives everything, then we have to!"

"I must assess it first!" JD's face flushed, and he clenched his fists. He was building up to one of his familiar rants.

Niel virtually picked him up by the scruff of his neck. "Let's go check it out, JD, and then we'll decide. And just to remind you, this is a group vote, so don't get ahead of yourself, or I might drop you from a great height."

Estelle had been so focussed on attacking Black Cronos, she hadn't realised she was freezing.

Although Barak's heat served to insulate her, the driving snow and wind was taking its toll, and she hadn't bothered to cast a spell to keep herself warm, preferring to focus her magic on the battle. She assessed the damage below.

Areas of the battlements were in flames, particularly some of the guard towers, but more and more men were arriving on the battlements to take control of the huge weapons. The good news was that the blizzard hid their position. The bad news was that it also hid the huge arrows and blasts of power emitted by the unusual guns. And she knew that Barak was itching to fight. So far he'd ferried her around, but he needed to do more than that. She was also becoming increasingly aware of Belial's jewellery in Barak's pocket, despite the fact that she'd cast a protection spell on it.

A strange glow below caught her attention. "Barak! Is the main castle on fire? What's that?" However, before he could answer, she felt the power it exuded. "Shit! It's a spell of some sort."

"It's coming from the wheel of correspondences! It's melting the snow—or am I seeing things?"

Estelle tried to sort through what it might be, separating the feel of the elements and magic within it. "There's air and fire, but there's also a lot I don't understand. He's harnessing planetary energies."

Barak flew wider to avoid it, but it advanced quickly, spreading outward like an umbrella. "It looks like a shield. I have a feeling if I get caught in it, we'll burn."

"And if we stay out of it, we'll be trapped outside for good."

"Inside it is, then. I hope Zee and Nahum have spotted it."

While Barak swept around and under it, Estelle scoured below for sign of the others. "I see Zee flying in from the north. I can't see Nahum at all, but the helicopter is on fire. Oh shit, and the soldiers are changing again! They're taking power from the wheel!" Despite all the havoc they'd achieved and the soldiers they'd killed, they were failing. The soldiers kept coming, and their power kept adapting.

"What say we dodge the fight up here completely and head for the castle?" Barak asked.

"I'll blast out a window."

As the coppery light bloomed above them, encompassing the battlements, Barak honed in on a window on the second floor. Estelle shattered it. Unfortunately, the blast drew the attention of their attackers, and with the narrowest of margins, Barak swept through the gap and skidded into a stately room beyond. They both rolled across the floor, landing in a tumble of limbs and wings.

"Keep running!" he yelled as arrows flew in through the opening.

Estelle rolled on her back and threw up a protective shield. Arrows thudded against it and fell to the floor. Barak hauled her to her feet, and they ran out of their attackers' view. Seconds later, Zee arrived, landing with a great deal more grace than they had, and ran to join them.

Barak gripped his shoulders, checking him over for injuries. "Brother! Are you okay?"

"Slightly singed, soaking wet, and covered in bruises and cuts after a few close calls, but I'll survive. You two look bedraggled."

"I feel it!" Estelle patted her head, and realised her hair was plastered to her scalp. Collecting her wits, she cast a spell to dry them all off, and delicious warmth oozed through her. "That's better." She took a deep breath and looked around the room. After the chaos of the previous hour, it was good to have a breather, no matter how short. Every part of her felt bruised. "So, we're in the belly of the beast, although, it looks very civilised in here. I suppose we should get moving, though. The question is, where to?"

Barak edged closer to the window and looked out. "That weird shield seems to be in place, so we're stuck here now. That means the count is, too, although I doubt anyone will go anywhere in this storm."

Zee nodded. "I agree. He won't abandon his castle, especially with his super-soldiers outnumbering us. We need to stop them from getting in. Block every door we can."

"I can do that," Estelle volunteered. "Simple sealing spells will work well."

"Good. Then, I suggest we head deeper into the castle and disable the wheel's mechanism. At least that means we can escape. Being trapped in here is making me nervous."

"I think Nahum may already be down there, somewhere," Estelle told him. "The helicopter is destroyed, so he must have done that."

"I'd like to find him," Barak said crossing from the window to the door. "It's not safe to be alone. Let's get moving, because we have only seconds before a stream of soldiers are at the door. Once we find Nahum, we go from there."

"Wait!" Zee studied Barak's face. "You're carrying Belial's ring. Is it affecting you in any way?"

Barak glanced at Estelle, then back to Zee. "I feel him, but I'm fine."

Barak normally had an open expression, his beautiful, dark eyes honest and guileless, but they weren't now. Estelle rested her hand on his arm. "Don't lie for my sake. I can add another layer of protection to it."

He considered her words, then shook his head. "No. I'm okay. Being aware of it all the time is not a bad thing. I'm fine, honestly!" He edged the door open and looked down the corridor. "All clear. Time to go."

As he stepped into the hallway, Estelle looked at Zee for reassurance. "Well? Should we worry?"

"You should always worry when Belial is involved."

Shadow gripped her swords, ready to fight. The staircase from the barracks ascended a long way, finally opening onto a small landing with another sealed door. The siren was louder on this level, and it was obvious they were in a more populated area of the castle.

Lucien released the door again, and they entered a series of offices. Even over the sound of the siren, they could hear shouting. Without speaking, they hurried towards the noise. Shadow motioned the others behind her and eased open an office door. On the other side was a corridor where a large group of people were arguing furiously. In the middle of them she saw two Black Cronos soldiers, Stefan Hope-Robbins, and a figure she had hoped never to see again. She ducked back inside and shut the door.

Shadow sighed. "The good news is that we have caused chaos. I think the staff are trying to get out. The bad news is that I saw The Silencer of Souls."

Gabe glared at her. "You couldn't have. I killed her."

"She promised there'd be more. She was right."

Eli was already crossing to another room. "Block the doors and leave them out there. Let's see what we can do in here."

Shadow wedged a chair under the door, and they headed into more offices and lab rooms. "This place is a maze!"

"Unfortunately," Lucien said, "it is horribly like the lab I was imprisoned in, but much bigger." He was pale and breathing heavily. "I hate it! We must destroy it all."

"We will," Gabe reassured him. "Let's keep going."

The next room they emerged into was a long, hospital-style room with beds on either side, all empty. Shadow barely had time to take it in when the far door burst open and a Black Cronos soldier appeared. He raised his weapon and fired, and Shadow dived under the closest bed. Gabe landed heavily several feet away, but Eli and Lucien were trapped in the office.

The soldier shouted for backup and advanced. Under the bed, Shadow watched him approach. Pulling a throwing knife out of her fatigues, she rolled, stood, and released it. The soldier ducked with incredible speed and fired again. She hid beneath another bed as more soldiers arrived.

Herne's horns. Time to try JD's weapons.

Shadow whipped the small, silver device from her pocket and fired wildly over the bed. On the other side of the room, Gabe did the same. But the men kept advancing. Risking a quick look, she counted at least eight. Rather than aim at the soldiers, she fired at the wall above the door. The wall exploded, rubble shooting everywhere, and the frame collapsed. *At least no more would arrive that way.*

She rolled under the bed and fired at their legs. Unfortunately, a soldier had the same idea, and another boom of firepower whizzed past her head. *Great. No shelter under the bed or above it.*

Eli yelled behind them, "Back this way!"

Shadow hated to admit defeat, but she had no choice. She scrambled back to the office while Lucien released a barrage of shots from the doorway to cover them. When they cleared the entrance, they kicked the door shut and dragged a table in front of it.

"I hate being shot at!" Shadow complained. "I'd much rather fight with my sword!"

"I am sure," Gabe said, as they ran into the next room, "that will happen."

"Keep blocking the doors behind us," Eli shouted as he dragged a bed this time behind them, wedging the other door shut. This room was smaller with just two beds in it, but another door provided an exit.

For the next few minutes, they ran from room to room. The sound of shouting and gunfire echoed around them, and it seemed that they weren't the only ones fleeing.

"This place is huge!" Lucien said. "It's like a house of horrors. But where are the people?"

The next door they opened answered that. It was another hospital-like room filled with beds, but this time people were strapped in them. A lone figure at the other end was desperately trying to get someone up.

Jackson.

He looked up, alarmed, and then relief swept across his face. "Shadow? Gabe!"

But as they ran in, the door at the far end flew open and Stefan entered, The Silencer next to him. He took one look at all of them and shouted, "Kill them all! *Now!* I don't care what the count says!"

Shadow didn't hesitate, throwing a dagger at Stefan. The blade embedded into his chest, and he sank to his knees, hands clutching the knife uselessly.

The Silencer of Souls lunged for Jackson, who was closest, but he leapt over the bed, throwing any object he could at her.

Shadow vaulted over the beds, eager to meet her head-on, sword drawn. This was one fight she would relish.

Twenty-Nine

N iel landed on the giant metallic circle positioned in the centre of the armillary sphere, and set JD down.

He looked around, taking in the scale of the enormous structure. It was easier to appreciate it from the dead centre of the construction. Huge, concentric circles radiated out from the central circle, all manner of sigils on them, just like JD's. The metal bands were also engraved, and glowed with different coloured lights. Gold, silver, blues... It was beautiful, and they emitted an unusual energy that made his skin tingle.

"JD, what is it doing?"

JD paced across the floor, scowling. "Right now, it's maintaining a balance. It's ready for the solstice."

"How do you know?"

"From the signs. I think if we stood here long enough, we'd see it move, but it's so slight as to be almost imperceptible."

"Like a clock?"

"More than that, but essentially yes." JD stood in the centre circle, hands on his hips as his gaze swept the cavern. "This is definitely what he needs to change his soldiers. In fact, look!" He marched over to indentations set into the wheel. "Human-shaped, with hooks for restraints."

"To tie people in?"

"I would assume so. If you're going to change the resonance of a human, you would have to use something large enough to do it. This would be it. God's pox. It's brilliant." He looked up, gaze sharpening, and pointed to a set of steps leading from a platform above. "And that's how they get down here."

"It's horrific. Are we in any danger just standing here?"

"No. Not yet, anyway."

"As much as I know you want to admire this, we have to break it! Where is the mechanism to make it work?"

"I told you!" JD threw his hands up. "It doesn't need one!"

"But something makes the discs move. If you want to change someone, you must align it, right?"

"Something doesn't add up. I don't understand how..." He trailed off.

Niel flew to investigate the area the steps descended from, and found that it led to the lift. Right above him, another level up, was the lift again. It opened onto a maintenance platform that ran around the entire cavern. That made sense. He'd passed one below. This contraption would need maintaining, no matter how it worked.

Next, Niel flew to the top of the sphere, examining how the bands were connected. In the end, it didn't matter how it worked; they just had to break it. But that was easier said than done when it was so huge. They could lay grenades where the bands met, and also on the alchemical wheel. That would blow the whole lot up.

But where would the count and all his lab staff be while all this was going on? Surely, they would have to watch from somewhere...

And then he saw it. A large, glass viewing pane set high in the cavern wall, directly opposite the lift shaft. It had been hard to see at first because the room behind it was in darkness. He hovered outside it, seeing blinking lights and a panel inside. They were some kind of controls, despite what JD believed. Niel studied the glass. They could probably shatter it.

JD was pacing the circle, but Niel ignored him and flew down to Ash, Harlan, and Caspian. "I've found something. Some kind of control room, up there." He jerked his head up. "I think we should destroy it."

"What does JD say?" Harlan asked.

"He's pacing like a crazy man."

"He *is* a crazy man!"

"Have you found anything down here?"

Ash shook his head. "No. This is it. Just the fixing for the sphere."

"I could use magic to destroy the housing," Caspian suggested. "Or just blast it?"

JD shouted from above. "No! Touch nothing!"

Niel rolled his eyes. "Let me see what he wants. Why don't you come join us?" Niel flew while the others used the lift and found JD pacing again. "You have good hearing."

"Your voices carry! We can't destroy it."

"Why not?"

"Because the power of the universe that this whole thing draws on is too great! The spheres aren't just any metal! They are enhanced metals, forged using these very processes. Likely made using the wheel Barak saw in the courtyard. They are all protected by the very power that they carry."

"I bet I could destroy it using Belial's jewellery. It's throbbing in my pocket. I think this place is making it worse."

JD's eyes narrowed. "I feel it too, but using it here would be a mistake. Best not."

Niel was tempted to argue, but decided against it. Mixing angelic power with all of this could kill them all. "Okay, but we must stop it from working! *Forever*!"

"Let me rephrase my last statement. We will destroy it, but we magnify the power contained here to destroy the *whole* place," JD proclaimed.

"You can do that?"

"Of course I can! This is the same as mine, just on a grander scale. And I have a little something that will help." He marched to the central wheel and wedged a huge, clear stone into the middle. "Quartz." He said to Niel's unspoken question. He straightened. "You need to get me in that control room. And then we need to get out of here."

"Well, you can't set anything to happen until I find the rest of the team. They're above us somewhere."

As they spoke, a shudder shook the platform, multiplying Niel's concerns for his brothers. He needed to see what was going on out there.

"Oh no, you don't!" It was like JD had read his mind. "That room you saw. Get me in it!"

"I'll have to blow out the window."

"Why don't you use your precious axe? It seems to be attached to you."

"That's actually a great idea!"

Five minutes later, they were all in the control booth, crunching on shards of glass. Ash was only there because Caspian used witch-flight, and now Niel was even more concerned at Ash's refusal to fly. He wouldn't even try. Niel didn't want to make things worse, so he said nothing.

"I feel like I'm in NASA, about to watch a take-off," Harlan said, sweeping glass off a seat. "This is nuts."

"This is the best seat in the house," JD said, flexing his fingers.

A panel of buttons and switches was arrayed before them, and Niel couldn't make out heads or tails of them, but it seemed JD could.

"This door," Niel instructed everyone, "leads to what looks like a series of cells. Ash, do you want to stay to protect this pair? Me and Caspian will try to find everyone else."

Ash tapped his blade. "No problem. I've got this. Don't forget to use Belial if you need to."

"You know what? You should have it."

"*What*?" Ash stepped back. "No, you need it."

"I have full strength, and a witch at my side. You have an injured shoulder and a wing you don't trust." He dug in his pack and passed Ash the clasp. "Don't hesitate to use it if you need to."

He swept out the door, axe raised.

Nahum found the way to the mechanism beneath the alchemical wheel in the courtyard easily, but he also found several soldiers guarding it.

Nahum raced in, sword raised, fortunate to have the element of surprise on his side. With a few quick thrusts of his blade, the first soldier lay dead, but then it became a lot harder. The passages were tiny, Medieval in design, and certainly not meant to house enormous

Black Cronos soldiers and Nephilim. In addition, despite the freezing cold outside, it was hot underground. Ahead of him, pistons screeched beneath the wheel.

The soldiers down here seemed to be affected by the weird cone of power emitted above. Their eyes flamed in the darkness, and real flames bathed the length of their swords. But Nahum could only think of one thing. *He was going to be a father.* It drove his every thrust of the blade, and with every sickening crunch of bone, it renewed his endeavours. In fact, Nahum moved as if he was still possessed by Belial. Perhaps assuming Belial's strength the other night reminded him of the true power he once possessed.

Stepping over their dead bodies, he raced under the wheel and turned off every crank and switch he could see. The great cogs spread beneath the wheel whined and ground together, their screams shrill against the backdrop of the still-whining siren. When they finally came to a shuddering halt, he heard pounding feet and saw another squad of soldiers racing down the narrow passage.

Nahum kicked the door shut and wedged a block of stone behind it, only realising too late that he'd sealed himself inside. Fortunately, he had grenades.

The circles of stone were mounted on metal rails, but the circle in the centre was fixed in place. The underside of it was scored with marks and cracks, and Nahum shoved the grenade into place, and ran to the far end of the room. The grenade exploded, and white-hot flames shot through the underground space. Nahum dived behind fallen blocks of stone that must have been used for its construction, flattening himself onto the ground.

The flames swept over him and then receded. Cold air rushed in, and with relief, Nahum saw snow. But the rest of the circles cracked and splintered, too. Only the rails were holding them up, and they were buckling badly. Ears ringing, and with stars in his eyes, Nahum dragged himself through the wreckage and into the courtyard, taking to the air just as the wheel collapsed beneath his feet.

But he couldn't stay airborne for long. The explosion had attracted attention, and once again, he was being shot at.

Then he heard yelling. "*Nahum*! Over here."

Barak's booming voice was calling him from below, and Nahum zeroed in. The huge entrance door to the castle was wide open, and Barak stood on the threshold. Nahum dived, wings close to his body, slamming through the gap and into the great hall. The door banged shut behind him, and breathless, he whirled around.

Barak's hands were on his hips. "You after bragging rights? You blew up the helicopter *and* the wheel?"

Estelle and Zee were next to him, laughing as they barricaded the door shut using furniture.

Once he had his breath back, Nahum laughed, too. "Sorry. I'm sure there's still plenty for you to do." He gestured at the half a dozen dead soldiers on the floor. "You've been busy, too."

"We were just coming to find you when we ran into these. The explosion caught our attention."

"And rattled every bone in my body," Zee added.

Nahum was suddenly aware that he was soaking wet and cold, and every part of his fatigues clung to his body. "Why am I soaking wet and you're not?"

"That's down to me." Estelle cast a spell, and a weird shimmer of warmth raced over Nahum until he was dry.

"Neat trick. Thank you." He took some deep breaths, observing the empty corridors and the continuing peel of the siren. "Where is everyone?"

"No idea," Zee said. "Every room is empty. No staff, no residents, no count, and no Stefan."

"And also no Jackson?"

"Nope." Barak pointed down the corridor. "But we found stairs leading down, and a lift. I suggest we get moving."

Jackson scrambled out of the way of Shadow's fight with The Silencer, fearing he would get killed accidentally. Or deliberately by The Silencer, who lunged for him every opportunity she could.

Gabe yelled, "Jackson, can you get to us?"

"Wait!"

He retreated to the far door that Stefan had arrived from and peered through it. So far, the room beyond was empty. With luck, the soldiers were still arguing with the staff. *Or maybe killing them.* Jackson didn't care; they were all monsters.

He wedged the door shut, and ducking and weaving beneath the beds and around equipment, finally reached Gabe. His huge bulk was reassuring. "How did you find me?"

"Sheer bloody luck," Gabe admitted, half an eye on Shadow.

"Do you think you should help her?" Jackson asked, watching the fight, too. They were both moving so quickly, it was all a blur.

"Are you kidding me?" Gabe said, appalled. "She'd kill me! Do you know the layout of this place? We blocked off the way we came, but there are soldiers all over the place, and we could be barricading ourselves in."

"I've barely explored any of this half," Jackson explained. "I came from back there. Is it just you two?"

"No. Eli and Lucien are behind us, defending our rear." Another explosion ripped through the offices, and black smoke streamed towards them. "What the actual—"

"Sorry!" Lucien came running. "Jackson! Good to see you. Gabe, problem! More soldiers. They blew out the door. But we've found more corridors."

"Of course you have! This is a damn rat trap." Gabe shouted at Shadow. "We need to move! Jackson, go with Lucien."

"No."

"What?"

"There are people here that we need to rescue." He gesticulated at the unconscious men and women in the beds.

"Not a chance. We have no way of taking them out of here. Nowhere to look after them."

Jackson appealed to Lucien. "Surely you understand. We have to get them out of here!"

"It's impossible, Jackson. We'll have enough trouble getting ourselves out."

"But if Barak and Estelle had left you, you'd be one of them now!"

"And perhaps I wouldn't know any better. I certainly wouldn't have had those agonising months."

Jackson stared at him in shock, struggling to find his voice, but Lucien didn't even blink. "You regret surviving?"

"Of course not! I'm glad to be here, stopping them. I would not wish anyone to go through what I have, but you could barely keep me safe, or everyone around me." Lucien gripped Jackson's arms. "Admit it! I terrified you. I probably still do! Where would you put them?"

Jackson closed his eyes, his hands over his face. Lucien was right. They couldn't deal with it. *But all these people...* He looked around at the unconscious men and women, some of them whimpering in their sleep. "We'll be monsters if we leave them."

"*They* are the monsters." Lucien marched over to the closest one, and pulled the sheets back. "Look at all their tattoos. They have far more than me! Barak and Estelle found me early on! *C'est impossible*! You know this."

Jackson's energy ebbed as the truth of the matter hit him. Lucien and Gabe were right. There were too many of them, and there was nothing they could do. Lucien pushed him towards the door as a sickening crunch announced that Shadow had killed The Silencer.

Shadow withdrew her blade, and the woman slid to the floor, blood pooling around her.

"About time," Gabe said.

"I didn't have the advantage of flight and gravity on my side," she replied archly.

They fled from the room and thickening black smoke, only to be met with a wave of soldiers charging on the other side. A door beckoned, but there was no way they would reach it before the soldiers were on them. Eli squared up to face the first one, and his blade sliced clean through his attacker's breast plate, piercing his chest.

Jackson gasped. "You cut through armour and their metallic skin?"

"We evened the playing field," Gabe shouted, pushing him behind them. "A witch called El enhanced our blades with magic."

Jackson retreated while the others fought, desperately looking for a weapon. He ran back to The Silencer and grabbed her fallen blade, then looked up in horror as the door was forced open at the far end. The soldiers had arrived from the other direction.

He staggered backwards, kicking the door shut and wedging it with a chair, before racing back to the team. "There are more coming."

There was only one way out of the room. The smell of smoke was strong, and he suspected that if sprinklers didn't kick in quickly, they would suffocate before soldiers could kill them. *Brilliant*. Gabe, Shadow, Eli, and Lucien were all battling furiously, and the door was being battered down on the other side.

"Gabe!" Eli shouted as he fought, "this could be the moment!"

"Not yet!"

"This is not the time to get cold feet!"

"I know!"

Jackson had no idea what they were talking about, but knew he was useless fighting with just a knife. "Has anyone got a gun?"

Shadow rolled and ducked, then threw a silvery object at him. "One of JDs. Don't point it at us!"

Jackson was familiar with JD's experiments. They had a couple of these weapons at The Retreat. He leapt on top of an empty bed and started firing at the soldiers. The door he'd blocked was kicked in and the others arrived. He had a good aim and hit the first couple before needing to retreat. There was no way they could fight all of these. It was madness.

And then a bloodcurdling cry rang out from the other room.

Barak stepped out of the lift into a full-pitched fight. No one saw them coming.

Barak knew they weren't all soldiers, but he didn't care, and neither did his companions. They dispatched the soldiers first, and as the staff ran, they killed them, too. They hunted through the rooms, chasing down anyone they found, following the sounds of battle and screams.

Then he heard Gabe's shout.

Barak yelled to his companions. "This way!"

They came upon a group of soldiers who were focussed on another room completely. Through the open door beyond them, he saw Gabe and the others, and with a mix of blades and magic, they fought the soldiers to reach their side.

By now Barak's blade was singing. He could feel it. It resonated up his arm and through his body. He wasn't wearing Belial's jewellery, but he could feel its effects anyway. Any empathy he might have felt vanished, and he viewed Black Cronos as dispassionately as they viewed him. Even the men and women on the beds. They couldn't afford to leave any of them alive.

He killed each one swiftly as he passed, wishing them peace in the afterlife. Anyone they left behind was a tool for the count. He caught Estelle's tight-lipped expression and tried to speak to her, but she shook her head. "Not now, Barak."

In another few minutes it was over, and they stood in the blood-splattered room, surrounded by the dead.

Gabe looked the same as he felt. Dead-eyed and impassive. Gabe clasped his hand. "You feel him?"

"I feel him."

"Then let's move on."

Barak noticed that everyone seemed to be eyeing them warily, even Shadow, but he didn't stop to consider it. He reached the rear door and looked into another corridor. "Empty. This way."

He marched through it, desperate to feel the slice of sword on bone again. He tried to shake it off. Maybe Zee was right. They shouldn't have brought the damn things. *But without them, would he have fought so well against such soldiers?*

A door burst open down the end of the corridor, and just as Barak was about to race to meet the enemy, Niel stepped out, followed by Caspian. "Woah, brother!"

Barak took a breath. "You found a way in!"

"We found a lot more than that. And so did you, by the look of it." Niel lowered his voice. "You used Belial's jewellery?"

"No."

"You look like you have. So does he." He jerked his head to Gabe. "What's happened?"

Barak shook his head. "A lot of death. A lot of fire. Have you found a way to end this?"

Niel looked warily at all of them, and glancing behind him, Barak suddenly saw what he did. They were all wild-eyed and bloodied, with torn clothes and smoke- blackened skin. Fighting Black Cronos had turned them all into monsters. But there was still more to do.

Niel addressed all of them. "We've found a way to destroy the place, but we need to leave now. Have you found the count?"

Barak shook his head. "There's no sign of him, but Stefan and The Silencer are dead."

"Thanks to me," Shadow piped up.

"Nice job, sister!" Niel congratulated her, "But I hoped we'd find him, too. There's no time now. Follow me."

Gabe pushed Belial's insistent beckoning to the back of his mind and focussed on the sphere. "You think that will blow this place up?"

"I know it will," JD said. "We've already aligned the wheel. I just need to make one more adjustment."

Harlan nodded enthusiastically. "I've seen JD's weapons' system. It's ingenious. He doesn't have a sphere, but it's the same principle."

"So, when you set it off, how long will we have?" Barak asked.

JD shrugged. "Ten minutes at most, although it's hard to be specific. It will need to charge."

"I don't understand. It's not a bomb!"

JD wouldn't meet his eyes—or anyone's, for that matter. He stared instead at the dials on the panel, completely focussed. "I have made a slight alteration. It doesn't matter what, but when it blows, it will be big."

There wasn't time to question him, and besides, Gabe would never understand the details. "How big?"

"Big enough to blow a chunk out of this ridge. Although, I deeply regret having to do it."

"You shouldn't. We found a huge lab upstairs." Gabe tried to shake off what he'd seen. "It all has to go."

"Okay. Then we leave as we came in. Through the cave's entrance. Go ahead. Perhaps Caspian could take me when I'm done?" JD looked at Caspian hopefully.

Caspian nodded. "Of course. I can fly us straight there. The rest of you, carry on. Ash?"

"I'll go with my brothers, thanks, if one could fly me to the lift."

So, Ash still wasn't flying. That was worrying, but no matter. Gabe would talk to him later. And then a horrible little voice whispered that a Nephilim who couldn't fly was useless. *Broken.*

Gabe gritted his teeth, silently telling Belial to get lost. *It was a shoulder injury. That was all.* His meddling was the last thing he needed. Shadow's warm curves would dispel him. He opened his arms to her. "Let's go."

But when they clambered down the ladder into the chamber to wait for JD, they all had a nasty shock.

A dapper man, dressed in a suit and with the eyes of a sociopath, was waiting there with what seemed like a battalion of soldiers. They were lined up in front of their only exit beyond a shallow lake. A row of flaming torches illuminated the space, casting their faces into grim masks.

The count had found them.

He smiled. "I knew I'd find you here. It was logical. And Jackson, of course. Did you think you would escape? You're a fool."

Eli made to move in front of him. Jackson, however, wouldn't let him. "No. You're the fool for thinking that you could keep getting away with this! You can't keep experimenting on people! It's horrific. If we didn't stop you, someone else would. Some other government would find out what you do."

"No one has bothered us so far. Until you, of course. And there are so *few* of you." The count studied them all. "All seven Nephilim, I see. How unfortunate our bombs didn't kill some of you in Aswan. And Harlan, of course. I know *you.* We came so close to capturing you and your friend the other night. And there's the witch, and the fey. And my interrupted latest." His eyes flashed with annoyance. "The soldier you stole from me."

Lucien snarled. "My name is Lucien! I am not a faceless, nameless man! You stole my life."

"I gave you a new one." The count extended his hands. "I will give you *all* one. My lab will survive the odd fire. So will the *château*. It survived the Albigensian Crusade, and it will survive *you*. Fire cleanses, you know. But seven Nephilim, with my advancements...that will certainly be something." He cocked his head. "I don't know how enhancements would affect a witch or a fey, but it will be interesting to find out."

"I will cut your balls off and make you eat them first," Shadow said, already edging towards him. "Not even Herne could contain me."

That wasn't strictly true, but it sounded good. Gabe knew that in this light, she could disappear easily. But there were so many men. *Too many.* And not enough time. Belial's torc beckoned.

He whispered to Niel. "The exit is behind him, I presume?"

"The only way. He must have got down here using the passage over there." He nodded to the waterfall. "I knew I should have checked it!"

"Then we use what we have. Belial."

"I gave mine to Ash."

Gabe eyed his injured brother, wondering if he'd be prepared to use it, when Estelle laughed, drawing everyone's attention as she challenged the count. "You certainly can't contain *me*! Do you really understand my power?" She raised her hands. With an enormous roar, the lake of water rose in front of them, and Estelle shouted a spell that made Gabe's skin tingle. She brought her hands down, and the water crashed around the soldiers, sweeping some out of the door screaming, while others smashed into the cavern walls, carrying their dowsed torches with them.

Simultaneously, Caspian arrived in a whirl of air, depositing JD on the floor, and instantly summed up the situation. He whipped up the remaining water, sending it spinning across the floor, sweeping up soldiers and flinging them aside.

JD yelled, "What are you all waiting for? Run!"

Gabe sprinted for the exit, leaping over fallen bodies and making sure his team was ahead of him. The count miraculously was still standing, and weirdly still looking cocky. *He wouldn't be soon.* Gabe knew the explosion would kill him, but a niggling part of him needed to make sure he was truly dead. Although a group of soldiers were struggling to their feet to protect the count, Gabe aimed straight for him.

But then the count saw JD. He pointed at him, his hand shaking. "*You* are here! What have you done?"

JD stopped running and faced him, lifting his chin defiantly. "I recalibrated your machine."

"You can't possibly understand it."

"You always were a fool, Germain. You think because you're immortal that you're better than everyone. Well, you're not better than I am. I have drawn on the coming solstice. I beckoned darkness, and it answered. Mars and Jupiter are bringing their war horses. Capricorn and Sagittarius will also join the fight. And I placed a certain gemstone right in the centre of your grid."

Gabe wouldn't let him elaborate. The surviving soldiers were recovering their senses and moving to block their exit. A powerful whirlwind that blasted out from behind him showed Caspian was still there. In the ensuing confusion, he pushed JD through the exit and into the narrow tunnel, sorely tempted to pick him up and fling him across his shoulders.

He pushed Caspian ahead, too. "Take JD to the house!"

"Don't wait long, Gabe!" Caspian grabbed JD, and they vanished.

Gabe pounded down the tunnel to the entrance, finding Ash and Shadow waiting on the lip of the cave. Beyond it, the blizzard still raged, the landscape swallowed by snow and ice. "That's it! We're all out. Go!"

Shadow hesitated. "Ash can't fly."

"*What*?" Gabe stared at him. "Of course you can."

"I'm not so sure."

"Have you tried?"

"No. It feels wrong."

Gabe was dumbfounded, and again, Belial's voice sneered. *Broken.*

"I hear him, too," Ash said, his eyes filled with sadness. "He's right. Take Shadow. Go!"

"I'll take both of you."

"Yes." Shadow agreed. "He can. He's strong enough."

"Not tonight. He won't be quick enough or get high enough. Not in these conditions. You go."

Rage and fear filled Gabe. "Why didn't you go with the others?"

"Barak took Estelle, Niel took Harlan, Eli took Jackson, Nahum took Lucien, and Zee had already gone."

"You didn't tell them?" Gabe grabbed Ash and lifted him up by his breastplate. "I could kill you myself!"

"I know you're angry, but this is for the best."

"Gabe! Take him! I can scramble down," Shadow argued. "I'm like a goat!"

"You won't get clear in time!" Gabe pointed out, furious at the whole situation. He knew he must take both of them. He had to try. He didn't need to go far. "Shadow, shelter under my wings, on my back."

Before Ash could protest, he pulled him tight, and as Shadow grabbed him, he leapt into the storm, just as an almighty roar ripped through the ridge.

For a long moment, Ash thought that Gabe could make it, the blast helping to carry him higher and higher.

But then the snow and wind pummelled them, and Gabe plummeted.

Although he furiously beat his wings, carrying both of them in these conditions was too hard, just as Ash had known. And it was impossible to see where to land.

Ash fought free so that Gabe could save himself and Shadow, and then was suddenly tumbling, end over end, in a maelstrom of snow.

Another explosion sent out a second shockwave, picking Ash up and carrying him like a feather on the wind. Stones rocketed around him like cannon balls. As he found himself falling, thinking on his life and all he still wanted to do, he heard Belial's cackle.

Broken. Useless.

Instinctively, he ripped his armour from his body, extending his wings.

But he was right all along. Only one worked. He plummeted toward the ground, wheeling like a sycamore seed caught on the breeze.

Then that laugh rippled through his mind again.

Ash remembered the clasp. He felt in his pocket and gripped it, and suddenly Belial's power flooded through him.

Light bled from every pore of his skin, and suddenly the wing he thought was gone forever unfurled. He finally stopped tumbling, and the wild wind carried him higher and higher.

Through the hail and snow, the castle was a beacon of light. Flames blazed from it, and the ridge appeared to have been cleaved in two. The wind threatened to drive him onto it, but he steadied himself, and like a shooting star, headed for the chalet.

When he arrived there, he saw his friends gathered below, staring up at him. He was still incandescent. The light of the Fallen Angel leaked from him. He wanted to flee, but he didn't have the strength to. Instead, he wanted to sleep forever.

He lowered himself to the ground, wings outstretched, and let Belial's clasp fall away from him. But there was more than that. As the light faded, he realised his usual honey brown wings had changed, and were now as golden as his eyes.

Thirty

Harlan had hoped they would be jubilant after defeating Black Cronos, and yet the mood in the chalet was subdued.

He'd just indulged in a steaming hot shower, hoping the atmosphere would have settled by the time he emerged. It hadn't. He rubbed his hair with the towel as he stood on the threshold of the living room, watching the various groups who didn't see him in the doorway.

Ash leaned on the sill of the picture window that looked out on the valley below. It was still lost in the blizzard that seemed like it would last all night. Eli was with him, both talking quietly. Ash's magnificent golden wings had been folded away, but the memory of them was burned into Harlan's mind. As was his descent in the storm, to be honest.

He was used to the Nephilim and their amazing wings, but seeing Ash lit up like a Christmas angel was something else. But at least he could fly again. Gabe had told them what had happened when they escaped, convinced that he had killed his own brother, and he almost cried when Ash returned. He'd hugged him fiercely and Harlan walked away, feeling like he was intruding.

However, as the joy of beating Black Cronos and Ash's survival leaked away, the memory of Belial lurked. Niel had resorted to what he normally did when faced with a catastrophe. He cooked. Caspian was helping him. A clatter of pans, voices, and music leaked from the kitchen while they worked. The others were all gathered in the living room, taking a grim inventory of their injuries, relaxing, or cleaning their weapons. The room reeked of oil. The only one still celebrating was JD, who was crowing like a cockerel and pacing the room with nervous energy.

Harlan crossed the space to pour himself a bourbon, trying to decide how to lighten the mood, when JD did it for him.

He stood, hands on his hips in the middle of the room, glaring at all of them. "I will not tolerate you all brooding on the night we should be celebrating! We have destroyed the count! The immortal *Comte de St Germain*, who has plagued civilization for centuries with his deadly whims! I won't even presume to take credit." He shrugged. "I mean, I might have masterfully reconfigured his wheel, but you all helped! You killed soldiers, blew up guard towers, destroyed labs. Stopped the count from escaping—"

"I think the storm stopped the count from escaping," Barak pointed out from his armchair by the fire. "We just managed to kill a whole lot of people that might have been able to escape and recover. I must admit, the lab haunts me."

"No!" Lucien leapt to his feet. "You did the right thing. I know it! *You* know it. Look at the months I have struggled to survive. There were times today when I still wasn't sure where I ended and these enhancements began. It will be a struggle for months, if not all my life." His hands were clenched as he faced them all and his raised voice brought Niel and Caspian to the door. He took a deep breath, clearly forcing himself to calm down, and then turned to Barak and Estelle, who sat cross-legged on the rug in front of the fire. "I will forever be grateful to you for rescuing me, and to JD and Jackson for helping me in The Retreat. But I am sincere when I say I would not wish this on anyone. The people lying in those beds were too far gone. I could tell. You have nothing to regret." He sat down, collapsing in the chair as if the final bit of his energy had vanished.

"Well," Harlan said, "as much as I hate to agree with JD, he's right. We survived. We took out the count, and destroyed his base. There might be other bases, smaller ones, but we can root them out. Without him at the helm, we can all breathe easy. And as for Belial, he saved Ash's life!"

"Not willingly, I'm sure," Ash said, a rueful smile on his face. He shifted to look at the room properly, and his shoulders that had seemed so tight earlier finally appeared to drop.

"Even better, right?" Eli said to Harlan. "That's exactly what I said. But the thing is, Harlan, and you won't get this, I know, but he is one of the strongest of the Fallen. He is the Angel of Destruction, delivering chaos and madness. We'd be fools to ignore his power."

"But you're not ignoring it! You know exactly what you're doing," Harlan protested. "You used it to save yourselves. You didn't advance *his* power, you advanced your own." Harlan knew the Nephilim had a thing about the Fallen and their fathers. It haunted them. Drove them. He downed a slug of bourbon, grateful that someone in this *château* had thought to stock some. "You know, we all have family issues. My father was an uptight son of a bitch who wanted me to go to law school, not become Indiana Jones. He's never forgiven me. It's sad, but I've gotten used to it. Also, can I remind you all, we saved Jackson!" He raised his glass. "My friend, good to have you back. I was very worried."

"I was very worried for myself." Jackson sighed, and Harlan sat next to him on the sofa. "Talking of family, I found out what happened to my grandfather. They caught him, like James Arbuthnot, and turned him in to one of them. I found out he had children, too." Jackson paused, and it seemed the whole room waited. "I met my uncle. I guess he died in the fight. At least I hope he did."

"Holy shit." Harlan felt terrible. "I'm so sorry."

Jackson shrugged. "At least I know the truth. My grandfather died years ago, so I'm glad of that. I still don't understand how the count reeled people in. A kind of indoctrination, I guess."

JD leaned over and patted his arm in an uncharacteristic show of affection and empathy. "The process would have changed brain patterns, I'm pretty sure of that, especially now that I've seen the scale of his set-up. Your grandfather would have changed, and probably didn't even know it."

"I hope you're right. I really do." Jackson stared into the fire, lost in his thoughts.

"So, dare I ask," Harlan ventured, "where Belial's jewellery is now?"

"Locked back in the box and spelled with protection," Gabe said. He was playing with Shadow's hair as she sat on the floor between Gabe's legs, leaning into him, her eyes half closed. They seemed intimate, close, as if they were the only two in the room, but Harlan knew both were following the conversation closely. Especially Gabe. He watched and listened to everything. Most notably, Ash. "And they'll stay locked away until we are able to follow it up properly."

"And what about you, JD?" Harlan shifted to look at him. "What will you do about the Emerald Tablet?"

"Continue to test the discs, of course. I refuse to rush it." His eyes sharpened with the prospect. "After all this time, patience is the key. Besides, I think I need a break to enjoy Christmas. We all do."

Niel cheered from the kitchen where he'd returned to cook. "When we get home, I'll make eggnog! Hey Caspian, how many eggs have we got? I could make some now!"

This seemed a safer topic, and soon, everyone was chatting about their plans. Harlan took advantage of the renewed chatter to sit next to Nahum and Zee. They were seated at the huge dining table, polishing their blades with a cloth. The metal gleamed, and Nahum put his aside and picked up another from the pile stacked next to it.

"You two are quiet," Harlan observed.

"Just processing everything," Zee said. "Cleaning weapons is a mindless activity that soothes me. I'm enjoying the chat, too. Although, I'll be glad to get home."

"Yeah, me too," Nahum agreed. He glanced at Harlan, quickly focussing on cleaning again. "Will you spend Christmas with Olivia?" He asked it casually enough, but Harlan knew the truth of it all now, and he didn't know what to think. Olivia was pregnant. With Nahum's child. And at present, they were the only two people in the room who knew.

"Yeah, I guess so. Might even catch up with Maggie. She texted me earlier after she'd seen Olivia." Nahum stared at him. "Yeah, seems we have lots to discuss. I'll see if Jackson wants to join us, too. We'll unwind, let off some steam, swap stories. All the fun stuff."

Harlan liked Nahum, but right now he was angry with him, and he found his protective instincts kicking in. It was weird. It was something he needed to process.

Before Nahum could respond, Niel yelled, "Clear the table, food's up, and someone grab some plates!"

Zee gathered the weapons and moved them aside, shouting, "I'm coming."

Harlan took advantage of the moment and leaned closer to Nahum. "You need to tell them your daddy news. *Now!*"

"With everyone here? I wanted to tell my brothers alone first."

"Shadow and Estelle will know straight after. Estelle will tell Caspian, and I'll tell Jackson. And well, it's JD. He's a crazy, mad alchemist. He might be able to help!"

Nahum's eyes widened with surprise. "With a baby?"

Harlan leaned in. "I need to talk about this, and so do you! It's good news, right?"

Nahum sagged in his chair. "Yes, but I'm not ready!"

"Well, you better get ready, because it's happening!"

Nahum sighed and closed his eyes.

"Nahum!"

"Yes, all right!" He slammed the blade and oil onto the side counter, and after a frenzied few minutes of table setting and dishes being brought out, they all finally settled around the huge table.

Nahum cleared his throat and Harlan sat back to watch.

This was going to be fun.

After the meal, Estelle found Caspian out on the sheltered veranda that ran the length of the house. He was sitting on a cane chair, wrapped in a blanket and watching the snow, while cradling a whiskey.

"Here you are! I've been looking for you." She sat next to him and pulled her own blanket around her shoulders. "Mind if join you?"

The light from the room that overlooked the veranda illuminated his beaming smile. His eyes were warm, and a sheen of dampness was on his dark hair. "Of course not. I've been reflecting on the night, and this stunning view."

"There is no view. It's all snow."

"But it's still beautiful. We don't get snow like this very often in Cornwall, and we certainly don't get a mountain backdrop."

"Or Cathar castles scattered on the ridges."

"Thanks for asking me to help you. I don't like to crowd you...you know, with the Nephilim and Barak. It's important to you." He raised his glass. "It works for you. I've never seen you happier."

Estelle knew she could be prickly, but she'd been trying very hard lately not to be, and she loved her new lease of life with Barak and his brothers. Even Shadow. "Thank you." She chinked his glass with her own. "I've needed the space, to be honest. It's given me time to reflect on my life and direction."

"If you don't mind me asking, Barak seemed a little wild-eyed earlier. Was that Belial?"

That was an understatement. "Yes. I didn't like it. I haven't discussed it with him yet, but I will."

"Don't be too hard on him. I'm sure he's struggling with it, too."

"Perhaps. He seems to have put it aside for now. I'll make sure to keep that box the jewellery is kept in well protected." She turned the conversation to lighter things. "I also wanted to thank you for attempting to reinvigorate our coven. I think it might be working."

He shuffled in his chair to look at her. "I agree. Our uncle and cousins seem happier. I feel more positive. Less like I'm relying on the White Haven Coven for everything."

"Don't tell me you're abandoning them?"

"Of course not! They're still my friends."

"Good, because you need them, like I need this bunch of reprobates!" She laughed. "What a night. You really helped back there."

"I don't actually feel like I did that much in the end, locked down in the engine house of the castle. You were in the thick of it on the battlements."

"Of course you helped. You ferried JD around, and waited with him to do his thing—whatever that was. And of course, attacked the soldiers, at the end. Without that we might have been caught in the blast."

"But did you notice that the count wasn't affected by our magic? He was like the unmovable eye in the heart of the storm. My wind whipped around him, and the waves crashed over him, and yet he just stood there."

"Of course I noticed, but what does it mean?" She voiced what had been worrying her all evening. "Do you think he could have survived the blast?"

"It obliterated half the ridge!" Caspian sighed and stared at the swirling snow. "However, it makes you wonder. Perhaps he's just the master of illusion, too."

"Or the universe aligns for him. He is a brilliantly evil alchemist."

"If he has survived, it will take him lifetimes to rebuild, but I think he's dead. We're witches, and that blast would have killed us." He squeezed her hand. "He's gone. The count likes to get in people's heads. Don't let him in yours." His eyes suddenly gleamed with humour, "Why don't you tell me how it feels to be an aunt? Perhaps it might have given you ideas!"

Estelle laughed, throwing her head back at the outrageous suggestion. "You are hilarious, Caspian Faversham! *Children*. You must be joking me..."

With both of them giggling like schoolchildren, the subject turned to much lighter matters.

Shadow laid her head on Gabe's broad chest, listening to the steady beat of his heart, her head rising and falling with each breath.

"I know you're not asleep, Gabe Malouf. Are you all right?"

"I'm going to be an uncle."

She laughed. "And I'll be an aunt! I'll be great. I can teach the baby lots of skills. But I do not do nappy changing. I like Olivia." She tapped his chest with her fingers. "I approve."

Gabe groaned. "But you know our history—"

She cut him off. "Yes. I know it and I am very sorry for your tragic losses, but this is thousands of years later. Everything might change."

"Curses don't."

"The power of angels has waned. You don't know."

"You're trying to cheer me up, I know. I'm not convinced."

"Then we will find a way." Shadow slid off his chest, nestling in his arm instead.

"What's wrong with you? You hate kids."

"I hate other people's kids. This will be Nahum's. And he's excited. You must be able to see that."

"He's terrified."

"Underneath all of that, he's excited. So is Harlan. So are your brothers."

"Perhaps Olivia should move in."

"Don't be an idiot! She has her own life and a job that she loves. She will want to keep her independence. It's important to her."

"I know."

"And *I* know that your protective instincts are strong. This is your brother's matter to handle, Gabe. Don't crowd him."

He nuzzled her ear. "When did you get so wise?"

"I've always been wise. You just get distracted by my curves and swaying hips."

"Speaking of which..."

He kissed her deeply, and she leaned into him and let the night's events fall away.

Nahum stared at his phone, wondering whether he should call Olivia, the silence of his bedroom pressing in on him.

He wanted to see how she was feeling, and also reassure her that he had survived and would fulfil his promise to help her in any way he could, and yet...he didn't want to be overbearing. Intrusive.

At least the news of his impending fatherhood had been well received. More than that, actually. There had been whoops of delight around the table, and Niel had found champagne to make toasts. Even Shadow and Estelle, those two staunchly independent women, had been pleased for him. Shadow had immediately offered her coaching skills, which was frankly terrifying.

No one talked about their past issues. Everyone had focussed on the future. If they believed it could happen, then maybe it would turn out well. Refusing to second guess Olivia's response further, he called her, heart beating frantically like he was a teenager again.

She answered quickly. "Nahum! Are you all right?"

"I am. I survived. It felt as if I might not at times, but I did. We all did."

She sighed, her relief palpable, even over the phone. "That's so good. What about Jackson?"

"We found him. In typical James Bond fashion, he's shaken, but not stirred." He laughed. "Does that even make sense?"

"It's strangely apt. I'm so relieved."

"More importantly, are you okay? The baby?"

"It's still a little blob, and we are both fine. No official scans or anything of course until at least six or eight weeks. I've told Maggie. I needed to. I hope you don't mind."

"Of course not. I just told everyone here. Harlan made me. But they have been sworn to secrecy for now. They were very happy. We all drank champagne."

"Maggie is happy, too. She toasted us. I drank water." Olivia laughed. "So, it's official then. They all know. Wow. This is so odd. Is Harlan okay? He looked...shocked. And then he was all protective!"

"Ha!" Nahum recalled his intense stare. "He's fine. He's aiming to keep me on my toes. Make sure I fulfil my duties. I think he'll be the most fearsome uncle of all. But it's all good, yes? No second thoughts?"

"No. I should probably visit you in Cornwall at some point, just to meet all of your brothers. I've only met a few."

"They're eager to meet you. I guess I should meet your family, too, at some point." He rushed on to cover his nerves. "I know you probably have Christmas plans, but what about New Years? We have plenty of room. You wouldn't have to lift a finger."

"I'm barely pregnant. I can do plenty! But yes, that would actually be really nice." He could almost hear her relax, as if she was snuggling under her sheets.

"Are you still with the witches?"

"Yes. They've been amazing, but I'm going home tomorrow to re-evaluate my space. I'm excited."

"So am I." Nahum felt his heart swell. *This was unreal. Unexpected.* "I better let you sleep. I need to, as well. I'm shattered. I'll be in touch, okay?"

"Sounds good. I'll keep you up to date, too."

He ended the call and flopped onto his bed, feeling like he'd flown from one end of the Middle East to the other. He flicked the bedside lamp off and stared into the darkness. Everything was changing, again.

But it was a good change. New beginnings. And no doubt, new enemies.

The coming year was going to be a very interesting one, indeed.

Thanks for reading *Immortal Dusk.* Please make an author happy and leave a review here.

This book is a spin-off of my White Haven Witches series. The first book is called *Buried Magic,* and you can buy it here for free!If you have already read this series, book twelve is called *Midwinter Magic,* and it's on pre-order now.

If you enjoyed this book and would like to read more of my stories, please subscribe to my newsletter at tjgreenauthor.com. You will get two free short stories, *Excalibur Rises* and *Jack's Encounter,* and will also receive free character sheets of all the main White Haven witches.

By staying on my mailing list, you'll receive free excerpts of my new books, as well as short stories, news of giveaways, and a chance to join my launch team. I'll also be sharing information about other books in this genre you might enjoy.

Read on for a list of my other books.

Author's Note

T hank you for reading *Immortal Dusk*, the sixth book in the White Haven Hunters series.

As usual, this one was quite the ride. I knew I wanted to move things along with Black Cronos, and that it was time to see the Fallen again. As for Nahum and Olivia... Well, I just knew I had to get them together, I just wasn't sure of the outcome. The future will certainly be interesting!

I'm not sure how many more books will be in this series, but I certainly have a few more storylines to explore, so I'll keep going for now. I love my human characters, so really wanted to draw them together. I also could not resist bringing in the Moonfell witches. I feel another spin-off brewing, but this one may be a little different. I'm thinking on it...

It was a big effort to get this one written in time for my planned release. This has been a busy twelve months, especially the last six months when we bought and moved into our new house. It seems almost unbelievable I actually managed it. I'm planning on a more sedate second half of the year.

If you'd like to read a bit more background on the stories, please head to my website, www.tjgreenauthor.com, where I blog about the books I've read and the research I've done for the series. In fact, there's lots of stuff on there about my other series, Rise of the King, White Haven Witches, and Storm Moon Shifters, as well.

Thanks again to Fiona Jayde Media who keeps producing such fabulous covers, and thanks to Kyla Stein at Missed Period Editing for sorting out my knotty sentences!

Thanks also to my beta readers—Terri, and my mother. Their reassurance as they read each new book always soothes my nerves. Also, thank you to my launch team, who give valuable feedback on typos and are happy to review upon release. It's lovely to hear their enthusiastic responses to my books, as I never know how a new book will be received. I also love hearing from all of my readers, so I welcome you to get in touch.

If you'd like to read more of my writing, please join my mailing list at www.tjgreenauthor.com. You can get a free short story called *Jack's Encounter*, describing how Jack met Fahey—a longer version of the prologue in *Call of the King*—by subscribing to my newsletter. You'll also get a free copy of *Excalibur Rises*, a short story prequel. Additionally, you will receive free character sheets of all of my main characters in the White Haven Witches and White Haven Hunters series—exclusive to my email list!

By staying on my mailing list, you'll receive free excerpts of my new books and updates on new releases, as well as short stories and news of giveaways. I'll also be sharing information about other books in this genre you might enjoy.

I encourage you to follow my Facebook page, T J Green. I post there reasonably frequently. In addition, I have a Facebook group called TJ's Inner Circle. It's a fab little group where I run giveaways and post teasers, so come and join us.

About the
Author

I was born in England, in the Black Country, but moved to New Zealand in 2006. I lived near Wellington with my partner, Jase, and my cats, Sacha and Leia. However, in April 2022 we moved again! Yes, I like making my life complicated... I'm now living in the Algarve in Portugal, and loving the fabulous weather and people. When I'm not busy writing I read lots, indulge in gardening and shopping, and I love yoga.

Confession time! I'm a Star Trek geek—old and new—and love urban fantasy and detective shows. Secret passion—Columbo! My favourite Star Trek film is the *Wrath of Khan*, the original! Other top films—*Predator*, the original, and *Aliens*.

In a previous life I was a singer in a band, and used to do some acting with a theatre company. For more on me, check out a couple of my blog posts. I'm an old grunge queen, so you can read about my love of that on my blog: https://tjgreenauthor.com/about-a-girl-and-what-chris-cornell-means-to-me/. For more random news, read: https://tjgreenauthor.com/read-self-published-blog-tour-things-you-probably-dont-know-about-me/

Why magic and mystery?

I've always loved the weird, the wonderful, and the inexplicable. Favourite stories are those of magic and mystery, set on the edges of the known, particularly tales of folklore, faerie, and legend—all the narratives that try to explain our reality.

The King Arthur stories are fascinating because they sit between reality and myth. They encompass real life concerns, but also cross boundaries with the world of faerie—or the Other, as I call it. There are green knights, witches, wizards, and dragons, and that's what I find particularly fascinating. They are stories that have intrigued people for generations, and like many others, I'm adding my own interpretation.

I love witches and magic, hence my second series set in beautiful Cornwall. There are witches, missing grimoires, supernatural threats, and ghosts, and as the series progresses, weirder stuff happens. The spinoff, White Haven Hunters, allows me to indulge my love of alchemy, as well as other myths and legends. Think Indiana Jones meets Supernatural!

Have a poke around in my blog posts and you'll find all sorts of posts about my series and my characters, and quite a few book reviews.

If you'd like to follow me on social media, you'll find me here:

Facebook, Twitter, Pinterest, Instagram, TikTok, YouTube

f facebook.com/tjgreenauthor/

P pinterest.com/Mount0live/

♪ tiktok.com/@tjgreenauthor

▶ youtube.com/@tjgreenauthor

g goodreads.com/author/show/15099365.T_J_Green

O instagram.com/tjgreenauthor/

BB bookbub.com/authors/tj-green

Other Books by T J Green

Rise of the King Series
A Young Adult series about a teen called Tom who is summoned to wake King Arthur. It's a fun adventure about King Arthur in the Otherworld, the world where Shadow used to live.

Call of the King #1
The Silver Tower #2
The Cursed Sword #3

White Haven Witches
If you love witches, paranormal mysteries, secrets, myth and folklore, you'll love this series that's set on the Cornish coast!

Buried Magic #1
Magic Unbound #2
Magic Unleashed #3
All Hallows' Magic #4
Undying Magic #5
Crossroads Magic #6
Crown of Magic #7
Vengeful Magic #8
Chaos Magic #9
Stormcrossed Magic #10
Wyrd Magic #11
Midwinter Magic #12

Storm Moon Shifters
Set in London, it features the Storm Moon Wolf-shifter Pack, and is a spin-off of the Hunters and Witches series. It has familiar characters and plenty of new ones, but can be read as a standalone.
Storm Moon Rising #1

Made in United States
North Haven, CT
04 February 2024

48285253R20182